# GRIOTS
## SISTERS OF THE SPEAR

Edited by

*Milton J. Davis*
*and*
*Charles R. Saunders*

# GRIOTS

## SISTERS OF THE SPEAR

ISBN 13: 978-0-9960167-0-4

Cover Art by Andrea Rushing
Cover Layout/Design by URAEUS
Copy Editing by Rebecca McFarland Kyle

Manufactured in the United States of America

First Edition

# SPEARING STEREOTYPES

By Charles R. Saunders


The woman in Andrea Rushing's evocative painting that graces the cover of *Griots: Sisters of the Spear* symbolizes the essence of the anthology. Although the painting is not a direct depiction of any of the characters in the stories, the spirit of this woman imbues all of them. She is a teller of truth, and a slayer of stereotypes.

As is the case with black men, black women have been subjected to invidious stereotyping for centuries in real life and fiction alike. For the most part, these characterizations have ranged from the condescending to the downright hostile – from the faithful "Mammy" of *Gone with the* Wind to the scornful "Sapphire" of *Amos 'n' Andy* to the degraded "Ho" made infamous in all-too-many rap-music lyrics. The fantasy-fiction genre is no exception. Until recently, black women have been either non-existent, or portrayed in ways that made absence the preferable alternative.

Real life defies the stereotypes. Throughout history, there has been no dearth of strong and courageous black women who have stood alongside – and sometimes in front of – their men and children during the course of a 500-year-long struggle against oppression in Africa, and the places in the rest of the world to which Africans were taken against their will to fuel economies with their forced labor.

A few examples: The Candace, or queen, of Kush defied the legions of ancient Rome. Queen Nzinga of Ndongo in central

Africa fought to protect her people from the depredations of European slavers. Harriet Tubman risked her life to lead slaves to freedom in the years before the U.S. Civil War. Fannie Lou Hamer endured vicious physical abuse from the authorities in her non-violent quest to win basic civil rights for black Americans. Women such as these – and many more like them – stand as living contradictions to the misrepresentations that persist to this day.

So do the women in *Sisters of the Spear*. When Milton Davis came up with the idea of a woman-themed sequel to our first anthology, *Griots*, I co-signed immediately. Like *Griots*, *Sisters of the Spear* presents an opportunity to bring more black representation to a genre that's still in need of more color. Thanks to *Griots*, we knew there were more than a few writers and artists of all racial persuasions who would embrace our theme of powerful black womanhood and create stories and illustrations that would be excellent by any standard.

Our expectations have been more than fulfilled. Our modern-day *griots* came through with – not to belabor the point – flying colors. The fictional warrior-women and sorceresses you will meet in the following pages can hold their own and then some against the barbarians and power-mad monarchs and magic-users of both genders who swing swords and cast spells in the mostly European-derived settings of modern fantasy and sword-and-sorcery. The reach of sword-and soul has expanded greatly with *Sisters of the Spear*.

It's time now to allow the woman on the cover serve as your guide through the anthology. The light she carries will illuminate the truth that is always inherent in the best of fiction. And her spear will slay the stereotypes.

*To Our Sisters*

*In honor of everything you are*

*and everything you do.*

# Marked

*Sarah A. Macklin*

*My markings itch. You'd think I'd be used to it by now. Yet I'm not. They itch like they're trying to leave me, like they're ready to be free from my body. Well, I'm ready to be free of you, too.*

\*\*\*

She walked into town like a specter, quiet and unassuming, and I was smitten from the moment I saw her. I was only ten, old enough to be bored by everyday life. A visitor, any visitor, would have been welcome in my small town on the border of the Sahel, but she was more than I could have ever asked for. I stared as she passed the town walls along with everyone else. She was tall and thin, obviously a foreigner, out of place among farmers. Her hair was cut close to her scalp; her hair the color of rich, wet earth. On her back was a spear and a large, round shield. She looked like some kind of strange turtle. Even her skin seemed like it was covered in scales.

I stood up to get a better look. No, it wasn't scales but marks, like a tiny bird had walked all over her body. Not even her face had been spared. I stepped out of the shade of my parents' house and into the main street. My grandmother always said that I was far too bold for a child. She was absolutely right. I felt no fear as I walked up to this strange woman. My smile couldn't have been any brighter. She gifted me with a small, patient smile and my heart grew three sizes. "Are you a traveler? Where'd you come from?"

"Are you the town guard?" she asked. Her voice was polished wood.

"My name's Ogisou," I replied, the giggle spilling out of me.

"It's a pleasure to meet you, Ogisou."

Now that I was closer I was mesmerized by the markings on her face. They weren't as random as I thought they'd be; they were arranged almost artfully, in a crude pattern. "Are you a warrior from the king?"

"No. I'm merely a wanderer."

I saw her eyes move at the same time that I felt my mother's protective arms around me. "Welcome, guest," my mother said from just above my head. If I hadn't been so caught up in the stranger, I would have heard the caution in her voice. "What brings you here?"

The woman -my woman I'd unknowingly decided- nodded. "I am only looking for a place to rest my head and a humble meal for my belly. I'll happily be on my way in the morning."

I looked up to my mother, hopeful. I wished with all my might that she would let the warrior woman stay with us. I'd never wanted anything so much in my short life. My mother's lips pulled into a tight line as the silence stretched. "My uncle has an extra room," I interjected before my mother could make her final decision.

My mother jerked me sharply. "Ogisou," she chided.

But I was undaunted. "He lets travelers stay there sometimes. And my aunt's a really great cook." I burst forth from my mother's protective embrace and grabbed the woman's hand. "Here, I'll take you to him." I rushed through town right past my mother, dragging the warrior behind me. I was oblivious to the stares of the other villagers. My people were suspicious of travelers and when you lived where we did, you had good reason. But this traveler was different, my young heart decided. She was special.

I glanced behind me. "What's your name?"

"It's not important."

I smiled again. "Everyone has a name."

She chuckled at me, one of the most glorious sounds in the world. "Some have called me Blade and many have called me the Lioness. For some I was Sleeping Leopard. You may call me what you wish."

"I like Sleeping Leopard." She made a sound. I'm still not sure if it was disapproving or if she was merely amused at my curiosity. My eyes traveled up the marks on her long, muscled arms. "You have a lot of marks."

"I do," she said hesitantly.

"What are they for?"

I remember that she didn't answer me at first. She slowed down slightly reining in my break-neck pace. "When you do evil things, sometimes you're punished."

I was old enough to recognize the tone in her voice. That was the end of the conversation. I followed her lead and was quiet until we reached my uncle's home. The mood may have been subdued, yet my excitement remained. I had a warrior to look after and learn all I could from her. She was a gift just for me and an omen of excitement yet to come. I had no idea the sort of excitement I was in for.

*** 

*The child is too trusting, like all children. One day in his village and he hangs on my every word, watches my every movement. He hasn't been jaded, broken by the weight of this world or crushed by life's many disappointments. How nice it must be to still have dreams unbroken, to still have a full hopeful future ahead of you. How I envy youth.*

*But wait. What is that noise?*

\*\*\*

I was still asleep when the damned ones came. Slumber only left me once I heard the low noises outside my family's house. It was an odd sound, half growling, half laughing interjected with scratches at the mud-brick walls. I sat up on my mat on the floor, my mind still under a haze. The growl/laughing grew closer. I leaned down to peer through the small crack underneath our door. Shadows passed in front of it, blocking the pale moonlight seeping through. Terror didn't grip me then. I didn't realize at that time the horror that waited for me outside.

I froze with the first shove against the door. I only had time to take the breath to yell out when the monsters burst into our home, spilling in like living shadows. They were on me before I could scream. Moonlight reflected from every sharp tooth. One clamped a flithy hand over my mouth and my nostrils were filled with their sour, rotting stench. They dragged me out kicking and punching to no avail. Each time I wrenched a limb free from one of their grasps, another latched onto me. My village didn't even stir as they carried me away.

I cried. I tried not to. I tried to be the little man my father urged me to be even while my ears were filled with the sounds of the monsters' growling laughter. I cried as I was carried out into the sahel over hills and shallow valleys, deep into the wilderness where I was sure I'd never leave. The moon hid behind passing clouds, casting the whole world into darkness. I was glad that no one, not even these damned monsters, could see my tears now.

I was jerked downward. I looked up just in time to see the moon emerge just to be blocked from view by the cave walls. The monsters were taking me deep underground. The air grew hotter around me, thick with their stentch which I've yet to forget. The memory of it makes me want to wretch even now. We twisted and turned through their lair, through what seemed like a lifetime of tunnels. Dispair weighed down on my small shoulders. They were going to eat me, or just murder me for the sport of it. I was going to die; a prospect to child should ever have to contemplate. Yet, when you're in the midst of creatures from your worst nightmares, what else can you think of?

A small, warm light grew as we hurried down a tunnel. Our group burst into a large room that had a fire pit in the center. Only then did I get a true look at my captors. I was finally able to scream. They looked like demons in the skins of hyenas. The size and shape of men but stretched out to the point that their muscles seemed to be straining to hold onto their bodies. All beady, gold eyes were on me as I was passed over head, each of them wanting to get a chance to hold their prize. Unearthly chants errupted filling the room with a malestrom of noise. Only when each had taken their turn, did they toss me into a corner.

There was no hope of escape. Two of the damned ones stood nearby as guards. There were several ways out, but none of them near me. I was sure that this was the end.

\*\*\*

*Does evil never rest?! Why do they never concern themselves with true battle, only seeking to plague commonfolk? Why can they not find satisfaction in fighting warriors? Why must they inundate my path of redemption with their filth? I've grown weary of them. All of them. The Jebaris, the Hatounas, the Keverii, and especially the changelings. I am sick of the changlelings.*

*But I can't leave the boy to his doom. My markings itch, urging me on. I agree. I have to move quickly.*

\*\*\*

I remember being sleepy, yet there was no possible way I could have slept. The hyena monsters had begun dancing around their firepit, some striking up a strange song in their language. The rhythm was steadily building along with the energy in the room. Goosebumps rose on my skin despite the heat and the hairs on the back of my neck lifted. They beat on walls, on gourds, on anything that could make a sound. Laughs echoed off the walls making the room seem fuller than it actually was. One could taste the excitement in the air. It was a maddening scene.

Every so often one of their number would dance his way close to growl and taunt me. I knew that they could smell my fear for it had trickled down my legs and pooled on the floor beneath me. They laughed in my face, fetid breath choking me. Then they would return to the mad dance twirling and jumping in the fire light.

The song and dance grew louder, more insistent. I watched the fire turn from a flickering orange to yellow and finally to a ghostly white. Suddenly, the dancing stopped, the monsters surrounding the pit still singing their beastly song. The crowd parted and I could clearly see one of their kind, an elder, standing near the flames. He held his arm up then bit it savagely. He held a small cup beneath his arm, collecting the thick, black looking blood. Hoots and howls started, mixed in with the song. The old one thrust the cup into the fire, not a sound of pain escaping him as his hand was engulfed in flame. His eyes then fixed on me and he began to approach.

I screamed, trying to run, but strong hands clamped down on either arm. The two demons held me fast as their elder came close. He dipped his long, leathery fingers into the cup which was glowing with the same eerie light as the fire. I tried to pull away in vain, half out of my young mind with panic. The old demon raised his blood covered fingers to my forehead and I could feel him writing. He marked my cheeks next, the glowing blood painfully cold against my skin. There was satisfaction in his eyes as he took a moment to inspect his work.

Then there was a scream at the back of the room. All heads turned to see the source of it. I looked too, but couldn't see past the crowd. I could hear; however, and my heart jumped at what I heard next.

"Let the boy go."

It was the warrior, my warrior. She'd come to save me. The demons began to growl now, not a hint of laughter in any of them. The two holding me let go to join the fight. I scrambled backwards, pressing myself against the wall. The room was filled with growls and the howls of the dying. I could see blood flying this way and that and soon I could see her. I know I must have held my breath for to watch her fight is mesmerizing.

She moved through them like water, flowing without effort from one opponent to the next. She used both spear and shield as her weapons. Her spear would find its way through one demon's belly just as the edge of her shield shattered the throat of another. They tried to claw her, to punch, kick, and bite her but few attacks made their mark. The few that did, she scarcely seemed to notice. She was fury incarnate. She was a goddess of battle. Truly, she lived up to all the names she'd earned and even more.

Nearly half of the monsters had been cleared out when she laid eyes on the elder. The old demon turned and ran toward me but he never made it. In an instant, my warrior's spear was sticking out from the front of his bony chest, dark blood dripping down. He was dead before he crashed to the floor, coming to a stop right before my feet. The other hyena monsters paused in their fighting, fear and anger playing across their faces. Some took this as their moment to run. But there would be no escape for them. My warrior flipped back placing herself firmly in front of the exit. She may have only been armed with her shield, but there wasn't a hint of apprehension in her eyes. Despite my fear, I knew that she would finish this.

The monsters descended on her. I could barely see her in the low light, but I could tell from the way the demons were steadily falling dead that she was a blur of movement. Soon, enough of them had died to give me a better view of my warrior. The last three tried to rush past her, but in one motion she whipped her shield around, striking them against the side of the head so fiercely their necks snapped.

The room was suddenly quiet, snapping me from my awe and jolting me back into the present. The entire horrifying night seemed to suddenly weigh down on me and I sunk to my knees. I grew weak at the smells of death, blood, and filth surrounding me. To my shame, I voided my stomach just as she touched my shoulder. I cried and watched my sickness slide into the blood pooling on the floor. After a moment it proved too much for me and I fell into her arms.

\*\*\*

I awoke to the blessed scent of fresh air and the warmth of the afternoon sun. I felt weak, ill, and still acutely aware of the almost burning cold writing on my face.

"You need to wake," came my warrior's smooth voice from somewhere nearby.

I reluctantly opened my eyes. We were in the shade of a large boulder, but the bright day stung. Squinting, I looked over to my warrior, my Sleeping Leopard. She stooped in front of a puny fire. I could smell cooking meat and my stomach turned uncomfortably.

"Here," she said quietly, handing over a small, slightly charred morsel. "It tastes horrible, but you need to eat."

I did as she bid me to, nearly gagging on it. "It *is* horrible," I croaked.

She chuckled. "It's good to see you still have life in you." Her expression sombered as she watched me eat. I followed her eyes as she studied my face and knew she was looking to the writing the old demon had scribed on me the night before. It still felt as cold as when he first placed the blood on my skin and now it sat on me like some kind of slime that refused to slide away. I reached up to rub it off. With the speed of a snake, she caught my wrist and shook her head.

I could feel tears starting to form again. "What's going to happen to me?" I asked, trying with all my might to keep the tears at bay.

My warrior sighed heavily, sitting down beside me. "I hope and pray that nothing will come of this." She paused and looked out to the landscape. "They were going to make you into one of them. I arrived in time to stop the ceremony, but not soon enough."

"Am... am I going to turn into a monster?" I asked, panic starting rise again.

To my relief, she answered with a firm, "No." A frown formed. "But you've been marked. You won't ever be the same again. People may fear you, what you might become."

"Is that how you were marked? By monsters?"

She didn't answer at first and I was afraid, even after all that had happened to me, that I'd offended her. I waited.

"No. I was given these marks as punishment." She paused again. "I've killed many people, not all of them evil. My only care was to follow the orders of the ones paying my fee. One day, a witch cursed me. I would wear a mark for each life I've taken and they will not disappear until I've saved as many as I've killed." She turned her deep eyes to me. "Since then, my life and my skills as a warrior have been dedicated to helping as many as I can."

I looked aside, taking in all she'd said. "Then I will help people, too. Whatever happens to me because of these... these marks doesn't matter. I want to help people, just like you."

Her expression was unreadable. She slowly turned away from me, putting out the fire.

She helped me to my feet passing me another piece of the foul meat she'd cooked. I realize now that it was to keep me quiet. "It is good that you want to help people, Ogisou," she said as we set out. "Very good. But don't try to be like me."

I nodded even though I had every intention of emulating her. Our trek back to my village was not as long as I thought it would be and we were walking through the gate by sundown. My parents wept at my arrival and the whole town rejoiced. Many thought me long dead, eaten by monsters in the night. I was overjoyed to see them and eager to tell them of my rescue. I looked back through the crowd for my warrior, but she was already on the road out of the village. I called out, but my voice was drowned out by the cries of jubilation.

***

People did treat me differently after that. My markings never faded and there began whispers that I was half-demon now. Not that I didn't give them reason to suspect it. I laughed more often, even at things no one else found funny. I started more fights with the other boys and could be heard growling in the midst of it. I grew tall and thin with taut muscles.

Yet, I also grew stronger and faster than any of the others. And when I had the chance, I left my tiny village to keep my word and help all those that I could find. I'm still on the road now following my Lioness, my Sleeping Leopard, my warrior. I hope that one day I find her and by that time, she's free of each and every one of her marks.

# The Antuthema

*Dennis Brown*

Awere slowed her breathing, relaxing in the seated lotus position as she allowed her mind and body to enter the meditative state.  She was a powerful adept, a natural talent highly developed due to her heritage.  Her life, such that it had become, demanded that she hone the meditative skill to the utmost degree.  She could feel the cold of the marble floor, an opulent addition in a corner of the world that was long ago even more luxurious, then barren of such luxury through heated war and conquest, only to come around again. She wore a red headscarf.  He breasts were deep brown, bare and full, exposed in glorious splendor.  Her halter and chain mail were in the corner folded neatly, as were her boots, mid-garment, waist-belt, simok blade, and sash.  She wore a short loose fitting sarong attached to a golden waist chain.

Her muscles tensed, then relaxed, and tensed again, she let the exercise of control wash over her entire body. There was no part of her that she did not control, that she did not command.  She opened her eyes one more time to take in the ostentatious luxury that surrounded her.  The curtains that billowed over the open windows, the walls adorned with fine designs, frescoes of ancient battles, gods as they moved among men.  There was the massive bed against the far wall, adorned with sheets and pillows.

Outside, the morning desert sun was a resilient reminder that above all, powers still held sway over the destinies of men.  The gods would not be forgotten.  Hot dry wind blew across the city of Aleocrates, a place that felt as though it existed on the border of all worlds, all kingdoms, all empires.

However, here inside, there was the gentle reminder that man would ever strive against the might of gods.  The so-called icing system was a Kiuerere import, a power that none of the desert dwellers or foreign invaders knew well.  But Awere knew it.  In her father's lands there had been many such wonders.  But she was no longer in her father's lands.  She closed her eyes once more and stood in one fluid motion.  Her body was unto a work of art, a thing of immeasurable beauty, and powerful resolve.  Her strength was evident as she began the warrior form, moving effortlessly one step at a time, arms in motion, her eyes shut, an exercise in total control.  She exuded energy, one not to be trifled with, despite her circumstance, despite her life, such as it had become.

She gained speed in her movements, her breathing controlled, silent, her body mesmerizing, arms moving to block, then to parry, then to strike, legs following, low kicks, mid-level kicks, a few strikes that would devastate the head of an opponent.  She was purity, ebony purity, form and deadly function the likes of which few had ever seen, at least none in this part of the world.  She was sensuality and strength, deep passion that tore at the hearts of men.  She was revered, she was hated, she was lauded, she was feared, and above all …wanted, wanted in the deepest ways.  She was power incarnate, and as such, she attracted power.

The door opened slowly, silently. The Kensu Prince stepped fervently into the suite, followed by his Grand Azari.  They were new to the land, less than a hundred cycles, but they came bearing power and wealth, and though they didn't hold sway as conquerors, the power of their far away land was well respected.  In this time, trade was paramount and there was no friction between the peoples of Kensu and the Western Kingdoms who held sway over this part of the Homelands.  In fact, the Kensu revered the Homelands and called it as such.

It was said that their academics asserted that all the hundred-hundred clans of the Kensu people from the great eastern throng of cold and grey iron mountains to the southern islands and mystical paradises; even to the Kensu's oldest enemy in the farthest reaches of the East, the Normin of the so-called end of the world, the Kensu believed all descended from the Homelands. It was here, that all the peoples of the world, in all its kinds began, so they believed.

The Prince had since learned that this Kensu theory was absolute truth. He learned this from Awere, who schooled him on historical fact like a teacher educating a child. It made him smile. She was his, yet she never acted so. He didn't threaten her. He knew he could not. And though she was pure warrior through into her heart and soul, and protected herself well enough, he could not bring himself to directly harm her as punishment for insolence. She was his pride, and though he must wait a thousand years to bed her, if that is what was required, he would do so.

"My Prince!" Erupted Tenzo, the Grand Azari.

Awere had not opened her eyes. However, as she moved through her warrior form, she had stepped close to him, turning swiftly; her foot a gliding graceful arc that appeared to be heading for the Prince's head.

Tenzo reached out to protect the Prince, but a swift hand rose. The Prince didn't move save for that one right hand. He held it out, keeping Tenzo at bay. Awere's foot missed the Prince's head by inches. His long black hair billowing from the wind created by the warrior's passing foot.

"No harm," said Prince Qiang. "Awere would never strike me."

Awere placed her foot on the ground and stood erect, head back, shoulders set. Her face had a regal bearing. She looked evenly at the Prince, but said nothing. His eyes beheld her, looking at her body from head to toe, and back up again, slowly drinking in her frame. Her breasts were a terrible temptation, stirring his loins to fire. Her barely clothed state was unto a siren, inviting men in, but bosomed within the welcome was a portent of doom. The Prince had wanted her since the day he set eyes upon her, nothing had changed. However, he stayed his hand, and his desire. He would not tempt fate. No, for in truth, despite the best advice, and in some instances direct intervention of his advisors, Prince Qiang loved Awere. He loved her without recrimination, unabashedly, even if his station prevented him from expressing as much. There had been times of weakness, but ... the Prince held fast to his desire, and kept it under control. He longed for the day when her eyes would look on him with the same admiration he had for her. Alas, that day would not be today.

"Awere," said the Prince. "I offer you this time daily to focus your mind, to hone your resolve. I would hope you would not seek to repay me with a foot in the face."

Awere turned her back on the Prince and strode over to the corner where her clothing was gathered. Behind her she heard the hiss of Tenzo, a sniveling reaction to her perceived indiscretion, to actually turn her back on the Son of Heaven.

"Your Highness," snarled Tenzo, through gritted teeth. "We have suffered this indignity long enough. A slave walking through the city armed. How long must we—"

"We must nothing, Tenzo," interrupted the Prince, silencing his Azari. "I must ... if anyone must. And I choose to indulge Awere."

They both stood silent as Awere dressed, waiting for her to speak. It was almost more than Tenzo could bear.

Awere looked at ... her owner, and breathed deeply. "As ever, Prince. I am in your debt."

"The Son of Heaven wishes nothing more than to please you, and be pleased by you."

Awere's eyes were cold. "If I'm not mistaken, it pleases the Prince greatly every time I take to the field."

"Not so much as you would believe. You are a wonder, Awere. A work of pure art, of untold value. You are wasted in the arena. But this is truly the way of things."

"You could free me."

"Would but the Son of Heaven be able to grant such a boon. Alas, it is not within my power."

Awere almost laughed. "Interesting thing, the limit of one's power, especially when one is unto a deity. Exactly how does that work, unlimited limitations?"

Tenzo nearly jumped out of his robes. "You mock Prince Qiang, you animal!"

As swiftly and as fiercely as Tenzo's words flowed, so to was the fluidity of the Prince's strong hand. His blow struck the Azari soundly on the chin, a powerful blow lifting him off his feet. The royal advisor landed soundly on his ass, a smattering of blood at the corner of his lip.

"Awere is mine, Tenzo! No one, and I mean no one, addresses her thusly!"

"But she is a slave, my Prince!"

"She is a warrior and she is mine! Now silence before I allow her to display her skills in the arena here ... now ... ON YOU!"

Tenzo calmed the fire bellowing in his belly. His anger was a powerful thing, none of it directed at his Prince. His life was meant to serve, and as he wiped the bit of blood from the corner of his mouth, his mind reeled at the state of his being. He served the Prince of Heaven. He adored him as one might adore a god. His hate, his inner fire, the bile that was threatening to spill over if he did not maintain control, was all directed at what he had come to call the *black whore*, the dark bitch of the West who had somehow ensorcelled his lord and master.

Tenzo was no prude, he recognized the beauty and majesty in the feminine form before him. But to him she was a lowly thing, a beast, like a powerful cat, something to be owned and cherished as property. In his mind, she was the lowest and most dangerous of slaves, and she could never be offered a position of favor. Slaves could be allowed to rise, to gain full rights in the world, but some slaves were dangerous. This one was perhaps the most dangerous of all.

"Stand up, Tenzo!" commanded the Prince. "Go see

to the celebration. Ensure all is in order."

Tenzo stood, and bowed deeply. "Of course, my Prince." There was no animosity on his face, none in his bearing. However, as he turned to leave, he looked the beauty that was Awere. He caught her eye, and she returned his cold stare. Unspoken understanding passed between them, words conveyed through the ether in their dagger-like stares. The portent was death, one to another.

*Black bitch!*

Awere smiled at the Azari as he left the room. She held no fear of him. Awere feared no man.

"I hope Tenzo didn't offend you," said Qiang.

Awere was stoic. "Your worm means nothing to me."

The Prince chuckled. "Of course, of course."

They stood there for a moment, silence between them. Prince Qiang simply smiled, admiration showing plainly on his face. It was a look Awere understood, but certainly didn't appreciate. It frustrated her to see his blatant love. This man had made plain his intentions, his desire. He had called her a queen, away from the eyes and ears of the prying and planning, that she would sit on the celestial throne. She listened to his endless prattling, his dreams. He was a strong and powerful man. She saw in him the potential to realize his dreams. However, she would never be at his side. He was allied with those that destroyed her home, something she could still barely conceive over two cycles later. However, she had come to know the cold touch of acceptance, something that sobered her soul, and her resolve. Though the path ahead was shrouded in shadow, she would stand, and in time, her people would rise.

"If you would again, take the place of honor at this evening's feast, I personally would be most honored," said Prince Qiang. "Will you do me this favor, my beautiful Awere?"

There really was no choice. "Yes, I will."

"Thank you," he said, bowing slightly. A move that would have sent Tenzo into waves of apoplexy, frothing at the mouth.

"May I take my leave?" asked Awere.

"You may."

Awere gracefully moved past the Prince, regal as she made her way to the door.

"And remember, Awere," said the Prince. "You are always welcome here. My home, is your home."

Awere said nothing as she left him behind, down the hallway, descending the stairs of the tower. She knew she was taking advantage of his largesse, even as he hoped to one day take advantage of her. No, that was not quite accurate. He hoped to make her something more, something of an equal in the far Eastern lands. She knew enough beyond just his words, and could sense enough, to see this was his intent. Clearly, it did not matter to the Prince that his desire was dulling his senses. He was plainly mad. Tenzo, was not alone in his hate of Awere. In fact, Awere was painfully aware of just how much she was hated by most peoples, by most powers. This was the result of how she appeared as a slave. It was not a good fit, clearly the result of her heritage. The irony was not lost on her. She firmly believed it was her heritage that nurtured her soul, and fortified her spirit. She knew without equivocation that it was her heritage that provided her with great physical strength, a gift from her ancestors that allowed her to keep the beasts at bay, even the barbarians that saw her as a beast, those who were truly beasts themselves. No, she was a person, surrounded in a world full of animals that walked like men. She knew who she was. She would never forget.

"This is the season of the Cororucabia!" The Prefect Druel yelled, a hearty bold declaration, opening the gathering to revelry. "The celebration of annual change, the time of dying, and eventual rebirth!"

The fat politician stood at the center of the reserved table on a raised dias. Officials sat on either side, beaming in their robes and accoutrements of luxury. The desert had brought prosperity to many a foreigner, merchant, soldier, and solitary warrior who could brave the expanse.

The Prefect had once been a warrior of some prominence. Now, he was fat with food and drink, his golden curls graying not just from age, but too much debauchery. His pale hand held his goblet aloft, a golden cup studded with jewels that was a prize of precedent, an heirloom that was said to have belonged to the family of a great King of the Western Homelands, an ancient power that was now ground to dust.

Druel had been assigned to Aleocretes several cycles ago. The ancient city was considered by some a backwater, but since the Etrusican Empire had restarted its campaign of selective aggression, the city had become a point of importance. It was one of many gateways to the oldest parts of the Homelands, great empires beyond the desert, kingdoms as old as human kind, powers that had grown old, staid, and some instances too decrepit to defend themselves. The Etrusicans held fast to the belief that the Gods justified the actions of the youth, that it was right for the young to replace the old, on their own time, by their own volition. Such was the root of Etrusican expansion, and their mission to stamp out the old things, to remake the world anew.

"Hold up your goblets!" commanded Druel, with a toothy grin. "Tomorrow, we watch those who satiate our lust, we watch those who pit themselves alone against death, by commandment of the Gods in celebration of their greatness and the cycle of renewal. They who will enter the arena for the Grand Iduma, the Game of Life Takers, the Gladiators …"

The Prefect paused, and looked at the assemblage of gladiators. They were on the opposite end of the dining hall, seated at a table against the far wall. The center of the table was reserved as a place of honor, directly opposite the Prefect across the yawning distance of the room. In this chair, surrounded not by wealth and citizens of status, but rather cold warriors, slaves to the last bound by fate, and doomed to death, in their center, at the place of honor, sat the lone woman of the West, Awere.

"Yes, they will fight and some will die." Druel looked directly at Awere with wonder, would she survive yet again? "Yes, tomorrow is the Iduma. But tonight, we revel! Tonight, WE DRINK!"

The bulbous sybarite brought the goblet to his lips and drained it. All around the room men and women joined him in drink. The room became suffused with the sounds of celebration, music and dance, food and wine, debauchery.

"He stares at you, Awere, as though he is certain," said Bosko.

"He is certain of nothing," she said. "The fat man is now a product of this world. This is what happens when we forget who we are."

Bosko nodded, saying nothing. He too was Etrusican. He too had once been a warrior. He had this in common with the Prefect, but this is where they commonality ended. Life happened to him, as it had to Awere. Bosko often wondered how the noble, the honorable, were charged with pain and suffering, a torturous life, while the corrupt prospered, growing fat in their wickedness, stepping joyously on the lives of those that lived with honor ... how did power gravitate to such people?

Why did the Gods allow things to be this way? He had discussed this many times with Awere, with no answer that satisfied. Yet somehow, Awere, who had been wronged most of all, yet defiant to the last, managed the lots of banality and venality that life cast at them all so effortlessly, she managed it much better than any of them, and for this alone, she was honored by each gladiator, and would be protected ... if she were in such need, which of course, she was not.

Bosko looked at his plate, he was hungry. Yesterday was yesterday, and tomorrow, they may very well die. After all, one could not outrun the eventuality of fate.

Awere glanced at Bosko, almost reading his mind. The tanned Etrusican ate with an even face, no joy, but a small sense of satisfaction did pierce his mien. It was the look of a man who had survived, and continued to survive for the moment, with the acknowledgement that the very next time he set foot in the arena, might very well be his last moments alive. She looked to her left, and it was the same. There was Devis, with his powerful muscles and long flowing blonde hair, a slave from the barbarian hordes of the far North. Only Prince Qiang's people were from farther away. Garesh, with his flowing black locks and deep dark brown skin hailed from the Northeast, the great nation states between the Etrusican Empire and Kensu, Empire of the Celestial Throne. Tome was from Encarf, his father a merchant prince, his mother a Htebian cortisan. Neither lived, and Tome, a fiery boy bereft of home and heritage, had found himself a man in Aleorcretes, another victim of deceit. Oberta was a warrior woman not unlike Awere, but with flaming red hair. Her skin had taken on an ochre color in the unforgiving sun of the Homelands. Her story had been one of kidnapping from a home of joy in the lands between Etrusica and Encarf, her family put to the sword by bickering warlords, tortured for pleasure; her world was horror and rape, no different than all the rest, save that like the rest gathered here, she had survived.

Awere took them all in. These few were closest to her among the other warrior slaves gathered. Each story was unique, as different as the places from which they came. It was not lost on her that in such a harsh world they each seemed noble, they each seemed innocent, the word innocent being the most grave to consider. There was darkness in each of their hearts, for it took cruelty and no small amount of callous evil to survive the arena. But each of them, each of them stood by her as people that sought mightily to retain their honor, despite their circumstance. Each of them, wanted to be good, even as they spent their time again, and again, and again doing what could best be called evil, against their own, for the amusement of others. If they survived long enough, they would have to face each other. One would live and one would die, whittling their ranks as part of the spectacle.

Awere closed her eyes, breathing deeply of the moment, in an effort to push it all away, and remembered another place, another time …

"Excellent, my child.  Your father and mother both will be very pleased."

Awere smiled.  "It's not that hard, Bregah."

"Not that hard, indeed," said the old teacher.  "I'm quite certain there are many in the realm, both young and old, who might disagree with you."

"Simple symbol maths?  Really?"

The old man looked at his charge and smiled.  His perfect white teeth were a stark contrast to his glossy ebony skin.

"Awere, I have taught children for more cycles than I care to count. I am the leading instructor on all things of physicals and philosophy in the realm, having ordained the children of the great families for generations in the ways of worldly knowledge, the foundations outside the realms of the mystics.  I leave that for my brother and sister, both highly adept in the mystic arts, as you know."

"I know, I know Bregah," she said, rolling her eyes. "You are proud of your family."

"It's a noble tradition."

"It seems everyone around here is all about noble tradition, and that's all."

Bregah chuckled.  "Child, you are the most precocious student I have ever taught."

"Is that so bad?"

"No child, it is an absolute pleasure.  Now, tell me as we look onto Osusa, The Great Western Sea, tell me of the first generation of men."

Awere turned her attention to the ocean, the breeze blew through the arium.  They were alone in the open-air classroom, student and teacher.  The Kingdom was old beyond reckoning, staid, but its rich history gave no shortage of pleasure in high art and culture.  Heritage and history were things the people were proud of. They were of the most elder peoples of the Homeland; they were the Antuthema, the children of the Theman, caretakers of knowledge and power.

"The Themans were not the first peoples of the Homeland," began Awere. "But they rose to be the highest. They excelled in all things, and in time considered themselves to be unto gods. They sailed away across Osusa, founding a new homeland of dreams and wonder. It is said they rose, and rose, until they rose too high, for they were not gods, but mere men, and they were claimed by Osusa in their hubris, and we who remained are the Antuthema ..."

There was no strength in the arms of the Antuthema when the young barbarians descended upon them from beyond the great wastelands of the eastern desert, mad plunderers with no regard and no respect, soldiers who came in waves of onslaught from new empires, Etrusican, Encarfican, the mad Appotrians whom all detest, even The Tygopians, brothers and sisters from across the waste, themselves conquered eventually by foreign children from beyond the middle sea, and the lands to the north.  When help came to hold the line, power from the southlands that could not, and would not be denied, it was too late. The cradle was decimated, the Antuthema was said to be no more, their old might gone after years of peace and tranquility, softness, their blood and bone ground into the dirt, their heritage robbed, bartered, sold, the remnants .... scattered to the winds.

Such memories would come to Awere unbidden in moments of introspection, even in a loud banquet hall. She worked hard to keep the memories safe, deep inside. Her identity was only of the moment; even as her true self provided what could best be described as incredible power and might. Her world was now, and she sometimes had to remind herself to acknowledge this, the facts of her circumstance, her life. She was a slave, a gladiator. And tomorrow, in the arena, she might very well die.

In another corner of the room, the Kensu representatives

were at their tables celebrating with abandon. The Prince was enjoying the attention of a host of women who wanted him, and men who wanted to be him. Seated at a table behind him, his Azari huddled with four of his advisors. Tenzo was speaking urgently with his men, but his eyes were firmly set on another, far across the room. He burned with a hate that could almost be felt, hate for Awere.

"The Prince will be most displeased," said one advisor.

Tenzo huffed. "It will not matter. He will soon forget."

"I'm not so certain," said another advisor. "The Prince has shown his extreme … interest for this one."

"And do you not see this is the problem?" demanded Tenzo, tense with frustration. "Do none of you see where this is going? I will say it, if you will not." They all glanced at the back of the Prince. "The Son of Heaven is in love with this dark skinned whore!"

Tenzo's teeth were grinding in disgust. "Would you see this slave bitch on the throne? Would you? Any of you?"

The all shook their huddled heads. There was the sense of fear, for the walls were said to have ears.

"Of course not!"

"Shhh!" urged the advisor closest to the Prince. "He might hear us."

Tenzo clamped his lips shut, struggling to maintain control. "I am Tanzo Tea'an Amura. I am Azari to the Son of Heaven. And here in this heathen land many of us see fit to actually call Home, I am responsible for the sanctity of the throne, of the line of destiny. This was my father's duty, and my grandfather's duty before him. This is my responsibility … and I will not fail."

The small throng of men became silent, considering the weight of Tenzo's words. They looked at each other and all nodded in agreement.

"Nevertheless, it is in motion," said Tenzo. "Any

moment now, they will be leaving, escorted back to their quarters. And there, the two Encarficans we've hired will fulfill their contract."

"It is done," said one of the advisors.

"Yes," said Tenzo, with a sense of satisfaction. "Yes, it is done. And by tomorrow, the exotic lure of this Awere animal will trouble me no more."

The advisor closest to the Prince looked at the back of the Son of Heaven's head, and wondered what he would feel at such a loss. He looked beyond him, far across the room to the sitting warrior, Awere. She was truly a wonder to behold, almost terrifyingly beautiful, and just as dangerous, as she had proven time and time again. He had not missed how the Azari said she would trouble him no more, as opposed to the Prince. A stirring in his loins at the sight of her reminded him that she troubled not just the Azari, but all men.

Desire mingled with hate, in a muted mumble. "She cannot be allowed to survive," whispered Tenzo. "She cannot."

He sighed, a sense of satisfaction overwhelming him. There would be an end, one way or another. As he fought the skulking desire that he so hated, he turned his attention to the Prefect. The man was laughing and stuffing his face with food and drink, *disgusting barbarian slob.* The Azari could not believe this man could be so conniving, so dangerous. It was a well-known fact that he was once a soldier, a supposedly venerated soldier. One could look at him and think him wallowing in senescence. But clearly, his abilities were still potent. The special surprise the Prefect had arranged for the Cororucabia would not only delight as well as terrify the crowds, but it would ensure death for any gladiators that remained standing. There would be a changing of the line, a wipe out and renewal. Awere had emboldened the rabble, mounting victory after victory. It was time for an end. The blood would flow, leaving none alive. If one plan fails, then another will fulfill the need.

Suddenly there was a commotion at the entrance to

the banquet hall. The doors were thrust open, several soldiers strode in, at their lead was a tall warrior with ebony skin, leather and metal adorned him, light armor of intricate design. The pelt of a lion was strewn across his chest, the head of the great beast serving as his breastplate, the mouth turned into a clasp, tying the garment to him as a sign of leadership and strength. His contingent of men was twenty strong, and as they entered the room, all in attendance fell into silence. The ebony soldier eyed the crowd slowly looking over the room. When his eyes landed upon Awere, he paused, but his face gave no indication of acknowledgment, or knowing. His gaze roved over the rest of the room, bold eyes that challenged the Kensu, Encarfican, and Etrisucan. His eyes settled on the Prefect, who immediately seemed to sober, stood and bowed.

"Great General, Crown Prince Tashaki. You honor us with your presence. Would you join us for food and drink, in celebration of the season, the Cororucabia?"

"That would be difficult would it not, fat man?" the General's voice boomed. "There appear to be no available seats for my men."

"General, there must have been some error. Please forgive me." The Prefect leaned over quickly, loudly whispering to the man seated next to him. The man got up and with a flurry started issuing orders. The next two tables, filled with Etrusicans, was hurriedly emptied. Servers appeared, quickly clearing the tables of food and drink, resetting, and placing, readying them for the General and his men.

"I did not know you would be gracing us with your presence," said the Prefect. "The Inqousu Imperium's Crown Prince is always welcome in this hall."

The General moved to the tables, followed by his men. The hall remained silent as they were seated, and food and drink were quickly provided. "You need not tell me what I already know, fat man. Instead, I would inquire about the massing of troops on the northern border."

The Prefect's face suddenly turned cold. "Garrison

replenishment, Your Highness, nothing more."

The General's look was equally cold. "One would hope that was all. The peace that is maintained in the northern Homelands is one of choice, not need. All of you from across the sea would do well to remember that."

The Prefect nodded. "We will be sure to do so."

Silence ensued ... the crowd waited.   Of the many assembled, merchants, politicians, spies, courtesans, warriors, and gladiators, what was unspoken was well known. The Etrusican hunger for war had been abruptly stymied by the might of devastating Inqousu.  Though the Etrusican march was considered the most aggressive expansion in an age, their penetration into the Homeland met a seemingly peaceful Inqousu Imperium, until the destruction of the Antuthema. The ties between those two nations were still not well known. But the devastation wrought by the Inqousu response was only halted by the Inqousu, and it was not an easy thing. There were those Inqousu who for some reason yelled of blood debt, and transgression, and a desire to sail their great ships filled with horse hoof, elephant, and Inqousu machinery of war, and lay waste to all of Etrusica.   But no, the Emperor Sisiwe forbade it.  Thus, was the peace.

"My father will ensure peace in this land, Prefect. And any other if need be. We are not to be tested in this. Our resolve is as it ever was. We are at peace. Let us remain at peace, for the safety of us all."

Again, the Prefect nodded. "Of course."

"Now," said the General holding up his arms, hands wide. "Let the celebration continue!"

The room erupted in release, music again blared, the revelry continued, as if the pressure in an earthen valve had suddenly been released. The valve struggled to maintain, to hold its integrity, but even with the release of the pressure, it threatened to burst.

"I like not, the looks of this," Bosko said to Awere.

Awere agreed. "Neither do I."

"There has always been the threat of renewed conflict.

I mean, did anyone even know the General was coming?"

"I don't think anyone knew the General was coming."

"But it does not matter," said Oberta. Awere glanced at her sister in blood and bondage, someone she had come to love as family. "Does it, Awere?"

"No, it does not," said Awere, understanding her meaning, both of them. "First, we are gladiators. Tomorrow, we fight. Second, the conversation between the Prefect and the Prince speaks to the inevitable. Who among us did not know? The Prefect has gone soft, perhaps so have the Etrusicans as a whole.

"Loose lips sink ships," said Bosko.

"But the Prince will wait," said Oberta. "He will wait, and again prove the might of the Inqousu."

Awere and Oberto both looked at Prince Tashaki, General of the Inqousu Armies. He was a man to be respected, and feared. Both women looked at this warrior with admiration, and no small amount of desire. They both had needs that were not at all being satisfied.

"It's time," said a guard, approaching the table. "Back to your quarters, gladiators."

As one, the assembled fighters stood, surrounded by guards, they were escorted from the room, with Awere in the lead.

The Prefect stood, "We salute you great warriors!" He held his cup aloft, a wide smile breaking across his face. "Tomorrow, warriors! Tomorrow the Iduma! It will be legendary, unlike any other! Be rested warriors! We drink to you!"

Everyone held their cups aloft, and drank to the gladiators as they left the room. Tenzo drank, and dreamed of a tomorrow that was bereft of Awere's presence, either by morning, or without question by mid-afternoon. There could be no mistake. Prefect Druel smiled, as he let the wine dull his senses, but only so much. He relished tomorrow, for tomorrow would bring so many surprises. He imagined the humbling of one Prince, and the showing of power to another. In the arena there would be a spectacle unlike any other, and raise his peerage in the eyes of the assembled, and the aristocracy back home that he could accomplish such a thing. But tonight, tonight before his women were brought to his chamber, he would satisfy his desires by cutting out loose tongues. He could not stand spies, even his own.

"Go with the gods, Awere!" The lead guard escorting them, a monster of a man, pushed her forcefully as hard as he could into a chamber on the left. Before she could react he closed and bolted the door. The bolt was placed just a second before the door shook as though struck by a thunderbolt.

"Too late, Awere!" He said, looking at her through the window grate.

"Let me out," she said, with cold calm.

The guard laughed, closing the grate. He turned and leered at the other gladiators. The main group had already been separated off and led away, taking another route back to the gladiator compound. Only Awere's group of contemporaries remained, the so-called Dreche. They each had two guards with swords drawn on either side of them, a blade at the neck. "Now, the rest of you, back to the compound."

Bosko snarled. "And if we don't?"

The guard's smile grew wider. "Heads will roll. And they will keep rolling until I say stop. Really put a damper on tomorrow's festivities. But, it's up to you."

"I don't think the Prefect would like it so much if you ruined his celebration."

"Kensu money buys a lot," said the guard. "More than you can possibly imagine slave."

"Go!" They heard Awere yell from behind the bolted door. "No more words Bosko! Go, and don't look back."

The guard shrugged. "Up to you." He raised his sword.

The gladiator exhaled. He slackened visibly. His hands opened and dropped to his sides.

"Shall we?" The guard asked.

Bosko, walked.   His broad shoulders and brutish look contained the quiet storm that he forcefully held at bay. Oberta was close behind, a blade at her neck.  Her red hair paled against the anger she kept in check.  Tome was next; his tall lean frame was a deadly weapon that he kept sheathed. Devis, the blonde mountain of pale skinned muscle was next. He looked at the door, at the guards, then at the door again.  He felt an arm on his shoulder, and he looked back.  Garesh, with his jet black locks was shaking his head. *Do not my friend.* Devis breathed heavily and nodded in acknowledgment.

"Hey, put your arm down," said the man guarding him.

Garesh lowered his arm and looked the guard in the eye.  They continued walking, but it was clear who feared whom.   As they were weaponless, one would assume they stayed their hands because the guards were armed.  However, though some gladiators were slaves that could only earn death as entertainment for the crowds, some had been warriors.  And for a few, it was in the arena that their true nature came alive, that in truth they were warrior born of incredible skill, no matter their beginning.  The guards and their weapons were no match for Awere.  Unfortunately, the truth of their situation could easily be lost in the moment, in the bloodlust.  Garesh was aware of this, as was Bosko, as was Awere.  If they killed the guards, what then?  Once they freed Awere?  What then? The question was one that needed no answer.  This was not the time or the place for such bold action.  Or, was it?  They vanished from the passageway, through the doorway to the compounds.  Leaving Awere to her fate.

On the other side of the bolted door, Awere had already turned, her back was to the door and freedom.  There was a dent, splinters where she had struck it with her fist.  Given enough time, enough anger, enough gathered will, she could probably kick the immense door down.  However, reason prevailed.  Her brilliant mind took hold. *How did I let him do this to me?*
She had become complacent.  She could feel the darkness in

the guard, but she should have been able to discern between his normal low-life criminal state of mind and his intention to act. There were any number of things she could have done once he had started leaning towards her. She knew she was just that fast. In fact, she could have made him miss her altogether. She would not forget.

*You never stop teaching me, do you?*

She could feel it. The room was a holding pen, wide and dark, high ceiling, with landings, three levels. Detritus thrown about, the room was not abandoned, but the occupants, tonight's prisoners, were gone. Given their proximity to the compound they were intended to be part of tomorrow's entertainment. *Murderers, then.* But the question was clear, *are there any murderers still here?* The answer was obvious, but that did beg another question. *How many?*

As if in answer, two men stepped into the light on the other side of the room.

"This, is what he wants us to kill?" asked the one on the left, a tall muscled man with greasy long black hair. He was wielding a huge broadsword. "This ... girl?" He wore a nasty brown tunic, black leggings and boots. His face was a tanned ragged mess, war wounds. His mouth was foul, all broken teeth. He was a horror show and clearly proud of it. "Can we play with her after we're done?" He guffawed, as dark thoughts flooded his mind and fed his humor, as well as his soul.

"Be careful, you ape," said the man on the right. He was dressed in all black, with a hooded cape. He had two long knives, one in each hand. "Do not take her for granted. I have heard of this one. She is to be respected."

Awere took their measure, *Encarfican assassins.* They stepped forward

"Respect who? Where? Why?" the man laughed. "Maybe I wasn't paying attention.Are we really getting paid all this money to kill this slip of a girl?"

Awere crouched, settling her breathing. They were armed. She had already scanned the room. There was no time to make something useful. She had no weapons save the gifts she was blessed with in mind, body, and soul. *Fine.*

"Stop talking you idiot," said the man in the cape. "Just kill her. Now!"

They ran forward with purpose. Awere didn't wait, but leapt forward to face them. The caped assassin's eyes widened as he lowered his blades, one out further than the other. She was incredibly fast. Awere ran low. She stepped to the right away from the oversized monster. Her speed an angle would ensure the caped man was between her and the big one's broadsword. The caped man got closer, angling to strike. Just before he was on top of her she suddenly brought her legs forward, sliding with one leg angled for his crotch. Her foot struck hard and true. She curled forward on the ground, twisting and bringing her body forward, while grabbing his leg. She quickly stood, up ending him onto the ground. Awere twisted jumping high into the air. She came down with her knee in the center of his back. There was a loud crack.

The hulking Encarfican stood there, his sword at the ready, but his face held a look of bewilderment. "Axus?"

Awere now held the caped assassin's blades. She faced the oversized monster, fearless.

"Axus?"

"Your friend is dead."

The Encarfican shook his head. "That can't be. That just can't be. You couldn't have killed him. Look at you. You're just a slave. A small woman."

"Not that small."

"Shut up! Axus has killed over a thousand men. He slayed the Ugolian beast single handed. He killed the guards of the Appotrian Oracle, and raped her for fifteen days.

"He did that?"

"He is a legend!"

"He is dead. Now what will you do?"

"You, you bitch! You can't have killed him!"

"I did. He is dead. Now?"

The Encarfican was breathing heavily.  His anger was threatening to explode.  His eyes were bulging.  Spittle was flying from his horrendous mouth.

"He was my friend!"

"Yes, he was," Awere said, a cold smile slowly spreading across her face.  "Your friend was apparently a great legend, a raping, killing legendary pig, who met his death in an instant at the knee of a woman.  Just reward for such a man ... a weak man!"

"ARRGGGG!!!!!"  The Encarfican's yell was a loud irrational thing.  "DIEEE!!!!!!"

He swung the huge sword like a man possessed, it moved quickly, with no delay, as though it were merely an extension of his arm.  His strength was astounding.  However, of the people he had killed, he had never faced one such as Awere.  Her strength was formidable as well.

She effortlessly stepped back out of reach.  He lunged and swung.  She ducked.  He swung again, and she did what seemed impossible.  He was almost twice her height, incredibly huge in comparison.  He should have cleaved her at the shoulders on the swing.  But she jumped up, jumped up high.  She jumped up high and actually stepped on his sword ... *SHE'S STANDING ON MY SWORD*!  She stepped not once, but twice, and then kicked him in the face, merely an irritating tap, and then she flipped over sideways to land on her feet.

"What .... what, are you?"

"I am your ending."

The killer yelled and lunged at her, consumed by anger.  Awere swiftly moved forward closing the distance.  She brought up the long knives and blocked his sword.  The killer's eyes went wide.  There was absolutely no way this woman could be so strong as to actually block his blow.  She stepped closer, jumping up with incredible force.  In one fluid motion, block, jump, thrust she plunged the knife into his throat.  He fell backwards, shocked.

She straddled him, still holding the knife, and frowned

as rancid fumes plumed up from this mouth.

"Impossible," he gurgled, as blood pooled and frothed flowing over his lips. "Impossible."

"No, "Awere said, raising the other blade. "It is not impossible Encarfican dog! I am Antuthema!" She plunged the knife into his eye.

The room was silent. Awere stood. She wasn't even winded. She looked at the killing monster she had just dispatched. *This was a vaunted Encarfican assassin?* Her knowledge of the world was that of the educated. However, her actual experience was limited. She knew of all the assassins guilds, perhaps had faced a few in the arena. She did not know the stories of all the people she had been forced to slay. These two were clearly not the best in the world. Yet the other was something of a surprise. She walked over to him and looked through his clothing. This one has apparently laid claim to the raping of the Appotrian Oracle. Awere recalled visiting the Oracle as a child. Despite the barbaric ways of her people, the Oracle was a divine treasure, a pleasure to meet and a riddle in conversation, a truly wondrous and quite magical person. She remembered her despair upon hearing of the rape, that some animal had so violated her, killing her guards and attendants, and ruining the flower of that most exceptional lady. The Oracle lived, but ever after she was said to be broken. Was this the man who had wrought such pain? Surely not. Awere pulled the money pouch from his belt.

"Kensu," she said, examining the coins. "That pig!"

There was no doubt in her mind of who was responsible for this attempt on her life. There was almost certainly more of the coin stashed somewhere. The Azari was sure to have paid handsomely to ensure the task was completed. And clearly more coin was spread around in order to ensure the deed was done in the dark, away from prying eyes and ears. The Azari had not spent his money wisely.

Awere dropped the coins, and stepped away from the bodies. The moonlight was shining from an open window on the upper tier. She sat down in the moonlight, closed her eyes, and controlled her breathing. Her awareness expanded. She could feel the two dead men behind her, bereft of souls, dark spirits now fled, yet … for the caped one, the rapist, there was something different. She opened her eyes, and looked back. She saw nothing, but he felt … not right. She got up, took the knife from the man-monster's eye, and shoved it into the back of the caped one's neck, up into his brain.

"Be dead Axus. Stay dead, Axus."

The body jerked once. Then, it was again still. She had been well educated, but she also had learned to trust her senses. Her awareness was fine-tuned, as special as her speed, her strength, and her skill. She went back to the moonlight and sat down. She closed her eyes and waited. The guards would soon return. They would come for her and do the only thing they could … return her to the gladiator compound.

The sun was high in the sky.

The arena was almost spilling over with spectators, filled to capacity with the rich and poor alike. In the time of the Cororucabia the Iduma was the ultimate celebration, wanton destruction that symbolized the life and death cycle of the world. However, the arena itself and the celebration were in truth a perverse corruption. The Etrusicans knew the power of spectacle, and how necessary entertainment was to the social order, how crucial it was to empire. If you keep them entertained, they will not lament the toil, and the yoke will rest that much easier, a necessary component for the preservation of the sybarite.

Druel was addressing the crowd from his honored perch on the noble terrace, surrounded by princes and dignitaries. He was holding forth to the crowd, rounds of applause punctuating his pronouncements. He sat down as the gates opened. To Awere, he was nothing more than background noise; a factotum of the aggregation of worldly stupidity, a caricature of the game of life that had been the norm at one time, and certainly was now the norm again, the love of the spectacle, with true civility and the benefits of advanced civilization consigned to the ash pit.

She drew strength from inside to fight the bitterness of this world she found herself inhabiting, this upside down place of ignorance, blood and pain. Bregah would have been incensed by this mad perversion of the rites of the cycle of life. What was precious was never meant to be wasted, dashed into the dust by blade, bone, stone, hand, whatever was available, a lust for blood. The irony of her ability, her voyage of self-discovery that through unfortunate fate culminated in her capture and enslavement had enabled her to not only survive, but to thrive.

"You okay?" Bosko asked her.

Awere nodded. "I'm fine, my friend. "Just thinking."

"Well, don't do too much thinking," said Devis. The huge man's blonde main flowed freely, as a sharp wind blew across their faces. Awere looked at him and for a moment saw the boy that must have been there, before the ax and hammer came to dominate his life. "Less thinking, more smashing, Awere." His huge muscles flexed as he squeezed the pommel of his war hammer. In his other hand was an outsized war ax.

Awere chuckled, as she deftly swung her sword with expert flourish. The simok blade seemed to sing in the wind. It was a slightly curved weapon, double edged, long-pommeled, chosen of her ancestors. A found gift from the Kensu Prince. He thought the gift would not only help protect her, but would comfort her with memories of her people. His special arrangement with the Prefect allowed her to keep such a weapon. She was very appreciative, but not as much as he would have liked.

The Prince had been incensed by the attempt on Awere's life. There had been no clue as to who had contracted the killers. The Prince's anger was a boiling thing, especially as the caped killer had presented some problems, his death a serious complication. In his anger, the Prince threatened to withhold Awere from the gladiatorial games, something he longed to do despite her incredible skill. He longed to hasten the time when she would be free. However, he had no power to remove her from the arena, even though she was his slave. The laws of Aleocretes superseded his authority, even as the Son of Heaven. As such, there was no reprieve from the Iduma. Awere never expected one.

"Indeed, Devis," she said. "More smashing, or cutting as may be required."

Her friends all shared a brief moment of laughter, a respite in the face of certain death. They knew something was coming, something far more dangerous than what they had faced in any other arena event. There was nothing funny about the moments before them, but as nerves became excited with energy, opening eyes and ears to the possibilities of life and death, laughter was … normalizing. It spread from Awere's friends to the other gladiators gathered around them. They were thirty strong. This was to be a spectacle unlike any other.

"Don't do too much smashing, Devis," said Oberta. "Leave some for the rest of us."

"I'll clean up what you leave behind," said Tome.

Bosko grunted, "Who, young one? Oberta or Devis? Neither will leave much for you to clean up."

"I would not worry," said Garesh, who had not shared in their laughter. "All of us have never been in the arena at the same time. This is the Iduma, but unlike any before. There will be more than enough, hopefully not too much."

His words silenced their laughter.

"Garesh is right," said Awere. "All of you, be ready." She looked over the entire assemblage, warriors and peasants, all gladiators, all survivors, all tested. "Steel yourselves."

As if on queue warriors slowly emerged from the gate on the far side of the arena. They were hardened, seasoned, dressed resplendent in gilded armor, but of no nation's armies. They were made to look like heroes, which was clearly the opposite of fact.

"Criminals," Oberta grunted. "Former soldiers dressed for the Last Battle."

"Tragedy and drama," said Garesh. "You're right, Oberta. We're participants in a play. Judging from the dress, it's from the final battle between heroes and demons, when gods stood side by side with men."

"Any guesses who's playing the demons?" asked Bosko, chuckling bitterly.

"Doesn't matter," said Devis, twirling his oversized hammer. "They will all fall."

"Awful lot of them coming through the gate," noticed Tome.

"Stop worrying!" Devis snapped.

Tome spit. "Who's worrying? I could give a damn!"

"Silence," Awere commanded. "Be focused. There's more to this than just numbers."

They understood her reasoning. The crowd required more than just one spectacular free for all between gladiators and former soldiers dressed up as gods and heroes. Even though the scale was larger, the need of the spectacle would demand shock and awe. The Prefect would no doubt provide. The Prefect stood, a vile beatific look spread across his face.

"The numbers are astounding!" He boomed. "The heroes of the Empire are poised to stamp out the demon vermin. You see them there, demons from the four corners of the world led by a devil!"

The crowd roared.

"But that cannot be all!" He boomed. "There must be more!"

The roar of the crowd reached new heights.

"I have personally taken it upon myself to make this the Iduma of an age! For you, the people of the Empire, I bring the greatest of spectacles! A war on the blasted sands between gladiators and warriors of right, heroes and demons! But the gladiator-demons are a horrifying lot, with awful strength. What can I do?"

The calls for blood were many and varied.

"How can I help our brave heroes?" Druel asked, milking the moment. "What aid can I render?" He looked toward one of the other gates near the rear of the so-called heroes. It opened slowly. Men with ropes emerged, dragging with them a nightmare from the wildwood, the deep jungle, something from beyond the deserts, something Awere readily recognized.

"By the Gods," said Bosko.

Awere felt the fire in her belly rage, her body stiffened unto steel. She gripped her sword in a vice grip. "Steady, Bosko. Steady all of you!" She yelled back to the gladiators.

"My people," said the Prefect. "With pride, I present to you the aide our heroes need to destroy the gladiator-demons to the last. I give you … THE RAT KING!"

"Awere?" Bosko's voice held the sound of fear.

"Steel yourself now!" Awere commanded.

"But—"

"There is no but. Nothing has changed. The stakes remain the same. Either they die or we die. And I say we decide fate this day. I say we control destiny, not Druel!" Her words rippled through the gladiator ranks like electricity, charging them against rising fear. No man had seen the likes of the Rat King in an age, if not longer. Such a thing was not to be believed, but there it was before them, a rat the size of three men, horribly strong, ferocious, and fiendishly intelligent.

The men dragged the grotesquery of a rat onto the field of battle. It was huge, easily fourteen feet tall standing. Its face was full of aggression, snarling hate. It wore a red tunic and nothing else. However, rats didn't customarily wear clothes, did they? Then again, none had ever seen a rat so large, so alarmingly aware. Its legs and arms were muscled. It wasn't fat at all, still ratlike in shape, but powerfully built. Once it was close to the far right flank of the gilded warriors, the men gave a little on their ropes and allowed the Rat King to stand. It hissed and spat. It was a horror of anger and hate.

It looked up at the Prefect and was motionless. The crowd grew silent.

The rat eyed the Prefect and suddenly ... it spoke. "Druel, I will end this, every human on this field. And then, you. You will die by my hand. This I swear!"

The crowd erupted in fear and horror, mixed with fascination and delight. Druel raised his hands as he laughed, calming the crowd. His smile had actually grown wider, if that was at all possible.

"My dear Pau," he said, addressing the Rat King. "That would indeed be something."

The crowd joined him in laughter. "My friends," he bellowed. "Have I not delivered for you today? Have I not satisfied the requirement? Is this not the Iduma of an age?"

The crowd roared.

"Now," he yelled. "Heroes of Etrusica, Rat King, do your duty, and destroy the gladiator-demons!"

Awere stood at the head of the gladiators, the tip of their deadly spear. "On my order," she said. "Steady ... steady ... steady ... steady ... NOW!"

*The War Dreche! The War Dreche! The War Dreche!*

Someone in the crowd had started the chant months ago. Awere had come to command the respect and admiration of the crowd. She was a pleaser, a prime bit of entertainment. The women admired her physical prowess, as did the men, and much more. A Dreche was a war leader's honor bound warriors, his or her closest allies, a bond forged in blood stronger than the bonds of family in some instances, and old term, an ancient term not reserved for the men and women of the arena. Awere and her companions had not become comfortable with the term, but their dedication to each other was above reproach. It was clear in how they fought, how they defended each other. The crowd was only waiting for the day when they had to fight one other. Of course, such a thing was complicated. You did not want to kill your best. It diminished the entertainment. However, today was different.

The chant grew louder as Awere arrayed her men and women. Like pincers the gladiators thinned their ranks to the flanks of the forward rushing horde. Bosko, Garesh, Oberta, and Tome stayed close. The so-called Heroes of Etrusica plunged forward into the circle Awere had created with no fear. Awere's simok blade sliced the air as her muscles coiled.

"Take them!" She yelled.

*The War Dreche! The War Dreche! The War Dreche!*

Awere was an ebony blade, flesh and metal. She led her warriors into the maw of battle and gave no quarter. Her simok blade was death's scythe, slicing effortlessly through the armor of the Etrusicans. Her Dreche was the tip of the spear, and they bore deep.

Devis's war cry was a thing to frighten even the most hardened warrior. His hammer smashed head and helm, even as his war ax cut through shield, broke sword, and separated bone from flesh, producing great gobs of blood and gut. He was an unholy horror on Awere's right. Oberta was just next to him out of reach of hammer and blade, claiming life after life with her sword. Her flaming hair was a beacon, a harbinger of doom to the soldiers who rushed headlong into her deadly embrace.

Garesh held their rear guard. With cold, calculating determination, he dispatched the Etrusicans that spilled on either side of their number. They were a deadly tip plunging deep into the ranks of the criminal soldiers. On the outside, the pincers of their fellow gladiators were making good work of the opposition, but these were still seasoned warriors, and from where Garesh stood, his tall height and well-seeing eye afforded him the cold truth. The Etrusicans were giving as good as they were getting. The gladiators were holding, but no without losses. Their number of thirty became twenty-five, by his reckoning. He swung his blade with even stronger determination.

Suddenly there was a heightened roar of approval

from the crowd, as though they could actually get any louder. Prefect Druel was standing waving one hand, in the other was a goblet of wine. On the edges of the great battle he had released animal predators into the arena. Dozens of massive starving lions descended on gladiator and soldier alike. Awere and her War Dreche, ensconced in the middle of battle knew nothing of the lions that were making short work of the fighters on the edge of the conflict. However, the gladiators though not of the War Dreche were still some of the finest. The Etrusicans, though criminals were still soldiers. They quickly turned the tide against the lions, slaying them one at a time, until beast cowered from man, and man once again turned his bloody focus back to man, and the cloying heat of battle.

"Awere, Tome!" Bosko yelled. "Stay on pace! You're getting too far ahead!"

The simok blade's silver was covered in deep red. Awere's strong and seemingly inhuman arm was a blur as she cut, and cut, and cut, deeper into the Etrusican ranks. Tome kept pace with her, claiming his own kills, fighting with everything he had to give, proving his worth again and again. They were leaving Bosko and the others behind.

"Cut the bitch down!" An Etrusican yelled from somewhere in the rear of their ranks. "If we kill her then we might just get out of here alive! KILL THAT BITCH!"

There was renewed vigor among the Etrusicans, and they swiftly closed ranks around Tome and Awere. They had never fought such a number, and in her desire to dispatch as many as she could as soon as she could, Awere had made a tactical error. A small circle of soldiers surrounded them. And then … a pause.

"Stay close," Awere told Tome.

"Where are the others?" He asked, breathing heavily as he put his back to hers.

"They're there. Still fighting."

"But not for long," said an Etrusican soldier, smiling with rotted teeth. "Slay the bitch!"

"Get down, now!" ordered Awere.

Tome quickly hit the dirt. He wasn't certain what he would see, but given Awere's skill, he knew it would be impressive, as well as save his life. He heard the warrior princess exhale, and then, he didn't see her, or rather she had been replaced by a blur that moved so fast it seemed impossible, even inhuman. Etrusican body parts seemed to litter the air as her simok blade slashed seemingly every direction at once. Tome's eyes were wide. He had seen her fight for a long time now, but he had never seen her move like this. He had no idea she was this fast. Suddenly, a tremendous roar erupted behind him, and Etrusicans fell onto the ground bashed and bludgeoned. The blonde barbarian Devis broke through their ranks, stepping forward on the backs of the slain.

"Missed me?" he asked, smiling down at Tome. "Get up, boy."

"You do realize I wasn't cowering."

"Enough," said Awere, finally coming to a halt. "We push forward."

The circle that had surrounded them was a broken thing, separated into sections as warriors fought for survival.

"Time to finish this lot," said Bosko. "Right, Awere?"

Awere was standing silently. Her War Dreche stood beside her, covering all sides. But no warriors dared confront them at this point. The arena was a roaring crescendo of barbaric delight, the crowd was glazed, eyes wide at this most inhumane of spectacles. But there were other things, and Awere could sense them, even as those around her could not. She looked over the fighting gladiators and criminal soldiers, and stared into the cold eyes of pure hatred.

"I had almost forgotten he was there," said Tome, his voice shaking. "Why is he just standing there like that?"

"He's waiting, "said Bosko.

Oberta cut down two soldiers that turned their attention towards their group, "You know we still have a fight here to contend with before we start worrying about oversized rats."

"You call that oversized?" asked Tome.

"Courage, "said Awere. "There is something else."

"What?" asked Bosko.

"Do you not hear it?"

Bosko couldn't hear a thing over the den of fighting, even though they stood, yelling to one another in a space of relative calm at the center of a blood-made human conflagration.

"It's coming from outside the arena," said Awere.

"You can hear something outside the arena?" He asked.

"Are you surprised?" Asked Garesh. He came up to stand beside her. "He's waiting for the ranks to thin," he told her, turning their attention back to the Rat King.

She nodded, refocusing herself on the matter before them. "Yes, and he has seen us fight. Pau is a legend, Garesh. I can't begin to tell you how shocked I am to see him here. This will be no easy thing.

"Is it ever?"

She chuckled. "No."

All of them looked toward the rat, now standing against the far wall, cold, stiff, red eyes staring them down. People in the crowd were pelting him with food. He ignored them. Some gladiators came close to him as they fought. He ignored them as well. The crowd was enjoying what was before them, and were not at all perturbed by the monsters intransigence. They were patient in their wait for ever more gore.

"When?" asked the tall, dark warrior.

Awere breathed heavily, readying herself. Her eyes remained locked on the Rat King. "I would guess … right about now."

Suddenly, there was an inhuman roar that cut through the den of death and applause. Pau barred his teeth and his long forearms, so very different from a normal rat's appendages. Powerful weapons, they flew out in deadly snatching and sweeping arcs, claws cutting, crushing, tossing and rending.

Now, the Etrusicans were undone. The gladiators closest to them followed suit. Fear had descended on them all, and there was no place to hide, no respite from the horrifying demon that was Pau. Bodies started to take flight.

Pau The Rat King stood well high above them. Hardened wariors now cowered in fear as he waded among them deep, using foot and claw to literally stomp, shred, disembowel and toss soldier after soldier from the field. Body parts and gouts of blood began to literally rain on the spectators. Horror, revulsion and delight filled the arena. Above the screams and yells there was obscene laughter. The Prefect was almost beet red, filled with sheer delight at the unholy spectacle he had created.

In the nobles section, the elite of Aleocretes were a broad mix across the emotional spectrum. Those closest to the Prefect mirrored his response. This was absolutely delightful, a feast for the senses. However, other dignitaries were not so pleased with the complete and utter horror that was taking place below.

"This is blasphemous!" Spat Prince Qiang. "Where did he find this abomination? And how dare he release it into the arena!"

"My Prince," said Tenzo. "One only knows where the Prefect found such a beast. This part of the world is full of such abominations. Consider your slave, Awere."

The Prince didn't respond. He was standing, riveted to the action below, as though he were willing the gladiators to survive.

"Perhaps it's only fitting that bitch fight this beast my Prince," said the Azari. "In truth neither of them are worthy of our attention."

With a vicious swiftness Qiang turned and wrapped his hand around Tenzo's neck. He slowly squeezed.

"Tenzo, I have tolerated your disrespect towards Awere. Tolerated! She is down there fighting for her life as she never has before. She has earned your respect and the respect of all those here gloating and howling. In case you

missed it Azari, the animals are all in the stands!"
He thrust his advisor back into his seat, over which the Azari quickly tumbled backward, leaving him with his ass pointed in the air.

"Not another ill word, Tenzo!"demanded Prince Qiang. "Not one!"

The Prince's second and third level advisors rushed to pick up the Azari. They helped him straighten his clothes, as well as his seat. Tenzo collected himself and quickly suffused the anger that was plainly written on his face. He was trained from childhood to serve, and he would do so nobly, and reverently, and without rancor for his charge. Quickly, his anger turned into a smile. The worried looks of the other advisors quickly changed as well. On the field, Pau The Rat King was facing Awere. The blood red arena was actually in a moment of pause, calm descended, only to be shattered by the sudden sound of thunder.

"What was that?" asked the Prince.

Over in the Prefect's perch, Druel's smile began to fade.

"Prince, I think we should leave," said Tenzo.

The Prince turned to his Azari. "Why, Tenzo? What do you know?"

"Nothing specific, my Prince," Tenzo said, trying to stretch the knowledge he possessed from lie to wise assumption. "Aleocretes has always been at the heart of conflict. The Etrusicans are again harassing the Inqousu. This, of course, is not wise, and I have said as much to our friends, but they do not listen."

Another sound of thunder, an explosion.

"Guards!" yelled Druel, over from his perch. "Guards!"

"The Lion Prince will not sit idly by as Appotrians and Encarficans join Etrusicans in so-called exercises," said Tenzo.

"What did you say?" demanded the Prince. A look of incredulity spread across his face. "Appotrian soldiers are in Aleocretes, with Encarficans?"

"I can't be certain, my Prince. Only the whispers of advisors and eunuchs."

"I would gather those explosions mean whatever exercise they were going to be engaged in, they have once again underestimated Inqousu resolve. Prince Tashaki will not be merciful."

"Again," said Tenzo. "I advise we take our leave."

"No," said the Prince. "We head down to the arena floor."

"WHAT?!?"

In the arena, Awere and her War Dreche faced the ultimate horror, Pau King of the Rats.

"Form lines," ordered Awere. "Circle him."

"For what!" demanded Pau, in his eerie guttural voice. "I'm simply going to kill you all."

"I think not!" yelled bold Devis.

"Northerner, I have no desire to kill any of you," said the Rat King. He eyed Awere. "Least of all you. I know who you are, and I am saddened to see you come to such a pass. You and are I much the same."

"Wow," said Bosko. "Did ya hear that?"

"Rumors of the noble rodents, rats mice and others, have reached even my land," said Garesh. "Though shocking to behold, it speaks to the truth of the great mysteries."

"I and my kind are no mystery, Easterner," said Pau. "We are as real as the one who leads you, a forgotten people and a forgotten cause, but we are not without purpose. And it is to that purpose that you all must be sacrificed."

"Enough," said Devis. "Time to end this."

"Do not break the line," Awere yelled. "Devis!"

The powerful barbarian threw himself at the rat king with hammer and axe. The rat king was quicker. He jumped back, but Devis followed. Two gladiators attempted to aid Devis and slipped behind the rat. The tried to strike with spears, but Pau swung his right claw out and downward. The men were cut in two. Devis launched at Pau, burying his axe deep into the rat's abdomen. The Rat King howled in pain.

Devis roared in triumph. "You die, like any other!"

As the rat staggered backward, Devis brought up his hammer to strike. Pau's eyes seemed to glow red, seething with anger. Before Devis could bring his hammer down, the Rat King shoved his foot into the abdomen of the roaring barbarian. The foot went through Devis like a spear. In one quick motion. Pau jerked his foot and tossed Devi's body back among the warriors, now so much useless flesh.

"Devis!" Oberta yelled, a cry of pain and grief that told the truth of her feelings, of moments past.

"Stay your ground, Oberta!' Awere demanded. "Heed me now!"

"But he's almost dead," said one of the Etrusican soldiers. "Your barbarian cut him to the quick! We can finish this. Follow me"

Four Etrusican soldiers followed him, a man who spoke with the authority of an officer. He led a charge, and the Rat King answered in kind. Blood flew, some from Devis's axe, which had now been dislodged, the rest from the soldiers, who the Rat King destroyed with tooth and claw.

"I am far from dead, Antuthema."

"I know," said Awere.

"It is a shame I shall have to kill you."

"I don't think I will die here today."

"Oh yes," said Pau. "For you must!" And with that, he leapt into the air. He landed with the intent of squashing Awere, but she was no longer there.

"Strike!" she yelled.

The Rat King was still faster. He cut Tome and Garash down with an evil claw that sliced five more men to ribbons. They all fell to the ground, fleshy parts, clothing and metal. Oberta, moving swiftly jumped and was on the rat's back, spear in hand. She yelled as she drove it deep, pushing it in as far as she could manage. The Rat King howled in pain and bucked hard enough to toss the fiery redhead off his back and away. She crashed into the ground unconscious.

"My Gods!" said Bosko. "My Gods!" Just that fast, the War Dreche had been decimated. Etrusicans tossed spears that found their home. The Rat King couldn't avoid them, but he showed no signs of falling. He descended upon the spear throwers, biting heads and disemboweling bodies.

"Pau!" Awere raged. "Face me!"

Pau turned. "Yes, little girl. Let us make an end of it." The Rat King glanced at the crowd. "Once we are done, there is a fat Prefect I intend to devour."

"You won't get the chance," said Awere. "Stand back, Bosko."

Bosko scrambled backwards. "You don't have to tell me twice!"

She controlled her breathing and gritted her teeth, pushing down her anger, anger at herself for not thinking, for not acting faster, anger at the loss of those she had come to consider family, anger that threatened to open the door to the deep pain within, a pain that could consume her whole, if she lost control. She exhaled, and closed tight the locks on her anger, that which could very well make her go berserk. Her eyes became wide orbs, as she launched herself at the rat.

Pau extended his claws, barring his teeth. He was pure ferocity. As Awere closed the distance, he moved swiftly to strike, both claws extended to deal the death blow. Awere ran between his hands, moving ever faster. She held the deadly simok blade with both hands, bringing it down with dizzying speed first to the right, and then to the left. Pau howled in pain. She didn't break her stride as she ran forward, leaping high into the air, her blade held aloft readying a killing blow. The Rat King moved his mouth like a weapon. He bit at the blade, moving his head back and to the side. Awere's blow was powerful. It didn't kill, but it did cut deep. The rat king staggered back, and fell to the ground howling, hissing and spitting, as he tried mightily to control the pain that burned throughout his body.

Awere stood next to him, glancing back only for a moment at what she had wrought, two long arms with clawed hands still twitching in the dirt, and part of the Rat King's lower jaw. Blood was spattered everywhere. She didn't let it show, not to Pau, not to the gladiators, or the soldiers; however she was very surprised by what she had done, the swiftness of skill, the sheer power she was able to bring to bear with the simok blade. Then, in that moment, amidst so much death, for a moment she remembered the girl who played among the flowers, danced on the shore, never did she see herself as she is now, a pure and potent weapon of destruction, able even to stand against the ancient and powerful Pau.

"Finish it, girl," said the Rat King. "Let it be done."

It was at this moment that the warriors in the arena noticed what was going on around them. People were fleeing. Thunderous noise from outside reverberated against the walls, echoing all around them. To the soldiers, and many of the gladiators, the sound was all too familiar. This was the sound of war, mighty siege engines. As if in tandem with this realization the sky was filled with fireballs, sailing high. Some arced over the arena. Others, were clearly aimed in their direction. Balls of Theman fire collided with walls that had stood a thousand years, and seen generations of blood. Today, they were falling, and the people couldn't leave fast enough to follow them into oblivion.

"Finish me," repeated Pau. "I'm done. And if you don't move fast enough, you'll quickly follow."

"This," said Bosko, coming to stand by Awere, "is perhaps the worst day of my life."

Awere held her sword firmly, but stayed her hand. First, she wanted answers.

"Noble King, how did you come to be here?" As the question fell from her lips, her demeanor changed. She became respectful.

"Ahhh, little girl," sighed Pau. "Deadly little thing that you are. You words warm my dying heart. I see you know the old ways.

"I was not always as you see me."

Pau smiled, a grisly sight from only half a mouth.

"But this was always to be your fate, in the end."

"Why do you say this?

"My dear, I know all about you. More than you know about yourself. Is Druel still here?"

Awere and Bosko looked to the seats. As the fireballs fell, and walls shattered, the crowd was now only a remnant, the slowest and those considered the least in importance were all that remained. There was no sign of the Prefect of Aleocretes. Around them, the remaining gladiators and soldiers were fleeing as well. Some of the remaining Etrusican soldiers attempting to leave through the far wall ran into death, as shining warriors of the Northern March poured through the opening.

"The Inqousu!" said Bosko. "This is just getting worse. The world is coming to an end all around us. Awere, we've got to get outta here!"

"Come," said Pau to Awere. "Take my foot. I know much, and will share with you what I can of my own free will."

"Awere, don't!" warned Bosko. "It's a trick!"

"No," said Awere. "King Pau is Rafusku.

"Yesss," said Pau.

"Low humans came to call them rats, because that is how the simplest of us, so many of us, see them. But Bosko, did you know that it is said the Rafusku thought us to be nothing more than overzealous monkeys?"

Pau laughed, chucking blood. "This is true, Awere. But all that is done. Come, take my foot now. There isn't much time."

Awere took the foot of Pau, King of the Rafusku, and her body shook. Her mind was flooded with images, visions of the past, of great heights, and terrible falls, of freedom and slavery, bold betrayal, and wicked murder, magic and realms unseen. She fell backward, and as she fell into darkness she saw men running towards her.

"Awere!" Bosko yelled. "Awere, are you alright?"

Awere shook it off quickly, getting up to one knee,

and clearing her head. She blinked twice, and found herself surrounded. Bosko was there by her side, as well as the Crown Prince of the Celestial Throne, Prince Qiang of the Kensu Empire. Beyond them, stood the Inqousu. The soldiers of the Great Imperium formed ranks, and down their center walked the Lion General of the Northern March, Crown Prince Tashaki Nqobi son of the Emperor Sisiwe Nqobi.

"Pau?" She asked.

Bosko shook his head. "He's dead. Whatever he did to you finished him off."

As the eastern wall of the arena began to crumble and fall under the barrage of Theman Fire, the Prince of the Heavenly Empire and his retinue stood across form the Prince of the Great Imperium and his fearsome warriors, but there was no anger, no recrimination. They assessed each other, and there was an instant feeling of kinship. One knew Awere, as did the other, but differently.

"Awere, you are safe," said Prince Qiang

Awere stood. "Yes, I am fine, Qiang."

The Prince smiled. "I never had a doubt."

"I too, am glad to see you safe," said Prince Tashaki. "To know this has been your fate …"

The words trailed off.

Awere looked at him with an even smile, barely any emotion. He was clearly a man of great power.

"You are free to come with us," he said. "My father and I would be honored to have you stay in our home. I would accompany you back to the Imperium myself, and together, you and I, we might rebuild what barbarian invaders have torn asunder."

A sense of wonder and surprise spread throughout. The Prince's words were powerful, very meaningful. They almost had the sense of a proposal.

"The slave is the property of the Prince of Heaven," Tenzo said haughtily, standing behind Prince Qiang.

Two of Prince Tashaki's lieutenants drew their swords. The look of anger on their faces was terribly powerful.

"Silence!" Commanded Prince Qiang. "Let us all be calm."

"Kind of hard with it raining fire and all," said Bosko.

The Prince ignored him. "Awere," he said. "I don't have the words. You know how I feel. I can never replace what you have lost. I can never right what has been done to you. A thousand apologies and all the wealth in the Empire would not be enough. But know this, you are free. And I will forever be yours to call upon in time of need.

The Prince of Heaven bowed low to Awere, leaving his retinue in abject shock.

"I will be leaving Aleocretes," he said. "Perhaps even the Homelands. But if fate be kind, we will see each other again Awere, as equals. And in this time, perhaps I may earn your love.

"Prince Qiang," said Prince Tashaki. "Your actions show your true nobility."

The General of the Northern March extended his hand to the Son of Heaven. They shook hands firmly. Prince Qiang looked upon his beloved Awere one more time. Then, he turned and left the arena.

The Prince of the Imperium turned his attention back to Awere. "Kaya Akosa Se Awere Antuthema, have you considered my offer?

"Kaya?" asked Bosko. "I thought your name was Awere?"

"She is the Princess of the Antuthema, of the old race," said Prince Tashaki. "She is to be honored and revered, and though apparently she needs no protection, I and my soldiers are readily willing to provide it."

Awere considered his words. Suddenly, in a world gone insane, she was free. She had choices, but she was filled with sadness and lost, as the fire and heat of battle wore away.

"Where is Oberta?"

"I'm here, Awere," she said, coming to stand next to Bosko. Her eyes were red, holding back the pain of loss, of what was never realized. "I am by your side."

"And this is all that is left?"

"We're it," said Bosko.

"You are all welcome in my home," said Prince Tashaki. "I suggest we make our leave. My troops are making short work of the remaining Etrusicans, Encarficans and Appotrians We will secure the city and finish tearing down this monstrosity. Then, we will head home."

"Prince, your offer is well received," said Awere. "We will accompany you."

"I am honored," he said. "Prince Qiang was right. I can do nothing to redress your tremendous loss. However, please but if you would only allow me to try.

"The world has much to answer for," said Awere. "But the world is as it is, and nothing will change that. I can't live my life in the past. However, I will honor it, with all that is required."

"I would expect no less of the Antuthema."

Awere cleaned and sheathed her simok blade. She took one more look back at Pau, at the gladiator arena that her been her home for what seemed like untold ages, ages of blood and metal. She would gladly leave it behind, but respect it for what it had made of her. Never again would she be a slave. She didn't know what she would be. There was no certainty. But she could accept this truth. In time, she would find her way.

# THE NIGHT WIFE

### *Carole McDonnell*

The Queen of the Southern Kingdom had six husbands; a seventh was needed. Aged, ugly, and fatigued with life, the queen would have gladly remained without the seventh. She had no wish for yet another consort whom she did not truly love. But rules are rules, and ancient laws existed for sensible reasons. The thing was required; the thing had to be done.

Heralds were sent far and wide throughout the kingdom, declaring that any youth of good standing, unmarried and free of any taint in his mind and body, should travel to the city and present himself to the queen. None were compelled – because the queen was as wary of being unloved as she was of loving. But, as might be expected, many young men presented themselves at court. And why not? To live as a Queen's consort would bring gold aplenty, and riches. Although the land was peaceful, blessed, and fertile -- gold, good food, honor, and riches are not to be sneered at. So young men – beautiful and strong (and some neither so beautiful nor so strong) ventured to the city to make their fortune in marrying the old queen.

Among them was Amar, a dancer from a small village in the east. When he entered the throne room, the old woman smiled in spite of herself. The boy was handsome, with kind eyes, with a slender body made for women to look upon. When he spoke, his intelligence, insight, and ready wit --combined with a radiant joyfulness and easygoing laughter-- touched the old queen's heart. He was not wise in the ways of the world, being from a tiny village, but even as he spoke of commonplace matters, the queen found herself clutching her heart. It had been years since her heart felt it had met its true companion. No wonder then that, after a year --notwithstanding being warned in a dream-- she chose Amar as her seventh husband. Because the young man loved her, her heart was truly happy.

But, as often happens, trouble loomed. The boy had a spirit who coveted him, a night wife who had seen him dancing upon the hills and who loved him. This spirit guarded him jealously, and made it clear to the entire palace that none should lie with him but herself.

Now, as I have said, the queen was old and ugly and tired. Indeed, she had always been old, having battled hardship all her life. But she had also been engaged in a great war inherited at her coronation, a war begun when her father sought to invade the peaceful lands surrounding his kingdom. She had fought victoriously and had crushed many lands and was tired of warfare. Her recently-dead husband had been a great warrior and had died in battle. She had no desire to war with either humans or spirits. She had long forgotten what passion was, having lost all patience or trust in her husbands, having put aside love to make war. The reborn fire in her heart terrified her and because the spirit asked for nothing else but that the youth should not lie with the queen-- the old woman was inclined to compromise.

But, the queen remembered her younger days before her ascent to the throne, before she had fought her father's war and decimated kingdoms, days when she was bullied by the children of her father's other wives, days long gone now that those siblings had been dispatched to lands beyond the queen's territory. She did not wish her young husband to be bullied by a spirit. For Amar would rise from his bed bruised and battered from the spirit's cruel lovemaking. Worse, if the youth so much as kissed the old queen –for the youth himself wished to lie with the queen-- the spirit would pierce him through with many spirit lances and leave him in lingering pain for days. So, because the queen disliked suffering and cruelty and because of the sudden late-blooming passion in her heart, she resolved to rid herself of the jealous spirit.

But to battle one from the spirit realm is not a thing easily done. Spirits are stubborn folk and not inclined to easily part with what they possess. Vindictive and cruel are they also, and prone to enjoy triumphing over humans in all matters great and small. It was said that to battle a spirit was to invite death to feast on one's family.

The queen, therefore, sent word that all the magicians, soothsayers, charmers, and advisers in the land should present themselves before her throne. And from within the palace, she called forth her three daughters, her two sons, and her six husbands to hear their opinion on the unprecedented battle. Meanwhile Amar lay in the queen's chamber recovering from the attack inflicted upon him by his night wife. Thus, the room sealed by magical herbs within and without to block the ears of spirits, one proposed this and another proposed that.

Then, one stood up who claimed he had encountered such battles before. A bearded man from the eastern country with hair braided and shiny with shea oil, he was a man the queen considered too handsome and too glib. But he was a cousin of a cousin of a cousin of the queen's third husband and his glibness was to be endured. His name meant The One Riding at the Water's Edge and this was his advice:

"Great Queen, it is obvious what should be done." He advanced toward the queen's throne without asking for permission. "These spirits do not leave one home or one lover unless they find another. Therefore, find some other boy – one as pretty or prettier than the one you now have—and bribe the spirit to take that boy as her lover."

All universally considered the suggestion a worthy one. Except the queen.

"Should I sacrifice another life that my own sorrow might end?" she asked. "No, that I will not do."

The One Riding at the Water's Edge answered her. "As always, Great Queen, you are noble. And yet – let me speak plainly—spirits have always existed in this land. Indeed, the world is full of them. When your young husband dies, will this selfsame spirit not find herself a new love?" He shrugged, stroked his glistening beard.

"Therefore, why trouble yourself with such scruples? Find the Night Wife a new love, and rest happily with the young husband of your old age."

But the queen turned to the others. "Is there no other scheme?"

No one answered.

She looked at her oldest husband, the husband of her youth, a man whose name is translated "Light," a weak, willful, jokester with a good heart, but one who was never much of a warrior. "What is your advice?"

"Give up the young man," he told her. "Find yourself another husband and let the spirit triumph over you. Or do you not know how much trouble you could bring upon our land if you insist on battling spirits? True, our kingdom is large and our army great. But who can fight a legion of spirits?"

"And how do you know this spirit has a legion to command?" she asked him, annoyed as his usual weakness.

"Because it is the way of spirits to league together," he answered her, raising his voice, forgetting his place as usual.

The queen looked at her fourth husband – now "third husband" because her third husband had so recently died. This husband was a deceitful man who had once taken her handmaid as a lover. (The lover had subsequently had her feet boiled in oil; thus no other handmaid had dared to supplant the queen or triumph over her.) "And what do you think should be done?" she asked him.

This one – named The Warrior Who Revenges— answered her. "I know your heart, Wife Queen. You do not like anyone triumphing over you. Therefore, you will not give up the boy. And even if you were to give the boy over to his spirit lover, you would still fear for him. Because you know others will love him, and he may love others. Thus, even if he is left in the hand of his spirit lover, he will continue to be harmed. And that is your wish, is it not? That this boy not be harmed? Therefore, I say, Fight this spirit! Or else, ask her what she wants and give it to her."

"The spirit wants the boy!" the Queen's eldest son, a boy of twenty and three years, said. "There is nothing else she wants."

"Perhaps there is something," the Queen began.

But the boy shook his head knowingly. "A woman will not easily give up one she loves. And this spirit has taken the form of woman and believes itself capable of understanding human love. Therefore, she will not allow a human woman to take what she considers rightfully hers."

"Perhaps, Mother," the first-born daughter said, "perhaps you should find the Night Wife a spirit husband. One who is as lovely, as witty as Amar, but long buried, one who sleeps alone in his grave and would not mind walking the spirit-world with her."

"Not so," said the second-born daughter.

Now this girl was intelligent and beautiful to look on. She also had a fierce spirit, and she also loved Amar, although Amar's eyes and mind were full of nothing but his love for the old queen.

"Mother," she said, "spirits do not want dead bodies to lie with. They desire warm flesh, hot blood. Why should this spirit leave a vibrant young man to lie among corpses?"

"You have only challenges," the queen said, furious that none in the royal room could help her. "Have you no remedy?"

The second-born Princess approached her mother. "I will battle this spirit, Mother-Queen. Let me lie tonight in your bed, beside this young husband of yours. And when the spirit appears, let it meet my lance."

"And what use is a lance of iron against a spirit woman, Daughter?" the now-fourth husband, a fat and stupid man from the northern lands, asked. And though generally quite stupid, he had asked an intelligent question.

The Princess answered, "Let my lance be bathed in all such herbs that are said to be weaponry against evil. At such time when the spirit is near me, I will retrieve my lance and pierce it through."

"Could your mother not do that?" the fourth husband asked with concern. This he asked because his features and the Princess' so resembled each other that all deemed him the Princess' true father. "Why should you risk the spirit's anger?"

"I am young and swift," the girl replied. "And already, the royal lance lies within the queen's bedroom. Many herbs as well. Already weapons lie within reach of her bed. The sorcerers can enter and work their lore and the spirits will not know."

But the old queen would not hear of it. "To battle a spirit? No, my daughter. Why put yourself in danger because of me." She turned to the others present. "Is there no other counsel?"

But the Princess pushed hard at the idea, unrelenting. Because her heart was full of yearning for Amar. Because she thought to lie with him and win his heart from her mother. Therefore, she spoke earnestly of desiring her mother's happiness, and --because all knew her skill with the lance and arrow-- at last the queen was forced to relent.

It was agreed that the plan should not be spoken off outside those doors, that the evil spirit should not hear the schemes they schemed against her. (For it was evident the spirit had many spies, both human and otherwise, who might prevent the success of the exploit.)

And so the thing was done.

That night, the Princess lay beside Amar, and how lovely she thought him to look upon. His braided hair flowed along his dark arms like rivulets of dark honey. His words and wit made her heart leap with joy. Yet, all he talked of was her mother, and her heart broke with sighing, filled as it was with envy that her mother had won the love of so gracious and kind and handsome a man.

At midnight, the Night Wife arrived. How shall I describe her? A torso only, headless, legless, with large breasts. A misty pale body of white fog and light, smelling of love and death. The headless spirit hovered toward the bed then turned itself to the Princess.

A voice issued out from where the head should have been, the spirit's breath filling the royal bedroom with the odor of putresce and death. "And why are you here, Princess? Do you think you can destroy me?"

The Princess sat up in bed, kept her right hand firmly on the lance hidden under the royal covering of silk and satin. They spoke of this and that as warriors are wont to do– and all the while the Night Wife hovered near the girl, taunting. At last, when the spirit drew near, the Princess -- her hand, quick and deft-- grabbed the lance and struck. The magical poison struck deep and the Night Wife fled the room, wailing, disappearing through the walls and into the corridor.

Amar, amazed that the spirit who had taunted him for so long was routed, said to the Princess. "Truly, you are strong and brave. Tomorrow, I will sing songs and create a dance proclaiming your victory."

"Sing no songs for me, Amar," the Princess answered. "And dance me no dances. Only, love me and take me to your arms. All that I have done, I did for myself and not for my mother."

Amar shrank back from her, aghast, disgusted. Truly, the Princess had never seen such a look on the face of any man. No, no one had ever shamed her so. She rose from the bed, bowed, then exited the room, leaving the lance atop the Queen's bed.

The next morning, before the sun rose, a great wailing

was heard through the palace halls. It came from the depths of the soul of one of the servant women. She had found the youngest daughter of the Queen, the daughter of the Queen's old age, the one all called "The Unexpected One," a child of five years old hanging from a hemp rope which swung from a high beam of the child's chamber.

"But how could a child have known to do such a thing?" the queen asked, weeping and tearing her gray hair with grief. "How could she know to tie the noose just so?"

"The Night Wife taught her," the fifth husband said, and broken into tears for he had loved that young daughter who bore such resemblance to him.

"Put the boy away!" the Warrior Who Revenges shouted, he too awashed in tears. "Or will you kill all your children and all your people for the love of this one boy?"

The funeral of the young princess broke the heart of even the most hardened. Broken flowers strewn on the processional death march could only be interpreted as the young girl's broken life. The Queen, herself, was so despondent she could not rise from her bed to attend the ceremonies.

She lay in her royal bed, weeping and growing grayer and more listless as the days continued. At last, her young husband came and pleaded with her.

"Wife," he said, "You must cease this grief or it will drag you to the grave."

The queen answered, "How blessed my life would be if I could indeed join my child in the underworld." No, she would not cease her wailing for all his pleading, but instead found her blaming both him and herself for the death of the child.

So love and sorrow strove in the old queen's heart, but anger as well. The Night Wife had killed the child of her old age: the Night Wife had to be destroyed, humiliated, and made powerless.

Amar then left her room and gathered together all his belongings, putting all he had brought with him into a bag upon his back, and left the royal city. But when he was some great distance from the city, the queen's warriors caught up with him and urged him to return, saying, that the queen had learned of his departure but yet she loved him still. So he returned with him.

Days passed and again the queen called her counselors to her throne room: what was to be done with the evil, vindictive spirit?

Once more, the Queen's second daughter knelt before her. "Mother," she said, "I beg to battle this spirit again."

"This you cannot do," the Queen answered. "Or have you not seen the evil she has done against us?"

"I have indeed seen," the daughter replied. "And, for this cause, I must battle her. Or then, how shall I live knowing myself the cause of the death of my young sister?"

And yet, the Queen did not wish to send the Princess to battle the spirit again. "What will she not do if you battle her again?" she asked, fearing the answer.

But the Princess spoke convincingly of her desire to avenge her sister, pleaded that she would find greater poison and more powerful spells. At last, the Queen relented. But Kaymar, the son of the Queen's counselor spoke to the Princess. He had grown up with the royal children and had loved the Princess from afar.

"Princess," he said, "You must not fight this demon. Or else, let me help you fight against her?"

The princess laughed. "And where should you hide that she would not see you? This demon lives to draw men's hearts and bodies away. Would she not turn your heart toward her?"

"She has not turned Amar's heart toward her," Kaymar answered. "Because he loves our great Queen. And I love you. Am I so weak that my heart can be turned to her from you?"

The Princess shrugged. "Even so. Why should you

fight against her? Why should you harm yourself by causing her to be aware of you? Let her live unaware of you. It's safest. But as for me, I go to protect my mother's husband and to free him from this demon."

"Do you go only for your mother?" Kaymar asked, holding her gaze. "Often I have watched you when you thought yourself unwatched. Do you not love this boy? Tell me truly."

"And what business is it of yours if I do?" the Princess asked and commanded her old friend to leave her side.

So all the remainder of that day, the magicians and sorcerers and wisemen read  and chanted spells over the lances in the Queen's room, and made their potions stronger with the names of all their gods. That night, the room was filled with spells and charms as heavy as  any unguent, spells that called the warriors of heaven down, charms that made the warriors from beneath the earth powerless.

Again, the Princess lay beside Amar. But this time his soft voice did not lull her heart with tales and song. He had no heart for the Princess who sought to save him. Yet, she loved him even more.

"Why," she asked, "should such a lovely man waste his youth on an old woman?"

"Your mother," Amar corrected, eyeing the Princess with disgust.

"I am a woman as she is."

"You are no woman I want. Young women are as bad as spirit women to me. Let your heart find itself another love."

All evening they argued until the Night Wife arrived. Fuming the demon was, angry she was, wounded she was.

"You again?" she asked the Princess. "Why do you want to free this boy from me? When he was hungry on the hillside, was it not I who fed him? Where was this queen? Who taught him to dance so well that the stars stopped in their course to look upon him? None but I! And yet you will deprive me of him?"

And they argued back and forth while Amar remained silent hating them both. But as the night continued, the Night Wife tired of the verbal battle.

"Ah," said she. "Do you not know that I have seen your heart? I know how it is. You love the boy. What spirit, good or evil, human or divine, can not but perceive the deep love you have for your mother's husband! Understandable, because you and he are of an age. And yet you cannot have him. I will not allow it."

"Even if she could have me, I would not want her," Amar chimed in.

The evil spirit ventured toward him, hovered. "I shall enjoy you tonight as I always have," she said. "As I always will."

"I have greater poisons and greater spells with which to war against you," the Princess shouted.

"Indeed?" the Night Wife asked. "And I have greater shields, for the spirits of the dark have all gathered here to protect me."

She removed then the veil that rests upon the eyes of men and the Princess and Amar saw the horde of armed spirits surrounding her, all writhing and pestilent like a nest of vipers.

The Princess grew silent. Then suddenly she said to the Night Wife, "You who know my thoughts, what thought lies within my heart now?"

The Night Wife did not answer, but faded into the night.

"She is no longer here," the Princess said. "She is gone forever."

Amar eyed the Princess suspiciously. "Or so," he said, "it will have us believe."

The next day, the Queen was told the spirit had fled, had been rendered harmless and would no more return to attack the boy. But only the Princess and the Spirit knew that the spirit had covenanted with the Princess to enter her body.

Happy though she was to have her husband, the Queen was much grieved at the loss of her youngest daughter and so would not sleep with her young husband. In the meantime, the Princess who had now given the Night Wife permission to use her body sought to take Amar as her lover, but Amar was immune to her charms.

"Why do you not love me?" she asked him one day in the Queen's garden. "Have you not seen how I sacrificed my life and my body to free you from her assaults?"

"It is no sacrifice," Amar answered her. "True, she no longer attacks me. But it is because she believes she will have the use of your body to seduce me. She and you are allied against me. Do you think I am a fool and unable to see the schemings of human and demon alike? Why should I love you?"

"So you know?" the Princess asked.

"I surmised," Amar answered, disdain in his voice.

"But have you not benefited from my covenant with the spirit?" the Princess asked. "And what and if I should send her from my body? Will she not return to you again in spirit form to destroy you with her nightly passions?"

Amar laughed. "That I do not fear. I do not think you will renounce the spirit so easily." He walked past her toward the garden gate. "It was not I who made the covenant, and when the spirit put the thought within your heart to covenant together, you should have rejected her counsel. Even now, you will not reject her and cast her from you because you are as she is, selfish and covetous."

So he left her there, but his words were true enough. For the Princess was now irresistible to all men. No man could see her and not wish to lie with her. And the Princess herself enjoyed seeing the passions she inflamed in warrior, servant, ambassador, and statesmen alike. And yet, for all her exploits with commoner and nobles, native and foreigners, the

Princess and the Night Wife could not seduce Amar. Because Amar had no place in his heart for either of them.

The Princess then sought advice from Kaymar, the boy raised with her in the palace. To him, she told all her heart.

When she finished speaking, he said to her, "My Princess, I had heard the rumors of your exploits with men in and around the palace, but I did not think them true." He shook his head. "So, they are indeed true? And yet, I feel no great desire to use you as others have. Nor do I feel any desire to be used by you. How strange this spell is!"

"Strange indeed. For I have the love of all I do not wish to love. But those who love purely will not have my love."

"My friend," Kaymar said, "since this evil spirit has tricked you, renounce her. Truly, she will never give you what you desire. Isn't it apparent that she never intended to give you the boy? Now she comforts herself with many lovers, but what will become of you? In time, you will be broken and crushed, like a flower trampled by passers-by. The diseases of those in the palace, pestilences brought by soldiers from foreign lands – those infirmities will tear and destroy your body. And when you are dead – which will be soon enough-- she will have the boy once more to herself. Your covenant will be ended. Therefore, renounce the spirit and cease from loving your mother's husband."

But this is not the answer the Princess sought. Although she did not want a spirit living within her, hearing all her words, using her body as it willed, she would not give up the hope that Amar would love her.

"Friend, friend," she pleaded, "tell me. How shall I make Amar love me?"

The boy answered her roughly. "Do you not see that you will never have him? Your mother has brought this curse into the palace. Cease from loving him and set your heart on freeing yourself from this evil spirit! Do you think the Night Wife will be able to bear it when the Queen and Amar lie down together at last? Will she not use your very hands to slay your own mother?"

But the Princess would not heed the words of her friend and walked daily beside Amar, hoping to gain his love.

Now, the queen was no fool. Often she would see her daughter walking among her gardens, following after Amar, lovesick. She was unclear what manner of love bound them together – affection, passionate love, friendship—and although she did not like for any to triumph over her, she was not one who was prone to jealousy. She determined, therefore, to study the matter and to reserve judgment until the truth was clear.

One day, when the hills around the palace glowed green, the old queen saw the two in the royal gardens. All around them was youthfulness and life, and in her palace was her own old body. It began to dawn on her – or perhaps some ally of the Night Wife whispered it to her—that perhaps she was being deceived. So she called her daughter to see her in the throne room.

"Daughter," she said, when the Princess arrived. "I often see you and Amar walking the hills together. Tell me now, and do not fear…either for your life or for the young man's…if there is any love between the both of you."

"Oh, Mother," the girl answered, "on the night I battled the night wife, after she had fled, Amar took me in his arms. There, in your bed, he told me all his heart, how he was tired of his life in poverty and sought a wealthy wife. He told me he loved you at first, but --because his soul had been inflamed by the passions poured onto his body by the Night Wife-- he grew to understand that giving of his love to an old woman would not satisfy him. So he took me, Mother, and lay with me. He forced me, Mother, and after I had lain with him – because he was gentle to me and so blessed with beauty and charm—I fell in love with him."

"Indeed?" the old queen said.

"I speak the truth, Mother," the girl answered. "Often

we have met together and I have told him to speak his heart to you. But he refuses, although I have told him time and again that you are kind-hearted and have been betrayed more than once, that you would not kill him or turn him away."

"Has he spoken of love?" the old queen asked, leaning on her throne. "You have not said if he loves you, only that he desired passion. When he speaks with me, I feel his love. Would you be happy with one who desires passion alone but not love?"

"Truly, Mother," the girl said (but she lied.) "he has told me he loves me. He declares, when we lie together, that I am all he dreams about."

The old queen nodded, then pointed to her daughter's stomach. "And is he the father of that child? I had not seen, had not known, before you entered the room. But now as you stand before me I cannot help but see that you carry a child within you."

"Indeed, Mother, he is the father of this, your grand-child, for I have lain with no one else."

"Go then, Daughter," the Queen said, "and call my young husband to me. I will hear you again, at a later time, on this matter."

So, after that, the queen called Amar to her throne room. He entered the room, his hair long and braided and glistening with oil. The old woman's heart rose and fell at the sight of him. It leaped because he was so nature-blessed and handsome; it tumbled because she feared he did not love her.

"Dear husband," she began, "I am an old woman."

"Old and young should walk together," Amar answered, walking toward her and taking her hand. He sat at the foot of her throne looking up at her with eyes that seemed to behold only her.

The Queen smiled. "Tell me, my husband, what do you think of my daughter? She saved your life and did rid the land of that evil spirit."

Amar answered, "I hear it said the spirit is fled, yes."

"But you do not believe?"

"It is not something I easily believe, Wife Queen."

"Still, let us not speak of that odious spirit. Consider carefully, my husband. Hear what I say."

"I am listening, Wife."

"I am old. And perhaps it is good that I have not lain with you as a wife should lie with a husband. Have you seen the way my daughter looks on you? What do you think of marrying her?"

Amar's mouth fell open. "I think very little of it," he said. "It is you I love."

"And yet," the queen persisted, "it has been reported to me by one who should know that you have lain with her.'

"Then the one who should know knows nothing. I have not lain with your daughter." He rose from the floor indignantly. "And why do you push her into my bed?"

"Can you not open your heart to her?" the Queen asked. "Since you already desire her body?"

Amar wished to tell the old queen the truth of the matter that the Night Wife now lived within her daughter. And yet, he could not speak the words. Perhaps a spirit held his tongue. Perhaps wisdom itself held it because he feared the Queen would attribute the "loss" of another daughter to him. He only said, "I do not wish to marry my wife's daughter? What will your people say? If you do not want me, say so. Let me return to my village on the hillside."

"If the child within her belongs to you," the Queen pressed, "you should honor the mother. And do not fear, I will not harm you. As for the common people, they only know what the palace tells them. Neither have they seen your face to know which Amar I have married. It would grieve my heart to divorce you, and yet . . .is it not best to…"

"I tell you I am not the child's father!" he shouted. "And do not force me to marry one I do not love." He knelt, stroked the Queen's wrinkled cheek. "Do you not love me, My Wife? You have sacrificed much for your kingdom. Let your old age be filled with happiness. Why sacrifice love?"

"So you have not lain with her?" the queen asked. "Why should she lie?"

"So it is she who has told you this great lie?" Then could Amar no longer keep his secret.

"That daughter of yours was a liar from the start and now an even greater liar lives within her. Understand, my wife, I have always loved old women. It has always been my way since childhood. And for that reason alone, I cannot love your daughter. She is too young for me. But the greater reason is this. The Night Wife now lives within her, and both have covenanted together to take me from you."

When the Queen heard this, she hardly knew what to say or think. Yet she believed Amar and she called all her servant girls and ladies-in-waiting to her throne room. There she charged them that if any did know some secret about the Princess they should plainly speak the truth, that none would be harmed or charged with defaming the Princess.

They told her all, about the Princess' trysts after the evil Night Wife had entered her. The Queen listened calmly, her hand to her forehead, burning with hatred against the Night Wife and sorrow that she had brought this curse upon her kingdom by loving a man so much younger than herself.

At last, one of the handmaids spoke to the queen, a young girl recently taken captive from a northern country. The girl was dark-eyed, with skin red as the earth, and hair braided to her waist, a gentle girl to look upon.

"My Queen," she said, "If you would call for the Prophetess who lives in my country, she would be able to deliver the Princess from the power of the spirit. This Prophetess is a woman of great power, tall and graceful, bruised and broken from many battles. They say the very power of God lives within her. Seek her out and call her to deliver your kingdom from this curse."

To find a true Prophetess is a difficult thing, but to find a true Prophetess from among the people one has been warring against – oh, such a thing is impossible. Nevertheless, the Queen sent word – conciliatory words—to the king of that northern country telling him all her state and begging him to find the Prophetess and to send her to the Queen's country. The king of that country, happy that some reconciliation between their nations loomed, sent his warriors to search for the Prophetess.

Yet even this king, who had seen such wonders wrought by the hand of that Prophetess, feared failure. After all, who could stand against a Night Wife?

Meanwhile, the Princess was bound by the Queen's great warriors and tied with chains strong enough to bind three strong men. She was kept in her room with the Queen's female guards all around her. No man was allowed to see or speak to her. There she lay, imprisoned until at last the Prophetess was found.

The Prophetess entered the palace, reeking of camel urine, and wearing rough clothing. But she carried no weapon, no lance, no arrow, no sword. But her weathered sun-wrinkled face made the old queen shudder with fear.

When the Queen saw her, she stepped down from her throne and bowed, knelt prostrate, before her. "I am honored," she said, "to have one who represents the God of Heaven in my throne room. Truly, my throne room is nothing compared to the throne room of Heaven which you have surely visited."

"Where is this daughter of yours?" the Prophetess asked, looking around at the regal room with indifference.

The Queen rose from the ebony floors. "She is within her room, locked up with many chains.

"And tell me why I should help you?" the Prophetess said. "You who have recently killed so many young warriors in my kingdom?"

"It was war," the Queen said. "Should I not have completed the task my father gave me to finish?"

"No, you should not," the Prophetess replied. She approached Amar, though how she knew him none knew --for the Queen had not introduced them. "So you are the one the Night Wife loves? Are you willing to do all that is necessary to rid this kingdom of this curse?"

"I will do all but marry the girl," Amar answered.

"Even for love of your wife?"

"Even so."

The Prophetess looked at Amar from head to toe and seeing him, she loved him. "I understand," she said at last, "why the Queen loves you so." She turned to the queen. "Bring me to your daughter, and to the Night Wife within her."

The Prophetess was led to the deepest dungeons in the pit of the prisons inside the royal palace. When the Queen saw her daughter, tears fell from her eyes. That she should be made to bear such sorrow in her old age – the Queen was almost at her wits' end.

"Unbind her," the Prophetess said, "and let her go."

So the warriors who kept guard of the dungeon unbound the princess  and immediately raced outside.

The Princess strengthened her back, lifted her eyes to look at the Prophetess. "I know you, who you are," she said, "You serve the Lord of all."

The Prophetess shrugged.

All at once, an eerie voice full of hatred and spite spoke up. "This body is my clothing, the apparatus I intend to use. It was covenanted to me by the Princess herself. You cannot cast me out. Moreover, I have at my side eight thousand spirit princes who will destroy this kingdom if you send me forth into the darkness."

The Prophetess answered, "No, I doubt you have so many." She smiled. "But I understand your threat." She clapped her rough hands loudly. "Let us see how powerful you and your allies are. Leave this apparatus of yours."

Immediately the Princess' body slumped to the ground and a loud wind blew all in the dungeon to the ground. An instant later, the air around the palace and indeed all around the city grew dark as a mighty windstorm, bringing hot sand and cold hail, blew into the kingdom.

For forty-nine days, the Prophetess did nothing as the hot sand, cold hail, and mighty wind destroyed the city. While others remained inside and the flocks died in the field and the fruit died on the vine, she walked throughout the city, seeing only the limping warriors and women left widowed by the war begging in the marketplace. Then on the fiftieth day, she climbed to the highest turret of the palace.

"Is that all you can do?" she shouted to the winds.

Then flies came, settling in on the cows and goats --lice as well, crawling on the skin of rich and poor alike. Then frogs. Everywhere. The frogs were in the ovens, in the troughs, in the jewel boxes of the rich, in the ointment boxes of apothecaries, in the travel sacks of wanderers. The whole kingdom stank from the reek of them. Because of the thick multitude of the lice, an unsettling and heavy and terrifying darkness covered the whole kingdom. None could go out for all the darkness.

Again, the Prophetess said, "Is that all you can do?"

After she said this, great cancerous boils grew upon the flesh of man and animal and fowl alike. From the young to the old, all in the land were afflicted.

At last, when all the land was destroyed and the ground itself seemed to move because of all the lice and flies walking upon it, the Prophetess shouted into the darkness. What she spoke none understood, except that the words became a flood of light, dispelling the darkness. She spoke again and the words fell from her mouth like water, flowing over the land, washing all the frogs and lice away. She spoke again and the words came from her mouth in the form of a two-edged-sword cutting and turning every which way. None saw how –none saw who-- but a blood-curdling shriek sounded throughout the city as if a spirit body was being scattered and rent and sent to the ten directions.

Then light came and darkness left the city, and the flesh of those who still survived the plagues became whole again and clean like a little child's.

The Prophetess descended the turret then walked to the Queen's throne room. "It is finished," she said. "And my land is avenged."

"Your land?" the Queen asked. "Was it you who sent the spirit to destroy my land?"

"Not I," the Prophetess said. "But it was convenient for me to wait until these spirits thoroughly ruined your city. You have, after all, destroyed my land. Saint, I may be; holy I may be. But I am human, and my sons and husband were killed in your wars. The opportunity for revenge was there. There has been great war between our peoples. Should I not have taken it?"

She walked outside the palace gates. "It is enough," she said. And as she walked through the ruined streets, she said to herself, weeping, "It is enough." And as she walked through the damaged fields, she said, weeping, "It is enough."

# The Blood of the Lion

## Joe Bonadonna

Men screamed in horror and agony. The smell of blood hung thick and bitter in the air, drifting closer to us on a gentle breeze. We looked up from the fresh water spring where we were refilling our water bags. Morning sun cast spears of golden light through the treetop roof. Once again we heard the cries of dying men. The coppery scent of blood called to the beast. A sharp howl of pain was followed by the rending of clothes. I looked away as Lion emerged, there in the dark heart of the Gundardrune—the Maze of the Spirits.

Lion roared and took off running. I chased after him as fast as my long, slender legs could carry me. Monkey and bird took flight as I tried to keep pace with Lion. But then he was gone, off in another direction. I did not follow, holding true to my course until I reached the clearing and our campsite. There I found the bodies of four of the warriors who had accompanied us on safari. *But where is the fifth member of our band?* I wondered. *And where is Lion?*

Our campsite lay in ruin, our warriors pinned to death by their own spears. They had not been given time to draw sword and defend themselves. Blood pooled everywhere, their bodies torn and mutilated beyond my ability to tell one from the other.

Something had feasted on them before they died.

I knelt beside each warrior to close their eyes. I folded their hands upon their breasts. Then I noticed the paw marks left in the earth of the clearing, and the *membo* of fear breathed on the back of my neck. I knew then what had attacked and killed our warriors.

Silence cast its mojo over the great rainforest of the Gundardrune.

There came a soft rustling in the trees surrounding the clearing. The crackling of a crushed leaf was almost too soft to hear, yet my ears captured the sound of it. I set my hand to the hilt of my scimitar, but waited to draw steel. Once drawn, a sword must soon taste blood. Then a thing like the wings of the hummingbird sped past my ear—and the head of an *assegai* buried itself in the trunk of a banyan tree close to me. I leapt into the air and spun around, landing on my feet in a fighting stance.

My eight foes emerged from the trees and stood facing me.

"By the Holy Tree—I knew I smelled female among the humans," spoke the tallest of the eight. No doubt he was the leader. He was also the ugliest.

Tulonga Na'Koor, they are called—the Monkey Men. They look much like the mandrill, but when armed with wooden clubs and other primitive weapons, they walk like men. A savage and vicious race, they are beasts of the wild who hate us and eat our flesh before killing us. How they learned to speak our words, only Almighty Vizna could say.

"I like her hair," said a fat one. "The color of dried blood and braided like a rope of vine."

I looked around, wondering what happened to Lion and the fifth member of our party.

"Don't look for the one who fled," the leader said, tapping the palm of one paw with the stone head of a tomahawk. "He won't get far. Two of mine give chase."

"Do we kill before we play?" asked the smallest of the Monkey Men.

I watched them staring at me, their yellow eyes burning with the flames of hunger and desire. Wearing only my deerskin halter and knee-length skirt, I felt naked before their eyes. My arms and legs rippled with chills, yet sweat glistened on my dark brown skin. I knew the Monkey Men took great pleasure in the smell of my fear.

"First, we play," said the leader.

They came toward me, steady, slow, and sure of purpose. I drew my scimitar from its leather sheath. Sunlight danced along its sharpened edge. The Monkey Men laughed at me, but I was a warrior trained and seasoned by many feuds, though I had not yet seen twenty summers. I was as good as any man of my clan—and better than many.

I threw their laughter back into their faces.

By their own law, the leader of the Tulonga Na'Koor would be the first to taste my body, my flesh. He would also be the first to taste the metal of my sword.

He came at me in a rush, waving the tomahawk over his head. But he was reckless: my sword flashed quicker than the blink of the owl's eye and met his attack. I feinted and lunged the way my father and older brother had taught me. The Monkey Man parried my stroke, but I ducked beneath his next blow, slipped in under his guard and sliced open his belly from hip to hip. He stood there a moment, watching his entrails spill to the ground, mouth opened wide in a scream he could not voice. He was long dead before he hit the ground.

The seven who remained howled and rushed toward me.

Then Lion sprang from the forest, all sharp claws and teeth. The great cat slashed and bit with savage fury. Monkey Men screamed and fell—disemboweled, throats torn open, heads ripped from shoulders. I slew two more with an equal number of sword strokes, and then watched Lion take apart the others, one by one, giving them no chance to flee or defend themselves. Blood erupted, red and bright under the light of morning sun.

When it was over, Lion walked slowly toward me, jaws, teeth and paws slick with the blood of our foes. He growled as he drew close. I wiped my sword clean with the fallen leaf of the palm tree, and returned it to its sheath. Lion squatted beside me, leaned into me, and rubbed his massive, shaggy head against my leg. I scratched behind his ears.

"You certainly took your time," I told him. "And time is something upon which we cannot rely. It moves swiftly against us."

He purred like the kitten, his soulful eyes searching my face. I reached inside the pouch hanging from my belt and took out one of the two remaining red beans I must give to him.

Lion is Vidaro, my older brother.

I am a proud warrior of the Churengari Clan of the great Turquangi Tribe. I am the daughter of a renowned chieftain.

My name is Nidreva C'Mora, and this is my tale.

***

Seven of us had set out from Churenga, the village of my clan. We walked across savannah, trudged through marsh and bush, and hacked our way through dense forest on safari to seek the aid of the great Juju Queen, Kijazura Alae.

Seven of us there were. Only two of us now remained.

As Lion pawed me gently, I lifted his head, and he opened his jaws to me. Then I placed the red bean upon his tongue, the mojo bean made from Vidaro's blood and sealed with a powerful spell. Now there remained only the one red bean. I prayed to Almighty Vizna that I would not have need of more.

I waited for Lion to swallow the bean. A moment later, he roared in pain. My heart wept bitter tears, and I turned away to search through the supplies scattered over our campsite.

What food and water we would need I gathered and placed in a pack made of *raffia* and strapped it to my back and shoulders. I found the leather kilt, vest, and boots that Vidaro had worn during his days as a mercenary with the Wandering Swords and still favored over all other attire. When I heard him capture a deep breath and then set it free in a long, drawn-out sigh, I turned around. I laughed at his embarrassment: where Lion had been, now stood my brother, naked to my eyes.

I tossed to him his clothing. "Get dressed."

"Thanks," he said, turning his back to me while he dressed.

"Why did you leave me at the spring?"

He finished dressing and turned to face me. "I picked up the stench of two Monkey Men chasing a warrior whose scent was familiar to me."

I was not slow to guess what had happened to our fifth warrior. "Who was it?"

"Young Ezril." Vidaro shook his head. I knew his heart was heavy with sorrow and regret. "I was against his coming with us, but he was insistent, and I was too weak to deny him."

"Now he sleeps with the others, in the arms of Vizna," I said.

We held a moment's silent vigil for our warriors, our companions, our friends. When the moment passed, I gave my brother a stern look.

"Ten years older than I, and yet you are as stupid and reckless as a child half my age!" I slapped the side of his head. "Five warriors of our clan are dead—because *you* had a plan."

"My sorrow and regret run deep, little sister." There were tears in his eyes, which he did not bother to wipe away. "But my plan did save many lives."

"Yes—but who knew your plan would turn and bite you in the hindquarters?"

"I knew the risk, Nidreva. I agreed to chance it."

I sighed and shook my head. "Orella should have known. I wonder what else she did not tell you. I wonder what you may be keeping from me."

Vidaro shrugged and lowered his eyes. I knew he was hiding something. But drawing it out of him was akin to pulling a tusk from the jaws of the elephant.

\*\*\*

It all began with a rogue lion that had been raiding Churenga for twice seven nights. It had slaughtered our cattle and killed three men. The lion had even killed a woman and her baby. Our hunters had failed to track the great king of the rainforest; it eluded all attempts to capture and kill it. But then my brother, my brave and foolish brother, was struck by the lightning bolt of inspiration. To track the lion, one must think like the lion, he told me. To think like the lion, one must *become* the lion.

So with his wit and his smile he charmed Orella, our old and frail Juju Mother, and talked her into helping him. She made a powerful mojo to shape-change him into Lion.

Seven black beans she gave to Vidaro, made from the dried blood of a lion that she kept sealed in a jar made of clay, and these she marked with a spell to change him. Then she gave him seven red beans made of his own blood, so that he could change back to himself.

"Heed my words, and heed them well," Orella had warned Vidaro. "You must always take the red bean before sun gives way to moon. If you are still the lion by moonrise, you will remain the lion until you draw your last breath."

And so Vidaro swallowed the first black bean, and once he became Lion, our hunters followed as he tracked the rogue beast. Against our father's objections, I accompanied them because Orella told him I would be needed. Vidaro and

I, sharing the same parents, shared the same blood. Thus, when he was Lion, he would obey only me, and he would understand my words. So for three days we tracked and hunted the rogue lion, and I made sure to give Vidaro the red bean before each sunfall, so he could change back into my brother again. On the morning of the third day, he found the great beast, and we captured and killed it.

But then we learned that old Orella's magic had a flaw in it, one she had not foreseen.

As we carried the carcass of the rogue back to our village that day, Vidaro suddenly changed into Lion—without having swallowed another of the black beans. It was the scent of blood from the many wounds that had killed the rogue lion that caused my brother to change, I reasoned. So I gave to him one of the four remaining red beans, and then we left the carcass of the beast for the vulture and the hyena, and we continued our safari homeward.

Late the following day, while we stopped to rest and refresh ourselves, the mojo of Orella's making once again turned my brother into Lion, without need of the black bean.

One of our hunters was honing the metal head of his *assegai,* and cut himself on its sharp edge. Almost at once Vidaro smelled the man's blood, and the horrible shapeshifting claimed him. I realized then that the smell of *any* blood—man or beast—would bring about the change, and the *zsaleel,* the Spirit of Lion, would take possession of my brother's soul.

I gave Vidaro a red bean, and thanked Almighty Vizna that I still had two beans left.

Two days later, without further incident, we returned to Churenga.

Our father and our people greeted us with joy and fanfare, but Vidaro and I rushed to the wooden lodge of Orella and told her what had happened. She studied the hairs on his head, read the leaves at the bottom of the cup of chai she gave him to drink, and read the palm of his hand. To pile one trouble upon another, Orella told me a thing my brother had not shared with me.

"Each time Vidaro becomes Lion, he loses a piece of his soul to the Spirit of the beast that sleeps inside him," she said, coughing heavily after every few words. "In time, not even the mojo of the red bean will have the power to change him back."

I moaned in frustration, seethed with anger, and slapped my brother on the head. "You knew this, Vidaro? You knew all along that this would happen?"

My brother looked sheepish, as well as surprised. He had not expected Orella to betray him. "Yes, I knew," he said. "It was my choice to do this."

I wanted to strike my brother again, but to unleash my anger any further would not serve us anything. Yet I sensed that Vidaro was keeping something else from me, something he did not want me to know. A thing I was not to learn of until much later.

"Can you fix this, Orella?" I asked. "Can you reverse this magic of yours?"

Our old, wrinkled Juju Mother coughed again. Her breathing was labored, as if her lungs were filled with water. When she spoke, her voice was a raspy whisper.

"I can," Orella answered. "But you must heed—"

Before she could complete her words, she coughed again, and then gasped for breath. A moment later, Almighty Vizna called Orella to her everlasting home beyond the clouds and the stars. The Juju Mother's ancient heart had failed her at last.

"Vizna's mercy!" Vidaro cried, kneeling to see if there was something he could do.

My thoughts were not concerned with the dead, but for the living. "Do you know what she might have been about to tell us?" I asked of my brother.

He glanced at me but quickly turned away and shook his head. "No, I don't."

I knew there was something she had told him in

private before we set out to track the rogue Lion, but I was not of a mind just then to press him further.

"Come with me," I told him. "We need to undo Orella's magic—now!"

In a panic to save Vidaro, I threw the four remaining black beans into Orella's fire pit, told our father what had happened, and dragged my brother from village to village, seeking help from the Juju Mothers of our neighbors. But none could aid us: they were unfamiliar with the mojo Orella had made and did not possess her skills or her knowledge.

Then Zalla of the Sarangi Clan told us of a great Juju Queen named Kijazura Alae, who lived to the east, near the Tulavaga Plains. She wrote a message for us to give to this Juju Queen and drew a map for us to follow. However, the shortest and quickest way to the lodge of Kijazura was through the lands of the Tulonga K'Adru—the Men with Two Horns. They were a race unfriendly to the tribes of men, save for the white-skinned Shuunakai. But Vidaro showed no concern for this, saying that he would make a plan that would take us safely through their lands. My brother and his plans . . . ever a source of trouble for him and for all those around him.

The next morning we started on our journey, Vidaro and I and five of our warriors. Zalla had promised to send word to Kijazura to prepare her for our coming. I did not ask her how she would do this thing; Juju Women have their own secret ways.

As we took leave from Churenga, I turned to look back.

Our people had gathered along the wooden stockade that topped the stone walls of our village, waving farewell and wishing us good fortune. Through the opened gates, I could see the stone houses painted with the colors of every flower in the Gundardrune. The great dome of our temple to Almighty Vizna rose sparkling white beneath the morning sun above the walls of Churenga. And high atop one of the tall towers on either side of the gates, all alone, stood my father, Obalu, our great chief, watching us leave hearth and home.

As tears stung my eyes, I looked away and followed my companions. I gripped the pouch hanging from my belt, the pouch holding the last two red beans. If Vidaro should smell blood and become Lion more than the number of red beans, and if we failed to reach the Juju Queen in time, he would remain Lion until old age or the spear of a hunter ended his days.

That was five days ago.

***

After we buried our dead companions and sang the Song of Parting over their graves, Vidaro and I prayed to Vizna and the Spirits to greet them in peace when their souls crossed the River of Golden Light. The Monkey Men we left for the ants and other carrion eaters of the Gundardrune. I was ready to continue our journey, but Vidaro wished first to break his fast.

"You *are* aware that time is no friend to us, are you not?" I asked. "That our need is urgent and we still have a very long way to walk?"

Vidaro's handsome brown face stretched into a wide smile. Not even the scars of battle could spoil his beauty. His bright blue eyes—a sign of our family's royal bloodline, as were my own green eyes—sparkled in the light of the sun.

"I am well aware of that fact and all your insinuated consequences," he said.

"I worry for you, Vidaro. It concerns me that you often act like the fool who has lost all ties with the world around him."

"Are *you* aware that you always sound so formal and pompous when words come out of your mouth, baby sister?"

I slapped him on the head, as I had done many times since I was a young girl. It had probably rattled his brain and knocked all common sense from his brain.

"I prefer the High Tongue, brother. It is a sign of intelligence and breeding—unlike the easy way you have with words that you learned from your fellow mercenaries."

Vidaro's great laugh sounded very loud in the quiet forest. Although he could be as stubborn as the mule and as stupid as the ox, his laugh always made me smile.

"We'll make it to Kijazura's house in time," he said. "Trust me."

"So said the serpent to the fowl."

He rolled his eyes at me. "I don't know how you managed to talk father into letting you join in the hunt, but then, you've always managed to wrap him around your little finger."

"That is because father loves me best." I grinned at him. "He had no choice but to listen to Orella. I am the only one who can control you when you are Lion."

"I should have strangled you in your cradle, Nidreva."

"Even then I could skin your hide and make you weep like a small girl." This time I punched him in the chest.

"Hey—that hurt!"

"And mother always loved *you* best, may her Spirit know peace." My manner became more serious. "In three days, we reach the lands of the Tulonga K'Adru and their village of Streegora. I wish we had the time to circle around and avoid their realm."

"You know that would cost us another week of travel."

"How far is it to the Midorna? We could travel by river."

"Tell me—what would we use for a canoe? Or do you plan on swimming?"

I raised my hand to hit him again. But he ducked and

laughed at me. "I was thinking we might build a raft."

"You're just full of ideas today, aren't you?" he asked. "Still, it would take us another fortnight to reach the Midorna. And we can't afford to waste time, as you keep pointing out."

He was right, and I knew it. If he kept smelling blood and changing into Lion, I would quickly exhaust my very limited supply of red beans.

"Then how do you plan to get us safely across the lands of the Tulonga K'Adru?" I asked of him. "Streegora lies directly in our path."

My brother fell into thoughtful silence and then smiled quickly. I did not much care for the way he smiled at me.

"The Men with Two Horns believe that the lion is a good omen," he said. "The king of beasts is sacred and holy to their kind."

I did not much care for what he was thinking, either.

\*\*\*

The forest is a living thing, its voice the chatter of the monkey, the hoot of the owl, the song of the bird. Panther and leopard lurk in the shadows and strike without warning. King Lion rests and guards his pride while his mate hunts for meat to fill their bellies. Hyena laughs and jaguar roars. The voice of the elephant is like the Trumpet of Vizna, announcing Time's End.

The Gundardrune runs from the Mahama Hills in the east to the western shores of the Darkvale Coast, where our major cities were built long ago. Northward lies the Tiga Wilderland, the Scarlet Desert, and the realms of Marl, Rojahndria, and the other five kingdoms of the Aerlothian continent. Far to the south runs the wide Midorna River, the Heartblood, which courses east to west across the whole of the mighty Gundardrune; another city stands at the mouth of the river, where it flows into the Sea of Shadows. South of the Midorna stands the Shamiri Rainforest, and beyond that, at the southern edge of the world, stretches the vast kingdom of Bungagoll, the realm of the Quotida Hamar—the People of the Black Skin.

For the next two days, Vidaro and I followed the map Zalla of the Sarangi Clan had drawn for us. We traveled quickly, stopping only to relieve ourselves and fill our bellies with food and water. At night we would rest, taking turns sleeping and keeping watch. Awake, I would stare at the moon, which we call Undala Gobar, the Left Eye of Vizna. It seemed to be a great white pearl set amidst an ocean of stars that sparkled like diamonds too numerous to count. Asleep, I would dream of having wings so that I could fly up and touch them all.

We had no more to fear from the Tulonga Na'Koor, for the Monkey Men are not fond of the dark of night. They love only daylight and give worship to the sun—Undala Kozar, the Right Eye of Vizna. As for other dangers, like the snake and crocodile, these are threats we of the Gundardrune are born to and live with all our days. My brother and I were no children new to the tall grass of the pampas and the realm of towering trees. We knew the forest and its denizens. We knew how to survive.

This was our world.

By the grace of Almighty Vizna and the Spirits that counsel and guide our people, we encountered no threat, no obstacle to bar our passage. And we came upon no dead or wounded animal whose blood scent would cause my brother to change into Lion.

Early morning it was when we finally reached the edge of the forest and the hilltop ridge overlooking Streegora, the main village of the Men with Two Horns. It was large, without walls, and squatted in a great basin surrounded by the Stonefall Hills. There were many different types of dwellings where the Tulonga K'Adru lived, from bamboo huts and tents made of animal skins to great lodges built of earth and log, mud, and stone.

"Give me one of the black beans," Vidaro said to me.

I frowned at him. "But I threw away those that were left. If you had told me your plan before we left our village, I would not have done so."

"Leave it to you," he said, sounding impatient with me. "Then give me your knife."

"What do you intend?"

"Just give me the knife, Nidreva."

I guessed what he had in mind, but kept tongue locked firmly behind teeth. I handed the knife to him and then watched him prick his finger. When a small drop of blood appeared, he held the finger to his nose and inhaled deeply. For a number of many heartbeats we waited, but nothing happened. Vidaro licked the blood from his finger. Still nothing.

"I guess it doesn't work with my own blood," he said.

I thought he was going to ask me to cut my own finger, to use my blood, but he knelt on the ground instead and began to dig with the knife. A moment later, Vidaro rose to his feet, holding a fat worm between his fingers. He cut the worm in half and returned the knife to me.

I wiped the blade on his vest, and then punched him in the arm. "By Vizna and all the Spirits of Undala—you are too much in love with tempting Fate, Vidaro."

He pinched my cheek, smearing me with worm guts. "You worry too much, baby sister."

"And you are an ox with the brain of the cuckoo!"

"This is the only way we can safely pass through the lands of the Tulonga K'Adru. I'm telling you, Nidreva—don't worry. I know what I'm doing."

"The last words of many a dead man, I am sure."

"Come on, be reasonable."

"I *am* reasonable, Vidaro. And I *do* worry. You know

I must give you the red mojo bean before sunfall so you can change back into your own skin. And there is only *one* left. What if the scent of blood wakes the beast in you again?"

His smile was cocksure and his manner full of bullheadedness. "This is *my* life, Nidreva. It's mine to risk."

"Selfish fool! You think only of yourself!"

"Was it selfishness that I chose this path for the good of our people?"

I could not answer that, for his generosity, his bravery could not be denied. "But—"

"Trust me, little one. You'll be fine. We both will."

With a heavy sigh of frustration, sharpened by concern for him, I stepped back to give him room. Then he held the still-wriggling halves of the worm up to his nose, inhaled deeply, and then tossed them aside. He undressed quickly and handed his clothing to me. This time I did not turn away as the *zsaleel* of the lion that slept inside his soul was awakened.

Vidaro cried out in great pain and dropped to his hands and knees.

First his flesh began to change and turn into the coarse-haired, golden hide of the lion. Then I heard the sound of his bones grinding together as they made themselves over into a different form. A thick mane began to grow around his head, his face widened and his teeth grew long and sharp. Claws tore through his fingers and toes as his hands and feet twisted and curled into paws. A tail emerged from the base of his spine. His ears lengthened like the leaves of a fern. Long whiskers sprouted from either side of his nose, and his eyes became the eyes of Lion.

He voiced a low growl and rubbed his great, shaggy head against my leg. I still found this unsettling but never once was I afraid. Lion always obeyed me.

Stuffing my brother's belongings inside my shoulder pack, I scratched the top of Lion's head. "Come then," I said. "Let us go where even the Spirits fear to walk."

***

The Tulonga K'Adru stopped in their comings and goings to stare as Lion and I entered their village. Many more there were who came out of their homes to watch and point at the lady and the King of Beasts that walked among them. Then they did a thing that surprised me, though I suspected that my older and more worldly-wise brother had counted on it: the villagers bowed their heads or went down on their knees as we walked past them, thanking their gods for the Visitation of the Lion. Many threw palms leaves and flowers in our path as if we were gods. In spite of our situation, I must tell you that it pleased my vanity.

The Tulonga K'Adru are like and unlike men. Bearing a faint resemblance to the rhinoceros, they have long noses, grey and leathery skin, and two horns jutting from the center of their brows like a pair of sharp daggers. They favor long, colorful shirts and pantaloons, and their feet, like those of the rhinoceros, are bare. But unlike the centaur, minotaur, and other halflings of the land of Khanya-Toth, the Men with Two Horns did not come to our world from some Otherworld but are native to the Gundardrune, and have lived in the forest since First Dawn.

One of them, who stood very tall and walked with pride and purpose, accompanied by a retinue of four others who carried spears in their six-fingered hands, came toward us. His clothing was adorned with feathers and beads, and he wore a leather torc carved from the ivory tusk of the elephant. I took him to be the hetman, for he wore a headdress made from the teeth and jaws of a great crocodile. A moment of fear cast its shadow over my heart.

We stopped as the Rhinomen approached.

The hetman bowed to us. "Welcome to our humble village of Streegora, Sacred Lion," he spoke in the Common Tongue of Men. "You and your Lady Fair honor and bless us with your presence. I, Rigonaka, leader of this village and its people, assure you that you shall pass unhindered and unmolested. Go in peace, Holy Ones."

He bowed and stepped aside to let us pass. His four guards did the same.

"Peace and prosperity to your tribe, great Rigonaka," I said.

Lion purred and acknowledged the hetman with a nod of his great head. Glad I was to see that a part of my brother remained aware of his surroundings from inside the soul of Lion.

We continued on our way and passed through Streegora without incident. But then, as we neared the village outskirts, I noticed a long-legged woman and eight grim-looking men with skin as white as the milk of the goat, watching us.

They carried long swords that slept in leather sheaths and tall spears, the heads of which were concealed by leopard-skin hoods. Two of the men had great bows, their long arrows hiding inside quivers made from the skin of the cheetah. They wore jerkins, breeks, and boots made from the hide of the antelope, adorned with the teeth, claws, and ears of other animals. Turbans covered their heads, and the left cheek of each man bore a lightning bolt of red paint.

These were people of the Shuunakai—fierce hunters and warriors of the Tulavaga Plains, beyond the Mohama Hills. They are the only tribe of men on peaceful terms with the Tulonga K'Adru, and they did not hunt the Rhinomen. I did not much like the look of these hunters.

As for the woman . . . her head had been shaved to the scalp, and her skin was the color of polished ivory. She was armed with a long sword, and she carried a small wooden dowsing rod in her belt, which told me that she was a medicine woman. Silver rings hung from the lobes of her ears, and around her neck were hung the shrunken heads of many diverse animals, as well as a few men. One of the shrunken heads she wore was that of a lion.

The woman boldly stepped forward but did not bow

to us. Neither did she smile. Something crawled down the back of my neck like a cold drop of winter rain, even though I knew we were safe from harm while passing through Streegora. Lion and I kept walking.

"A handsome animal you keep for company," she said, keeping pace with us as we walked quickly through the village. "My name is Glira, of Clan Dromada. What would you accept in trade for your friend?"

I had to think quickly. "Lion is a gift to me from Almighty Vizna, may all give praise to his name," I told her. "We are on a holy pilgrimage. I cannot and would not trade my companion for even a sack of the gold your people use for barter."

Glira gave me a long look, and then shrugged. "More's the pity," she said. "He would have blessed my village and brought fortune to my people." She stopped, and this time she bowed, letting us pass. "Peace unto you."

"May you and your people know prosperity," I said to her.

Lion and I continued on our way. I knew Glira wanted his head gracing a wall in her lodge, and I did not much care for the way her men kept staring at me as we passed.

\*\*\*

I followed the movement of the sun as Lion and I pressed on, and eventually we crossed the Ushom Creek. No less than four hours had passed since leaving Streegora, I reasoned.

According to Zalla's map, we would reach the Mohama Hills and Widru Pass, which opened onto the Tulavaga Plains, by moonrise. Now it was safe to eat and rest since we had passed beyond the lands of the Tulonga K'Adru. It was also time to give Lion the last of the red mojo beans so that Vidaro could return to me while time was still our ally.

We stopped in a small clearing, and I laughed at Vidaro's embarrassment as he emerged naked from the soul of the great cat. I handed him his clothing, then searched through my shoulder pack and found some buffalo jerky and a few stale but still edible biscuits.

After we had eaten and taken our rest, Glira and her companions emerged from the thick woods behind us. Though swords were still sheathed, their spears were now without covers.

Glira looked at us, the late-afternoon sun casting an evil glow upon her eyes.

"I see you've found another companion along the way," she said to me. "Where's your companion? Where is the lion that walked beside you?"

This unexpected encounter filled me with dread. There were nine of them, only two of us. Vidaro had no weapon, for in our haste to leave the graves of our warriors we had neglected to take one of the swords for him to carry. All we had were my sword and knife. But no matter—we were outnumbered, and two of them were armed with longbows.

"Hunting," I said to Glira. "This man we encountered not long after leaving Streegora."

"You lie, *mekizio,*" she said.

She called me a word of hatred usually reserved for the halflings of Khanya-Toth. When it was used to insult the centaur and minotaur and all their kind, it meant they were animals. When the white skins threw the word in our faces, it meant that we were even less than animals. I knew what Glira and her men wanted. I knew what they had come for.

They were headhunters. They would have Vidaro's head hanging from a wall—whether he was Lion or not. As for me . . . the men might pass me around until they grew bored, and then mount my head next to Vidaro's. Or they might kill me, first.

Anger seethed in my breast. Vidaro spat on the ground and started forward. I pulled him back. Now was not the time to fight.

With her eyes mirroring the fire of the falling sun, Glira approached us. She studied Vidaro with great interest and then brought forth her dowsing rod and pointed its forked end at him. Then she gave a howl like the wolf and fell back a few paces. Her eyes went wide. Their color darkened, and she pointed a finger at Vidaro.

"He is *enspelled!*" she shouted, moving back a dozen or so paces. "The Mark of the Beast is upon his soul."

The men of the Shuunakai glared at us, fear and hate blazing in their eyes.

Vidaro looked at me with great sadness on his face. "I'm so sorry I got you into this."

The egg of the Muse had hatched an idea in my brain. I would be putting Vidaro's life at risk, but there was no other way. It may not have worked with his blood, but with mine...

"You worry too much, brother." I smiled and squeezed his hand.

With the thumb of my left hand pressed against the hilt of my scimitar, I slowly pushed upward, sliding my sword free of its sheath, just enough to expose its sharp edge.

"A demon?" asked one of the men.

"Yes—a shapeshifter!" Glira cried. "A Devil of the Dark Places!"

I pressed one finger against the edge of my sword until I felt its bite. When the finger began to bleed, I placed my left hand upon Vidaro's shoulder.

"Breathe deeply," I whispered to him.

"Draw steel and arrow, boys!" Glira called out.

"Kill them and cut off their heads!" another one of her men shouted.

The hunters came toward us . . . and then I heard my brother cry out in pain, heard the tearing of his clothes, the roaring of his anger. Before any man could draw arrow, Vidaro fell to his hands and knees—and Lion emerged from within his soul.

All things moved as swiftly as running water. I drew my sword as Lion took a mighty leap and landed in the midst of the Shuunakai hunters. Men screamed as Lion bit and slashed his way through their flesh. They tried to defend themselves, but this was no ordinary cat of the rainforest: this was Lion, my brother.

One man broke away from the others and came at me, howling like a starving hyena.

Before my sword kissed his blade in loving combat, I saw Glira fall, gashed across face and shoulder by Lion. It was a pleasing sight. My smile infuriated the hunter.

"Now you die, witch!"

Then I did battle with the man, our swords echoing throughout the forest in the song of Death. He was stronger than I but less of a swordsman. My scimitar struck his longsword with a flashing and sparking of steel. But he surprised me with his speed. His weapon circled around his head and would have sheared through my neck had I not moved aside in time. Still, the edge of his blade took a small piece of my left shoulder with it as it hissed past me.

Biting my lower lip to keep myself from screaming, I moved like the antelope and easily slipped inside his guard before he could bring his sword back into play. My sword flashed once and cut him open from shoulder to hip. He fell at my feet to lie among his own intestines.

Another man then took his place, armed with a spear. I blocked each thrust and swing of his *assegai,* but he was tall and strong, and his furious assault forced me to give ground. Then suddenly he wailed. Blood spurted into the air, and he toppled face down.

Lion had taken him from behind.

It was all over. I looked around. Not a body was moving, not a sound could be heard. I wasted no time making sure that none of our foes still lived. I had no red beans left to give my brother. Time, I feared, was no longer our friend.

Hastily I wiped the blood from my scimitar on the shirt of a dead man. "Lion—come!"

The great cat approached me, covered in the blood of Glira and her men. His dark, soulful eyes were filled with the love and trust my brother held in his heart for me.

"We must go, and we must move quickly. We need to reach the house of the Juju Queen before night falls or you will remain Lion until your eyes close and never open again."

Lion bowed his head in understanding.

"Do not be afraid," I said. "But now you must run—run like the gazelle!"

I mounted his back as men mount the horse and the camel, grabbed the coarse hair of his great mane, and off we rode in our race against time.

Sunfall was closing in upon us.

*** 

While the dying sun still reigned like a torch in the western sky, we reached a parting in the trail where one fork continued eastward and the other turned toward the south. We held true to Zalla's map and continued eastward. Not long afterward, we came to the River Kalur and the small bridge that spanned it. On the other side of the river stood a simple lodge nestled within the gentle arms of the Mahama Hills, close to where Widru Pass led to the Tulavaga Plains. The lodge was built of stone and mortared with clay, with a roof of timber and palm fronds. A chimney fashioned of stone exhaled smoke like the snout of the last dragon that sleeps somewhere beneath the hills of earth.

At long last we had finally reached the house of the great Juju Queen, for it could only be her, standing outside the entrance to her dwelling.

"I've been waiting for you," she said, coming forward

to greet us. "Zalla of the Sarangi sent her familiar with word of your coming."

She spoke our language as if born to the rainforests of the Gundardrune, which, by her appearance, I could see that she had not been. Her skin was like the velvet the caravans from the north trade to our people, and it was as black as the space between the stars. She was of the far southern lands of Bungagoll, a realm of cities, tall ships, and great seafaring nations.

I bowed my head to her. "Greetings, Kijazura Alae."

Then Lion did a thing that surprised me. He walked straight up to her and rubbed his massive head against her leg. The Juju Queen scratched his ears and the muzzle of his nose and stroked his ears most gently. Lion purred and lay beside her, his tail swaying back and forth like the cobra listening to the music of a snake charmer.

I stared at the wonder of it.

Tall and slender of limb, Kijazura looked strong and not much older than I. Her black eyes, like polished jet, mirrored the sun, and she wore her hair as I did, in braids that caressed her back. Her long dress was made of leopard skin, and she wore a necklace of shells and beads; silver rings adorned her wrists, ankles and ears. In her right hand she held a staff almost as tall as she—a staff of cedar that had been sanded and polished so that it gleamed in the moonlight; two short, sharp branches stuck out just below its knobbed end. Unlike most people of the Gundardrune, she did not wear shoes or sandals.

A moment later, I found my voice. "Then you know our story and why we have come, O Juju Queen," I said.

"So formal and so endearing!" Her laughter was sweet and calming music. "But I am no queen, Nidreva C'Mora. Call me by name. You may even call me Kija, if you wish."

"Yes . . . Kijazura." I felt that I did not know her well enough to call her Kija. But I liked her, and I liked her easy manner. "I bear a message for you," I added quickly.

She nodded. "Drowah told me everything. I'm glad

Zalla sent him—it saved us precious time. Come, come inside. Let's tend to this quickly, before the stars come out to play."

I had no idea who this Drowah might be. "Then we have not come too late?"

"No, you arrived in the sliver of time."

The Juju Woman turned and entered her dwelling. Lion followed. I followed Lion.

Inside, Kijazura's lodge was a single room containing furniture, rugs, and sundry odds and ends. Tables and cupboards were piled high and filled with all those items a medicine woman would own: bones of small birds, lizards, and other animals, a variety of colorful feathers, serpent heads, dead insects, and the eyes of frogs and chameleons held in jars made of blown glass. An aroma of pine, cedar, and a pleasing blend of spices hung in the air.

A large, green parrot perched atop the mantle of a stone hearth paid no attention to us while it chattered away and groomed itself.

"Meet Drowah, the parrot that Zalla sent with word of your coming," said Kijazura.

I did not ask whether Drowah spoke to her or had carried the message in writing, for I do not meddle in the doings of Juju Mothers if I have no need. Instead, I sat in a chair at a small table and stared at the orange flames dancing in the hearth. Lion curled up on the floor next to me. The Juju Mother stood between us.

"Can you help my brother?" I asked Kijazura.

"I can and I will," she replied. Then she he held out a hand, and in her palm rested a small, brown bean. "Why your Juju Mother didn't give this to you in the first place is something I fail to understand."

"Maybe she was confused. Orella was old and often forgetful. She was well over ten times ten summers when she died."

"That it explains it." Kijazura smiled. "Well, shall we get on with it?"

"Yes!" I said eagerly. "I fear that too much time has already been lost."

"You worry too much, Nidreva." Kijazura's words echoed the words of my brother. Then she knelt beside Lion. "Please, my handsome cat, open your jaws."

To my amazement, Lion spread wide his jaws. Then Kijazura set the brown bean on his tongue, and he closed his jaws and swallowed.

The change came upon him quickly, a reversal of old Orella's original magic.

Lion roared as his bones ground together and readjusted themselves. His fur and claws receded and retracted. Long, sharp teeth returned to normal. Whiskers and mane disappeared, skin stretched, and flesh reshaped itself. Then a hazy outline of my brother emerged from the beautiful, golden skin of Lion . . . a spirit leaving a body. His form was clear as fresh water and shimmered with blue light. Then Lion slowly vanished like mist under a morning sun. The blue light gradually faded, and my brother's transparent form became solid flesh. He stretched his limbs and yawned, unmindful of his nakedness.

"Well, that felt good," he said, winking at me. He looked at the Juju Woman. "Kijazura, I presume? You're a vision of loveliness, young lady."

"My, my—you *are* the flirt!" she said with a laugh.

"By the way, brother," I said, trying not to smile, "have you forgotten that you are standing there wearing the clothes you were born in?"

Vidaro glanced down at his naked, walnut-colored body, and then turned his back to us in embarrassment. Kijazura and I laughed at him. She turned to the cupboard and gathered in her hands a long blue shirt and a pair of white pantaloons and handed these to my brother.

"I have no shoes or sandals for you," she told him.

While Vidaro quickly dressed, Kijazura took down a small, clay jar with a lid sealed in wax. Breaking the seal and removing the top, she held the opened jar beneath my brother's nose.

"Inhale," she said to him. "It's fresh bat blood."

He took a deep breath and then slowly released it from his lungs.

We waited for a long space of time . . . but nothing happened.

"All done," Kijazura announced.

"That's it?" Vidaro asked her.

"That's it."

"It is considered bad manners not to thank one who has helped you," I scolded him.

Vidaro frowned at me but bowed graciously to Kijazura. "Thank you, Juju Mother."

Kijazura nodded. "My pleasure."

"But we have nothing to give you in return," I said to her.

"Don't worry about it," she told me, once again sounding like my brother. "I'm happiest when I can help people. Your own Juju Mother, she was Ajubunga, wasn't she?"

I nodded. "Yes. Orella was from your land."

"So there. We keep it in the family, so to speak. Now, join me for a meal. It's still many hours until dawn, and I think it best that you rest here a few days."

"We can use the rest," Vidaro said. "Now that we no longer have Lion to see us safely through the lands of the Tulonga K'Adru, we'll have to travel far out of our way."

"Which is all well and good after what almost happened to us," I said.

Kijazura turned her shiny black eyes on me. "What are you talking about?"

I told of our encounter in the forest with Glira and the other Shuunakai. "We were forced to kill them all," I said. "They left us no other choice."

"They're a bad lot, those head hunters," said the Juju Mother. "But you can avoid them by turning south for the Midorna River. There are good men with boats who will gladly take you down river as far as you need to go. Tell them I sent you, and they won't ask for payment."

"Thanks," Vidaro said before I could say the words.

I looked at my thumb, which I had hastily wrapped with a piece of a kerchief I found in my pack. But I had not bothered to dress the wound in my shoulder.

"Tomorrow morning I'll send Drowah back to Zalla with word that you'll be returning home," said Kijazura. "And now, Nidreva—let me take a look at those wounds of yours."

\*\*\*

Vidaro and I spent two days with Kijazura, resting, eating, talking, and becoming better acquainted with her. Then the time came for us to bid farewell and begin our journey home. The Juju Queen gave us food and water for our safari, and we set out on a day bright with sunlight.

We had already crossed the River Kalur but were still within sight of Kijazura's lodge when Vidaro and I heard voices and the pounding of heavy footsteps. A moment later, our path was blocked when a great number of Tulonga K'Adru emerged from Widru Pass.

The Men with Two Horns were armed with spears and weapons that looked like the great battle axe hanging on a wall in my brother's lodge. Hetman Rigonaka led his warriors, a spear in one hand and a tomahawk at his belt.

Next to the hetman walked Glira of the Shuunakai. The wounds on her face had been sewn closed, and her arm was wrapped in bandages and held in a sling. Lion, my brother, had not killed her, as I had believed. Once again we were greatly outnumbered, but this time Lion could not be called upon for help. Neither could we flee, for they would surely have run us down. That they had tracked us this far spoke well of their skills.

"Do you now see, Rigonaka?" Glira shouted, pointing to us with her good arm. "There is the *mekizio* witch and her demon—who tricked you, who tricked us all with her mojo!"

I could almost feel the heat of Vidaro's rage over Glira's insult. "We're neither witch nor demon!" he shouted. "A bad mojo—"

"Be still, shapeshifter!" Rigonaka told my brother. "The Shuunakai are on friendly terms with my people. Glira would not lie to us."

"We do not claim that she lies, O great hetman of the Tulonga K'Adru," I said. "But I do say that she is mistaken in what she saw, in what she believes. Please, allow us to explain."

"You and your demon slew my companions—and nearly killed me!" said Glira. "Deny it if it's not true. Deny it, and *you* will be the one who lies."

"That is the truth," I said. "But you and your head hunters came to capture a lion, and when you saw there was no lion, you attacked us, believing my brother to be a demon. We fought and killed to defend ourselves."

"There's another lie!" Glira cried out. "First this demon was a man the witch said she had met on the trail. Now she calls him brother. And there is no lion to prove he is not a demon."

Rigonaka shook his head. "Brother or stranger on the road, it matters not. Glira tells us that he shape-shifted into a lion. Is this not true?"

"No, that is a truth I cannot turn into a lie," I said.

"But you must let us explain," Vidaro pleaded. "It was a spell cast upon me. Go to the lodge of Kijazura, the Juju Queen. She'll confirm what we're trying to make you understand."

"We know of no such Juju Queen," said Rigonaka. "Where is her lodge?"

I dared not turn my back to them. "There, behind us, still within sight."

"There's nothing there but emptiness and morning mist," Glira said.

Then I turned to look back, and Vidaro turned, also. But there was nothing there, no sign of Kijazura's lodge. All we saw was a veil of silver mist floating across the River Kalur. It was as if Kijazura and her dwelling had never existed. My heart fell into my stomach.

"Now do you see, Rigonaka?" Glira asked the hetman. "The witch and her demon are tricksters who have made fools of you!"

My brother and I looked at each other. His face was grim, his eyes without hope. *Where is Kijazura?* I wondered. *Why does she not see our peril and come to our aid?*

Vidaro put his arm around me. "Once again, I beg your forgiveness, little sister."

I stabbed him in the ribs with my sharp elbow. "We shall get out of this somehow," I whispered to him. *But how?* I asked myself. "And when we do, I will give you a severe beating."

Tears rolled down my brother's cheeks. He turned to face the hetman of the Tulonga K'Adru. "Please, let me sister go free," he said. "It was I who wronged you. Not her."

"Vidaro—no!" I yelled at him.

"Be silent, witch!" Glira shouted.

"You lied to us, woman—you tricked us and slew Glira's men," Rigonaka said to me. "You committed blasphemy against our gods. You mocked the Great Lion we hold sacred and holy. You are demon and witch. For that, you both must die."

Glira smiled with devilish delight. "First, they will burn your brother, so he won't be given the chance to save you from the same fate," she told me.

"Take them!" Rigonaka ordered his warriors.

I handed my knife to Vidaro and drew my scimitar. "You will lose many warriors before you bring us down, hetman."

Rigonaka laughed and Glira smiled as great nets made of hemp were thrown over us: another band of the hetman's warriors had crept up behind us, taking us unawares. Before I could lash out with my sword, Vidaro and I were overwhelmed and captured.

*\*\*\**

It was past sunfall when we were brought back to Streegora. The Tulonga K'Adru then locked my brother and me inside a small hut made of white stone. This bore resemblance to an eggshell broken in half, with a stout wooden door that had been locked from the outside. Inside, it had a dirt floor and nothing else. There was a small window with three bars made of strong wood opposite the entrance, but it was too small to squeeze through. It did, however, allow the silver light of Undala Gobar to enter so that Vidaro and I might see each other.

We were held in this place for what seemed like many turns. From outside came the sound of talking drums, the singing of the Men with Two Horns, and the chanting of their priests. The whole of the village of Streegora was making ready to celebrate and attend the ritual that would lead to our execution by fire.

Vidaro and I sat cross legged on the dirt floor, facing each other. He took my hands in his own and gifted me with a long, loving look.

"I'm so sorry I failed you, Nidreva," he spoke to me.

"We had great and urgent need to seek healing for you," I told him. "We succeeded in that. Our fate now lies within the palm of Vizna's right hand. You are a hero."

"I'm no hero. You see me through the eyes of a baby sister."

"You will always be my hero, brother."

We embraced and held onto one another for a long moment of silence. I took comfort in the arms of my brother and gave what comfort I could in return. After a time, we loosened our embrace but continued to hold each other's hands.

"It troubles me that the Juju Queen helped us and then abandoned us," I said.

Vidaro shrugged. "She did what we asked of her. Maybe she didn't know, didn't see Glira and her friends take us captive?"

"That I find difficult to accept. Why would she veil her lodge with a great mojo so it was hidden from all eyes? She may even have fled when the Tulonga K'Adru came for us."

"I don't know, Nidreva, and I'm not going to dwell on it." He set free a heavy sigh of regret and resignation. "It just saddens me that you have your whole life ahead of you. As for me, it doesn't matter. My years are few in number, and Death and I are old friends."

"If I am to die, then it is good that I die with you." A thing I could not put a name to touched the deep places in my mind. I stared at Vidaro, looking into his eyes in hope of reading his thoughts. "What do you mean when you say that your years are numbered?"

Vidaro lowered his eyes and shook his head. I was near to pressing him further when the door was unlocked and pushed open. Rigonaka and Glira of the Shuunakai, accompanied by four of the hetman's warriors, entered our stone prison.

"It's time for you two to say goodbye to each other, witch," Glira said to me. "First the demon you call brother will burn—and then you will follow him to the Dark Place."

Rigonaka nodded. Two of his warriors seized Vidaro and dragged him from the hut.

*"No!"* I shouted.

I leapt to my feet and threw myself at Glira, one

hand clutching her throat, the other curled into a fist that hammered her jaw. As if I had lost my wits, I screamed and beat her until her knees began to fold. Yet I held her upright, gripping her throat.

"Stop her!" I heard Rigonaka say.

The remaining warriors grabbed me by the arms and pulled me away from Glira. She staggered backward, swayed left and right, and then stepped toward me, bleeding from nose and mouth. Her eyes flared like torches as she wiped blood from her face.

"I'll take great pleasure in watching you burn," she said to me.

Then her fists slammed into my face and belly. The breath was loosed from my lungs, and my head snapped to one side. The Rhinomen released me, and I fell to the ground.

Lying there, I could see through the opened door, see the torches burning in the night as the Tulonga K'Adru sang and danced around a great firepit filled with kindling. In the center of this pit, standing in the midst of all that kindling, stood a tall, wooden post.

"Five pearls I'll give you, Rigonaka, if you roast her slowly over hot coals," said Glira.

"For five pearls, I'll even put an apple in her mouth," the hetman told her.

I tried to stand, but Glira kicked me to the dirt again. "Too bad you won't be able to watch," she said. "But you can still enjoy your brother's screams."

Outside, the singing grew louder, and the drums talked faster.

Glira and Rigonaka turned and left the hut, followed by the two warriors.

Before they closed the door behind them, I saw my brother, still helpless in the grip of the hetman's warriors. Two priests of the Tulonga K'Adru then walked toward him. One stripped him naked, and then the other began to paint strange symbols in white paint upon his brown skin.

I lay there and wept, unable to free myself, powerless to save my brother. I prayed to the Spirits who guide and counsel, begging them to intervene and save Vidaro.

A familiar voice then called out my name, almost whispered it, from the small window behind me. I rose to my feet and turned—and then I ran to the window.

I gripped the wooden bars. "Kijazura! I thought you had forsaken us!"

"I'm sorry you thought that," she said. "But there was nothing I could do at the time. Your foes are no friends to me. Years ago, I cast a spell so they would never learn of my whereabouts or existence. I was forced to cast a new spell, which also affected you and Vidaro."

"But could you not have cast a spell to save us?" I asked of her. "Could you not have conjured some demon to do your bidding?"

"No, girl. I'm not a witch or sorceress who plays with dark things." She placed a hand on one of my own. "Quickly now—we don't have much time. There is only one way out, and you must take this in order to free your brother and leave here alive."

"How? What do you want me to take?"

"This." Kijazura's other hand reached through the wooden bars of the window: in her palm was a small, black bean.

"You want me to—"

"Yes," she said. "But first I must ask you—are you willing to sacrifice three years of your life, in order to save your brother?"

"What are you talking about?"

Kijazura stared at me, and then her black eyes went wide. "You don't know?" she asked. "Your brother didn't tell you?"

"Please—I beg of you! What are you talking about?"

It seemed like an eternity before she gave answer. "Each time your brother changed into the lion, it cost him three years of his life."

In anger, I cursed my brother and promised myself that I would crack his skull should we survive the night. But then my eyes shed tears of sadness, and I quickly added the number of times Vidaro had become Lion. My heart ached and nearly shattered into pieces.

"Vidaro is known to be foolish," I said. "But this was a stupid thing for him to do."

"The stupidity of fools is often the courage that saves the lives of wiser men."

"But . . . twenty and one years," I said in a quiet voice.

"So it is, and there's nothing I can do about that," said Kijazura. "Your brother accepted this, and now I ask if you're willing to do the same."

"If my brother can sacrifice so much for our people, can I do any less? Three years is nothing when weighed against the years he lost."

"Then hurry, Nidreva! Take off your clothes and hand them to me."

I quickly undressed and gave my clothes to the Juju Queen. "Where will you be? What will you do?" I asked her. "What shall *I* do?"

"Your instincts will guide you, Nidreva. You create the diversion, and I'll free your brother. We'll escape into the forest, and you can follow our trail."

My hand shook as I let go of one wooden bar and took the black bean from her hand.

"But before you take the bean, I must take a drop of your—"

I wasted no time in swallowing the black bean.

"—no, wait, Nidreva!"

A moment later, the change was upon me.

The *zsaleel*, the soul of the lioness, entered my being, and I felt a brief moment of sharp pain. Lightning flashed before my eyes, and red-hot lava flowed through my veins. Then there was no more pain. I felt my bones move and shift to form a different body. I felt my flesh stretch and sprout coarse fur. My body kept changing from what it was to what it must become.

And then it was done.

No thoughts. No emotions: instinct now ruled.

I was Lioness.

Yet there remained a small part of me, the part that remembered who Kijazura was, that knew to trust and obey her . . . and that I had a brother who was in great danger.

*"The celebration is over and soon they'll light the great pyre."* Lioness heard the words of the Juju Queen, and understood those words . . . deep inside her, Lioness understood. *"Go, save your brother, first—and then I'll find a way to save you. We'll meet you in the forest. Follow us. Now go!"*

Then she was gone, and all Lioness heard was the pounding of drums and the singing of song. Lioness, Queen of the Hunt, sensed what she must do.

With an angry roar, she threw herself against the door. Wood cracked and splintered, metal hinges bent and twisted with a squeal. The door shattered and fell.

Lioness was free.

Two guards outside the hut panicked and fled when Lioness growled. Yet there were other Rhinomen who saw her and made ready to throw spear and tomahawk. But she was among them before they could attack or flee. Rhinomen toppled as Lioness crashed into them. Claws and teeth bit and slashed with savage fury. The Men with Two Horns howled with rage, cried out with fear, and screamed in agony. Arms bled were hands had been. Rhinomen fell with missing legs. A head flew from its body in a fountain of blood. Bellies torn open dripped with intestines. Lioness was big. Lioness was fast. Lioness could not be stopped.

Females and their younglings wept and screamed in fear as they ran seeking shelter. But Lioness had no interest in them. She did not care to harm them. Males raced to find places to hide from her, but there were others, armed warriors who sought to slay her. Lioness tore their limbs from their bodies and ripped their flesh to shreds. Panic took hold of the village by its throat and shook it the way a cub will shake the mouse in its jaws before killing and eating it.

Small flames danced in the night as the pyre started to burn. Rhinomen ran back and forth like the rooster without its head. Some fled. Others, braver or perhaps more foolish, stood fast with their weapons, ready to face the demonic beast running amok in their village. Lioness galloped like the horse across the open place of the village, running straight for them.

Then Lioness saw the Juju Queen kick the flaming kindling out of her way. She reached the post to which Vidaro had been tied, and with two slashes of her knife, he was free. Vidaro and Kijazura cast a glance at Lioness. She nodded, and then they fled the village, vanishing into the darkness of night.

Lioness roared with joy—and then slaughtered the enemies who thought they could stand and fight and kill her. Many more Rhinomen came to help them, some with huge nets. But the claws and jaws of the Lioness sent the Men with Two Horns screaming to their gods.

Rigonaka, Hetman of the Tulonga K'Adru, fled before the attack of Lioness. Mighty paws with claws like thorns made of ivory brought him down. He tried to call out for help as Lioness ripped out his throat and tossed his body aside.

Then all alone, trapped against the burning kindling that was to have been Vidaro's funeral pyre, Glira stood with an *assegai* clutched in the hand of her one good arm. She screamed in rage and fear when Lioness turned toward her.

*"I see the witch inside you, demon,"* she said. *"Now it's back to the Dark Place where you belong!"*

She cast the spear at Lioness, who rose to her hind legs and battered the weapon aside as if it were nothing more than a mosquito.

Before Glira could turn to flee, Lioness made a great

leap and was upon her, slashing her face and knocking her into the very fire that was meant for Vidaro.

When it was done, Lioness looked around.

Pools of dark blood, severed heads and limbs, and the bodies of many dead and mortally wounded Rhinomen were left in the wake of the mighty she-cat's vengeance.

Lioness then turned from the village of the Tulonga K'Adru and followed her friends into the dark forest of the Gundardrune.

\*\*\*

Lioness knew the scent of those she followed, those she must find. She tracked them as if hunting prey, and before the moon rose much higher, she found them. They had stopped to rest and wait for Lioness in a small dell. Vidaro now wore now only a small loincloth. His feet were bare, however, and so was his chest. Kijazura wiped painted symbols from his skin.

Approaching slowly and quietly, Lioness reached them and then sat on her haunches to watch what they did and listen to what they said.

Kijazura finished cleaning Vidaro and then turned her black eyes to the great beast sitting near her. There was a great sadness in her that Lioness could sense, could understand.

*"I'm sorry, Vidaro,"* spoke the Juju Queen. *"In her rush to save you, Nidreva took the black bean. Your sister didn't stop to listen to me."*

*"You told her about the years she would lose?"* Vidaro asked. *"She understood?"*

*"Yes. She understood. I didn't know that you hadn't told her."*

Vidaro's shy, humble smile was pleasant to the eyes of Lioness. *"I was hoping to keep that from her, from our father and our people,"* he said. *"Orella had agreed not to speak of it."*

He reached to scratch the place between the ears of Lioness. She enjoyed that, was warmed by the familiar scent of him, and she licked his hand.

*"But you must understand, Vidaro—I can't save her. She was in such a hurry to save* you *that she gave me no chance to explain that I needed a drop of her blood in order to make the red bean."* Kijazura set free a heavy sigh. *"Lioness she is, and lioness she may well remain."*

*"So we're caught between the hammer and the anvil."* Vidaro smiled again. *"Lend me your knife, Kijazura."*

The Juju Queen handed her knife to him. *"What do you have in mind?"*

*"My own blood didn't work when I needed to become the lion. But Nidreva's did."*

*"So you're hoping—"*

Vidaro cut his thumb. *"We share the same parents. We share the same blood. With the Mercy and Blessing of Vizna, this may work."*

Blood dripped from Vidaro's wound as he held his thumb beneath the nose of Lioness.

The smell of his blood was sweet and calming. Lioness purred, but then a lance of hot pain pierced her soul, and she roared in agony. Light as red as a setting sun, as red as Vidaro's blood, blinded Lion to the night. The pain grew sharper, hotter—and then was gone in a flash of blue light. Coldness gripped the soul of the Lioness and hurled it away into some vast, dark place deep in the mind, deep in the soul of the young woman named Nidreva.

I opened my eyes and saw Kijazura and my brother standing in front of me, smiling with relief and joy. Then Vidaro laughed at me.

"What is so funny, brother?" I asked.

He pointed to me. "Now we're even. It's your turn to be embarrassed."

Kijazura laughed softly. I looked down and realized

that I was naked. I felt myself blush, my face turn warm. The Juju Queen handed my clothes to me, and then I spun around and dressed quickly. When I was finished, I turned back to them.

"Thank you, Kijazura," I said to her. "Thank you for all you've done."

"You're most welcome, Nidreva," she said, bowing to me.

Then I threw myself into my brother's arms, embracing and kissing the cheeks of his face. He was alive, he was safe, and his soul was free of the *zsaleel* of the lion. And then I remembered what the Juju Queen had told me, about the years of his life that he had sacrificed for his people. I pushed him away from me and started hitting him.

"Idiot! Fool! Stupid ox!" I shouted. "What can I do? What *shall* I do with you?"

My brother took my arms and kept me from hitting him further. "There is nothing you can do, sister. But what you *will* do is say nothing of this to anyone. Tell no one, understand? This is a secret that must be kept between the three of us."

I looked at my brother and realized the truth of it. He was nearly twenty years older than me, and he was a warrior; I had always accepted the truth that he might die before me. But now his life had been shortened by twenty and one years, and it was heavy stone to carry in my heart. But for him, for Vidaro, the weight of it on his shoulders was much too painful to even think on. So I embraced him again, my proud, brave, foolish, loving brother.

Vidaro kissed the top of my head and then moved aside, though he kept one arm wrapped around my shoulder. "Thank you again, Juju Mother," he said, bowing to Kijazura.

"You're welcome," she said. "You were quick in thinking how to bring her back to us."

"Are you certain the smell of blood won't cause her to change in the future?" he asked Kijazura. "I have only so much blood to give, you know."

My brother's meaning was not lost on me. "Yes, maybe you should return to Churenga with us, Kijazura, just to be on the safe."

"I've been giving that some thought," she said. "I'm tired of living alone, and there's nothing in my lodge that can't be replaced. You need a new Juju Mother, and I need something to keep me busy." Kijazura took my brother's hands into her own. "I promise you this, Vidaro—I will do all that I can to find a way to return to you those years you have lost."

So we began our safari to the village of my people, and our home. And that is how Kijazura Alae became Juju Mother to the Churengari Clan of the great Turquangi Tribe.

My name is Nidreva C'Mora, and even unto this day, there are times when I can still feel the blood of the lioness burning in my veins.

# Lady of Flames

**LaTreka Cross**

3296 B.C. – Year of the Raging Lion, Nine days after the Helical Rising of Sodpet (Sirius Star Cluster).

*'I am the lady of the place of the beginning of time. I am the Lady of Life. I am the Mistress of the Dead. I am the Lady of Slaughter. Death and destruction is balm for my warrior's heart. I am the Eye of Ra. I stalk the land for my enemies and destroy them with my arrows of fire. My flames ignite thee. I am the Inflamed Lady, Nesert. Know me. I am Sekhmet, the powerful one, and vengeance is mine.'*

Even as I voiced aloud that last sentence the burn in my belly grew hotter. My hands curled into tight knots as I stared at the hieroglyphs carved into the limestone pillars at the entrance of Sekhmet's Temple. Justice was a right and one of Ma'at's principles. Although I read Sekhmet's edict a thousand times, I never could relate to those words until tonight. Fourteen years ago, Ammidagu-the Asiatic from Yaqaru, murdered my father in cold blood and usurped the Papyrus Throne in Pe, the city of the cobra goddess. For fourteen years, I've been silent. Waiting.

I felt the lightning charge in the air as every aspect of Ra's light ignited my chakras, starting at my lower spine and climbing still to settle in my heart chakra. My chest exploded with heat, spreading through my valves, crawling through my veins and forcing my fingers to tingle as if urging a weapon to fill the void. I've felt it before in the past, but tonight was different. Ancient war chants and chiming sistra echoed throughout the temple as my temple-sisters sang in praise to the great goddess, Sekhmet. I followed the sound through the narrowed halls, allowing the energy to guide me through the inky darkness.

Alas, I reached the end of the corridor that spilled out into the open courtyard. The evening sky bled bold shades of red and orange in the west as the glorious sun descended into the mountainous regions of Manu. The elders in the surrounding village of Imau called nights like this Nights of Slaughter, but worshippers of Sekhmet knew this night as the Rise of Sekhmet.

The gleaming black marble felt cool underneath my bare feet as I descended the many steps into the square. Vivid red poppy grew in a garden to my right and scented the air. A small pride of tamed lionesses lounged underneath the canopy at the northern edges of the enclosure wall, napping. In the courtyard's center stood the seven foot statue of Sekhmet looking down upon us all. Made of black diorite, her stone flesh shimmered against the fire blazing atop the pillar urns. In her extended left hand, she carried the papyrus scepter symbolizing her as a primeval deity. In her right hand resting at her side, she carried the ankh, the symbol of eternal life. A gift that was not granted but earned.

My eyes feasted upon the goddess' leonine face. Her fiery ruby eyes set against her black stone flesh denoted her power over all that looked upon her. The glowing orb balanced upon her head brewed internal flames and encouraged the flaring cobra made of Ta-Seti gold to shimmer light on her brow. Although she possessed the head of a lioness, her body bloomed as a female with naked breasts that offered the sustenance of life and wide hips that seated the gate to the heavens beyond. In other words, feminine power.

Sekhmet was both creator and destroyer and I am honored that I am her chosen.

Surrounding Sekhmet's image stood my sisters. Like

me, they dressed in red linen honoring the goddess and our purpose. Long stemmed red poppies littered the alabaster altar before Sekhmet along with jugs of red-tinged beer. I watched as High Priestess Tiye poured libations into the sunken pool around the goddess and when she turned to place the jug on the small bench, she noticed me standing at the edge of the square.

"Come, Neitaru. We've been waiting for you."

My sisters parted as I approached. Shaded from the bluest black to the lightest brown, each sister greeted me with a bowed face acknowledging my status over them. Although Ammidagu lorded over the north, I am a descendant of the original bloodline. My ancestors, Heru-Shemsu or Followers of Heru, assumed the throne after the Great Heru ascended the heavens. To see those women, my sisters, acknowledging my right to pursue the throne strengthened my will to succeed.

Tiye, mother when I had none, stood before the altar. I've known her all of my life. She and my birth mother, Makena, grew up in the Temple of Sekhmet together. Upon the death of my parents, Tiye and her brother Djer, the royal treasurer, snuggled me from the palace in Pe to safety in Ineb Hedju, *the white wall,* and Tiye raised me here inside temple.

"Are you ready, my child?"

"I am." I nodded feeling my braids skimmer against my bare back and creating sensations down my spine. Breathing slowly; my eyes could barely stay open. The dense energy felt like the milk of the poppy in my veins. Addictive, yet soothing.

"Come." Tiye gathered my hands in hers and encouraged me to bow before Sekhmet. My sisters formed a circle around us, each representing an hour in the day and shadow night. Sadu, the oldest temple-sister started chanting with the others joining in until their voices harmonized. I could feel the earth tremble beneath me.

"Rise, Eye of Ra." Tiye recited from the *Book of Adoring Ra of the West* and touched my forehead.

Sweat beaded down my spine as the chanting grew louder, deeper.

"Drink this."

I accepted the chalice of foaming crimson beer and looked up at the statue of Sekhmet. I felt my sisters' stares as they waited for me to drink. When I took longer than necessary, Tiye guided the cup to my lips. The taste tingled on my tongue as the warmth seeped into my belly.

Tiye raised her hands in supplication. "Oh powerful, mistress of Imau. Here our call for justice. We offer, Neitaru, daughter of Seka to do as you please to right the justice in the land of the Ancient Ones."

As soon as Tiye ended her proclamation, the earth trembled beneath me and the columns lining the causeway swayed slightly. At the edge of the courtyard, the lionesses rose from slumber and made abrupt roaring noises. They paced from one end of the yard to the other, but never displayed aggression.

Luminous discharge crackled from the sun globe balanced on Sekhmet's head and sputtered out the cobra on her brow. I watched in awe as the current ripped down the statue reacting to the quartz solidified in the diorite. Bands of blue current undulated around the statue in a wobbly motion that sped up and steadied with each second.

Mist rose from the pool surrounding Sekhmet's statue. Tendrils of blue current crawled out of the water and latched onto my sisters. Gasps echoed around me as the energy covered their bodies and arced between them. The current continued, rippling across the marble floors, along the granite walls and every inch of the courtyard until everything around us charged.

As I looked down, pure energy danced over my brown skin. My senses intensified. The smell of frankincense burning at the four corners of the courtyard grew stronger with each breath. My ears chimed hearing the vibration of the earth pulsing beneath my feet and all around me. I glanced up at Tiye and the blue current whirled around her black braids until they transformed into blue-black light. Her dark brown skin shimmered as her essence conducted the violet light surrounding her body.

"The goddess is near." Tiye said and stared ahead at Sekhmet's statue.

I saw the ripple between the two dimensions. It moved like liquid without gravity. The gate between the two worlds parted and in the distance pure white light reflected off all surfaces inside that realm. Pyramids of light and other forms of towering buildings dotted throughout the wheat fields and large hawk-shaped barges hovered in the blue sky. The Sekhet-Hetep, Field of Paradise. It was the place where the ancestors went if their hearts balanced with the ostrich feather on Ma'at's Scales.

A woman clothed in a red dress knotted at the shoulders and hugging every inch of her curves all the way to her ankles, waited on the portico of an opalescent temple with two muscular warriors in full golden armor flanking her sides. She descended the tiled steps and strode towards the veil, but the men stayed behind. Deep in my gut, I knew that if they sensed any impendent danger on our end, those two lions wouldn't hesitate to engage in battle.

As the goddess stepped through the veil, the golden dust painting her light-brown skin shimmered in the torchlight surrounding the statue. Underneath the solar crown atop her head, her short hair, curled out from the roots as if forming a short ruff mane like a lioness. Her kohl drawn eyes enhanced the brown irises flickering crimson in their depths and they seemed to see right through me. I bowed my head instantly, not knowing if I was permitted to look upon the goddess's beautiful face, but yet already knowing that was a moot point now considering I had gawked at her since the veil opened.

"Mistress of Imau." Tiye fell to her knees with her red dress splaying around her like a pool of blood.

"Tiye, you have served me well," Sekhmet's strong voice said above me. "Rise, Neitaru, daughter of Seka."

Each syllable she spoke caused my soul to churn

and burn brighter. My legs trembled as I stood up to greet the powerful one, but I kept my face bowed, not wanting to offend her greatness any further.

"You're the last of your father's house. My heart weeps for your lost in this realm. You fear loneliness. Fear not, loneliness is not forever."

Tears fell down my cheeks unchecked.

"So much pain wounds your spirit, but your heart boils with anger. You cannot defeat your enemy with only rage for it will consume you and everyone around you."

Sekhmet's hand covered my heart, and the anger of growing up parentless leaked from my pores like sweat. She siphoned the hate and words of malice I've heard over the years choking my soul in darkness. In its place the flames of courage, strength and power surged through my veins, righted my spine. The heat emitting from the light ignited every inch of my skin until a film of fire hovered over it, but didn't burn.

She lifted my chin and I found her eyes burning with flames.

"Your enemies are my enemies. Ammidagu and his horde are spreading their infectious poison throughout the North. But I have a remedy for this illness. The lion of the south sails on the winds of Hapi with Heru's falcon on his shoulder. Ra's light covers him. Like you, he is my chosen. Together, you and the lion will extinguish the darkness from Ta-Mehu and resurrect the power of Wadjet."

\*\*\*

Dawn had crested in the east when Sekhmet finally returned through the veil. No one expected her to stay as long as she had. Now that Sekhmet granted me with the powers to defeat my enemies, I refused to wait a day longer to remove Ammidagu from Pe.

Remnants of light particles still shimmered on my skin in the darkness as I made my way to my bedchambers. While my sisters went off to their quarters for a few hours of rest, I had another mission.  Lowering on bent knee, I looked under my bed and pulled the leather bundle towards me. I handled the leather with care, tugging the ties and unwinding it until a gold hilt with a cobra's tail peaked out of the bundle.

Tears brimmed in my eyes as I stared at the perfection of the scales.  On the pommel, hieroglyphs spelling 'Seka' glinted in the sunlight peaking through the small window over my bed. This beautiful sword and the matching ceremonial dagger was all I had left that belonged to my father.

A soft knock on my door interrupted my thoughts and I placed the bundle on the cedar chest in the corner. When I opened the door I found Kadja standing before me. Her curious hazel eyes looked around my room and settled on the traveling sack, and the pile of leather lying next to it.

Her eyes found mine again. "It's true. You're leaving, aren't you?"

I returned to the cedar chest and she shut the door behind her with a soft click.

"Let me come with you."

"You, young lady, still have to attend school." I continued to place a few articles of clothing into my sack for the trip.

"We all would die for what you believe in, Neitaru. School doesn't matter to me anymore."

"What is this talk? School is important. You cannot grow up dumb as a donkey. Tiye isn't having that and you know it." I slowly turned and accessed my foster sister. Barely twelve summers old, Kadja with her lanky posture and hazel eyes brighter than Sodpet's light probably weighed less than my pinky.  Kadja had so many things to look forward to like marriage and children.  Fighting wasn't one of them.

"But I want to go." She whined and lowered her tone when I eyed her. "You. Need. Me."

This beautiful soul had a huge heart just like Tiye. "I

need you to stay here and look after Mama."

She approached and her long white halter dress with tiny embroidery beads along the bodice tinkered in the silence. After roping her slender arms around my waist, she embraced me in her warmth. I breathed in the subtle coconut oil scenting her twisted hair, relishing all the love she felt for me. I never had the opportunity to know my older siblings for I was too young to remember them. This girl made me wished I had known them and Kadja did as best as she could to fill the void of my loss.

"I don't want anything to happen to you," she said and I felt her hot tears on my shoulder. She hugged me tighter and I fought back the tears clogging my throat.

I leaned back and cradled her baby face. "Nothing will happen to me. I promise."

She closed her eyes and more tears fell. "Don't make promises you can't keep, Neitaru."

"Have I ever promised you something and not held it."

She shook her head.

"Then don't expect me to start now." I pushed her kinky twists away from her face and kissed both of her sharp-angled, brown cheeks. "I will return, little sister. You will see. I will return."

The door creaked open behind me. I glanced over my shoulders and found Tiye and Sadu standing there waiting.

"Kadja, go help your sisters clean the kitchen." Tiye's tone brooked no argument.

Kadja kissed my cheek and left the room without another word. Sekhmet willing, I would return and not forfeit on my promise to her.

"Horem is preparing your reed boat for travel." Tiye's husband had always been kind to me. He never tried to replace my father, but loved me as best he could. I would miss him. I returned to the cedar chest to finish packing and Tiye placed a small wicker basket next to my sack. The pleasing smells of fresh baked honey bread teased my nose.

"I brought you food for the travel. It's not much, but it should aide you until you reach the city."

"Thank you. It's more than I have now." I pulled the beaded ties on my sack to secure it.

"Sadu and Kema are coming with you."

I stiffened. Tiye cocked an arched eyebrow at me and folded her arms over her chest. I angled my stare towards Sadu standing quietly at the door. Before, I paid no mind that her ceremonial robes no longer draped her body. Instead of soft linen and dainty sandals, leather armor now covered her ample bosom over the short linen dress and she had a short sword strapped her back. "This isn't your fight."

"Isn't it? Are we not all in bondage?" Sadu asked.

"You are from Nekhen. Ka-Sekhem is your king. Your freedom isn't relevant--" I choked off my words when I saw Sadu flinch. Although Sadu was born in Nekhen, the city of the Falcon, she had lived in Ineb-Hedju most of her life after Sekhem-Hor, Ka-Sekhem's father, banished her family from Ta-Shemu, *Upper Kemet*.

Hand on her wide hips, Sadu approached me. Her pierced nose flared with anger. "Where am I, Neitaru? Am I not standing here with you? Do I not have to worship an imposter that stole the Papyrus Throne, *your* father's throne? We are sisters, not by blood but definitely in spirit. If you suffer, I suffer. If you win, I win. If you die, I die. However it may end, we fight as one."

"I don't know about you two, but I don't plan on dying anytime soon." Kema walked in bringing along with her enough weapons to start a war. She leaned the leather sack of obsidian tipped-arrows, flint daggers, short-handle spears, and curved swords against the wall and plopped down on my bed. Battle ready, leather sheaves covered her short legs and arms and she too had on a leather breastplate. She had pulled her long braids into a high ponytail atop of her head and twisted them into one thick, braid.

Where Sadu was tall and thick, Kema was the total opposite, short and petite. I ranged in the middle of their sizes, standing at five feet six inches. If I had desired two warriors to stand at my side, these two would fit my requirements. Kema learned how to defend for herself at an early age living as an orphan on the streets of Ineb Hedju. Sadu had more courage than most men and she sided with me more times than I could count. But my decision was final. "As much as I appreciate your help, I can do this on my own."

"Sekhmet never said you had to," Sadu countered. "And I'm not letting you do this alone."

"Neither am I." Kema frowned and dared me to say any more with her golden stare.

I balled up my fists and Kema stood up from the bed.

Tiye stepped in between us before the battle begun. "They are going or you're not going."

I set my jaw and stared off in the corner, as my thoughts took over.

"Stubborn," Kema murmured.

Stubborn, possibly but the truth was I didn't want anyone's blood on my hands, especially the people I loved.

"Having confidence is good, but don't let your ego ruin your purpose. Your sisters can aide you against the enemy." She turned my chin to gain my attention and I saw the worry lines creasing her brow. "Djer will meet you at Takisa's Tavern, in the slave's district of Dep right after sunset. He knows the blueprint of Ammidagu's palace. Follow Djer's instructions to very glyph." She turned to my sisters. "Follow Neitaru to the meeting point. If you see any spies, you take them down. Don't let them report your presence to Ammidagu. Stay on the move and don't linger in the city longer than a few hours. We don't want to alert that bastard that you are coming for him."

\*\*\*

The glorious sun ascended at its peak overhead, imparting its burning rays down upon us as we sailed down the fast moving water. Clusters of huts and mud brick house sprung from the thick foliage along the shore. Farmers stood out in their fields with oxen, plowing the countryside. Fishermen drug their nets down the river for today's catch. My arms burned with fatigue of rowing for the later part of the trip. The limestone mile markers along the riverbanks gave me the only indication that we made progress.

"I thought we'd never get here," Kema said.

Anticipation rushed through my veins and heat coiled up my spine. The twin cities, Pe and Dep, rose along the east and west bank like papyrus stalks. High walls made of gleaming limestone surrounded Pe, but Dep lacked protection. Large foreign ships docked along the wharfs of both cities indicated the inverse of power over the years. I maneuvered the reed boat to a small cove and Kema and Sadu jumped into the knee-deep water to push the boat ashore. A barge full of Asiatic soldiers turned the bend just as we hid our boat amongst the dense foliage. Kema and Sadu crouched beside me as I pushed back the tall papyrus sedges. Our feet sunk into the fertile layer black silt Hapi brought along with it during its annual flood season.

"They're looking for something." Kema whispered.

"Or someone," I added.

Sadu reached into her sack and pulled out a magnifying crystal. She held the crystal out before her face and squinted. "How sure are you about, Djer? Can we trust him?"

That same question popped in my head, but I had to believe Djer was on our side.

"It doesn't look like it. Traitorous bastard! Isn't that him on the barge with them?" Kema asked and had already pulled an arrow out of her quiver and notched on the curved bow.

"Are you insane?" I snatched the arrow out of her hand. "We stick to the plan and we meet Djer at sunset."

Kema lowered the bow. "Clearly, that is a bad idea."

"You are paranoid." Sadu rolled her eyes.

"I'm practical." Kema hissed.

We dipped below the foliage as the barge sailed by.

"What is your instinct telling you?" Sadu whispered over my other shoulder. "Tiye trusts Djer and you should too."

Kema gripped my wrist. "Never trust anyone who has a greater advantage than you, Neitaru. Djer eats with the imposter and is paid by the imposter. Even dogs don't eat and piss in the same place."

I shook my head, although Kema's logic had implanted seeds of doubt. "What choice do we have? Djer is our way inside the palace. He is Ammidagu's advisor and he must act accordingly so he isn't suspected of treason. Besides, we don't know what they're looking for."

Foreign language echoed across the waters. Although I didn't speak the gruff Asiatic language fluently, I understood certain words. The young man who wore the black cloak sitting under a netted canopy said Ka-Sekhem's name repeatedly followed by the words 'war' and 'battle'. Clearly upset, he jumped up from his chair and paced an agitated line before the men.

"We are the least of their concerns, ladies. Apparently, Ka-Sekhem is a thorn in Ammidagu's ass."

"Should we watch and wait then?" Sadu asked.

A smile bloomed on my face. "Ka-Sekhem can have his war, but Ammidagu is mine."

\*\*\*

I entered the tiny tavern nestled in the poorest section of Dep a little before sunset. Kema and Sadu patrolled the outside perimeters, watching for any of Ammidagu's men. Swirling incense smoke, a strong mixture of myrrh and bdellium, poured from many clay urns along the walls. Probably to hide the stench of the ale stained floors and smelly bodies gyrating all throughout the place. Not that I mind the poor attempt of freshening the air. Smelling funky ass and armpits ranked low on things I wanted to encounter tonight, but I digress.

As I moved through the crowd, I found an empty table at the back and sat facing the door. Sensuous music played in the background of raucous laughter of lewd men throwing copper shards at naked dancers performing on top of the tables. I realized now why Djer suggested we meet here. This seedy part of the city overwrought with thieves, vagrants, and whores was the last place Ammidagu expected Djer to linger.

Fine hair on the back of my neck rose and my skin prickled. Slightly to my left, that part of the tavern lacked the luxury of torchlight. Soft giggles and sighs floated from the darkness and then a slim sister with knotted hair walked out with an empty tray. Curiosity stoked, I waved her over.

"What's going on over there?"

She cocked a brow at me with a toothy smile. "Depends on whose asking. The patrons in that corner paid extra coin for discretion. You want ale?"

I declined and she walked off to attend the paying customers.

Something about that dark curtain unnerved me so I kept my eye on it, and my fingers resting on my dagger. Looming shadows passed over me and the click-clack of metal dropping on the table pulled my attention away from the corner. A pile of gleaming copper coins lay before me and two men of Asiatic origin hovered over my table.

"Dance," the taller one with startling gray eyes said as his eyes raked lustily over me.

"Move on. I'm not for sale."

The short, stout one, moved closer. "We didn't ask you that."

I stood and towered over him, my hand curling into flaming fists at my sides. "And I told you to move on."

"This whore thinks she's better than us. Once a

whore—" My flaming fist slammed into his face, followed by a swift right to his temple. The fat man fell over and crashed into the adjacent table, sending wood fibers across the floor.

Letting out a battle cry, the taller Asiatic rushed me, and we both spiraled over the table. He landed on top of me and tried to roll him over to no avail. After his first punch landed square in my mouth, I deflected his backhanded cuffs to my face. Hatred gleamed in his eyes as he wrapped his fingers around my neck. Burning air trapped in my lungs. I fingered for the dagger at my waist, not finding it there. I battered my fists against his arms, but he wouldn't let go.

I dug my fingers into his face. Flames lit up on fingertips. My opponent screamed in terror as the heat burned his face. He tumbled back, kicking and screaming. Gasp hard, I sucked air into my lungs and watched as the brawl raged all around me. Kema plunged her sword deep into a man's belly, coming away with stinky entrails as she removed her sword. Sadu fought with her opponent, blade striking blade until she swiped his limbs from under him, and delivered her sword through his beating heart. Men that I hadn't realized was there brandished swords and fought against the foreigners to the death. Asiatics against Kemetu, the clear distinction of ethnic divide cut deeper than a knife.

Someone grabbed me from behind and wrapped their beefy arm around my neck in a choke hold. I twisted sideways and elbowed the aggressor in his stomach. The moment he doubled over, I launched a spiraling kick to his face. He dropped flat on his back, out cold.

I spotted the jeweled handle of my dagger underneath a broken chair. I dodged swaying fists and dangerous swipes of swords as men fought to their deaths. As soon as I wrapped my fingers around the jeweled hilt, someone struck me from behind. The blow sent me hurtling to the floor and I shook away the sudden dizziness that assailed me. I never answered the attack because my temple sisters chopped him down before he could belt out another blow.

Sadu and Kema grabbed my forearms and pulled me

to my feet.

"Now that was a wild ride." Kema laughed—great, panting filled laughs and I heard traces of nervousness in the mirth.

Sadu bent over, catching her breath. "And to think this is our first night here. I wonder what tomorrow has in store."

"Let's not get ahead of ourselves," I said as I surveyed the damage. The stench of death stifled the air with its presence. Crumpled bodies of the dead, and severed limbs scattered about without a care. Puddles of blood stained the tiled floor, and streaked down the walls like a poorly painted mural. Not one piece of furniture remained in a usable state.

The naked dancers and a quartet of lyre players huddled in the corner, shaking with fear. A small fire, caused by overturned oil lamps, blocked the only exit and several men stomped it out before it grew wild. As soon as they extinguished the fire, the women and lyre players sprinted for the door.

When the dust settled, a tall man swathed in fine linen and gold wristbands emerged from the shadows. Muscles rippled throughout his lean body. He reminded me of a lion, with his regal countenance and keen eyes. Dark like the night's sky and too handsome for his own good despite the ridged scars marring his left cheek that ended at his proud lips. Thick dreadlocks corded around his head. At his waist, a long curved sword dangled dangerously with light catching on its shiny surface as he prowled through the throng of surviving men.

"Burn the bodies in the desert." His deep voice commanded authority.

The men moved about without a word and did as he ordered, clearing the tavern of corpses and the injured. He approached me and I took a measured step back.

Unease settled deep in my gut as his eyes scrutinized my round face, and lingered over my full lips. As if he had my permission, his eyes continued roaming over the swells of my breasts hidden under the thick leather, swept down the taut muscles of my exposed abdomen until they flinched and then he quickly averted his focus to my face.

"Are you all right?" he asked.

I swiped the blood cornering my throbbing lip with the back of my hand. "I'll live."

He slightly inclined his head. "So you will. You handled yourself well. What is your name, raging lioness?"

Kema and Sadu protected my sides with their swords brandished, interrupting the lie I was about to tell. In response, his men drew their weapons and flanked in to defend the stranger.

"Her name is unimportant to you," Sadu snarled.

The stranger held his hands out in front of him as if seeking calm. "Lower your weapons. You are amongst friends."

"You and I are not friends," Sadu spat and raised her weapon higher.

"You don't want me as your enemy." His cool tone sent shivers down my spine and his eyes grew unrepentant.

"We already are by law."

Realization dawned on me as I dissected Sadu's words. The man standing before us was Ka-Sekhem, ruler of Ta-Shemu. I drew my dagger, unsure if we could defend ourselves against these warriors.

"Shit! Do you think we can take them," Kema whispered.

"I don't know about you but I'm going down swinging," I said and kept my eye trained on their leader. He, I would do first.

"No harm will come to you," Ka-Sekhem said and ordered his men to put their weapons away. The scraping of metal against leather broke the silence until each man sheathed their swords away.

"Neitaru?" Djer stood at the door, mouth agape. "What is going on here?"

I noticed Ka-Sekhem's eyes narrowed at Djer's mention of name. Did he know who I was?

"Have you all gone mad?" Hunched over and supported by an ivory staff, Djer hobbled inside. He lowered as best he could on bent knee before Ka-Sekhem. "Heru Shemsu, Son of Ra, I'm glad you received my correspondence and agreed to the meeting. Please forgive my nieces behavior. Exhaustion makes them a little crazy at times."

Correspondence? Kema, Sadu and I exchanged worried looks. Had Djer set us up?

"Rise, old friend. After what just happened they probably fear for their lives. It is understandable."

Djer grunted as he pushed himself upward.

"Old *friend*?" Kema hissed under her breath. "I told you we couldn't trust him. You should've let me plug his eye when we had a chance."

"Put your weapons down," Djer admonished over his shoulders. His face flushed with embarrassment.

I slid my dagger into my leather sheath first and eyed my sisters urging them to do the same.

"If I die tonight, we all die tonight." Kema eyed Ka-Sekhem with warning and then dropped her sword arm.

"Don't even ask me. I feel comforted armed," Sadu said and raised her weapon a hair. I reached over and pushed her wrists down until the blade pointed to the floor. She and I exchanged heated glares until we came to a mutual understanding. If anything jumped the wrong way, heads would roll tonight.

"Feisty lot you have, Djer. Not exactly what I was expecting."

"They're unconventional, but skillful at what they do."

"From what I saw, I'd have to agree. Perhaps, we can combine forces," Ka-Sekhem's eyes found mine and held.

"They are honored to have you consider their worth, Son of Ra." Djer turned and hobbled towards me. A balanced mixture of silver strands twined through his thick dreads rioting about his curved shoulders. The layers of white linen belied his thin frame. He had aged considerably since the last time I saw him. He pulled me into his embrace and kissed both of my cheeks.

"The beauty of Queen Makena lives on. It's been a long time since I've looked upon your face." Djer gathered my face in his hands, examining my lip. "And now it's bruised."

"I assure you my prey looks worse than I do. They didn't stand a chance," I said and winced as I tried to smile.

"That's my girl." Djer chuckled low in his throat.

"We should leave," Sadu said, growing quite twitchy beside me.

"I'm afraid I can't let you do that." Ka-Sekhem's deep voice echoed in the silence and no one moved.

"Are we prisoners?" I asked as my fingers wrapped around the dagger's hilt.

His eyes followed the movement and a smile cornered his lips. "No, you are not prisoners."

"Then you have no grounds to hold us captive."

Ka-Sekhem smirked, nodded once and his troops parted in halves allowing us to leave. This was too easy. The fact that he kept smiling sent tiny shivers down my spine. I backed away slowly and then turned to make a hasty retreat. Kema and Sadu walked backwards, sword raised until we approached the exit.

"Wait." Djer moved faster than I've ever seen him as he cut in front of us, blocking the door. "The Lord of Ta-Shemu can help you defeat Ammidagu, Neitaru. Sure, you can gain entry inside the palace. Maybe even get close enough to Ammidagu, but you have to go through five hundred of his troops to do so. Use Ka-Sekhem's resources. Let him give you the advantage and the distraction on the battlefield."

I looked over my shoulder at Ka-Sekhem. If the rumors were true, he commanded over one thousand Abtu soldiers, not counting the hundreds of warriors from the other nomes in Ta-Shemu. Yes, I probably could use his troops to remove the vermin from Pe, but at what costs? Power hungry rulers like Ka-Sekhem never raged war for anyone unless the results benefited them.

"I want revenge. I'll leave the fighting over land to the men," I whispered for Djer's ears only.

"You can have your revenge and your father's crown." He spoke with conviction.

I paused, and tendrils of hope wormed through my soul, igniting cinders that long since extinguished. Like a fool, I tried to stamp it out, but once the fire detonated, I saw peace at the end of the tunnel.

"Give your ears to his words, Neitaru."

An eerie calm had befallen the tavern as every eye trained on me. Pivoting on shaky legs, I stepped forward and stared up at Ka-Sekhem. He affixed his confident gaze upon me and my breath caught in my chest. I averted my face when the power in Ka-Sekhem's stare grew too great for me to bear. Tiny splotches of blood stained his tunic and shenti covering his lean hips. Not that I was surprised that he joined the fight, but disappointed that I hadn't seen this lion in action.

"What if I decided not to use your troops to gain the advantage?" I asked Ka-Sekhem and Djer sighed with a shake of his head.

"I'm marching on Ammidagu whether you agree or not." He folded his arms over his chest.

I cocked an eyebrow at him. "And if I consent with your proposal?"

"You must marry me and unite the two lands as it were in the time of our forefathers. The city of Pe and the city of Abdu united as one ruling Heru Shemsu."

Incensed, my eyes shot fire daggers at him. "Unacceptable. I have no use for a united kingdom. I am content as a maiden in Sekhmet's Temple." I turned and my sisters followed me out of the tavern. Djer trailed behind us, trying to get me to reason.

"Neitaru." Ka-Sekhem called after me. I stopped and regarded him over my shoulder. His wide-legged, arm-crossed pose was starting to piss me off. "You are aware of my terms. If you take Ammidagu's head, I will consider that as a consummation of our relationship."

"You can consider it as whatever you want, but it doesn't mean that I consent. As a daughter of Seka, I have no living king."

I walked off and I could feel the heat of Ka-Sekhem's stare boring into my back. The cool night air charged the rivulets of sweat beading underneath my clothing. I knotted my fingers into fists hoping to ward off the tremors erupting in tiny waves throughout my body.

"You're stubborn as a mule and disrespectful." Djer chided. "After what you've just done, I don't think Ka-Sekhem will welcome any further proposals."

I ignored Djer's complaints and continued south towards our camp outside the city.

"I'm surprised he didn't take your heads for treason."

"Ka-Sekhem and Ammidagu are both foreigners with no stake in this land."

Kema and Sadu chimed in with approval of my words.

"Would you rather have Ta-Mehu ruled by someone who has the glory of its people in mind or by devils who seek to strip her of her riches?"

"I alone should rule this land."

"Which is it? Are you seeking to rule as queen, or are you content as a temple maiden?"

"I can do both and without the likes of him. My father imparted a legacy I must resurrect--"

"Your father was a good man, a follower and upholder of Heru's law. What happened to him those many years ago was tragic, but you cannot undo the past."

Air deflated from my lungs in a rush as if Djer had kicked me square in my chest. I turned away with tears brimming in my eyes, ashamed at my weak display of emotion.

Djer laid a frail palm on my shoulder and squeezed. "See reason. No land is ever gained without bloodshed. Don't think Ka-Sekhem will give you Ta-Mehu without stipulations."

I whirled on Djer and pounded my fist in my palm. "Then I shall take it."

Djer shook his head. "Ka-Sekhem's power grows with each rising sun. You are a one woman army—"

"Three women, thank you very much," Kema interjected.

Djer waved off her comment. "Ka-Sekhem leads thousands of men. Who do you think the people will bow to?"

"I am a daughter of Seka. The people will support my cause."

"The people don't know that you even exist."

I turned away from the truth staring me in the face. I remained hidden in Sekhmet's Temple so long that no one outside my sisters knew my birthright.

"How does Ka-Sekhem know who I am?"

"The princes of Ta-Shemu have always known you existed. They searched for you after Ammidagu invaded the city. Tiye and I decided that your existence and your location were best kept a secret until you were able to make your own decisions."

"Pressuring her is not allowing her to make her own decisions," Sadu said in a quiet voice.

"I'm afraid time is not on our side." Djer regarded Sadu over his shoulder and then averted his attention to me. "You must make the decision quickly before our window of opportunity closes."

"Why are you so eager to marry the two nations? What are you receiving from the deal?" Sadu had asked but I cared not for Djer's answer. I had already made up my mind.

\*\*\*

The next night just after dusk, the horns of Pe blew with alarm as dozens of Ta-Shemu's ships closed in on the city. The glow from the half-moon cast enough light that I saw Ka-Sekhem standing on the curving prow of his large vessel sluicing down the river. We watched from the banks of Dep and waited the perfect opportunity to slip into the adjacent city.

Standing in the midst of battle, Ka-Sekhem proved his worth as he slashed and maimed, kicked and punched his way to the secured gate. The moonlight danced on his dark skin. I stared, captivated by his gleaming dreads swaying with his swift movement. Met with minor opposition, he and his troops fought with courage as they demolished the Asiatic soldiers and overtook the limestone wharfs. Their shouts of victory echoed throughout the marshes and sounded like a lion's roar.

Their victory cries were short lived. Flaming arrows rained from the battlement upon the Ta-Shemu warriors. Shields rose and surrounded Ka-Sekhem as they formed an arch and rammed against the door with the battle ram of Ra. My heart pounded in my chest, knowing his troops were seconds from battering inside.

"Come on, Neitaru," Sadu shouted. And when I didn't budge, Kema grabbed my wrists, and pulled me behind her at a dead run. The instant the gate broke free, Ka-Sekhem led his men inside the city and we hopped into our reed boat.

Sadu and Kema quickly maneuvered the boat near the northern irrigation tunnels running beneath Pe and dropped anchor. After constant begging and a little fibbing, Djer finally imparted the irrigation maps earlier that morning and Kema had prepared the underwater gates for our entry.

"Remember, fifty strokes south and the water empties into an underground well underneath the palace," Kema said as she secured her sword on her back.

"Stick to the plan," I said eyeing both of them with hard stares. "If I'm captured, you are to flee to Ineb Hedju."

"Ka-Sekhem doesn't want to feel the heat of my

blade," Sadu said as she slid several knives into the leather sheaves strapped to her thighs.

I grabbed her arm and tugged her close. "Flee."

Sadu said nothing as she back flipped into the water, snatching out my hold. The boat rocked with fervor against the rippling waves.

"You really think he'll capture you."

I snorted. After what I had planned, Ka-Sekhem would uproot every foundation stone looking for me. I shrugged for Kema's sake.

"Then we shall prolong it. We'll make him squirm a little before he does." Kema smiled as she slipped into the water.

Now or never. With one last gulp of air, I dove into the cool river water.

***

I swam downward at first and then suddenly the tunnel inclined. My lungs burned from the lack of air, but I pushed on fighting exhaustion. Darkness surrounded me until I saw a glowing light at the end of the tunnel. When I broke the surface, I gasped a harsh breath and watched as Kema swam to the rocky edge. Muted torchlight flickered along the cave walls. Rough hewn stairs bracketed by towering stalagmites rose out of the water, while crystals and pink granite covered the remaining concave wall.

I swam to the edge and Kema and Sadu pulled me up on the narrow ledge. After changing into dry clothing that Djer surprisingly left for us, we headed up the steep limestone stairs. A large door at the top landing would lead us through the royal wine cellar. Sadu listened before turning the lotus shaped knob. I nodded and she pushed the door open.

I slipped through first, and the thick aroma of fermented wine assailed my nostrils. Countless alabaster jugs lined the stone walls and wooden shelves. We wove through food supplies and wicker baskets until we reached the exit. Despite the war brewing outside, the palace hummed with stillness.

We cracked the next door open and I peaked inside. Two burly guards paced an agitated line back and forth in the recess, apparently guarding the back door. Their polished bronze breastplates and armbands glimmered in the moonlight streaming through the large window. I held up two fingers and Sadu slipped inside.

Brisk Asiatic language rose through the door as Sadu pretended to weep with fear. I heard a gasp and then a body falling to the floor. When Kema and I stepped into the palace, Sadu had plunged her knife through the victim's skull and slammed her other blade up through the other guard's chin. Gurgling blood, he dropped face first at her bare feet. She deposited her blades back into her thigh sheathes and searched them for additional weapons and coins, pocketing what she could use.

Fanning out, I headed down the main hall, while Kema and Sadu branched off in opposite directions. I reached the end of the hall, turned left and the corridor emptied into a grand colonnade. Limestone statues of Ba'al and gold-leaf statues of the cobra goddess, Wadjet intermingled between the papyrus-shaped columns. Ahead, my father's old throne rose on a blue tiled dais. I held my emotions in check as I ambled down the blue carpet runner towards my father's past.

"Have you come to kill me," the utterly deep voice asked from the eerily dark shadows behind the throne. I stopped walking; standing about twenty feet from the throne.

I watched in silence as my enemy emerged welding a sword in his outstretched hand. Ammidagu had completely disregarded his former identity as a man of Yaqaru. His light complexion had darkened a deep golden brown from years of living in Kemet. Like most foreigner who docked on our shores, he assumed the way my people dressed, with a short loincloth riding his hips. His flabby chest was bare save for the colorful row of beads making up his neck collar. Resting on his graying brown curling hair, he wore my father's circlet made of gold and emeralds with the flaring cobra just above his brow.

"Have you nothing to say? He sends you, a woman. He couldn't bear to face me himself. I deserve the honor of fighting that Ta-Shemu bastard man to man." Sudden rage flashed in his gray eyes.

"Ka-Sekhem didn't send me."

My statement deflated the air from his lungs. He titled his head to side as if studying me. "Then, what do you want."

"Vengeance."

His eyes narrowed. He descended the dais, his golden sandals clicked with each step. "Little girl, you're playing a man's game."

I unsheathed my sword from the leather scabbard dangling on my back and twirled the curving sword before him. "Is this man enough for you?"

My eyes flashed fire and Ammidagu roared with anger. He swung first and our swords clashed mid-air. We danced and swiped, neither of us landing a maiming blow. We lobbed, sword against sword until Ammidagu head butted me, sending me hurling to the floor. I rolled over as Ammidagu rammed his sword into the carpet, where my head had rested milliseconds before.

"Did you think you could walk into my house and kill me?" Ammidagu said through wheezing puffs of air.

I jumped to my feet and held my sword out before me. "Your house?" I roared as we circled each other. His pudgy belly and flabby arms, the side-effects of years of living in luxury, had become his disadvantage. Sweat poured down his face and matted his curly hair to his scalp. He wheezed and coughed as he tried to catch his breath.

"You have stolen my father's legacy. By rights, all of

this is mine!" I opened my arms wide, enraged that he had the audacity to claim my birthright. "I am Neitaru, daughter of Sa Ra Seka, a princess of Ta-Mehu and your death dealer, asshole!"

Heat rippled up my spine. The fire of Sekhmet churned through my veins and emitted through my fingertips until the golden hilt melted into my palm. Color drained from his face and his eyes widened into twin moons as a thin film of fire covered my body.

"Do you deny that you usurped the Papyrus Throne from Sa Ra Seka?" I swung down with powerful aim and his sword caught the blow before I sliced his skull in half. The ringing vibration of our blades echoed off the large metal urns nestled against the walls. He staggered, and then slipping to the ground on one knee. "Have you not an answer to my allegations. Stand and face me."

I stepped back and allowed him to push to his feet. His sword trembled in his outstretched hands. Swinging downward, he caught my blade as I chopped, and prodded. I dodged his countering swing, barely missing the deadly pass by my right shoulder. Before he could lift his blade I swung high and swiped through the top of his head with a death blow. His sword dropped to the floor at his feet as he stood motionless. Stunned.

My battle cry raged through me until I shook with it. Fire poured out of my mouth and crawled down my skin in whirling torrents. Blood pumped through my veins like molten lava. Hot and boiling. Everywhere I looked, the film of fire blurred my vision, until my gaze caught the moonlight spreading its radiance over the Papyrus Throne.

The fire settled inside me and extinguished as I inhaled cool air into my lungs. I watched with utter satisfaction bright red blood drip from Ammidagu's head wound in tiny rivulets. My panting breathes echoed in the silence as his knees kissed the carpet. The top of his head, severed brain and my father's crown slid in a heap beside him. Kema and Sadu called my name as his lifeless body listed to the side, dropping to the floor. I heard them screeched to a halt at the throne room's entrance.

"We have to go. Ka-Sekhem is at the palace gates." They said at once.

I picked up my father's serpent crown and followed my sisters out the palace through a small courtyard, and prayed that I didn't run into Ka-Sekhem.

# A Subtle Lyric

### *Troy Wiggins*

Rain threatened on the day they met. Back then, the middle of market season was frequently marked by ripe skies, plump clouds as round as a goat's belly. It happened on the Cassa Road to Medina market. Medina was the biggest market in Osu, frequently full of clucking aunties and hawkers pushing chalky white mounds of jackalberry flour, or giant snails out of multi-colored woven wicker baskets. The Oba's soldiers, dressed in khaki and studded jerkins, scanned the market crowds with sharp eyes and sharper steel. Ava looked back on that day and called it strange, strange because under normal circumstances, she would have paid as much attention to Kazhara as one does to the dust on the road.

Ava had just escaped the market crush, wary of the anvil of black cloud that threatened from the east. Usually, clouds such as that rolled along the fresh green grasslands with spears of wind that ripped the clothes off the backs of unwary travelers. Ava did not want to be one of those, the naked ones that had to take the tall grass back to Farm Nine. There were dangers in the tall grass, both animal and human. No, better to leave before the rain came.

And so she departed well before the close of market, only earning two sacks of gold dust for her vegetables. The sum was barely enough to last a month, never mind paying her day laborers. Cassa Road was full with elders, dirty children, wives and uncles, the occasional soldier picking his nails or staring at someone's daughter with smoldering eyes. She'd glanced back every so often, the beads in her dreadlocks click-clacking, scanning the road to take stock of fellow travelers, and always taking note of the cloud glowering on the horizon.

The heat the cloud pushed before it was nearly unbearable, so Ava sang. It was something she did, singing old songs when the day aligned in a way that brought the spirit of her mother rushing into her body, manifesting in her voice and the set of her shoulders. That day, that gray-black day, Ava recalled the lyrics that her mama had let roll from some red place within her all those years before, tumbling through the yam garden where Ava splashed in mud while mama washed the family's clothes in a slick black tub with a rock-shaped chunk of soap.

She sang low, her voice lacking the earthy baritone that her mother's possessed:

> *Anin, dunmaso, jahanba-le hadamaso*
> *A-mala a-marala wo Angani-ala caapi*
> *Dunmaso, tama fuyaa*
> *Le taa dondi ko le suuto*
> *Batu Karoo-aja sumbu*

And Kazhara heard. And Kazhara parted the crowd, despite Ava's low singing, despite the groans of trundling uncles, despite the many-toothed storm cloud that bellowed oh so near in the sky. Kazhara came close, close enough for Ava to smell her frankincense oil, with her red-black skin and her thickly braided knots of hair hung with bells and her and her roundly muscled legs, the outline of them visible even beneath her skirts…and Ava felt as thin as whipcord, a black, ugly thing.

"That was a wonderful song, sister," Kazhara had said. Kazhara, a stranger then, touched Ava's arm with a gloved hand, gloves made of supple brown leather that would cost Ava too many seasons to afford. Ava slid slowly away from the slickness of them, of that touch.

"Mind singing it again? That one hasn't been heard around here since your mother's time, to be sure."

And so Ava sang again. Kazhara glowed.

"Actually, My mother used to sing it," Ava volunteered.

"Your mother spoke with Angani? Walked the path of the moon and sky?"

"I don't know what that means; it sounds like poetry, like something the marabouts would sing." Ava shook her head. Her hair rattled merrily. "My mother did enjoy nighttime, though. She went on long walks each night, longer when the moon was out." Ava decided not to tell Kazhara, sweet Kazhara who was still a stranger, that the night had swallowed her mother whole and left no trace, and that her father had gone to find his wife and had never returned.

"And you?"

"The night is hot and full of biting things and no-good boys with fire in their bellies. Some of them even have swords and a decree from the royal stool to carry them. Too much trouble. I stay inside, eat, have a cup of wine."

"Ah. I see."

"I'm sorry," Ava said, shifting her basket as they came to the Cassa Fork. "I'm headed west. I have to get home before the rains come."

"Now, that is a shame," Kazhara had said, running her eyes up and down Ava's iron-lean body.

"I'm sorry." Ava muttered. A long, silent moment lived between the two women. Sweat escaped from the coiled tangle of her hair, traversed her neck, gathered its companions as it slid beneath her tunic. Finally, Kazhara nodded, and turned back toward the storm cloud, as if she dared its elemental rage to smite her. Ignoring the stick of her clothes, Ava wandered away, down the road to her farm.

\*\*\*

Ava saw Kazhara again at Medina the next week, wearing gloves—black this time—and *trousers*, of all things, trousers that would take a leatherworker much time and effort to create, and would need much gold to procure. Ava shook her head in disbelief at the woman's unbridled display of wealth.

Kazhara was a mountain in the middle of a sea of bodies, shoulders thrown back, hair knotted, trading quietly edged words with on of the merchants, a scrivener by the looks of his robes.  Every so often, the scrivener would glance around at the crowd, spot a soldier, drop his eyes, and the whisper all the more harshly at Kazhara, who planted her hands on her trousered hips and met his words full force.

Ava smiled as she recalled a memory of Mama, who spat at women that wore trousers. Mama had said she knew an old mchawi woman in the hills with herbs that could grow them a pecker if they wanted one that bad. But then, mama had disappeared. Where was the mchawi with Mama-finding herbs? Ava avoided the stranger like she was collecting taxes for the Oba, weaving through market traffic to her stall while ducking frenziedly, doing her best impression of the scurrying thing hiding from the shrike. She flipped over her table, brushed it hurriedly, laid out greens in sporadic patterns, stacked knolknol. Had the stranger seen? Ava wasn't sure. Then she was *there*, towering, legs splayed, looking even more mountain-like than before.

"I saw you come into the market, sister, but I wanted to wait until you got your table set up before I came to visit."

"Hello." Ava futzed with her basket, her blankets.

"It is fate that we meet again. Tell me your name and I'll tell you mine."

Not wanting to be impolite, Ava said, "Ava." One word.

"Ava. Your name is a circle. Ava. I'm Kazhara."

"Hello, Kazhara."

"Do you mind if I sit at your table with you?"

"Will you be able to sit on the ground in your nice

trousers?"

Kazhara guffawed, a thunderclap of a thing. "Of course I can. As long as you don't mind."

And so she sat. The market passed. So did the day. The Mese cowherd at the next table traded her candied bissap for a couple of yams. His scarred face wrinkled from smiling at Kazhara. Ava popped a candy in her mouth, enjoying the way her teeth squeaked against the purple texture of the sugary flower. Kazhara gingerly removed her gloves before taking one, studying it. As the stranger exposed her hands, Ava swallowed a gasp, forced it deep down, and locked it away. Deep violet whorls and designs danced along Kazhara's long brown fingers, forming an intricate pattern of ancient art that few understood, and even fewer had seen. Ancient patterns thought dark by some, deadly by others. Ava had seen it. One word thrummed in her head.

*Mama.*

"Do you find my tattoos odd?" Kazhara asked.

"No—no, not at all...they're just...so unique. So pretty." Ava tore her eyes away. She'd been staring. Stupid. Kazhara smiled again, this time tucking it away behind a sweep of hair. A hot moment buzzed between them.

"Your lips are purple," Kazhara said.

Ava grinned. "So are yours. Your teeth are, too."

A Khemeti courier materialized from the hive of bodies, bathing them in his shadow, all linen tunic and kohl-lined eyes and sun-browned skin and pride.

"Kazhara? You are Kazhara?" he purred, staring at Kazhara's bosom.

Kazhara thrust a tattooed finger toward her face. "Kazhara is here. What you're looking at are my breasts."

"Ah. Yes. Ahem—a message for you." He produced a red-lacquered papyrus scroll from his green satchel. The scroll was far too beautiful for the dust of Medina, Ava thought. Kazhara took the scroll from the boy, produced an almond-sized nugget of gold from her trouser pockets, and tossed it to him. The boy bowed so deeply that his topknot brushed the dirt, then ran off.

"Sad what happened to those Khemeti, what, with the Oba smashing their land to bits and throwing their people all over unified Ifria to work as mailmen. But ah, no need for gloom on a beautiful day like this, eh?"

"My mother used to say the same. Baba cursed them, usually, for their pride. But mama always looked a little sad." Ava said, leaning over to look at the scroll. "What is that, anyway?"

"Ah, little sister, this is for my eyes only," Kazhara said, tucking it away. She rose to her feet all at once, dusted the ground from her trousers. "In fact, it's calling me away at this very moment."

"Is that how you make your gold, and afford your nice gloves? Are you a scrivener? I saw you talking with one of your fellows earlier."

"Aha! You're sneaky, eh? What am I supposed to say?" Kazhara tapped her long fingers against her lips. "My gold doesn't come from the writing of the scrolls as much as it does from what's on the scrolls. I hope that was vague enough."

Ava narrowed her eyes. "It certainly was."

"Will I see you again?"

Ava felt a thrill in her fingertips. "I'm at market every week until the dry comes."

"Then I'll be here," Kazhara said. She turned on her heel, walked a few paces, and turned back, squatted in front of Ava's table. Close, so close that Ava could smell the clove and shea and under it all, the warm scent of Kazhara's skin. "Before I go…will you sing for me, sister?"

And Ava sang.

\*\*\*

"*Dunmaso, tama fuyaa…*" Ava sang. "*Le taa dondi ko le suuto…Batu Karoo-aja sumbu--*"

"Miss Ava," one of the day laborers called.

Ava had taken to wearing bells in her dreadlocks. As she looked up at the laborer that had called her name, only the tips of her dreadlocks tinkled, woven through with silver bells, a gift from Kazhara. The rest were tight under a red scarf. The day laborer that had called her name fidgeted above her, blocking out the sun. Was it Arubo? Mahmoud? The Zoolooman or the Mese, she couldn't tell. She rose to her feet.

"What is it?" It was Amadou. Amadou the New, they'd called him. Hired at the beginning of summer, after mama had gone. The Toahreg, his head wrapped in a *laget*, the traditional deep violet colored turban of his people.

"There's a…visitor at the gates."

"Who is it?"

"A woman…one of my people." He licked his cracked lips. "Ava, you really shouldn't deal with someone like her… they're a bad sort."

Ava frowned. Amadou never said more than a few words to her. Why so loquacious?

"She's one of the *Tamesh-atek*," he continued, unbidden. "Angani-Mwisi, in your tongue. A woman who's thrown off her ward-scarf to walk with the sky. Moon-kissed. The tattoos on her hands. You didn't know?"

She had heard. Heard, but did not know. She furrowed her brow at the well-meaning man. "What are you talking about, Amadou? I don't pay you to tell me tall tales like I'm a child. I pay you to tend my crops and make sure that we have food to sell and eat."

"I'm concerned—"

"Amadou. I appreciate your concern," Ava huffed in her annoyance, "but I am capable of handling myself. Kazhara is a dear friend."

"Just be careful, Miss Ava. You have always been kind to me. I only seek to repay that kindness."

"Thank you, Amadou. That will be all." Ava peeled off her gloves, hop-trotted to the front of the farm. She nearly started at the throng before her home, but realized that they weren't there for her.

"Ava! Ava!" Kazhara's voice was a lion's roar among the yips of jackals.

"Here!"

"Come! Come see!"

Ava pushed through the sweaty, dark bodies—someone caressed her thigh—until, finally breaching the press, she came face to face with a *farasi*, a tall, creature with steely cords of muscle under a hide that was as black as night, and gleamed just as much as the darkness. Kazhara stood next to the beast, her bell-less hair hanging loose around her face, a proud smile glowing against her brown skin, her gloved hands holding its reins tightly. A thick stack of woven blankets was lashed to the creature's back. It shook its mane, bared its great white teeth at the crowd, and pawed the earth with its iron-shod hooves. Ava stared in awe. Such a beast would take much gold to transport across the balmy northern sea. She wasn't surprised that Kazhara owned such a thing. Kazhara was full of surprises.

"Where did you get a *farasi?*"

"From a friend. Come on, let's ride."

And then they were, speeding down the Cassa Road, leaving Farm Nine far, far behind. The beast's hooves thundered against the road, each step sending a jarring rumble up Ava's legs and into her back. She circled her arms around Kazhara's midsection as tight as she could, holding on for dear life. Kazhara's response was to yell her pleasure into the fist of oncoming wind as they sped away.

"You'll never enjoy it with your hair tied up so! Let it free!" Kazhara yelled over her shoulder, barely audible over the punch of hoof on earth and roar of wind. Ava buzzed all over, like she was passenger on a lightning bolt. She reached up, tugged her headscarf free.

And made beautiful music in the wind.

*** 

They rode until the harsh sun relinquished the sky to a soft sliver of moon, and the world was painted in muted shades of slate and silver and deep, deep black. The women had ridden up a rise deep into the rocky desert, a landscape that was cold and unforgiving during the night; Ava tingled from the soles of her feet to, surely, the tips of her swinging dreadlocks. Kazhara grunted as she slid out of Ava's grasp and swooped off of the pile of blankets atop the *farasi*'s back like a cloud on a breeze. Ava giggled and tried to do the same, without the benefit of litheness. Kazhara reached up, grasped Ava around the midsection, and lifted her off the creature, which rumbled deep heaving breaths after the long run.

Ava screwed her eyes shut, wracked through with more giggles, more tingles. She felt rough hands clasp her face, cup her cheeks, then, butterfly wings on her eyelids. Kazhara stared only inches away, iron in her gaze. She had let the black beast roam free; it snuffled around the sand cropping at the short, rough desert grass. Kazhara's eyes were full of fire--she didn't seem too concerned that the creature would wander off. Kazhara held out Ava's scarf, beckoned her to tie her dreadlocks down.

"Sing for me now, Ava, sister. Sing now, but sing soft. This is not a night for kindness."

Ava shoved her giggles deep into her belly, pulling up a deep breath in their stead. Wrapping her hair in the scarf, she sang softly.

*Anin, dunmaso, jahanba-le hadamaso*

"Beware, daughter, the sinister son," Kazhara whispered,

*A-mala a-marala wo Angani-ala caapi*

"That burns his rule in Angani's embrace,"

*Dunmaso, tama fuyaa*

"Daughter, tread light,"

*Le taa dondi ko le suuto*

"Through the drape of night,"

*Batu Karoo-aja sumbu*

"And await the moon's soft kiss."

All the giggles dissipated from Ava's middle in a whirl. She returned Kazhara's hard gaze. "What was that? How do you know what that means? I don't even know--"

She stood at Kazhara's insistent pull. "I'll tell you everything you want to know, but you have to follow me and *stay quiet.*"

Ava nodded, crouched as Kazhara did, stole away from the place that they had dismounted, slid slipshod between tall claws of rock and earth that sprouted sharp from the sand.

"Where are we going--" Ava started, then cut her words short as Kazhara whipped a long black dagger from the belt of her trousers. The weapon was wicked, with jagged silver swirls etched into a blade blacker than the night they crept through. Kazhara poked one tattooed finger into the middle of Ava's lips. Her eyes followed the other finger's pointing into the blue darkness, toward a squat, sad shack that pushed a dirty yellow glow against the night.

"*Dunmaso....tama fuyaa,*" Kazhara whispered. Ava's lips bloomed with tiny pricks of fire, the soles of her feet buzzed angrily in a flash. As soon as the pain sprouted, it ceased. "Staying quiet will not be so hard now."

"What was that?" Ava wanted to yell through her burned lips, but found that nothing more than a whisper was possible. She made her whisper razor-harsh. "What are we doing here in the middle of nowhere? Where have you taken me?"

"I—" Kazhara sighed, shook her head. "I have not been totally honest with you, sister. That day we met on the road was not coincidence. I had been—have been—watching you."

"But that is not cause for this behavior—"

"Watching you because your mother asked me to."

All the air left Ava's body in a flash of heat. She stumbled, nearly crashed to the ground, but Kazhara's strong hands wrapped around her shoulders and lowered her gently into a crouch.

"Where is she?" All of Ava's being manifested in three words.

"She's gone, child. Walking with Angani, with the night, like she used to. But she was a dear friend to me, and she left a message for you. I am to tell you everything I know, but I need you to follow me and remain silent. Okay?"

Ava closed her eyes tight against sudden tears. "This is too much, Kazhara. Too much—"

"Ava." Kazhara's voice was steel. "Follow me. Please? This is your mother's wish, not mine. Please? You look so much like her, Ava. Both of you, black as the night's song, thin as a needle, with those eyes that belong on a lioness but are still gorgeous on your face, and that thick hair that I only wish I could grow. Angani knows I loved your mother. She was my best friend. And I am doing this because of her. Now, you agreed to follow me. I need you to hold good to that—no, your mother wanted you to. Will you follow?"

"How do I even know that you really know my mother?" Ava felt the hysteria building in her belly. "You could be a demon, this could be a prank. I don't even know who you are right now! I can't stay here and—"

Kazhara held up her hands. The foreign marks splayed across her fingers seemed to glow in the moonlight. "You've seen these before, haven't you? You've seen, and you've heard. You didn't want to believe. But you've seen them… on your mother. In a place that no one besides you and your long-lost baba ever saw, ever could see. Am I right?"

Ava could only nod.

"I will tell you everything that I know about your mother, I promise and promise again. But I need you to follow me. Will you?"

Ava found steel from some place deep inside herself. "Yes. I will."

\*\*\*

"Your father loved your mother, but she didn't love him in return, at least not his person. She appreciated what he represented—stability, order—but she couldn't resist Angani's call. That is why she left so much during the night... among other reasons. She always said the only thing that he ever did for her that she loved was help to make you. She loved you so much, Ava." Kazhara pulled a key from her trouser pockets and jammed it into the half-rotted door to the shack.

The door clicked and creaked as it swung open before catching on the uneven earth so hard that one of the bottom slats nearly cracked off. Kazhara pulled herself up to her full height, striding into the shack. After a moment's hesitation, Ava followed. A fat tallow candle guttered a grimy light throughout the room, softly illuminating a lone figure sitting cross-legged on a fur pallet in the middle of the dirt floor. He was thinly muscled, with blue-black skin and a cone of white hair atop his pointed head. A reedy cord bound his hands at the wrists. His eyes were rheumy, his lips cracked. Hungry fires danced in his sun-hardened face.

You've returned," he gasped weakly. "I am to die now, then? I will not lie, I am afraid. But I will not beg, nor will I run."

"You wouldn't get far," Kazhara said coldly. She walked over to where the man sat, placing a strong hand on his round black shoulder. With a flick of her wrist, she sank the knife deep into the earth near his gnarled black legs.

"Who is this man?" Ava asked. "I will not be a part of any crime—"

"He is the only criminal in the room," Kazhara growled.

"But not the only one with blood on my hands," he muttered, and then was silenced as Kazhara buried her boot deep in his midsection. He exhaled a draught of musky air, doubling over, his black flesh quivering.

"Kazhara! Stop!"

"He knows why I do what I do, sister. And soon, so will you. Ava, your mother was moon-kissed, as I am. These tattoos are the marks of our order. I got mine on my hands, because I'm haughty. Your mother was a little more conservative, and got them on her belly. Did you ever see them?"

And Ava did recall. She furrowed her brow, bit her lip. At baths, during dressing, when the breeze caught the hem of her mother's tunic and lifted it to expose the glorious brown of her stomach, she recalled. The same patterns, the same swirls and lines. "Yes," Ava whispered.

"Yes, I have seen them. Every so often someone would whisper, but I didn't believe. So I never knew what they meant."

"And she never told you? Ah! Stubborn girl, she was always so stubborn! No other flaws except that." Kazhara advanced on Ava, arms spread wide. "We are an order—no—a sisterhood. There are many in power that look to keep their power, and still many more that would look to keep that power on the backs of women. We disrupt the balance of power, right wrongs done to us in the name of 'equality'." At this, Kazhara waved her hands in front of her face, as if trying to rid the air of a noxious odor.

"That's where your mother got the idea to start her farm, you know. She always said, we take so much from the world; we are obligated to give something back. So she built a farm, married a man, had you…I never saw it the same as her, but of course, I'm not as cultured as she was."

"So you're thieves? Assassins?"

"Some say the best—" The old man piped up. A solid crack resounded through the shack as Kazhara drove her knee into his temple. He slumped again. Ava bit back a curse, fearful.

"Thieves and Assassins are crude terms, used by crude people." She eyed her captive disdainfully. "Think of us as a movement, a sisterhood of progress, embodied in thousands of women all around Ifria. And your mother was one of us."

"You're lying, Kazhara." Or was she? Ava shook her head in an attempt to clear her jumbled thoughts. "What happened to my mother, seriously?"

Kazhara shook her head, put her hand on top of the old man's head, and wrenched it up so that his eyes could meet Ava's. They were bloodshot, yellow, bruised. "Oromo? Would you like to pick up from here"?

Oromo cleared this throat. The rolling motion of his gaunt neck flesh sent green waves of nausea through Ava's stomach. "As much as I hate to confirm this terrorist's story, she is correct. Your mother, I'm sorry to say, was moon-kissed."

Ava shook her head, waving the old man's words away from her ears.

"I can only imagine that it is difficult, child," Oromo continued, "but it is true. And…furthermore, I can verify that she is…because…five rains ago…you would have been a girl then… purely by chance, my men-at-arms chanced upon her stealing through my *tondyaro,* my father's home—my home. I recognized your mother as the infamous *Anga Nyisi*—your mother was famous outside of her order, death from her was a sure as the night sky being black, hence the nickname "Black Sky". She lived up to her reputation, and killed several of my men before we could subdue her, two of them my own brother's sons. It soon came to light that she was making an attempt on my life…so I had my men order her death--" and in that moment, the ghost of a smirk flitted across his wooden features. "

Ava was black lightning, flashing across the small space that separated them, snatching blade from earth, driving it toward that soft place in the man's neck where she knew that his blood would mist hot and free--

And as quick as she became lightning, she was rooted again, her wrist gripped in iron. Kazhara's rough hand wrapped held hers in an unwavering grip. The blade quivered inches from Oromo's throat.

"What are you doing?" Ava wheezed.

"You both have the same temperament. You rush in when angry. You just believe him? You'd kill this man on his word, but wouldn't take mine?"

"This is different—ow!" Kazhara squeezed Ava's wrist, forcing her to drop the knife. It made no sound as it hit the packed dirt floor. "This is different! This man has no history of lying to me! And besides, I can read it in his face. He's proud of it, proud that he took my mother--" She spat her fury at him, it splattered across his nose. "Who were you to take my mother away from me?"

"He was no one, a minor wart on the ass of this nation--Ava! Calm yourself!" Ava tried to fight against Kazhara's grip and was roughly shaken as a reward. She wondered at Kazhara's intent, bringing her here to face the man that had taken her mother, and not allowing her to kill him in return. She pushed a small pocket of rage away, a tiny sliver dedicated to the woman that she had considered friend.

"Your mother asked me to do this. When she and I were younger—closer—we traded blood oaths and tattooed our love on each other. When you were born, she changed. Our original blood oaths were swift revenge, like Angani's wrath flashing from the skies. Once she had you, instead of just killing the person that took her life, in the event that she was taken—because she knew she would be—she wanted me to bring that person to you so that you could mete out your own justice. Because the Oba never would, never will. I am only doing what my most dear friend asked of me."

And then Ava was released. Her rage spent, she crumbled into a pile of muscle and sweat.

"I also want to extend an invitation. Your mother was one of the best we had. She had worked long and hard toward disrupting the status quo of corruption and insolence, of poverty and death. The thievery of her life by this—worm— left a gash in the world almost as big as the one it left in us, Ava. And it's still there.

"But you can make it right, both in here, and out there.

Join me. Join us, as we work toward fulfilling Angani's will for this world." She stretched tattooed hands toward Ava, reaching, reaching. Ava had trusted those hands. Still did, if Kazhara's words were true. And she believed. Ava grasped Kazhara's hand, allowed herself to be pulled off the ground. Kazhara enveloped her in a hug, held her close. The scent of Kazhara's body crowded out all of the sweet smells that had covered her earlier, the perfumes and oils worn away by stress and exertion.

Ava let go of Kazhara, moved away from that warmth, traded it for the cold of Kazhara's black knife. She advanced on Oromo, moving like a silent wave of darkness. The old man stared at her approach, a black glob of blood dribbling from a patch of flesh above his eye. His gaze was flat, but his features were fixed solid, death dancing in the corners of his mouth. Ava gripped the knife as she closed on him, the slim weight of the metal and leather hot in her hand. Oromo pulled himself into a sitting position, scooting away from Kazhara, closer to Ava.

"If I am to die tonight," He rattled, "I die ready. I have lived a long life, and I have left my mark on this world. You only kill a piece of me, girl. My spirit lives on."

Ava knelt before him. Her skirts bunched uncomfortably beneath her knees, itching her. She traced the knife along his black, black skin, heard the rasp of it against his dirty gray stubble. It would be easy, so easy, to push the knife slowly into the soft space beneath his jaw, or in his belly, or his back. So easy. And like that, Mama would be avenged. But would Mama be pleased?

Her mother's smile flashed in the corners of her vision, an ephemeral memory. Mama was full of life, and loved the life around her. She tended her garden and her daughter meticulously, and was always fair in paying the day laborers that couldn't find work elsewhere. But she also had steel in her, and wasn't afraid to do what was necessary to survive, to thrive. How would Mama handle this? What would her mother do?

Ava pressed the edge of the knife against Oromo's throat, leaned in close with that wickedness between them, looked into his dead eyes.

"You did a terrible thing to my mother," She whispered. "A terrible thing that you thought—no, that you felt was right. My mother also felt that she was right. I can smell the blood on you, Oromo, like one can smell the blood on an old simba that has eaten his fill of life and is ready to give himself to the dust."

"I have never denied my crimes," Oromo muttered.

"Nor have you admitted to all of them," Kazhara interjected.

"It doesn't matter one way or the other," Ava said softly, pressing the knife tighter against his flesh. "None of your other crimes matter to me. Only this one. Answer me true, old man. Did you kill my mother?"

Ava felt his throat move the knife slightly as he swallowed. "Yes. I sentenced her to death. I'd do it again, and again. I have no regrets."

His yellowed eyes spoke truth. The foul sweat that streamed from his pores confirmed his words. Ava slid the knife down his neck, over his collarbone, the blade dragging along his parched flesh.

"You took something dear from me, Oromo," Ava said, lightly trailing the knife along his stomach, his arms. "My mother was my life, the root of my family, and you took her."

"I'd argue that your mother's friend took her. The people she worked for, the Oba himself, they played a part in taking her from you as well."

"But none like you. Your hand directly took her from me. Kazhara says that her wish was for me to mete out my own justice," Ava's eyes were dark and full of storms. Her face was stone.

"And so I will."

Ava looked back at Kazhara, noted the bloodlust in the set of her forehead, the thrill that quivered her lips. She pulled the knife along his arms, and then, with one clean stroke, severed the rope that bound Oromo's wrists. The old man gasped at the sudden release of pressure. Ava leaned in, quick as a gust, and pulled him close.

"My mother's friend would have you believe that I would kill you without hesitation, because that's what my mother would have done. But I am not my mother. I am freeing you as part of my own justice. You took the one thing in my life that was dear to me—it only fits that I do the same to you. Again. And again. Until everything that you hold dear is gone. That sounds fair, right?"

Oromo coughed unintelligibly, clutching his chest. Ava stood, palmed the knife, and walked over to Kazhara. The older woman inclined her head, biting her lip in an effort to hold back some extreme emotion. Was it disappointment? Rage? Ava kindled the ball of anger inside her, holding it ready for Kazhara

"Is this truly what you wish?" Kazhara asked. "That is definitely not what your mother would have done."

"You said yourself that she wished for me to mete my own justice. I am not my mother. But I am ready to learn more about how to be like her, ready to learn more about the side of her that she hid from me. *Dunmaso, tama fuyaa Le taa dondi ko le suuto.* Teach me how to walk with the night, like she used to."

Kazhara nodded, and with a light touch, ushered Ava out of the door of the shack. Ava reached up and pulled her headscarf away from her scalp, freeing her lush dreadlocks and sending the peal of tiny bells through the graying skies at each step.

# Zambeto

### JC Holbrook

I couldn't believe that I was back again.

I held my sword in front of my body as I carefully walked along the forested trail. The Earth was a rich black, there were eucalyptus trees that had been brought to Africa by Europeans mixed in with date palms, vines, and leafy bushes like elephant ears that swayed onto the path. The forest was alive with birds calling, insects humming, and an occasional fly near my face.

Sweat beaded my forehead and started a march downwards to my eyes only to be stopped by the drab green bandana tied around my forehead. My hair was pulled back from my face so that my vision would be clear.

I stepped at an angle with my body facing the left side of the trail for about twenty meters then I would angle the other way for another twenty meters. I wanted to present the smallest silhouette for any attacker coming towards me, yet I had to also be ready for an attack from the forest. I had to be careful to not let my outfit rustle. My muscles were tense, but I kept my breathing slow and even.

Here I was courtesy of a fast jet from Nairobi to Accra. In Nairobi, I was with the Bank of Africa working as a high level accountant. I had the books from the last three months at one of our branches waiting for me when I returned.

"Phone call for you, line one." The general office assistant had walked down the hall and stuck his head in my office to deliver the message. He was short and thick but all muscle.

I gave him a smile and a "thank you" as I reached for my phone. "Hello, this is the accounting director. How may I help you?"

"Zambeto! Can you come to Accra on the 2 pm flight? Someone will meet you at the airport."

My stomach tightened, so I took a deep breath. Concern, fear, and excitement warred within me. I focused on the clock, 11 am.

"Yes, I am on my way."

I wrote notes for my supervisors saying that I would be gone for a few days. I did not give an explanation. I never took vacations so I used my vacation time for when I got calls like this. My supervisors were happy as long as I made my deadlines, I hadn't missed one, yet.
I left the notes with my assistant.

"Any idea when you will be back?" He asked.

There was always a chance that I wouldn't come back, that something would go wrong and I was killed or worse.

I smiled at him and answered, "In a few days. A week at most."

A whir brought me back to the present. My attention snapped to the tree where the sound had come from. I stopped and kneeled slowly down until only my eyes and the top of my head were above the bushes facing the tree.

I waited.

I had been educated at the best universities on the continent. My first degree was in economics followed by a business degree. I was hired before I had completed my degree for more money than I imagined. Upon graduation, I had taken the job and quickly had been promoted and promoted again.

There was a whir and a swirling near the tree that halted, and then was still and quiet.

Zambeto.

I slowly stepped off the path into the brush away from where it was hiding. I shifted my eyes to the left of it until my peripheral vision could see it clearly. It was a big light brown bushy form that appeared to be dried grass stuck to something, similar to a sniper's camouflage. Except this was no camouflage. It was what I was hunting: a Zambeto.

During the day, the Zambeto rested and was slow. As the sun set, that would change.

I turned my head the other way to see if I could see more with my other eye.
Zambeto could alter light in order to disguise itself during the day. Therefore, it felt itself to be safe during the day. The peripheral vision of the human eye was sensitive enough to detect the Zambeto, if one knew where to look, or really knew where not to look.

As I assessed the size and danger of the Zambeto, I remembered tracking my first Zambeto with my older sister. I must have been about ten years old. She was ten years my senior. Unlike mine, her hair was a deep bright red and her skin was a milky brown. She stood out in our family from the day she was born. In our community, a child with hair like hers was expected to have special powers, supernatural powers. Hers was hunting Zambeto.

It was a foggy day and my sister was hunting a Zambeto and allowed me to help. I had begged her to take me with her. She had armed me with a small sword and the two of us had entered the forest.

"You lead." She told me.

My excitement rose. This was my chance to show her and my family that I was grown up, that I could do things that my older sisters did. I jogged ahead along the trail into the fog. All I felt was happiness and excitement.

The trail was damp and slippery at points under my bare feet. The trail split, I followed the right fork without thought. I heard a hiss behind me. I froze, the hiss was a signal from my sister to stop.

I turned my head slowly trying to see her as she came closer. She was moving smoothly and quietly as she stepped around me and disappeared into the fog further along the trail.

I remained where I was. I just stared down the trail where

my sister had disappeared. After several moments, I sat down on my hunches and waited. Later still, I let my sword rest across my knees. I was starting to feel damp and a little cool waiting in one place so long.

I started inspecting my toenails and stretching my toes as I waited for my sister when I heard a whir coming from the direction where my sister had disappeared. I flinched, but quickly held my sword up and slowly stood up.

The fog gave the forest a twilight feel, it was hard to tell what time it really was. The whirring got louder and my sword pulled me towards the sound. I had to follow or lose my sword. It pulled me towards the whirring. I needed to know where my sister was, I clicked my tongue as I followed my sword.

In front of me was a swirling mass coming towards me out of the fog. No head, no eyes, no arms. I froze as my sword changed direction and veered to the right of the Zambeto. It appeared to be made entirely of dried grass whipping in all directions as it spun. It was hypnotic. I was frozen and entranced as it moved closer and closer. My sword pulled again to the right.

Suddenly, my sister leaped out of the fog between me and the Zambeto. This Zambeto was about the same size as my first one, its coat was a lighter color.

I took my phone from my pocket and sent a text to the team that was waiting back at the trailhead. I kept glancing between the phone screen and the Zambeto. A light flashed on my screen showing that I had a new text response.

Good, they were ready.

I stood up and crossed the trail towards the Zambeto. My sword pulled me closer and closer. Light on my feet, I moved forward. I took a deep breath in preparation.

This Zambeto had gotten free last week. A few days before, a group of young men had isolated a young woman in order for one of them to force her to have sex. The women of the village had been furious and disappointed that the young men had so little respect for the young woman. The young man was not known for such bad behavior which had made the situation more complicated along with the fact that the young men insisted that she had agreed to have sex with the young man. The elders had gathered after sunset that night and the next three nights to debate what should be done and if it was rape or not. The fourth night the Zambeto had arrived. As was sometimes the case, no one had called it. It came on its own.

The Zambeto woke up and started to spin. I turned my attention away from the moving mass and onto my sword. Over the years I had learned to not let Zambeto hypnotize me. I had learned to follow my sword.  It wasn't the same sword that I used when I was ten, this sword was about two years old. It had been given to me by a sword maker as I walked through a street market in Kumasi. I should have been used to such things happening, but my life at the bank filled my head with numbers, computers, money transfers, and ledgers. A young boy put the sword in my hands and then grabbed my arm and led me to a stall in the metal working part of the market. I knew what it was about. It was about me and the Zambeto. A smiling man welcomed me into his work area and over the next hour we refitted the sword to my specifications. By the time I left it was sharp, the perfect length, and balanced for me. The hilt was decorated with a golden cowry shell at the end, what looked like a haystack etched in the leather on one side, and a woman on the other. He would not take any money for the sword.

The sword pulled to the left. So, it was begun.

The Zambeto rushed towards me as I swirled away to the left. The sword moved me in a tight circle. I went into a series of spins.

The Zambeto stopped its charge and spun in place. My movements evolved into the dance. It was my turn to entrance the Zambeto.

That day long ago, my sister slashed the Zambeto with her sword to stop it from getting closer to me. In my fear, I blacked out, that is my mind blacked out, my body followed the sword. Then as now, I entranced the Zambeto and moved it towards the trailhead. Now I could follow the sword in the intricate moves of the dance without blacking out.

I held the sword in my left hand as I swirled in that direction. I wore a grass skirt and a grass shirt that created the same effect as the whirling Zambeto as I wove through the dance. I switched the sword to my right hand as the sword changed directions. The sword took me into a leap along the trail, and another spin.

The Zambeto docilely followed my dancing form. My sister had been sent into the forest to destroy the Zambeto. Instead I led the Zambeto back to our community, as I was doing now. As I danced, the grass of my outfit rustled and flowed like a live thing. I was sweating and I tried to control my breathing. I had no idea how long I needed to dance. I felt warmth in my chest as I did what my soul demanded that I do. That feeling of past, present, and future, connected within me in the moment that I was dancing with the Zambeto.

From that point forward, my sister lost her power and status. She insisted that she had not changed, and I knew that she hadn't. It was just that my community had never seen anything like me. There were not even any myths, legends, or rumors that people like me could exist – one that danced with the Zambeto.

Since my first time when I was ten, our relationship with the Zambeto had changed. Zambeto had always been the force that kept social order in our community. Our elders would call the Zambeto to evoke fear in those wrongdoers among us. The Zambeto would come into our existence when called. The Zambeto never failed to travel directly to the home of the guilty person which allowed the villagers to ensure that justice was done.

I heard the drums in the distance, we were getting closer to the trailhead. A few minutes later the drums were loud, I gave a cry to signal our approach. The tempo of the drums changed some deepened their tone while others beat higher notes. Some part of me felt the Zambeto transfer its attention away from me to the drums. My dance took on another form, I now flowed in a series of dipping movements with the sword, as if the sword were gathering up invisible strands attached to the Zambeto.

Then the sword took the strands and connected them to each drum. I spun and arched into a slow movement that ended with a light tap of the sword on each drum. The drummers, like me were sweating.

There were five drummers: two tall drums, two djembes, and one small drum. Two of the drummers were my cousin-brothers. The one playing the small drum had hair as red as my sister. His drum spoke to the Zambeto, just as my body and sword did. An old master drummer played one of the long drums, he kept all the other drums to the rhythm except for my red-headed cousin – his spirit knew what to play. He smiled as he drummed. On his face was a bliss that matched how I felt when I danced with the Zambeto. I danced a few moments more as my sword moved less and less until the drummers had the Zambeto under their control. I stopped, put my hands on my hips, and panted as I watched the Zambeto and the drummers.

When I first led the Zambeto back to the village all those years ago, no one was ready. My poor body danced and danced with the Zambeto until one of the elders realized what to do. He had the drummers assemble and begin to play the traditional song to control the Zambeto. It had worked and my sword had stopped moving and I had collapsed. I later woke in my own bed to find my mother anxiously by my side.

Over time, my red-headed cousin had been moved to join the drummers but had constructed a different drum – the one that he was using now. In my cousin's hands it had the power to control the Zambeto with a gentleness and delicacy that had been missing before. When my cousin was not drumming, he was a surgeon in Bamako. Like me, he flew in when we were needed to recover a Zambeto.

I watched as the drummers surrounded the Zambeto. The old master drummer was able to control the Zambeto when called but his hold was lost if the Zambeto reached the forest. Something about the trees or the undergrowth diffused the power of the drums.

One of my childhood playmates approached me. He

carried a cloth to dry my face and a cape.

"Thank You." I said as I took his offerings. I remembered that he had done the same the last several times I had danced. I turned my attention more fully to his face. There was something that he was trying to hide from me in his eyes. Attraction? I smiled and he gave me a slow smile back. I had to look away first, there was too much heat in his eyes.

I turned my attention back to the Zambeto.
My cousin changed tempo again and sang out a 'thank you'. Then continued with the more formal, "You are justice. Our actions will be swift and your justice will be done. Zambeto!"

As I watched the Zambeto winked out of existence. He said 'thank you' again and nodded to the other drummers that it was time to stop, which they did with stylish flare.

There was sudden applause as the community members, who had kept well back from the action, showed their appreciation for us ridding their forest of the Zambeto.

I bowed to each of the drummers to honor their help in sending the Zambeto home. The drummers returned the honor by each doing a quick drum sequence to me.

After we had showered and changed into our normal clothes, the community had a feast in our honor. I sat between my cousins and we caught up on our families. I was the only one still single, I looked for my childhood friend. His eyes were on me. I smiled an invitation, and he gave me that smoldering smile again. I would make sure that I made time to spend time with him before I left. But for now I talked with my red-headed cousin about the ritual that we had just completed.

I learned from my cousins that this Zambeto had arrived on its own in response to the communities' turmoil over the rape the week before. The community drummers had been able to control the Zambeto enough to keep it from hurting the guilty parties, but their guilt had been verified by the actions of the Zambeto. However, the community drummers were not able to prevent the Zambeto from going into the forest. As long as the Zambeto was in the forest, no one would enter. They had contacted my family for help. The people in my community and my family in particular were now famous for our ability to recapture Zambeto and send them home without bloodshed. My community acknowledged that me and my sword and my red-headed cousin with his drum had sealed that reputation during our generation.

I thought of my sister, who was now an artist in Lagos. I could only imagine that she was relieved to never have to find and kill another Zambeto. I hoped that she did not resent her loss of status. I wondered if her settling in Lagos was an attempt to put her past behind her.

I sometimes thought about where the Zambeto came from and what they thought about while in our world. It seemed that more and more were getting free of the drummers and my cousin and I were being called in more and more to send them back. Did they enjoy our dance and my cousin's talking drum? Why were they now coming when they were not called? What did they gain for helping solve the problems within our communities?
My sword was in my luggage checked for my flight back to Nairobi. I was going back to my world of numbers until I was called.

# THE PRICE OF KUSH

## *By Sylvia Kelso*

The Candace of Kush was in a vile temper that morning. In a quarter sun-span she had quarreled with her high priest, affronted her general, upset the queen mother, and the grooms had lamed her near-side chariot horse. Now her guard captain turned up pregnant at archery drill.

The Candace's horses were the best of Kush's twelve precious imported chariot teams. She had ordered the grooms beaten till they were lame as the horse. She fervently desired to beat Kasaqa even harder, but still more she wanted to scream, *You were my second archer! We swore to ride to battle together, your arm, your unerring eye to hide the defects in mine! I relied on you!*

She did say, "Who is he?" And kept the words almost under her breath.

Kasaqa stared at the ground. Dust, sand, beaten shapeless by a thousand thousand sandal prints. Upon the dust, the feet of the Candace's guard: seventy female feet at rigid attention, the grounded tips of eleven priceless composite bows.

The Candace tapped her own foot. Kasaqa muttered, "His father commanded Buhen Fort."

The Candace felt herself swell like an outraged toad. *Buhen Fort?* She wanted to yell. *Captive now to Egypt, once ruled by renegade Egyptians for us? An* Egyptian *has done this?*

Beyond the exercise field new sun caught the massive spine

of the outer city wall. Above it, priests' white kilts and capes fluttered like moths from the summit of Apedemak's temple, broad and high as a brick island above the inner city roofs. From the outer city, the harbor raised a chain of half-rigged masts. Donkeys, field-workers, artisans trooped past the archery butts, and over all spread the hubbub of smoke and shouting, hot bread and beer-scents that announced the city's day.

My city, the Candace told herself. My home. My kingdom, for the nonce. The incantation just served to contain her rage.

"You chose a *Fish-eater* to sire your child?"

"Sobekemheb is not a -! His great-grandsire served Kush, his grandsire served Kush -!"

"And now *he* thinks to serve Kush, much closer than Buhen Fort. Bringing the toll-reports from Sai, was it?" Fury blazed time and occasion vividly out of memory. First month of Peret, Sowing-time. Two, three months past. "*Kind* of him, to leave this message as well."

Kasaqa's eyes flashed and her chin jerked up. The dark-red archer's cap sat precisely on her tightly plaited hair, the short jerkin fitted close above the guards' version of an army archer's kilt. Her arm and thumb-guards were still pristine ivory against the dark luster of her skin. The proud arch of her nose and brows spoke the best blood of Kush. *Oh, my friend, my sister,* the Candace wanted to wail, *how could you gift a Fish-eater with all this?*

Kasaqa remembered herself just in time. The chin sank. The back stiffened to correct army posture. The Candace refrained from tearing at her own tightly plaited hair.

*You are dismissed your post.* The words hovered in the already warming air. *Return to the house of your father and mother and eat your shame.*

Beyond the buttes a long herd of cattle passed, hooves shuffling, brown and spotted hides blurring, tall horns steady above the dust. The cry of an obscured herdsman lingered like a bird's.

The Candace tightened fingers on her own bow and summoned the words. *You are no use as an archer now, to run on foot, or wheel in a chariot about a battle-front. You are no use to the guard. You have made this first women's troop a hissing and a mockery. The queen-mother will give me sympathy. The army will laugh us back to the querns.*

She opened her mouth and a household runner almost fell panting through the gate. "Kentakes! Kentakes! A messenger. From the Hyksos . . . requests instant audience!"

\*\*\*

"Kentakes Pelekh. Favored of Apedemak. Warded by Hathor. Daughter of Kings, Mistress of Kush." The messenger recited her titles in a rattle, head barely lifted from his prone position on the audience-hall floor. "King Apopis, Lord of Avaris, Master of the Two Lands, Favored of Amun, sends a message. By my unworthy hand."

*I miss my father*, the Candace thought. *I miss his presence in this throne, his size, his warmth, his smell, his noise. A year and a season since he died, and still it is not my place. I am Regent now; I will be ruler in three years. As the King's eldest daughter I am Candace in my own right. I will lead the army, should Kush go to war. And still, this is not my place.*

An image flashed by of her last target practice, the thicket of arrows outside the straw man's heart-mark, Kasaqa's mere two gone astray. She shook it fiercely off – *Not now!* - and lifted the ruler's mace.

"Kush hears the Lord of the Two Lands," she said.

*Though a Hyksos has less right to style himself Pharaoh,* she added silently, than I have to this crown. Minutely, she adjusted the tall white head-dress, symbol of Upper Egypt, half the Pharaoh's own, that her father had claimed the year

Kush regained the border forts. *And Apopis has even less right, with the supposed true Pharaoh roosting in Thebes, halfway from Avaris to here.*

The messenger had risen. Though he wore the plain kilt and sandals of a runner, his right hand bore a seal-ring, and his bearing never came from a peasant's hut. Nor did he relinquish the message roll to the court official bearing down on him. Instead, he broke the wax and read the contents, in reasonable Kushite, aloud.

The Candace had missed the repeated salutations and titles. His nuance now signaled the message itself.

". . . wherefore the Lord of the Two Lands sends to his brother and ally's realm, saying, This firebrand in Thebes has already singed us both. He is driven home now, to nurse his wounds from pillaging my fields. Once before we might have made this alliance, but my letter went astray. Now the Lord says again: summon your archers, your spearmen and your chariots. Raise the men of Wawat and Irjet, send emissaries afield to Punt. March downriver in Shemu season, and before harvest ends, you will see my tents under the wall of Thebes. Join with me there. Before the waters rise in Akhet we will drive this upstart into the Nile!"

***

"Naturally, you will not go."

The queen mother had caught up at last, on the palace terrace, under a rising moon. The Candace stared woodenly over the motley blur of inner city, toward the first bend of the river, a glittering scythe-blade pointed north.

"I shall consider," she said.

"Pelekh . . . –! Kentakes." *If your mother had not been Great Wife,* that smothered fury wanted to add. *If your father had not died untimely. If my son had been more than eight years old. If it was not Kush custom to accept the eldest child of the King and his Great Wife, male or female, as heir. Then I would be Regent, ruling for Shabako, and you would have the treatment your impudent, reckless, headstrong eighteen years deserve.*

"I shall consider," the Candace said again.

The moon domed the circular straw roof of the audience hall, vague against the bulk of temple whose shadow blotted lamps and datepalms alike. At length, the queen mother managed to speak temperately once more.

"The third month of Peret has begun. The crops are heavy in the ear. The men cannot be spared. To raise the army will take another month. How long to march to Semna? Let alone past the Cataracts, let alone to Thebes? The army of Kush, marooned by the inundation . . ."

*We will go by the western oases,* the Candace retorted silently, *if we go so late. We can raise a Kushite force in half a moon. We can summon Wawat and Irjet as we cross their lands. There is little to expect, and no cause to wait for Punt. Before Shemu is half over, we could be past the Ivory Isle. Into Egypt itself.*

*Where the harvests will feed us, and reaped fields will favor chariots, and the foolish young Pharaoh will find himself between the millstones. Kush to the south, the Hyksos to the north . . .*

"I must ask the messenger," she said aloud, forgetting herself, "about Kamose's wounds."

"Wounds!"

"My thanks for your counsel, Mistress of the Court." She gave the queen mother's full title as a sop. It was wonderfully easy, she discovered, to remain unbaited by the sort of badgering that a month ago would have had her shouting like a market-wife. Because now I see quite clearly. I, not you, have the power. Say what you choose. At the point, I shall do as I like.

She did manage a perfunctory joining of hands at her breast, before she paced almost slowly away.

A dozen yards along the terrace second thoughts froze

her to a stop. *Not as* you *like*, a voice whispered in the back of her head. *Not even as your city and your people like. You will do what is best for them.*

The Candace swung about and leant against the terrace rail. *But, O Hapi, Nile Father, O Apedemak, Kush's Father,* she thought dizzily. *What* will *be best for Kush*?

A sentry patrolled the outer wall, a firefly glitter of bronze arrowheads. The Candace bit her fingertips.

Am I thinking only what is best for me?

Is she right? Am I foolish and headstrong? Will I rush off like an unproven boy, just to take a chariot into battle? To lead Kush while I can?

Or stay home, because I am afraid?

She bit her fingers harder, seeing that target again. I am Candace. I have a chariot. Chariots are meant as skirmishers. If we go, I have no pretext not to lead the battle. But can I do it? Or will I bemock myself?

Worse, will I get myself killed, and leave Kush with no rule at all?

She pulled the shawl tighter. Third month of Peret, the sun had begun its return march, but the night was bleak. Bleaker still the prospect in her imagination: I fall on the field, the queen mother becomes Regent – but what of the army, left leaderless? Routed, pursued, perhaps destroyed, outside its own land?

*O, Father Apedemak, Mother Hathor. Is there no better way than that?*

On the terrace a shadow moved. She spun half about, heart leaping into her throat. Then she identified the profile, and smothered the gasp of relief.

When her heartbeat had nearly steadied, she said, as coolly as she could, "What are you doing here?"

The shadow answered, "You should not be alone."

"This is the palace."

The shadow let silence answer, *And we both know what safety that is worth.*

The Candace moistened her lips. Slowly, dully,

pronounced the words the morning had delayed.

"You will have to leave the guard."

"Not yet."

The Candace stared.

"I saw the harbor midwife." She sounded calm as if reporting a full barrack count. "She says I am, perhaps, not even three months gone. She says, I may drill, and march – and fight – for another three, even four months."

The Candace gasped aloud. "The child -!"

"The child will be at no less risk," Kasaqa answered evenly, "if I sit spinning at home."

The Candace caught her breath. More even than that sure eye at her elbow, she realized, she had dreaded losing the counsel of this strategist's brain.

Kasaqa said, "What do you mean to do?"

Unnecessary question, yet for courtesy, most necessary of all. The Candace felt her shoulders relax. *Ah, my sister*, she thought, *above all, I would have mourned for this. Matching a sister's wits and loyalty, teasing choices out to what I can, what I must do.*

To the distant city she said, "If we go. If we gather the army. If we call Wawat and Irjet to march with us. Whatever the season, before we ever enter Egypt, we must re-take Buhen."

Kasaqa let silence image the massive walls and towers of the Pharaoh's major southern fortress, king-post for the advance forts of Semna and Kumma. The only one that Kamose, that fiery young Pharaoh, had been able to reclaim.

In a moment, Kasaqa said, "If we can. If we pass the Cataracts. Then how do we aim?"

The Candace grunted as she saw the point. "You mean, are we the Hyksos' allies, or his gaming pieces? Hazarded from the south, so from the north he can sweep the board?"

"He might only wish to repay the Pharaoh's raids."

"To be sure." As always, her own wits roused to match Kasaqa's. "But what is it *we* want up there?"

"Plunder? Booty from rich Egyptian tombs, as the

kings have taken before? The 'Fish-eaters" grain?"

"We have grain enough. Booty?" She swung the other way. Across river the moon penciled in ripening durra and sorghum fields, the ranges of distant herds. The Candace stared past them, imaging the great ancestral tombs in the necropolis, hundreds of cattle, whole households, dispatched with their king into death.

"Rich grave goods? Is that our reward?"

Kasaqa came slowly to the railing beside her. Softly she said, "What if we do not go?"

The Candace followed her gaze north. North to the silver scythe of Nile reach, beyond which lay the Island of Sai and its market, where all Africa brought ebony and ivory and exotic beasts, where Punt sold the precious incense, where Kush and Wawat offered Egypt's even more indispensable copper and gold. And then the Second Cataract, fenced by Egyptian fortresses, Semna, Kumma, Iken, Buhen. The old Pharaoh who built them forbade us, all the folk of Ta-Seti, to pass the Cataract, or to trade save at Iken alone.

But the old Pharaoh's house has fallen, and the Hyksos have penned his successors in Thebes. They pay *us* trade-tolls. And my father pushed our border clear to the first Cataract, to the Isle of Ivory.

Whence Kamose has now repulsed us. Right back past the second Cataract, recapturing Buhen fort.

Her heart stuttered. The words felt cold on her lips.

"If Kamose need only fight the Hyksos, he has a far better chance to win."

Kasaqa did not bother to nod.

"He has come south once. If we sit still, will he think us cowards? Cowed by his last sortie? If he defeats the Hyksos . . ."

"Whether or not he bests the Hyskos," Kasaqa said, "one of them will remain."

The Candace stared. "You think he can win?"

Kasaqa made a tiny, almost impatient gesture. "If he wins, if Apopis wins, for us, the result is the same. A single

Egypt, with only Wawat between us and them."

The Candace gulped. Then she pulled the shawl tightly round her and pressed her knuckles to her cheeks.

"Then – do we stay home? Fight for the *Pharaoh*? Try to – to conquer them both?"

"I think we go north," Kasaqa said, "for ourselves. If we can retake Buhen. If we go into Egypt. Then we do not try to capture Thebes. If the Hyksos has ever intended that. Instead, we give Kamose a warning to remember. *Regard our strength. See what we can do to your land?* And then we withdraw to the Second Cataract. Make plain, that there we set our border. It may be, that will buy us time."

The Candace faltered, "Time?"

Kasaqa hesitated before she spoke.

"Sobekemheb and I – have talked. His brother is a scribe. He reads the Egyptian letters. In Buhen, he deciphered the inscriptions there. Sobekemheb told me what he told to them. That before our city, before our kingdom, the Egyptians have been taking trade from Kush. They will trade in peace, or like the fort-building Pharaoh, they will trade in war. But we have what they lack, and they need it. One way or the other, whatever our wishes, they will trade."

She broke off. The moonlight showed her hands clenched on the railing. Before she said, almost inaudibly, "Or they will conquer us."

The Candace gasped. "But the city! The kingdom! Our folk -!"

"We are strong now," Kasaqa answered bleakly, "but Egypt has been stronger. If we let Pharaoh meet the Hyksos alone, he may lose. If he loses, the Hyksos have Egypt. They will need the trade too. What will hold them from us?

But if Kamose wins, *he* will reconquer Egypt. We have seen the strength of Egypt. How long will Kush live in peace?"

The Candace had made a noise before she thought. Instantly Kasaqa's arm was round her. They clutched as they had in long night watches, in the young women's rooms, in the nursery where they had met.

"Oh, my sister," the Candace whispered at last, trying to laugh as a way to compose herself. "You always have such terrible dreams . . ."

Kasaqa's cheek was against hers. Kasaqa answered, yet more shakily. "I know."

Presently they disentangled. The Candace resettled her shawl, and looked north once more.

"So," she said, trying to sound like a Candace and not a scared young girl. "We must go to keep the balance. Not to destroy either side. To leave them unable to destroy us. Tomorrow, we tell the messenger. We raise the army. We march." She felt Kasaqa nod beside her, and set her teeth. "For Buhen, first."

Kasaqa said, "I also will train. I will march. We will keep our vows." To ride into battle together. "And when we come to Buhen . . ."

The altered tone made the Candace turn and stare. "When we come to Buhen?" What will be there, she did not have to add, but walls bigger than ours and a place impregnable to archers, which will cost more than enough Kushite blood to take?

The moonlight clearly showed Kasaqa's smile. A demure, almost smug expression, before she answered as demurely, "There is more use than one to a Fish-eater. Especially one such as Sobekemheb."

***

"Assuredly, Kentakes. I know Buhen's secret ways, yes. Our family built most of them."

The Candace decided she liked the 'our' family, rather than, 'mine.' And Fish-eater or not, he had composure, a steady, but not a liar's unwavering eye. Stockier than most Kushites, if his paler bronze skin trumpeted Egypt, he lacked the arrogance she had learnt to call Egyptian, from the Pharaoh's letters to the single prisoner she had seen as a child.

Still down on one knee, he awaited her reply. Calm as if the audience hall were not crammed with Kushite lords-at-council, as if her high priest and general were not skewering him with identical glares from her either side. As if Kasaqa were not in ambush behind the throne-dais hanging, heart doubtless in her mouth.

"Tell me of these ways," she said.

He glanced up, unamused but poised enough to return silently, *All of them*? She inclined her head, *No, not seriously*. "One," she said aloud. "Perhaps two. That might pass both the walls."

"The Kentakes knows how Buhen is." He sounded approving rather than surprised. "The main gatehouse faces west. With the drawbridge, over the ditch. Deeper than two men's height. Walled on either side. On the fort side, there are bastions, with loopholes for archers all around. Behind that, the main wall. Ramparts, buttresses, battlements, three men's height and more.

" Inside is the town. Bath-houses, bakers and brewers and bow-makers. Quarters for troops from Irjet and Wawat, and the Egyptian spearmen. Then the inner wall. Another drawbridge, another ditch. And the catapult."

Her general Alara winced. The Candace nodded. *Go on*.

"The inner fort has the Horus temple. The officials' houses. The Governor's residence. The freight stores. The Egyptian archers' quarter. And the Medjay."

Alara's face contracted in pure anguish. The Medjay were Wawat nomads, long enlisted in Egyptian armies, the best archers along the Nile. The Candace said, "And?"

"Two water gates open on the quays. The side walls run to the water, and the sentries kept good watch."

Sobekemheb held her eye, suggesting as little need to check the general's expression as the Candace felt. "Ah," she said.

*He read unspoken words,* she decided, *remarkably well.* He bent his head a little further. *Yes,* that gesture agreed. *No way for an enemy on land to attack on the water side. From the land side, a very expensive fort to take, if not impossible. Nevertheless . . .*

"Nevertheless?" she prompted, and that bowed head did not conceal a truly Egyptian smile.

"There is a water tunnel," he said.

\*\*\*

"Yes, Kentakes," he went on, when the sensation died down. "Just above the northern quay. Opening among the ships, under every sailor's eye." And secret outside Buhen, he did not have to say. "High enough for a man to walk. It descends just before the first warehouse, inside the fort."

General Alara's goaded bellow demanded, *Then what use is that?*

"When my grandfather rebuilt the temple for the Horus of Buhen, he dug a passage into the tunnel."

He and the Candace both ignored the high priest Aata's scandalized gasp. She said, "Concealed?"

There was an accolade in his flash of smile. "With care, a moderate swimmer could reach the tunnel mouth. There is a grating, but," he elevated one shoulder airily, "the chain has a key. And the temple passage is marked."

Very softly, the Candace said, "Ah."

Then she moved the mace that served for royal scepter and lifted her voice. "Let the lords take refreshment. The general, and the Server of Apedemak, be pleased to remain."

"Tell me, Sobekemheb," she said, when high priest and general finally shouted themselves quiet, "what chance, do you judge, of disaffection rising in Buhen?"

Sobekemheb was seated by then, on a lordling's stool.

He considered before he replied.

"With the Medjay, Kentakes, there is no chance." *You know*, that nod added, *that where the Medjay enlist, they remain, until they are discharged. Or die.*

"But the garrison now is little more than four hundred men. If we approach swiftly . . ." Alara's spate about signal stations brought an amendment. "Even if they have warning of our march, the Pharaoh can hardly spare more than – perhaps another two hundred men. Most likely, he will send Wawat troops, if he sends at all. And in the outer town . . ."

"What point seducing Fish-eaters, let alone men of Wawat, in the outer town!"

Alara's bellow produced an almost amused pause. Before Sobekemheb said, "If men went downriver to Buhen, before Peret ends. If they traded in the outer town. If they spoke to soldiers of Wawat there. If they told of a great outgoing toward Egypt. Of booty. Of grain and gold for Wawat. It might be, then, that a swimmer who came by the water tunnel could open the inner gate."

Alara erupted again. Such a ploy was too soon, too unlikely, the secret would never keep, no-one could manage such seduction, the entire scheme was beer-fumes and cow-pats, it would never work -!

The Candace said, "The key to the tunnel grate?"

Sobekemheb nodded. *That, we have.*

"One swimmer alone could not manage that gate."

"More," Sobekemheb answered softly, "could be arranged."

He has men of his own household, the Candace thought, who would do this for him. Who have been in these ways, who know Buhen as well as he does himself.

"And also, some who might appear traders – herders – who might know men, among the Wawat troops?"

Sobekemheb's mouth corners curled. Approval, however deferential, but knowing just where such presumption should stop.

The Candace ignored Alara's fresh uproar along with

the frozen hush that signaled the high priest's intent, when he had her alone, to singe her ear-wax out. Instead she watched Sobekhemheb. "And what avails such a plan for you?"

The smile vanished. He looked her straight in the eye.

"Buhen is my homeplace," he said. "My father's command. He sits now in the outer city, old, idle, broken by Kamose's spears. Whether he, or I, or none of our blood return there, whether we command or not, I will well that Kush re-take Buhen."

Alara blinked. Aata stared. Sobekemheb went on, still holding the Candace's eye.

"And the Kentakes knows – I would have a worthy deed as gift, next Akhet. When I have hopes to take a bride."

*  *  *

"There it is."

The tumult and shouting of Alara's, Aata's, the queen mother's, the council lords' disapproval, the trumpetings about rash youth and crazy hazards and suppressed curses at the even crazier whims of women were all two hundred miles and almost four months behind. It had taken the rest of Peret to alert Wawat and Irjet. To raise Kush's own levies. To assemble the multitude of donkeys and servants and armorers, the endless baskets of grain and arrows, the fletchers and shield-makers and other army craftsmen that must support the troops. It was almost another month since they had first mounted into the Candace's chariot, leading out the army, the royal archers' corps, and the Candace's guard.

Red plumes had tossed from the horses' heads as the twelve chariots of Kush filed from the inner city gate. There had been ululations along the outer streets, women wailing in praise and fierce encouragement, as well as forsaken grief. And then they had threaded the ripening fields of sorghum that those women would have to harvest, and the entire enormous serpent of men and beasts had begun its crawl into the north.

Now the Candace's chariot stood atop the last stony crest in the Belly of Rock, the belt of barren hills around the Second Cataract, and she and Kasaqa stared north under the heat-pale Shemu sky to the small, serrated shape perched like some grim child's toy on the west bank of the Nile.

Behind them, the army waited. Alara's fumings were confined at the hill's foot. By the right chariot wheel Sobekemheb stared with them, the eyes in his now bronzed face narrow as a hawk's.

They had been observed, they all knew, on the march. Like the southern forts, the Egyptian signal stations along the river were all in Kushite hands, but distant figures had wheeled and scurried like carrion beasts around their column, and now the hills toward Buhen bore a sequence of white curling smokes.

A new cloud shot up, closer to Buhen. Soundlessly, Sobekemheb sighed. The Candace looked down and said, "Do you hold by your plan?"

*Rather late*, his quick glance answered, *to ask that, is it not*? But his mouth replied politely, "The 'herders' returned from Buhen two months since. We have sent earnests of grain. We have pledges from within the fort."

"And swimmers?" the Candace wondered, struggling to sound as cool.

"And swimmers," he answered gravely. The faint incorrigible sparkle of amusement added, *Only do your part, Kentakes, as we have planned: make a great noise about the western gate. Shoot fire arrows into the drawbridge timbers. Frighten, focus, hold the fort busy through afternoon and evening and into the dark. And the rest will come to pass.*

The Candace glanced at Kasaqa, who was watching Sobekemheb. Not with infatuated adoration, but with a cool amusement that almost matched his own. She believes him, the Candace thought. And then: No. She has measured and gauged and decided. And she does not merely believe, she fully expects this will work.

The Candace drew in a great lungful of hot air and dust. Then she turned to the horn-bearers behind her chariot, and called, "Sound the Advance!"

\*\*\*

The Candace stood in the dark, listening to her troops attack Buhen.

The for-once concerted, "No!" of Alara, Kasaqa and Sobekemheb had banned her from the assault on the outer gate. Instead she stood with the signalers, on the nearest hill. Even from its crest, there was less to see than hear. Faint gleams inside the black fortress mass. Occasional flying sparks as fire arrows arced toward the vulnerable timbers of drawbridge and gate. But the night carried clearly the jibes and taunts of, "Troglodyte!" from atop the walls, the answering shouts of, "Fish-eater!" beneath, and the spike of cries and screams and orders from both sides as another sortie passed.

*Whether we prevail or not, we are losing men,* the Candace thought, *with every wave.*
Her stomach constricted yet again as she pictured swimmers spotted outside the tunnel. Unable to open the grate. Surprised in the temple, caught in the roused and wary inner fortress far short of the gate. *Madness, utter madness,* she told herself. *Alara was right. You should never have tried, never have dreamed of trying this. So many risks, so much reliance on the reed of suborned men's loyalty, such a complicated quagmire of a plan . . .*

*And the alternative?* Her own mind answered in Kasaqa's voice. *Another such frontal assault, with no support?*

*Or keeping Kush at home?*
The Candace shifted a hand on the chariot wheel and tried to stand as became her rank. A fresh outbreak of howls

and yells surged up from below.

Then, abrupt as a bursting gourd came uproar, full-throated cries of shock and horrified disbelief that surged across the outer fort, screams and shrieks mixed now with orders whose panic, whose futility, was plain as the terror they sought to countermand.

From behind the walls of Buhen light blazed up, red and leaping fiercely, a great deal of some inflammable substance kindled all at once. And from the enemy under the walls came a wolfish answering bawl.

\*\*\*

"Lord, it was like the ramp for some great statue – every load, every rope, every haul in place!" The three swimmers' leader used a wild mix of Kushite and Egyptian, worsened as he nearly frisked about Sobekemheb like an over-excited dog. "We found the grate, we used the key. The loose block was there, with the unsmoothed mason's mark. We crept from the temple, we ran swiftly to the gate. Not a spearman, never a Medjay did we see. Every F – every fool in the place was atop the outer walls! We opened the gate as it were our own house-yard, and when the Wawatis heard our signal, they threw down their officers!"

The Candace suppressed the urge to pinch herself. She looked down from her chariot into the inner fortress of Buhen, half lit by sporadic torches, half by a raging warehouse fire. Dim columns marked a street, the porch of the governor's house. Distant shadows sketched the water wall. Closer, the swimmer was still cavorting like a dancing girl at a feast.

"And the Kentakes too was wise, most wise! We did not block the water gates. We did not blockade the governor's house. We lit the warehouse nearest the inner wall and made a great noise in the gateway, and they ran – The F- the scribes, the officers, the priests, the governor, they ran like granary rats! Straight to the watergates and to ship!"

A cunning thought, Sobekemheb had said, when she proposed it in council. First in removing the head of resistance, second in clearing out a cumbrous load of civil prisoners, third, in sending advance notice, to both Apopis and Kamose, that Kush is abroad. And a good saving of our troops and friends, she added, that the Medjay were spread among the outer defenders, so they could not cost us dear for a last defense. Whatever it cost to lay them where they fell.

Kasaqa was a quiet core of satisfaction beside her. From Alara, at her other chariot wheel, came, rarest of the rare, a short, contented grunt.

"Kentakes," he said, "I believe you hold Buhen."

The swimmer's leader swung suddenly round and pressed both palms to his brows in obeisance. "Kentakes," he said, "you hold the favor of the gods."

The Candace stared. He looked up at her, the euphoria gone, torchlight glistening on the planes of his black-dark, thoroughly Kushite face.

"Lord," he said to Sobekemheb, "when we found the passage. We dared not light a torch. We were feeling our way up."

He stopped. Sobekemheb made a prompting noise, and the man looked up at the Candace.

"Kentakes, there came a light."

Now all of them stared.

"In the passage, before us. Where none had kindled it. A white, a golden light. As it might be, a midday Akhet sky."

He stopped, and began again. "And with it, shadow. On the passage wall. As it were a wing, that moved. That beckoned. Come. This way."

He swallowed. "We were much afeared. But the light led us. And by that light . . ."

He stopped again. When he went on, it was almost a whisper, low with awe.

"Kentakes, we saw His feet."

It was Alara who managed a brief questioning noise. As the swimmer looked up the Candace saw his eye-whites flash.

He said, "They were big as a man's. But they were the feet of a hawk."

The Candace heard several people gasp. She saw Sobekemheb's face. It was Kasaqa who spoke their thoughts.

"Nekheny," she whispered. "The Horus himself."

The Candace's head spun. Before she had worked out a quarter of the implications, Sobekemheb spoke.

"*Our* Horus," he said. "The Horus of Buhen. He led you through the tunnel, into the passage, into His own temple." It went up on a note of exultation. "He wants us – Kush, the Kentakes, our family – back."

*** 

The Candace had grown up in the palace, cheek-by-jowl with Apedemak's House. Aata had been her father's high priest before he was hers. As became the Candace, she had sat, silent but attentive, through more than one secret consultation when high priest and king discussed how best the gods might deliver omens to steer the people as the king chose.

Next evening they were in the Governor's inner chamber, the fort ordered, wounded salved, prisoners stowed, an arduous day spent distributing the chief plunder, the warehouses of freight. Bestowed, for the most part, among the Wawat troops.

"A reward, yes," Sobekemheb had agreed with her, while Alara spluttered and his officers' faces spoke a more than shamefaced jealousy. "And some will squander it. But for some it will be their own gain, yet also Wawat's. And also for us. For the more that turn trader, the less will fight for Egypt, ever again."

And after a long, teetering pause, Alara had grumbled assent.

Now, under the scented torches, upon the elegant dining couches, the commandeered dancers and fearful household servers dismissed, Sobekemheb and Kasaqa gone, only Alara still drowsing at her elbow, the Candace said, "Do you think he saw a god?"

Alara wheezed. Then he sat upright with a snort. But he had lived between king and priesthood too.

"No matter," a short hand-wave, "what he saw. What matters is what he *said*."

The Candace considered that. Then she said, "Was it planned?"

"With the – with your adviser?" Alara hesitated. Finally, reluctantly, shook his head.

"It would seem – thrifty. He certainly took the omen pat. But . . . it is hard to mimic true surprise. True – joy."

The Candace considered that, too. Alara gave another grunt. "True or no, all Buhen believes it. Our men and theirs. The army is – eager. And she is clever, your girl." A momentary reluctant admiration. "'Nekheny', she said. The Hawk. Wawat has called Him so, time out of mind. But in Egypt, His own place is Nekhen."

The Candace dropped the napkin she was playing with. Nekhen, the great city of Upper Egypt, almost as rich and powerful as Thebes itself? "But – that is the realm of," she could not help her voice's drop, "Nekhbet, is it not?"

Alara tilted his hand to and fro. "*Now* it is so. Especially since She smiled on that Fish-eating governor to repulse your father's force." This time he growled like an ancient, irate dog. "Kush, Punt, Wawat, Irket, even the Medjay we had summoned. Had the gods smiled, he – you – would be sitting in Thebes now."

The Candace had heard these heart-burnings over and over. "But Horus?" she said.

"Ah." Despite himself, Alara almost might have smiled. "Now the army sees the Hawk as our patron. And

Nekhbet," he made the obligatory honoring hand-motion," is the goddess of vultures, yes. The Lady of Nekheb, the tomb city. But Horus is the god of Nekhen. And He is the god of war."

Thinking it through, the Candace felt her heart lift. *So whether He led our sortie or not, the army believes He did. And between Sobekemheb and Kasaqa, they also believe that we hold Buhen by His will. And more. They believe that He will smile on our further going. Because Nekhen is His own place, and He is the war-god. And we are going to make war.*

She retrieved her napkin and made the homage sign herself. "Horus has honored us," she said.

***

Wawat evidently agreed. Every morning past Buhen another cluster of bowmen, spear-carriers, or mere villagers with scythes and maces would have assembled at the camp fringe. Waiting for the Kentakes, her general, or her traveling priest's notice, silently ready to offer their allegiance, their weapons, their lives, in Kush's cause.

"Wawat bore the brunt of the old Pharaohs' attacks," Alara growled. "Their wells filled, cattle stolen, crops burnt. Women and children enslaved, men and boys sent to the Pharaoh's army. Not once or twice, but time and time again. They have long memories, in Wawat."

Compared to Kush, Wawat was still desolate. They had need of their stores, and the master of supplies was blaspheming at each influx of new Wawati mouths, well before the somber river plain narrowed into higher, rougher hills, and Alara pointed out a small pair of islands and said, "Pilak. The Boundary Isles. Beyond is the First Cataract."

The Candace stared up at the long, barren, lion and dust-golden hillsides either side the Nile's meager necklace of date palms and sycamores and dull harvest brown. The river was shrunken. The dust increased daily. She drew back inside her tent mouth and said "You wish to do *what*?"

Squatted on his heels over the dust map, Sobekemheb answered mildly, "The river is so low, the mules and donkeys will swim it easily. There are boats here, some of them Kushite, waiting to return upriver. The horses can be ferried over. It will not take more than a day to ship the archers. The spearmen can help load the baggage. Another two days, and they will all be across."

"Five days halt, much labor, more than a little danger? For what?"

Kasaqa shifted on her stool. The pregnancy was beginning to show, less in her body than in her sweaty, tired face. She let Sobekemheb answer, composedly as ever.

"I did not ask this at Buhen, with the news running fresh downstream. If we had taken to the water then, Kamose would have attacked, beyond doubt. But now he knows we come by land, and on the western bank."

"And?"

"So he will muster troops there, if anywhere."

The Candace frowned. The frown deepened as she saw the first inklings of comprehension already in Alara's face. "And so?"

"And so," Sobekemheb said softly, "Kamose's men will be on this side. *We* will be on the east bank, where the stone road runs from the quarries, clear round the Cataract and down to Swenet. Then we can skirt the forts on Yebu, Ivory Island, and keep going."

"And?" The Candace snapped, when his tone added, *There is more.*

Sobekemheb's lashes dropped. "Nekheb, the city of Nekhbet, is here, on the west bank. Nekhen is on the east."

The city of Horus, already declared our patron. The sister city of Nekheb. Which is the vulture goddess's actual home.

A long-distance strategy, the Candace thought, staring

at his lowered eyelids with reluctant admiration, and a plan with many faces. Cunning, yes, indeed.

*\*\*\**

After that things went as the swimmer said, like the ascent of some great temple statue up its ramp, so smoothly that the Candace's neck began to crawl. An uncontested river crossing. A steady march that Sobekemheb directed into the black and twisted hills, straight to the quarries road, whose six miles took them south in paven sweeps back to the Nile opposite Yebu. Whose small fortress garrison could only signal impotently as the peasants fled and the Kushite army spread into the river fields, happily gathering grain threshed and stored or standing in the ear. Before the horns called again, and the tall palmette standards resumed their motion north.

A bare two days later, the Egyptian army appeared.

Alara permitted it, the Candace thought, as her fingers slipped, clammily, on her bow-grip. Alara himself said, *Kamose will not hesitate. He is back across-river already. We can give battle now, or he will. And for the moment the wind is from the desert, marginally blowing away from us.*

He argued, when I announced, *This time I will not lurk like a child behind the line. I have trained five years with the bow, with the chariots. We will go as my father planned, to engage the first skirmishers.* But he yielded, when I said, *I am the Candace. It is my place to lead the battle front.*

The horses fidgeted under a sudden wind-flaw and her driver Bartare calmed them. The flanking teams settled in turn. Twelve chariots and teams, bought with Kushite gold and the king's foresight, smuggled all the way from Avaris, formed now in four barbs of three, as the Hyksos trainers had explained. Each chariot trailing a wave of six or eight runners to deal with enemy stragglers or wounded. And in each chariot, a driver and two archers, all from the Candace's guard.

That argument had been the most ferocious of all. Only the old king's original decree had prevailed when he died, that the chariots were skirmishers, they required lightness above all, that women, some women, could manage horses and draw bows, even the deadly armor-piercing Hyksos compound bow, as well as men.

And we found them, the Candace thought, steadying her breathing. Five years choosing, testing, discarding, but we have them here. Now, my father, comes the test. Now you and I must both justify ourselves.

Bartare tensed. Beyond her, Kasaqa was already still as a lioness in ambush, the compound bow not yet drawn. The Candace did not have to look back at the serried shields of Kushite spearmen, the clouds of archers behind and to either side. Archery first, then spears, to follow that damage up. She could hear the low chant already: "Hor-us, Hor-us, Horus . . ." Through the dust haze she scanned the thunder-dark mass of the enemy. Tawny hide shield-blocks, spiked ranks of glinting spearheads. Flickers of squadron standards, scarlet or emerald. Even as she looked, the Kushite horns pealed the single long note of the Advance.

\*\*\*

As so many veterans had told her, battle in memory became a blur of disparate sight, smell, sensation, sound. The fierce thud of hooves, the vicious whick! of a compound bowstring, the slap of her own string against her wrist-guard, lurch of the chariot, time stretched in the last moment's terrified pause. Then the geyser of faces, bodies, weapons, a blur of here-and-gone-again swirling violently past her, shrieks, screams, orders, and over all the dust, the unbroken whick-whick-whick of bowstrings. And the blood.

She did recall the first successful sweep, each chariot barb swirling in diagonal echelon along the enemy front. Other fragments remained from when the archers meshed, hands, faces screaming up at the chariot, the runners engaged hand-to-hand. A team going down, one horse hocked, the other tripped, a surge of struggling stabbing bodies that swept all three women out of sight. No time to pause, let alone to mourn. Only to reform and sweep again, and again . . . and suddenly as sun through ragged cloud, spaces opened round them, the Egyptian archers falling back, Bartare swinging the team with ingrained discipline, heading outward, clearing the spearmen's front.

And the spearmen came, striding steadily but fiercely past the panting, head-down horses, surging into the blood and dust, and from their mass the deep-throated roars went up. First, "Horus!" and then, "Kush!"

The Candace had one delirious moment to catch breath and find her quiver empty, to see the battle front almost whole, Egyptian archers running, Kushite archers harrying them, two ranks of spearmen moving together like reapers over the fallen, to realize the Egyptian front was sagging, to think, incredulously panting, We did it. We bested their archers. They fear our spearmen. They are going to break!

A white radiance blossomed ahead of her, clearer and brighter than moonlight, spreading out toward the enemy through the dust. Her own heart nearly leapt out of her chest. The spearmen leapt too, roaring like a thunder-peel, "Hor-us! Hor-us!" Running now, as the blades came down to charge.

In that moment another light blazed, over the enemy lines. If the first was moonlight, this was full noon sunshine, sun met eye-open and unshielded, dazzling, blinding, cruel as a spearblade. It struck the light over the Kushite lines and drove it backward. Defeated, outshone, overwhelmed.

The Candace had one teary glimpse of Kushite spearmen blundering, recoiling, hands up to shield their faces, one momentary deafness from the enemy's roar. Then the Kushite horns howled frantically around her, the two long double notes repeated and repeated. *Retreat, retreat, retreat.*

***

Sobekemheb knelt on the Candace's tent floor, striking his forehead over and over on the dusty rug. Repeating, smothered but steadily, "I have failed. I have failed. I have failed."

Neither the Candace nor Kasaqa had the strength, in body or soul, to deal with him. It was Alara who stepped past, saying brusquely, "Get up, man, and have done. Past is past. You did not fail alone."

The Candace wiped her eyes, blurry with tears and dust. Alara's shape came into clearer focus, but it was still outlined in a dancing white blur. "What – was that?" she got out.

"Amun-Ra," Alara answered curtly. The sound of his voice told her he was looking at Sobekemheb. "The Great Sun. Egypt's Lord."

Sobekemheb winced. Kasaqa caught her breath. Then she got awkwardly from her stool and knelt at his side.

"But . . ." the Candace thought she sounded small as a child. "But we had Horus. He came for us. As at Buhen, so here. And we were winning. How could even Amun –"

"We followed Horus, yes. But this is not his land. It is Amun's. If we called Horus, Kamose's men called Amun. And there are more of them than us."

Outside the camp rumored with chagrin, with pain and loss and fear. Inside, Alara's voice died bleakly into the hush.

Then Sobekemheb turned about on his knees and abased himself once more at the Candace's feet. "Kentakes," he said into the floor. "Forgive me. I have erred. I have been mistaken. I have led you – the army – Kush – astray."

The Candace bit her fingertips. They tasted of dust. Perhaps of blood. She bit her lip instead and said it baldly. "Then we have lost?"

Alara shuffled his boots. Kasaqa sat slowly up at

Sobekemheb's side, and at her face the Candace looked away. Sobekemheb let silence and stillness speak for themselves.

"But we retreated. We were not driven. We lost men, yes. Less than Kamose did." She felt a brief pride in that. "The army is whole. The camp is safe. Why did we lose?"

Their silence answered for them. *We have the men, the supplies, the position. We do not have the power to fight a stronger god.*

The Candace stood up. Suddenly, piercingly, as not even before battle, she comprehended what it meant to be Kentakes: a land's ruler and leader, who must choose its way in absolute loneliness. And find, in that isolation, a solution when all others had given up.

She heard her servants muttering outside. They would be waiting with water, wine, perhaps the means for a bath, everything that went on even in defeat. She looked at the laced tent-flap, and saw gods collide above her. And the solution came.

"Horus cannot defeat Amun alone. Then He must have help."

She had time to think, that is the first plan I have constructed, entirely alone, in my life. Now I am truly Candace. Then she saw the other faces, amazement, wonder from Sobekemheb, from Kasaqa the quick flash of delight, in Alara a first remarkable signal of respect. Before all become the same expression: the wakening of hope.

\*\*\*

"Who will you call?"

Try to call, the Candace amended silently. But it was Kasaqa who asked. And there would be no need to qualify, for her.

"I thought at first, Apedemak." She slid her arms carefully into the long bleached-linen vest. They had no priestly raiment, even were she a priestess. But as Kush's head, as well as instigator of the plan, she had been awarded the summoner's role.

"But Apedemak is of Kush. As the Horus is of Buhen. He might not . . ."

"No." Kashaqa settled the hem straight. "He might not hear us, abroad."

"So I will try to summon Hathor."

Kashaqa put down the plaited ribband meant for a priestly head-dress. The Candace spoke quickly into her stare. "Hathor is Horus' wife, and the Candace's guardian." She paused. "She has also been – Sekhmet."

Kasaqa sucked in her breath.

"I know." The Candace swallowed. "The Lion Lady thirsts for blood. She may prove – dangerous."

"Enough blood," Kasaqa said at length, "and She may not want to stop."

"No. But if I call Her as Hathor – you know the story Aata tells, that Hathor became Sekhmet to protect Re from assassins. That She ran wild and killed until Re poured red beer before Her instead of blood. Grown drunk, She returned to Herself." The Candace twisted the ribband through her own fingers. "If I call Hathor, the Lady of Joy may become Sekhmet, when She sees Her husband threatened. But unlike Sekhmet – She will come back."

Kasaqa stared at her, eyes glistening ovals in the half-light of the tiny tent-lamp. The Candace felt her heart beat, once, five times, ten. Before Kasaqa let out a long shaken breath and murmured, "I would call this madness. Except, it is for Kush."

And for Kush's sake, the Candace filled in, we cannot withdraw. We have to hold, if not outright defeat Kamose in the field.

*\*\**

Deprived of Aata's bastion, the army's scandalized official priest was eventually browbeaten to accept that a woman, even the Kentakes, should attempt to summon gods. He did consent to supply incense; and finally, to disgorge words for a summoning chant.

The time was just before dawn. The waning moon, Kasaqa pointed out, would be at its brightest then. The priest noted, with relief, that Amun-Ra would be traversing the underworld in his Solar Boat. Alara added bluntly that, "The less time we give the Lady of Joy to forget our supplication, the better for us."

They gathered under a sycamore on the nearest knoll. The tiny censer of incense fumed palely in the shadows, drowning the stench of army latrines, the tickle of dust, the rank odor of aging blood, and the scanty hint of dew. New bread and beer sat at their feet. The moon looked whitely in on them, her disk half gone, and the Candace whispered prayers, feeling foolish, insufficient. Foolhardy, to attempt to shape the course of gods.

"Lady of Joy, Lady of the Sycamores, hear me. Taste of this food, this drink. Favor me with your presence, this day, upon the field of battle. Come to our aid, this your faithful servant, and your own husband, great Horus of Buhen. Protect us, when the slaying begins."

Her whisper died away. For a rare moment, the dawn-leaning world was entirely still. Nothing, human, natural, or supernatural, broke the hush. The Candace looked up, between hope and despair, and saw a pair of naked branches, black and slender, crooked like horns across the falling moon.

\*\*\*

"So I cannot tell if the Lady heard. But I saw branches on the moon, where none were before."

The Candace picked up her morning loaf. Across the tent, Alara looked dour, Sobekemheb uncertain. The priest had been sent out. It was Kasaqa who finally spoke.

"Hathor is the Cow of Heaven. Her statues bear the sun-disk between their horns." Her jaw hardened. "So, we have done what we can. We must offer battle, whether She heard or not."

As soon as the army finished breakfast the battle-lines were called. "Kamose will look for noon-tide," Alara had said, "Amun's own time. We must not let him delay." The shadows were still long beside them when the Candace led her chariots into the Kushite front.

The horses were grumpy and stiff, the guard subdued, by weariness, memories, and that barb of chariots now a team short. As they drove by, the spearmen too were silent and dour, but the Candace felt the pressure of their eyes. They know about the invocation, she thought. They are ready to fight, perhaps to die. But still, they would have victory. Or a death with value. They want to hope.

The Egyptians could not ignore the challenge. The two armies deployed out over trampled grainfields, among the remnants of yesterday's unsalvaged dead, facing each other in the mid-morning glare. The Kushite horns called. The Candace cried to her guard. The battle fronts began to move.

For a little it was yesterday over again. More fear, perhaps, with increased knowledge, less spring in muscle and bone. But the same deadly whirlwind of dust and tumult and blood, the same maneuvers amid the same turmoil of flying arrows and skirmishing runners between the opposing spearmen. Except that this time, the Egyptian archers were not giving way.

"Medjay!" Kasaqa panted as their team swung at a sweep's end. "Saw them – in the centre. They have brought up Medjay!"

The Candace's heart sank. She shouted hoarsely to Bartare, "Again!" As the team gathered speed, she nocked the first arrow and prayed silently, *Now aid us, Horus, Hathor, lord and lady. Before they raise Great Amun. Come. Come!*

Strings whick-whicked, arrows boiled. Men screamed and fought and fell. The dust rose, dirty fog-mist, dun-brown, pallid. Turning white.

The Candace screamed in exultation and heard the cry come back from a dozen throats. "The Hawk! The Hawk!"

She heard the spearmen's answering roar. The dust glittered white around her, whiter, whiter, then suddenly the reeling enemy collected themselves, the light was coruscating, dazzling, the roars of "Horus!" fragmented and she heard the wave-thunder of "Amun!" beyond, the team stumbled, Bartare at a loss, archers all round falling back, half-blind.

Without warning, the dust turned red.

Rust-red, sullen red, the red of the Nile at the height of Akhet, that indefinable earth-color neither crimson nor blood. It boiled up over the battlefield, Amun's zenith brilliance suddenly obscured, the entire scene become a painting of the underworld. The Candace felt the chariot jerk as the team rallied, she heard Kasaqa's kite-hawk scream – and the surf-bellow from the Kushite spearmen: "Hathor! Hathor!"

Kushite horns screamed. The Candace slapped Bartare's shoulder and pointed forward, waved wildly to the rest. The chariots came round, headed into the Egyptian archers' midst, straight for the spearmen's line. The one thing the Hyksos had told them, over and over, not to do.

*Alara will have apoplexy*, she thought, *Sobekemheb will run crazy – but the Lady is here, She is moving. We must go too, or lose Her. Here. Now.*

The press thickened. Arrows flew like hail, impossible to dodge We will die like porcupines . . . The red light had become a volcano's lour, Egyptian archers on the inland wing had fallen back, swinging outward, backing away. Their spearmen's front showed rock-like in the distant glare.

And from the river wing a cloud of darkness came, lower than the great celestial god-lights that battled overhead. This slid like a kind of blot, barely man-height above the earth. The Candace heard cries of panic, saw archers Kushite and Egyptian run. The darkness slid in between the armies and she was still trying to make Bartare swing to face it when a spurt of Egyptian runners leapt up about her wheels.

A contorted face bawled into hers. A flying mace caught Bartare in the ribs. The off-side horse screamed, reared and struck. The Candace whipped her dagger out just in time to slash the wrist that grabbed for her belt. Then another mace flew above the chariot rim, straight into Kasaqa's waist.

Kasaqa collapsed. Her body slid sidelong from the chariot and the Candace shrieked and hurled herself after, kicking, striking, flinging men aside as she landed astride Kasaqa's back, screaming wordlessly into the snarling faces, *Mine, Mine, Don't touch*!

Another surge of bodies flooded in. But these were Kushite runners. The press dissolved in a welter of hand-to-hand blows, the team were tangled, traces caught, the chariot stopped, an island in the minor battle's waves, but for a moment she and Kasaqa and Bartare wheezing above them were almost alone.

The darkness swept swiftly down on them. The Candace saw wings inside it, great shadow-pale wings oaring steadily, and between them, the featherless white vulture's neck, the long hooked beak, and the cobra head of a uraeus, perched above the hairless skull. Eyes stared into hers.

Black eyes, bird eyes, yet a more than human sentience, indifferent to all that lived. To anything that could not be consumed. Eyes focused, she realized, on the woman between her feet.

The Candace screamed, "No!" Then she grabbed Kasaqa's shoulder and howled wordlessly, *Not yours! Mine! Mine!*

The wings arched, rose and held. The vulture's beak opened, but no sound came out. Nekhbet spoke direct into her mind.

*This, or victory. Which?*

And the Candace screamed back without the need for thought.

*This! This!*

The beak closed. The wings rose, drove down and beat. Pale in her darkness, Nekhbet swept past them, and the three nearest men fell silently, loose-jointed as dolls. As the light turned to a fading red and she struggled to lift Kasaqa to the chariot, the Candace heard Kushite horns behind her. They were calling the Retreat.


\*\*\*


Dusk was closing when the Candace finally reached the small healer's tent. As she came up, the door-flap opened. Sobekemheb came out, moving like an old man. His face was hollow with grief.

Terror shut the Candace's heart. She managed, "Is she...?"

Sobekemheb whispered, "She lost the child."

The Candace felt a dagger in her own side. *Oh, my sister, my beloved, my truest, dearest one.*

Sobekemheb closed his eyes. Tears glinted briefly down his dirty, sweaty cheeks. Before she thought the Candace gripped his shoulder, as she might Kasaqa's own.

His eyes opened. He managed a sort of nod. Then he whispered, "She sleeps now. They thought – but the bleeding eased. They think – they think –"

They think that she will live.

The Candace shut her own eyes, vowing incense, gold, a hundred-cow sacrifice to Hathor, Lady of Joy. And perhaps, she ceded, something to the Lady of Nekheb as well.

Then she let Sobekemheb go. "If she sleeps, we can do nothing here," she said. "Yet. And I – Kush – needs you now."

\*\*\*

"It may be I have lost the campaign," she said, holding Alara's stare. *It may be I have lost Kush,* she added to herself. "But given that choice – I would do the same again."

Alara looked away. After a moment he said gruffly, "A comrade. A shoulder-man. Whatever else was at stake – so would I have done."

The Candace felt something like an overstrained muscle ease inside her. She swallowed, and like Alara, looked away.

Then she cleared her throat and said baldly, "So, what now?"

Silence brought the camp noise closer. Voices, distant animal sounds, a clatter of pots, the unending susurrus of feet. The low surf of pain from the healers' tents.

Alara scrubbed at his beard. Shuffled his shoulders. Looked up at the roof and down at his feet. When her understanding became incredulity, the Candace turned to Sobekemheb.

Who could maintain composure, but whose sole contribution was a barely audible, "The healers say . . . for at least a day or two. She can not be moved."

He too dropped his eyes. More camp noise intervened while they all absorbed that. Win or lose, fight or decline to fight, for the next few days, they were going nowhere.

The Candace looked from one to the other. Neither would meet her eye.

Her heart sank. Her mouth went dry. My sage veteran, my subtle new adviser, both are useless. My cleverest counselor is lost. I alone must decide here. Must *discover* what to do.

She drew a long breath, and made herself sit upright on her stool. "When we retreated – after – Kasaqa fell" – after, she did not say, Nehkbet told me I had squandered a victory – "Kamose also withdrew."

Alara nodded.

She remembered the men who had fallen in Kasaqa's stead. One Kushite, two Egyptians. "Nekhbet did not distinguish enemies. Was Kamose – afraid of Nekhbet, himself?"

Alara could only shrug.

The Candace bit her lip. "May the general advise me. If Kamose takes the field tomorrow, what outcome does he see?"

Alara grimaced. "If they offer battle . . ." he managed at last. And paused. "We must try to refuse."

When it was clear he had finished, the Candace said, "If Kamose offers battle and we *cannot* refuse – would the gods fight for us again?"

Alara heaved his shoulders up. "Kentakes, I am a soldier. These are questions for the priest."

"The priest," the Candace sounded tarter than she meant, "can also say neither Yea nor Nay."

Alara pulled his shoulders to his ears, like a man caught in a bitter wind. The Candace looked at Sobekemheb, who dropped his head. I have asked them the impossible, she realized. Only the gods themselves could answer me.

Now, what am I to do?

The solution came in her father's voice, a remedy he had used time and again when some problem of law or tactics proved currently insoluble.

"We shall sleep," she said, rising to signal their dismissal. "And perhaps, with dawn, a god will tell us what to do."

But it was a young guard officer who told her, all but falling into the tent like that household runner with word of the Hyksos' messenger. "Kentakes – Kentakes! The Fish – the Egyptians want to treat!"

\*\*\*

The Candace stood at the margin of a devastated barley field, watching the knot of figures under the standard bearing what Egyptians called the Wedjat: the Horus-eye that signaled, *We come in good faith. In the sight of the gods.* Doubtless as new-painted as the one above her own head. The one certainty in her bewilderment.

Kamose has more men. He has Amun to fight for him. Perhaps, he has Nekhbet. He might have destroyed us yesterday. He could do it today. We are on his ground, for complete vantage he need only wait. Why has *he* asked to treat?

The Egyptians were half across the field. A leading fringe of men, the counterpart of her own officer and guard-squad, spears ostentatiously absent, maces or daggers sheathed. Behind their white kilts and leather protector straps, a handful of doubtless high officers shielded Kamose. Would he wear the khepresh, she wondered, the blue battle-crown, if he came to treat?

Alara suddenly stiffened beside her. She muttered, "What?"

For a moment he did not answer. Then he drew an audible breath. "That is a woman," he said.

"A *what*?"

The Candace gasped. She did manage not to babble. "But how – who?"

She could see now for herself. Not a blue battle-crown, but a low golden head-dress with a projection over the brow of the full black wig. Not a kilt and dagger-belt, but a full-length white linen dress, girdled in blue and gold, and not the warrior's mace or Pharaoh's crook and flail in hand, but a...

At her other elbow, Sobekemheb murmured, "That is a parasol."

Alara said something startled but the Candace already understood. Protection from sun, but a royal symbol as well. The bearer was at least a queen.

At half a bow-shot the advance guard stamped in unison and stopped. A hum of talk – argument? altercation?

rose behind. Then a single officer emerged, striding to the Kushite line.

"The Regent of Qimit will address your leader." Unarmed he might be, but national arrogance he had to overflowing. "With each side's interpreter. Otherwise, alone."

And what does that mean, what uproar did she override for that, who *is* this woman to dare such rashness? The Candace's brain spun anew. But there could be no delay.

"Tell the Regent of Qimit," she addressed her own guard officer. "The Kentakes of Kush agrees."

At close quarters, the head-dress imitated a flying bird, wings spread down either side the woman's hair, feet gripping the Sekh rings Horus would hold, head – the Candace almost recoiled as she recognized the uraeus and the vulture beak.

But the eyes beneath, painted and elongated with kohl and green antimony, were black and still with royalty and ruler's experience, but human, nevertheless.

Neither woman offered acknowledgement. The Candace did wish briefly for a similar shade from the now insistent sun. She also waited. The treaty seeker had the onus to begin.

The woman spoke. The interpreter repeated in fair Kushite, "Ahhotep, Regent of Qimit, Great Royal Wife of Seqenenre Te, Mistress of Nekheb, asks, to whom she speaks?"

At her elbow Sobekemheb recited the Candace's titles. The eyes under the uraeus did not blink. She knew, the Candace thought, who I am.

Ahhotep spoke again. The interpreter said, "Why have you come here?"

Blunt enough, the Candace thought, feeling Sobekemheb stiffen. Her own question was equally bald. "Where is the Pharaoh Kamose?"

Ahhotep's eyelids dropped and rose, once. Her voice was flat. The interpreter said, "Kamose, son of Seqenenre, Lord of the Two Lands, has become Osiris."

The Candace just managed not to gasp. The wounds,

I never did ask that messenger. But he has become Osiris. Kamose died of them.

Ahhotep added one short sentence. "He was my son."

The interpreter's version was flat as ever. In the Regent's, the Candace felt her own father's loss. Stupidly, for all of Kush and Egypt, war and menace and gods between them, for a moment she felt them only two bereft women. She could have let her own eyes fill with tears.

And in that moment, she lost the crazily shifting future perspectives, Kamose gone, what would the Egyptians do now, what has Apopis done, what could *Kush* do. . . She recalled only Kasaqa's words on the palace terrace, their original strategy, and saw what her answer to the Regent's first question should be.

"We seek for a treaty," she said.

Hearing Sobekemheb's startlement, she thought acidly, *Just as well Alara is not here. But she was watching* Ahhotep's face, harder than she ever tried to read an opposing fighter. Hoping, against hope, for what it might show.

Ahhotep's interpreter had been startled too. Ahhotep's eyes merely opened, piercing as an arrow-point. Before the lids dropped and she said something crisp but lengthy that the interpreter almost stumbled in rendering.

"Need we stand in the sun to discuss terms?"

* * *

"She haggles like a – a fishwife. We may have a border at the Second Cataract. But for that, we must cede Buhen. We may trade into Egypt, but only if we regulate the Sai Island tolls. And we may have peace – but only during her Regency."

Kasaqa's face was still the color of milk-stained mud, and her body under the sheet seemed shrunken all over. But her eyes were clear and if her voice wavered, her mind kept its dagger edge.

"How long . . ."

"'My son Ahmose is ten years old,' she said. 'When he comes of age, he will rule Qimit.' I do not think she meant, what they have now in Thebes. 'I cannot say what Ahmose will do,' she said, 'But that is eleven and more years away. I am offering peace now.'"

Kasaqa's lids sank on her dark-stained cheeks. The camp rumor drifted in to them. Even in the heat of early afternoon, with everyone who could find shade using it, the murmur had an indefinable uplift. News, excitement. Hope.

"What did Alara say?"

The Candace gave a short laugh. "At first, he gobbled like a gander. The gods defend him from women in the throne-room, we have both run mad, offering, let alone talking treaty! Kamose is gone. The boy is ten. Ahhotep is a woman. We are here in Egypt. The gods are with us! Are we purely cotton-headed, can I at least not see the opportunity? Seize it! Seize it! Now we know the truth, reject the woman's offer! Call for battle, sweep the Fish-eaters before us and do what my father could not. Capture Thebes!"

Faintly but identifiably, Kasaqa laughed.

The Candace snorted. And sobered.

"But I wonder, my sister, if he is right?"

Kasaqa's eyes re-opened. The Candace forestalled her attempt to move.

Kasaqa submitted. Then she said, "And Sobekemheb?"

They both knew the other officers were relative nothings. Aaata, the queen mother, the lords' council, all the other decision-makers of Kush were beyond contact. Sobekemheb was the one other voice that might count.

"Sobekemheb wavers. Yes, Ahhotep may parley because her situation is parlous. And yes, we could have peace. Except, perhaps only for ten years. Sobekemheb says, Is that fair balance? For a victory, and restoring the First Cataract border, or perhaps, exacting more of Egypt as peace's price?"

Kasaqa pursed her lips. The Candace reached for the jug of boiled water beside her pallet and found the clay camp cup. Unprotesting, Kasaqa drank. The Candace set the cup down. When Kasaqa was silent, she said, "And you, my sister? What do you think?"

Faintly, Kasaqa frowned. "I wish we knew . . . *why* she parleyed. The truth."

"Ah." The Candace sat up. "Do you know, she has some Kushite? We spoke much, today, face to face. And at the end, I said that. I asked, 'Why did you treat?'"

Kasaqa's eyes flew open. "And she said?"

"She said, 'I heard what you did. For your archer. One saw it, on the field. You bargained with Nekhbet. A life, for a victory.'"

Kasaqa was staring. She might have been holding her breath.

"She said, 'And I thought, Here is one who may see past blood and glory. Perhaps, a ruler who may put the people first.'"

Kasaqa breathed out, a long, soft, Aah. When the Candace could wait no longer, she demanded, "So, then. What do you think?"

Kasaqa shut her eyes again. It was a long pause before the answer came.

"I think – the Regent of Qimit is either a ruler in truth – or a very clever woman."

She opened her eyes again. "And I fear, my sister, which the choice of which – can only come from you."

*   *   *

A very great help, my sister, the Candace thought acidly, trying to control real anger. I might as well be entirely alone.

Except there is one voice that did answer when I called. One wisdom I have not tried.
She strode away from the little tent, calling, "Akinidad! Someone find the priest Akinidad, and send him straight to me!"

The Candace stood at the verge of dawn beneath the knoll-top sycamore, attired in vest and ribbands, the censer in her hand. Down the knoll the priest and Sobekemheb, Alara, guards and servants waited. This voice, she meant to hear alone.

The moon was a hand-breadth above the horizon. The Candace bowed low, and swung the censer, before she began to chant, in the barest undertone. "O Hathor, Mistress of the West, Shield of Kush, Spouse of Great Horus, hear me. Vouchsafe the splendor of your presence to your pleading servant. Hathor, come to me."

The moon was almost on the horizon when she stopped. The incense was guttering. She will not hear. She has not listened. She no longer favors me.

Somewhere toward the river, in the ravaged fields, a cow called. Low and softly, as to a straying calf. Then the moon began to grow.

Larger, higher, whiter it shone, as pure a light as Amun's but far gentler. And round it, the shadow of a cloud, indefinite, drifting, suggesting rather than shaping horns.

Like Nekhbet, Hathor spoke directly into the mind. The sensation of awareness equated to, *Daughter, I am here.*

The Candace swallowed her heart. Managed to stop the censer's shaking. And began to speak.

"So, Great Mother," she ended, "I beseech you, tell me how I should choose here. What will be best for Kush?"

And presently, the wordless voice replied, *Peace is always good.*

The Candace swallowed again. "Even – forgive your

servant – if it is short?"

*Even so.*

The Candace mustered all her courage. "Will the Great Mother tell me? What – what will befall Kush?"

The pause this time was so long the dawn light began to strengthen. A breeze hinted dust and dew. Far along the river, a cock had begun to crow, when Hathor spoke again.

*Kush will bear what Kush will bear.*

The Candace licked her lips. War, she could not say? Ahmose will be another warrior? Kush will be attacked once more? Kush will – Kush will be – as Kasaqa feared?

"Great Mother . . . I pray, that Kush will survive."

The sense of speech this time was more distant, almost sorrowful, as if Hathor, like the moon, was drifting, dwindling away.

*Even Pharaohs cannot last forever. The last Great House will fall.*

"And – Kush?"

The last words were almost indistinguishable.

*Folk will always dwell in Kush.*

The Candace stood watching till the censer was quite empty before she went slowly back down the knoll. As Sobekemheb came up, a cloak over one arm, a cup in the other hand, the query eloquent in his face, she said, "For the moment, we will have peace."

\*\*\*

"We *might* have won another battle, yes. We are leaving Ahhotep to settle the Hyksos, rather than balance them, yes. But we have what *we* came for. If it is only ten years . . . Hathor Herself could not promise more. And in ten years, much may happen. The river might overwhelm Thebes, Egypt, Kush. Ahhotep might die. Ahmose might die. *We* might die. I chose for now. For as much as we can be sure of having, now and here."

Kasaqa heard her out, nodding. When the Candace finished, she said softly, "My sister, you chose well."

The Candace remembered Ahhotep looking up from the treaty papyrus, saying in her peculiar Kushite, "Women in Kush, as well as Egypt, will see their men come home now, and their fields unburnt. They will be thanking you."

Then Kasaqa moved and sighed. "Though for one moment's decision, one life, one woman," she murmured ruefully, "it seems a very high price."

The Candace looked at her face, less mud and more bronze-color this morning, and thought, You are not just one woman, my sister. You are my right hand. The half of my heart.

And somehow, with your subtlety, your endurance, your stubbornness, you are Kush. While women like you live, Kush will survive.

So if this is the price of Kush, it is a price I willingly pay.

Kasaqa did not look away from the open tent door, though her voice was steady enough.

"And one, now . . . they say, who will never have another child."

The Candace looked across Kasaqa to Sobekemheb. He was still somewhat hollow-cheeked, and his hand had a tendency to hover near Kasaqa's. *He truly loves her*, the Candace thought. *Child or no child, he will go on loving her. All his life.*

In a way, he has lost more than any of us. The battle. All his labor. Buhen. The hopes of his father. Even his child.

He looked up, so their eyes met, and the idea clove her thoughts like a lightning flash. Yes, he deserves recompense. Some commensurate place in Kush, land, cattle, rank. A place in the palace. A place at my side.

We agree very well together, the three of us. We think the same thoughts.

And the next thought came as night after day, noon

after morning. She laid her own hand over Kasaqa's at the sheet edge and said, "One day, my sister, I will give you another child."

Kasaqa looked startled, then half-resigned. *A foster-child, she thinks I mean.* The Candace lifted her own eyes to meet Sobekemheb's, and saw he understood.

They had always been very good at understanding without words.

*A child of his body, if not of his beloved,* the Candace thought. *A child of her beloved, for Kasaqa. A child they, we might even raise together. And one day, perhaps, an heir for whom I need not marry. No risk of splitting Kush over a husband's choice. Or of a fool sharing the throne.*

She leant down and kissed Kasaqa on the brow. Nodded to Sobekemheb. Then she went outside, where her general was waiting.

"Alara," she said, "Tell the horns to sound, Break

Camp. The army of Kush is going home."

# Old Habits

*Milton Davis*

Kadira tucked her braids under her head wrap for the fifth time, holding back a vile curse. The vendor before the poultry cart waited patiently, for he was used to the worries women suffered with their fashions. Kadira, however, was annoyed beyond concentration. She was tempted to tear off her head wrap and shave herself bald on the spot. She should have never let Nguvu talk her into this silly hair style. She was a warrior, not a trollop.

"What can I do for you, sister?" the vendor asked.

Kadira placed her hand on her wide hips as she concentrated on the various types of edible birds hanging from the wagon. It there was one thing about Sati-Baa market it was food was never in short supply. The farmers of Kenja kept it well stocked, especially since their new formed militia succeeded in deterring the once frequent slave raids. The rumor was that a female priest organized the militia, a woman trained by the Dogon to heal and to fight. A rivulet of adrenaline coursed through her sword arm and she bit her lip. Those days were done now. She was a wife and a mother now. Best she concentrate on the job at hand, which was buying food for her huge, greedy husband and their growing greedy child.

"I can't believe what I'm seeing!"

Kadira grinned then turned. Omari Ket stood with his arms folded across his chest, his head tilted. He was draped in armor and weapons that told of journeys throughout Ki Khanga, an outfit appropriate for a journeyman weaponeer. Kadira struck a similar pose.

"Believe it, Snake," she answered.

Omari held his arms open and she hugged him. She smiled until one of his hands found her backside. A quick jab to the stomach sent hem stumbling backward.

"None of that," she said. "I'm a married woman now."

"Two shocks in one day!" Omari exclaimed.

Omari assumed his skeptical stance again. "Who's the lucky man?"

"Nguvu."

Omari's face twisted. "I don't know him."

"You shouldn't. I met him long after you and I parted ways."

A wistful look came to Omari's face and Kadira felt embarrassed.

"So what brings you to Sati-Baa?"

"Money, what else?" Omari replied. "I thought that's why you were here.

"Sati-Baa is home now," Kadira said. "Nguvu and I have given up the road. We have a child."

Omari slapped his forehead. "Okay, I understand now. I'm dreaming. No, I'm having a nightmare. Excuse me while I go wake up and find the real Kadira."

Kadira laughed out loud. "You always made me laugh, Omari." She reached out and touched his hair. It was straight like a horse's tail.

"What happen to your hair? It looks like a horse's ass."

Omari slapped her hand away. "I spent some time serving with the Mikijen in Kiswala. Most of them are wearing their hair like this now, and the women seem to like it. You know how I am about pleasing women."

Kadira ignored his words. "Well, it was good seeing you, Omari. Don't get killed."

She turned to leave, but Omari grabbed her arm. A pleasant tingle raced from his touch to her chest and she smiled before she realized it.

"Aren't you at least a little interested in why I am here?"

Kadira hesitated. Of course she was interested. The reality was she was terribly bored, despite her feelings for Nguvu and their child. She reluctantly faced Omari.

"Okay, so why are you here?"

"A Menu-Kash priest put out a call for all those skilled in weapons to accompany him on a journey to Wadantu. He's willing to pay eighty stacks each...if we return."

Kadira's eyes went wide. "Eighty stacks?"

Omari grinned. "Eighty."

She shrugged. "For that much, I'm sure mercenaries are falling over themselves"

"True, but none of them have your skills or experience."

"You don't need me."

"I need you," Omari admitted. "You're the best archer in Ki Khanga, even better than that Dogon priest woman in Kenja. You would also be the only person I know, and I need someone I can trust."

"Any other reasons?"

"I did have a few others, but they've been dashed to pieces by your news of husbands and babies," Omari admitted.

"Eighty stacks is life changing money, but I have to decline. Besides, Nguvu wouldn't hear of it."

Omari looked shocked. "Since when did Kadira let a man stop her from doing what she wished?"

Kadira pointed out to plump chickens to the poultry seller and he quickly cut them down.

"Since Kadira became a married woman," she answered.

Omari shrugged. "I'll be at the Simbala hostel, if you change your mind, or if you want to revisit old times."

Kadira smirked. "You have no shame."

Omari winked. "Of course, I don't."

Kadira paid for her chickens and headed home. She glanced back; Omari stood watching her, his compelling smile fanning a flame that had recently re-emerged. She was bored and restless, but had done a good job keeping it in check. By the time she reached the farm, that flame was a raging fire.

She was greeted by the rhythmic clanging of a familiar hammer striking a worn anvil. Kadira crept to the smithy and peered at Nguvu as he worked over a long red hot length of steel. Olea's cradle sat on the opposite side of the cramped shed.

"What took you so long?" Nguvu asked. "You know I had work to do. I had to bring Olea out into this hot shed. I'm surprised she's still asleep."

Kadira placed the groceries on the cluttered table and went to her daughter. Olea stirred as she lifted her from the crib and held her close. The babe instinctively nuzzled her chest and Kadira began to feed her.

"I met an old friend in the market," Kadira said.

Nguvu continued flailing the hot steel. "Really? You have old friends?"

"Of course, I do," Kadira replied.

"What's his name?"

"How do you...Omari."

Nguvu stopped hammering. "I've never heard you mention his name."

"It was a long time ago, before the war," she said.

Nguvu began hammering again. "So what is he doing in Sati-Baa?"

"A Kashite magic man is gathering men for an expedition into Wadantu. Omari is going."

Nguvu placed his hammer down, satisfied with his work. He took the steel to his brine barrel and dipped it. Steam rose from the barrel obscuring his face.

"How much he paying?"

"Eighty stacks."

Nguvu whistled. "That's a lot of stacks."

He placed the steel down on the table. Nguvu was a decent blacksmith, but it was not his true trade. He was a killer, a very good one, in fact. He was also a rogue, like Kadira. She knew what ran through his mind. He sat on a metal stool he'd built himself then wiped his sweaty hands on his dingy apron. Kadira watched his massive muscles ripple across his bare upper body and grinned.

"You want to go, don't you?"

His question caught her unaware.

"Of course not!' she barked.

"Don't lie. I know you do because I want to."

Kadira looked away from Nguvu, stroking Olea's head as she continued to feed.

"We're not the people we used to be."

Nguvu stood. "Yes, we are. We just have a child now."

"Exactly."

Nguvu walked to her. "I think you should go."

Kadira blinked in shock. "What?"

Nguvu stood and folded his massive arms across his chest. "I said, I think you should go."

Olea still fed so fainting was not an option. "I can't go. You know that."

"We could hire a wet nurse for Olea," Nguvu said. "She's still young so she won't miss you too much. If she does, you'll have plenty of time to make things right...if you come back."

Kadira stepped closer to her man, raising her head to look into his eyes.

"Are you trying to trick me into staying?"

"No," Nguvu answered. "I'm giving you an opportunity to do what you want to do."

She felt the pressure ease from her nipple. Olea drifted back to sleep, so she placed her back in her cradle.

"You seem anxious to get rid of me," Kadira said. "Is there something I should know?"

Nguvu chuckled. "Now that's funny. Kadira is playing

jealous."

She rushed him and punched him in the stomach. She hurt her hand, but at least she made her point.

"I would think you would be worried, especially with Omari going along as well."

Nguvu's eyebrows rose. "Should I be worried?"

Kadira massaged her sore hand. "No."

"Then, I won't." He hugged her and her arms fell to her side in surrender. She'd fought all her life, confident in her skills. There was no place in Ki Khanga where she was not prepared for danger in any form, but for some strange reason, Nguvu made her feel safe.

"We have survived because we trust each other," Nguvu said. "We also know how we feel. You have not been happy here. At first I thought it was because it was such a big place. But it is because you miss the road. I have never seen you this excited since we settled."

He released her.

"You can't tell me you don't feel the same?"

"I don't." Nguvu went back to his stool and sat.

"I was raised to kill," he said. "I deserted and fell in with you because you offered something more. Now that I am away from it completely, I've had time to realize how terrible my life has been. This is good for me. You are good for me. But I want you to be happy."

Kadira became nervous. "It's not like I won't come back."

"So you're going?" Nguvu asked.

Kadira looked into her lover's eyes. He was sincere, she knew. But he also knew he wanted her to stay.

"Yes," she finally said. "I'm going."

Nguvu nodded thoughtfully. "Then you'll need weapons, potions and talisman."

"Do we have the money for all that?"

Nguvu smiled. "You don't, but I do, at least for the potions and talisman. We'll have to make the weapons ourselves."

"I still have my bow," Kadira said. "I will need arrows and blades."

"I'll make them," Nguvu said.

"No offense, lover, but I'll need something more dependable."

Nguvu frowned. "You haven't seen my best yet. I'll give you a stack to purchase the best, and I've give you my best. I hope you don't have the opportunity to see which is better."

Kadira couldn't hide her joy. A broad smile cut across her face as she grabbed Nguvu's hand.

"Come inside. The baby's asleep. There are other things I need to store up before I go."

Nguvu swept her up into his arms. "I should have sent you away a long time ago."

Olea's hungry wail woke Kadira. She slid from atop Nguvu, dressed then pattered across the floor to the cradle.

"Hello, hungry girl,' she cooed. "You may have my looks, but you have your baba's appetite."

Kadira winced as Olea took to her breast. "I think it's time to put you on solid food."

The statement made her sad. If she went on this journey, she wouldn't be the one to do just that. Some strange woman would be taking care of her child...and maybe even her man. She had no idea how long she would be gone, or, like Nguvu mentioned, if she would return. It was a sobering thought, one that added weight to her shoulders and forced her to sit. Did she really want to risk this gift?

And it was a gift. Her first pregnancy was unexpected. It was the sickness that alerted her that something was different. She told Nguvu after she was sure and he was overcome with joy. He announced they would settle down immediately, which sparked a three-day argument that almost came to blows. Kadira insisted she was still healthy enough to travel, but Nguvu wouldn't hear of it. The argument was ended by her increasing sickness. She became so ill she couldn't stand, let alone walk. They settled in a nearby village and Nguvu hired a house nurse to no avail. Kadira miscarried. They both grieved the loss then immediately set out to have another child, this time deliberately. When she announced she was pregnant again, they moved to Sati-Baa and became 'normal' folks, as Nguvu liked to say. Now she was tired of being normal. The road's call drowned any protest she could muster. Even as she fed Olea, she felt its pull. Seeing Omari was the tipping point. This hunger would not go away until she satisfied it.

"I hope you only have to miss me for a moment," she whispered to Olea. "If not, I hope you'll forgive me."

Nguvu rose from sleep as she lay Olea down. He strode naked across the room for a drink of water, leering at her over the cup as he drank. She wanted to take him to bed again, but there were things to do.

"I'm going into the city for shaft wood and feathers," she said. "I'm going to the Fez bazaar as well."

Nguvu nodded. "You always preferred their potions."

"I think I'll look at their swords, too."

Nguvu's eyes rose. "That's going to be expensive."

"I want to come back home. I'll splurge for the best."

Nguvu strode to her and slapped her butt. "I'm going to make you the best. It'll be a sword as good as me."

Kadira returned the slap. "There's no such thing of a sword that good."

An hour later, she walked the wide paved avenue that bisected Sati-Baa headed for the main market. The Fez bazaar was just beyond the local stalls, tucked down a narrow alleyway. She stopped to buy a ripe soursop when once again a familiar voice interrupted her bargaining.

"I must be the luckiest man in the world!"

Omari came to stand beside her. "It's destiny, Kadira. I know it is."

Kadira smirked. "Either that or you're following me."

"Sati-Baa is a big city, but it's not that big," Omari said. "Where are you headed?"

"To the Fez bazaar."

Omari smiled. "That means you're going with us! You always seek out the Fez before you go on the road."

Omari bowed. "I'll accompany you. There are a few things I could use from those sorcerers myself."

Kadira bought her fruit and they headed for the bazaar. An old feeling crept into her head and she smiled. This was good. This was very good.

The vigorous market crowd thinned as Kadira and Omari neared the Fezzan market section. The folk making their way down the street with them were not wives seeking food for the day's meal or children hunting toys and trinkets. These were folks seeking more ominous and powerful items. Kadira frowned as she walked between stalls of talismans, potions, powders and other charmed items. Her visit was a necessary evil for someone who traveled the road as she had. A skilled sword and intelligence were the foundation of any mercenary, but there were some challenges beyond the physical and one had to be prepared. Fezzan charms were some of the best available at a decent price, rivaled only by those of Menu-Kash, but paled in comparison to the items of Kamit. But Kashite items were tainted with the evil of the Cleave and Kamitic talisman were virtually impossible to find and expensive to obtain. Fezzan origins were obscure, but Kadira didn't dwell on it too long. She used what worked and so far her Fezzan talisman had not failed her.

Omari looked from stall to stall, his face crinkled as if walking through a pig sty.

"I remember why I haven't been to a Fez market. These places reek with dread."

"Don't be so superstitious," Kadira said. "I remember saving you a few times with a few of these dreadful concoctions."

"And I've never forgiven you for it," Omari retorted.

"I'll remember that," she said.

Kadira finally found what she was looking for, the Fezzan armory. Unlike the wooden stalls, the armory inhabited a stone structure with an arched entrance. A sturdy metal studded wooden door guarded the entrance. Two Baatian constables stood at either side of the door, their swords cradled in their arms. They looked at Kadira and Omari suspiciously as they approached. Kadira reached for the door when one of the constables extended his hand.

"I am advised by the denfari of Sati-Baa to warn all those who choose to enter this armory that the laws of our city do not extend beyond this door. Once inside this armory, you are subject to the customs of Fez. We have no jurisdiction beyond this point."

"I understand," Kadira answered. She walked past the constables then knocked on the door. She looked back; Omari remained beyond the constables.

"Are you coming?" she asked.

"I don't need any weapons," Omari answered.

"That's fine. You can wait for me here, coward," she said with a sweet smile.

Omari growled. "I hate you!" He joined her at the door.

The armory door opened to a damp, cavernous dimly lit room. Kadira strode inside, ignoring the long wooden tables stacked with hundreds of knives, swords, shields and various other implements of death. The Fezzani were no different than any other merchants, displaying their cheaper creations to distract an unsuspecting shopper. The real jewels were behind the thick wooden counter which slowly came into view as she walked closer. As she neared, a door opened behind the counter. She was temporarily blinded by a bright light escaping from the door. She shielded her eyes; when they cleared, a bearded man wearing a red tasseled conical hat stood behind the counter, his predatory smile bordered by a voluminous mustache and narrow beard.

"Welcome, sister," he crooned in perfect Trade Speak. "How can I serve you?"

Kadira leaned on the smooth counter top. "I'm here for a sword."

The man swept his arm before him. "As you can see, we have many weapons of the finest Fezzan craftsmanship."

"I'm not interested in that junk on the table," Kadira said. "I'm interested in what you have behind this counter.

The Fezzani grinned. "I see you have dealt with us before."

It was Kadira's turn to smile. "I have."

The man nodded. "Then I will not waste either of our time."

The man reached under the counter. The sword he revealed rested in a silver scabbard, its handle decorated with creamy ivory and jewels. Kadira grasped the hilt, drawing the sword out partially. She frowned.

"Pretty, but useless," she said. "Stop playing with me, Fezzani. I came here for a real sword."

The Fezzani's eyes narrowed. He reached under the counter again. This time, he walked around the counter, approaching Kadira with an object wrapped in a thick woolen blanket.

"I see you are one not to be fooled," he said. He removed the blanket, revealing a sword encased in a simple leather scabbard. He drew the sword and Kadira smiled. The sturdy steel blade emitted the slight blue glow of Fezzani nyama. Omari joined her, his arms full of weapons from the tables.

"This place is a gold mine! I found...ooh, what's that?"

"That is what I came for," Kadira replied. Kadira turned her attention back to the Fezzani.

"How long will it retain its nyama?"

"It depends on its use." The Fezzani lifted the blade, running his calloused hands along the flat. "Years if used only against normal blades, less if matched against a similar weapon."

"How much?"

The Fezzani's face grew cold. "A sword of this type must not be just purchased. It must be earned."

He threw the scabbard aside and attacked. Kadira dodged to the left, the blade barely missing her scalp. Omari dropped his armful of weapons and rolled into the darkness. She had her sword out and ready by the time the Fezzani took a second swipe at her, but she still dodged. Her sword was not charmed yet; if it clashed with the Fezzani blade, it would shatter. She reached in her bag, snatching out a small vial. Sidestepping a quick thrust, she flipped the cork from the vial, and then spilled the liquid in her hand. The Fezzani saw her move and pressed his attack, but Kadira's dexterity thwarted him. She managed to coat her blade just as her luck ran out. The blades met with sound of metal and the flash of magic. Kadira kicked the Fezzani in the stomach and he stumbled back. To touch a Fezzani with the sole of a shoe was the ultimate insult; the weapon master spat in anger.

"Aziz!" he shouted.

The door behind the counter swung open. Another Fezzani leaped from the blinding light, a battle ax in one hand, a shield in the other.

"This bitch has insulted me!" the Fezzani shouted. "We shall pay her with death!"

Aziz lifted his ax. A sudden booming sound echoed through the room, accompanied by a flash of light from behind Kadira. Aziz jerked up and backwards as if someone pulled him away with a rope then crashed into the wall behind the counter.

Kadira dared to look back. Omari stood with a smirk, a smoking piece of metal in his hand pointed toward where Aziz had been.

"Hand cannon," he said.

She jerked her head back to the Fezzani. He looked where Aziz had been, his eyes wide. Kadira rushed forward, knocking his sword free. She swept his feet and he crashed to the floor. The impact jarred him from his trance. When he looked up, Kadira's sword was at his throat.

Kadira took a pouch of cowries from her waist belt and tossed it beside him.

"I'll take it." She kept her sword on his throat as she picked up the Fezzani's sword and scabbard. She backed away, searching for Omari at the same time.

"Omari, where are you?"

"Here!" she heard him say. He peeked from behind the counter then emerged with Aziz's ax.

"This is a damn fine weapon," he said.

Kadira rolled her eyes. She suddenly remembered why she left him years ago. He was a beautiful man and a talented lover, but he was a scavenger and a rogue. She hated that about him.

"You have a new toy, now let's get out of here," she said.

They walked backwards until they exited the Armory. The Baatian guards greeted them with curious looks.

"What happened in there?" one of them asked.

"Nothing," Kadira answered. "I bought a sword."

"And I won an ax," Omari said, grinning.

Kadira and Omari strolled away from the armory, ignoring the glares of the Fezzani merchants. Kadira gave her new sword a final inspection, and then slid it back into its sheath while Omari spun his new ax, playing with the weapon like a new toy.

"Thank you," Kadira said.

Omari shrugged as he twirled the ax. "It was nothing. You've saved my life often enough. It's about time I returned the favor.

Kadira laughed. "You didn't save my life. I would have eventually beaten them both. You just shortened it."

She looked at his waist belt at the metal tube he called a hand cannon. "Where'd you get that thing?"

"Kiswala," Omari replied. "The Mikijen are in love with them. They have bigger ones installed their dhows. To be honest, I'm surprised I hit that Fezzani. Hand cannons are very inaccurate. A crossbow is much more reliable."

"So why do you carry it?"

Omari unleashed one of his signature mischievous

smiles. "It makes a grand impression. I've gotten out of quite a few tight spots because of the noise and smoke."

He reached out and grasped her wrist. "Come with me. I did you a favor, now you can do one for me."

Kadira snatched her arm away. "Your lucky shot isn't worth that much!"

Omari laughed. "I don't mean that! Unless you're thinking..."

"No," Kadira snapped.

Omari frowned briefly, and then his smile returned. "Since you're here and decided to go with us, we might as well get it settled now. I'll take you to the Kashite."

"Makes sense," she agreed. "Lead the way."

Every nation of Ki Khanga possessed a district within Sati Baa with the exception of Wadantu. The Baatians controlled the city center and the docks, with the other nation compounds arranged in order of most to least important to the merchant city. Those closest were considered valuable allies. The district the furthest away from the Baatian center was that of Kash. If the Baatians had their way, there would be no Kash district, but the mysterious warrior priests were not ones to offend. Their intrigues had ruined Aux and kept Haiset under constant armed vigilance. A request by Kash was rarely denied. Only Kiswala and Kamit seemed immune to their demands; Kiswala because of a suspected alliance; Kamit because they feared no one.

It was a long trek. The two stopped briefly at a small market to eat and rest, Omari reveling Kadira with stories of his journeys since they parted ways. His words stoked the fires of freedom inside her even more; by the time they reached the Kashite district, she was eager to be on her way.

The Kashite wall was a formidable thing, a structure of large granite blocks punctured by a towering metal gate festooned with gold and jewels. Eight heavily armed guards stood on either side of gate, two spearmen on each side accompanied by two man chariots. The guards edged closer to the gate as they approached. Omari stuck his hand into his pouch, and then rustled around for a moment. He eventually extracted a flat golden tablet inscribed with the symbols the Kashites used for words. The men cleared the way and they entered the district.

Kadira was immediately swept with a sense of dread. She'd only traveled to Kash once, and one time was enough. The episode was one that she was not proud of and she'd tried her best to scour it from her memory. Walking down the pale brick streets between the stone pyramid-like buildings brought the memory back in full details. She was regretting her decision. She was about to turn away when Omari stopped before a building shaped like a stylized jackal. He showed his tablet to the guards and they waved them inside. Hieroglyphs covered every part of the wall. A man sat in the center of the room in a high back chair before a wicker table, dressed in a simple white robe that bared one shoulder then fell to his bare feet. A snug white cap covered his bald head as he read a papyrus scroll.

"Omari," he said without looking up. "To what do I owe this visit?"

Omari bowed. "I have another person for our expedition, Sebe."

Sebe looked up. "Ah, I see. She cannot go."

"Is there a problem?" Kadira asked.

"Yes. You will be a distraction."

Kadira boiled. The Kashites were known for their strict codes, one which frowned upon women warriors.

"This not Kash," she replied.

Sebe lowered his scroll and looked directly at her. Kadira suddenly felt vulnerable.

"You are right...Kadira," he said to her surprise. "This is not Kash, and you are not just a woman. I have no doubt that you are more than capable of protecting yourself. I also have no doubt that some among our team will make you prove your skills. I do not wish to have to replace men unnecessarily."

"I will speak for her," Omari said. "I will tell the others I am her companion."

Kadira jerked her head toward Omari. "No, you will not!"

"It is a good idea," Sebe agreed. "Omari is well respected and the others like him. If he claims you, they will not challenge his claim."

"I won't hear of it," Kadira shouted. "I'm not his. I'm married!"

"Then, stay home with your husband and child," Sebe said. "If you wish to go on this expedition, you will accept the terms as given."

Kadira fumed, but the prospect of the journey and the pay overruled the insult.

"So be it," she finally said. "But this arrangement is in word only, not action, Omari."

"I could care less," Sebe said. "We leave in three days at sunrise. Meet us beyond the south gate. Do not be late."

Kadira stormed out of the jackal house, Omari chasing close behind.

"That went well," he said.

"No, it didn't!" Kadira snapped. "I should have cut that bastard's throat!"

"I don't think you would have gotten that close," Omari said. "He's a Kashite priest, you know."

"I would have gotten close with this." She snatched out her Fezzani sword. The blade felt heavier than she remembered, and the blue glow was gone.

"What in...That bastard drained my sword!"

Omari slid beside her and placed his arm around her shoulder.

"Okay, it's been a bad day. How about we go to the nearest tavern and drink the rest of the day away?"

Kadira shoved his arm away. "I'm going home."

Omari nodded. "That's probably a good idea, too."

"Goodbye, Omari," she said.

"That sounds so final. You are still coming with us, aren't you?"

Kadira didn't answer.

It was nearly dark when she arrived home. Light emerged from the windows of her house; a faint glow peeked from the cooling embers in the forgery. When she entered, Nguvu sat at the table, fussing with and object she couldn't clearly see.

"Did you get your Fezzani sword?" he asked without turning around.

"I did, for what good it will do."

Nguvu turned his head. "What's wrong with it?"

Kadira pulled a chair from the table and plopped down. "Not only did I have to fight for the thing, the damn Kashite priest drained its charm."

Nguvu's eyebrows rose. "Kashite priest?"

"His name is Sebe. He's the leader of the expedition. Omari took me to see him today to confirm my place." She decided not to tell him about the arrangements.

"So you were with Omari?"

Kadira's stomach churned with nerves. "I ran into him on the way to the Fezzan market."

She studied Nguvu's face, looking for some sort of disapproval. She found none.

"Well, since your Fezzani sword is broken, maybe you can take a look at mine."

Nguvu turned around completely, holding a beautifully wrought leather scabbard. Kadira stood as she grasped the scabbard and pulled the saber free. It felt perfectly balanced, the hilt fitting her hand naturally. The blade shimmered like a mirror.

"This is beautiful!" she exclaimed.

Nguvu smirked. "Thank you."

Kadira cut a few strokes in the air. "You made this for me?"

Nguvu nodded.

She slid the sword back into its scabbard and placed it on the table. She then straddled Nguvu and kissed him deeply.

"Ask me to stay and I will," she whispered.

"That's your decision," he said. "I won't deny you what makes you happy."

"You make me happy," she purred.

"You love the road. Go. I will be here when you return."

Kadira looked into his eyes. "What if I don't come back?"

"Then I will come find you," Nguvu answered.

Kadira was about to place a kiss on Nguvu's lips when her daughter wailed for attention. She went to the cradle, lifting her into her arms and feeding her. As she took her fill, Kadira looked at her closed eyes and her beautiful face. How could she leave this lovely child? She was a mother with responsibilities far beyond that of a wandering merchant. What treasure could be worth more than the one she suckled in her arms? Her life was hard, like Nguvu; she had no recollection of her mother or father, and she did not know what a mother was supposed to do. But she knew she loved her daughter more than anyone or anything, even Nguvu.

"I'm not going," she said. "I can't"

Nguvu stood. "Don't decide tonight. It has been a long day. You may feel different in the morning."

Kadira stayed with her daughter most of the night, playing with her bright eyed child until daybreak. She went immediately to bed, falling into a pleasant dreamless sleep. For the next three days she repeated the sequence, making love Nguvu, feeding and caring for Olea. On the third day, she awoke, her mind swirling with confusion.

"Go," Nguvu said.

"I..."

Nguvu sat up in their bed. "If you don't go, you will always wish you had."

Kadira faced him. "Why are you so eager to be rid of me?"

"I'm not," Nguvu said. "I want you to get this out of your system once and for all. I need you here totally."

Kadira took a deep breath. "Are you sure you are okay

with this?"

Nguvu shook his head. "No. But you must do this."

Kadira went to the water barrel and washed. She woke Olea then fed her. Once she was done, she dressed, slowly donning her armor and weapons. When she was done, she searched for Nguvu.

"I'm out here," he said, as if reading her thoughts.

She stepped outside; Nguvu held the reins of a magnificent red stallion.

"The stable master owed me a favor," he said. An expensive saddle rested on the horse's back and a quiver of throwing spears rested on its flank.

Kadira stood on her toes and kissed him.

"I'll miss you both," she whispered.

"Come back soon or I'll come to get you," Nguvu replied.

"I will."

She kissed him one last time then mounted her horse.

"Wait for me," she said.

"I will," Nguvu replied.

Kadira couldn't bear to look at him any longer. She reined the stallion about and galloped away toward the city walls.


Kadira knew she was late, but did not spur her mount. She took her time passing through Sati-Baa's busy streets, stopping at each market to purchase last-minute provisions. A part of her hoped she would be too late, and then she could return home with an excuse that would satisfy her husband and her conscience. As she passed through the eastern gate, she took one last look backward. She knew herself; once she appeared at the Kashite camp there would be no turning back. She was a woman of her word. She would commit to the expedition until it returned.

They were waiting where the Kashite priest said they would be, a gathering of camels, horses, ox drawn carts and men. As she neared, she recognized the clothing of almost all the northern countries; the bare chested kilt wearers of Kash, the blue quilted armor and conical helmets of Haiset, the chain mail wearing bowmen of Aux and even the nearly naked frog hunters of the Sati-Baa marshes. Standing out among all of them was Omari. He wore a red robe that challenged the sun in its brilliance, his head capped with a feathered monstrosity that made him resemble a harlot. Yet he was as handsome as a god, which made her smile despite herself.

He kicked his mount and galloped to her.

"I thought you weren't coming! I'm so happy to see you."

"I'm here," Kadira said. "What the hell do you have on?"

Omari lifted his robe. "Oh this? It's a long story. The woman who wore it before I removed it wished for me to keep it. It's a memento of our night together."

"And you're supposed to be my companion, showing up to camp in another woman's clothes?"

Kadira slapped him hard.

"What as that for?" Omari rubbed his jaw.

"That was for show," she said, smiling. "Now they'll believe I'm your woman."

When they reached camp, the men were smiling, whispering and snickering. Sebe was not amused.

"You are barely here and have already stirred trouble. This will reflect on you, Omari"

Omari nodded. "I have things under control."

Sebe's frowned deepened. "I don't believe you, but we are in Ba's hands."

The Kashite waved his whisk. "We must leave. Time is of the essence and we are behind schedule."

Shrill horns blared and the camels replied. The trained beast rose in unison and fell in step behind the lead camel. The mercenaries gathered around Omari and Kadira, a few of the men winking at her. She marked their faces in her mind so she would know who she would have to make an example of.

"Okay warriors," Omari shouted. "Time to go on a stroll!"

The men laughed and fell in behind them.

Kadira took one last look Sati-Baa. She was actually doing it. She was leaving.

The first days of the journey were painfully uneventful. Kadira assumed they would take a dhow to the southern end of the Lake Sati then cross overland to Wadantu. Instead, they took the land route, traveling east from the city to the bridge at the Kash River. The route would add weeks to the journey, something that Kadira didn't anticipate. She confronted Omari as soon as she realized the direction.

"You should have asked," he answered nonchalantly. "No one travels to the marshland during this time of year. You've lived in Sati-Baa long enough to know that."

"Apparently, I haven't," she retorted. "Enlighten me."

"It's bata season," he said.

"Bata season? What does that mean?"

"I see you spent too much time under that husband of yours," Omari said. He instinctively ducked the punch meant for his face.

"Keep your insults. What in the Cleave is a Bata?"

"You mean you never noticed those enormous Bata legs hanging in the market?"

"Of course, I have. So what?"

Omari smiled. "I think it would better if you heard it from the source."

Omari cupped his hands over his mouth. "Kunta, Bangiri!"

The frog hunters ambled over to them. Even miles away from their marshland homes, they carried the stench of marsh and fish on their bodies.

"What do you want, pretty man?" Kunta said. The frog hunter was a foot shorter that Omari but twice as wide, all of it hard thick muscle.

"My woman," he winked at Kadira, "wishes to know

why we won't travel through the marshlands."

Kunta flashed a yellow grin at Kadira. "I wondered that, too, pretty woman. The Kashite claims to be a powerful priest, but he trusts no other."

"You haven't answered his question," Bangiri cut in. "The Bata are hungry this time of year, pretty woman. They will eat anything they can fit in their mouths. Anything."

Kadira thought back to the size of the legs in the market and she grimaced.

Kunta smiled. "Now you understand. Bangiri and I could take a few, but we would lose some of you. We have only four hands."

Omari grinned. "Now you know."

The two frog hunters lingered, their eyes on Kadira. Omari approached them.

"Is there something else?" he asked.

"Yes," Kunta answered. "We were wondering if you were going to share..."

"NO!" Kadira answered. "Don't make me show you what I'm capable of, frog eater."

Kunta grinned. "I was hoping you would."

Kadira's foot smacked Kunta's mouth. Teeth flew into the air as he collapsed onto his back unconscious. Bangiri hustled to his friend's side.

"Make sure you tell him what happened when he comes to," she said. "Tell him it will happen again if he comes near me."

"Yes...Kadira. I will tell him." Bangiri answered.

She stalked away, Omari close behind.

"You're not making many friends," he said.

"I'm not here to make friends. I'm here to make money."

"It would go easier if you didn't try to kill anyone who speaks to you the wrong way. Let me handle it."

"Like you handled that?"

Omari smiled. "I'll do better the next time."

"Please do," Kadira warned.

She went back into the tent and began cleaning her weapons. She would give this expedition one more day. If things didn't get any better, she was heading home. For good.

The next morning they crossed the Joliba River into Kenja. The Haisti lead them for they were very familiar with the country. The peaceful villages that inhabited the savanna grasslands were frequent victims of Haisti slave raids. Kadira and Omari rode close to the center of the group, close to the Kashites. She smirked at the priest and his entourage, the group obviously not experienced with the rigors of the open road. They resembled more a procession that an expedition with their gaudy headdresses, ceremonial horns and drums and dozens of servants carrying various containers and chests filled with all types of talisman and other powerful items. A good sorcerer would have whittled her list down to a few effective items then relied on the goodness of other mages of the destination for whatever extra needs. But then again, they were travelling to Wadantu, a place as mysterious as the Cleave, but for different reason. The Cleave was a result of the Creator's anger toward buKhangans, whereas Wadantu was the result of His Wife's love and sympathy. Both were forbidden; what the Kashite priest planned to do could have bad results for an opposite reason.

A fog rose before them as they ventured further into Kenja, a thick moist cloud that eventually enveloped them and clung to their garments. The sudden change in conditions unnerved Kadira, but the others seemed not to notice.

"This is strange," she commented.

"The fog. It's appeared suddenly."

Omari shrugged. "It's almost rainy season."

"Yes, but..."

Cries rose from up ahead. Kadira spurred her horse forward, galloping toward the source with Omari close behind. When they reached the front of the caravan, a wall of fog greeted them. The Haisti were dead to a man, each impaled by an arrow to the throat. The others looked about fearfully, shields raised, swords drawn and lances held ready. The Kashites arrived soon afterwards. Sebe arrived in his elaborate chariot flanked by Auxite horsemen, their compound bows loaded. His face was grim.

"What is going on here?" he fumed. "Are bandits roaming Kenja now?"

The fog faded quickly after Sebe's words. At first, Kadira thought the sorcerer willed it away, but his expression was as perplexed as hers. The mist gave way to a ring of warrior surrounding them, armed men garbed in a variety of clothing and brandishing a myriad of weapons from swords to throwing irons. They were obviously a militia, a fact that made them no less dangerous despite their irregular appearance.

The men parted and a woman emerged from their ranks. She wore a grey pange about her hips, her upper body bare with the exception of a swath of cloth covering her breasts. Her head was bare of hair; she walked calmly to them carrying a massive bow, the arrows bouncing inside her hip quiver. She scanned their party, but her eyes lingered on Kadira.

"Dogon witch!" Sebe shouted. He punched his hand at her and the Auxites fired their arrows. The woman waved her bow, knocking the arrows aside. Just as quickly she loaded her bow with two arrows and fired. The Auxites jerked then fell from their mounts, their necks skewered by her arrows. Kadira was very impressed.

"That's the woman I told you about," Omari whispered.

"What woman?" Kadira replied.

"The woman I said was the only person who could match you with a bow. Nubia."

Sebe opened his mouth then his eyes went wide. He clutched at his throat as he struggled to breathe. Kadira looked at Nubia. The woman's right hand was extended, her fingers gripped tight.

"Apparently the bow is not the only thing she is good at," she said.

Nubia halted before them.

"Your mouth will get you killed sooner than later, Kashite," she said. She looked at Kadira.

"You will come with me and explain why you have trespassed. The others will stay here."

Kadira's stomach churned. "Nana, I am just a hired sword. I have no idea..."

"You ride with this group with no idea of its purpose?"

Kadira lowered her eyes. "No."

Nubia smirked. "Then you will come with me or you will all die now."

"Go with her already!" Omari urged.

Kadira nodded. Nubia turned her back then sauntered away. Sebe let out a gasp; apparently he could breathe again. Though he glared at Nubia, he made no other gestures.

"Go on, then," Sebe said to Kadira. "I hope you are a better diplomat than you are a companion."

Kadira followed Nubia into the rising wall of mist, hoping that she would live out the day.

The warrior woman stopped in her tracks, grasped her head and swayed. The line broke as the men rushed to her, but Kadira reached her first. She eased the woman to the grass. Nubia shared a thankful smile.

"The Kashite was more powerful than I expected. I thought I was going to collapse before him."

Kadira took her water gourd from her waist then handed it Nubia.

"Kashites are reputed to be powerful sorcerers. Apparently not as powerful as the Dogon."

Nubia sipped her water, and then wiped her mouth. "Their nyama comes from a tainted source. It will be their doom."

Nubia stood before her warriors reached her. One of them, a tall broad man with a natural scowl approached them, his eyes on Kadira.

"You should not take water from her," he said. "It may

be poisoned."

"Your warning is too late, Rabana," Nubia chided. "But this woman is good. It is why I chose her."

Rabana shared a reluctant smile with Kadira. "What is your name?"

"Kadira."

"Come with us, Kadira," he said. "We go to the village."

The village occupied a shallow valley just beyond a cluster of low hills. A deep moat filled with thorn bushes surrounded the gathering of conical huts capped with pointed thatch roofs. Warriors patrolling the perimeter rushed forward with relieved looks on their faces. Kadira walked beside Nubia, her head filled with a thousand questions.

"You may ask me what you wish," Nubia said.

"Why did you kill the Haisti?"

"They were leading you to this village," Nubia answered. We tracked you from the moment you entered Kenja. We would have let you be if you avoided our villages."

"They could have just wanted to replenish supplies," Kadira argued.

Nubia stopped, her eyes suddenly hard. "The Haisti never come to trade. They come to take. They knew the danger. Your 'companions' probably felt confident with a Kashite priest in their midst. They were wrong."

She had angered Nubia so she decided to hold her questions. She followed the baKenja into the village and to a small hut in the center. The men dispersed to their homes; Nubia went inside the tent then returned with two mats. The women sat before each other.

"Your reason on this journey is different from the others, despite what you tell yourself," Nubia said. "You will find what you seek, but it is not what you expect."

She handed Kadira a scroll. "This map will lead you through Kenja without encountering any villages. There are clearings designated for trade. If you are in need of provisions send a person and someone will come."

Kadira took the scroll. Nubia reached into a pouch on her side and extracted a crudely cut amber piece threaded on a simple leather strip.

"Wear this," she said. "It will help you when you enter Wadantu."

Kadira took the necklace and immediately put it on.

"How do you know all this?" Kadira asked.

"This is my home," Nubia replied. "There are no secrets to me here. Now go. Your companions wait."

Kadira bowed to Nubia then turned to leave.

"One more thing," Nubia called out. Kadira turned to receive her words.

"Trust no one," Nubia said. Her eyes narrowed. "No one."

When Kadira reached the village edge a wagon with provisions waited, she managed to harness her horse and pull the wagon to the expedition. The fog wall persisted, but immediately faded as she approached. Omari was the first person she saw.

"Kadira!" He galloped toward her, a brilliant smile on his face.

"I assume the baKenja will let us live?"

"Only if we do as we are told," Kadira replied.

She continued riding to the Kashites, ignoring the stare of the others. Her status seemed to have risen among them because of Nubia's summons. Maybe they would stop leering at her and focus on the journey. She hoped so.

Sebe and the others looked in her direction as she approached. The Kashite sat in his throne-like chair flanked by fanning acolytes and the Kashite warriors. Kadira dismounted and approached. The guards did nothing to impede her.

Sebe looked up at her, his arrogant stare replaced with the hint of worry. This unnerved her. He was the leader of the expedition. If he was losing his confidence they might as well go back to Sati-Baa.

"What did the baKenja witch have to say?" he asked. The bitterness was gone from his voice.

"She knows where we are headed," Kadira replied. "Her quarrel was with the Haisti, not us. She gave me this map. She said it will lead us to Wadantu and keep us away from baKenja villages."

She took out the map. Sebe looked at it and waved his hand.

"She gave it to you which means she trusts you. You will lead us through Kenja."

Kadira laughed. "I'm not a pathfinder."

The hard look returned briefly in Sebe's eyes. "You are now. Take your place at the lead of this expedition or we all go home."

Kadira bit back her words then turned to walk away.

"Wait," Sebe called out.

Kadira spun about then folded her arms across her chest. "What?"

"What is that you wear?" he asked.

"What are you talking about?"

"The necklace."

Kadira had forgotten the amber necklace. "It's a piece of amber given to me by Nubia."
Sebe's eyes widened then he smiled.

"You may go."

Kadira rode back to the provision wagon. The men were helping themselves to the food, Omari among them.

"Omari!" she called out. Omari looked up, his mouth smeared with honey.

"You pick the worst times for conversation," he snarled.

"Sebe wants me to lead the expedition through Kenja and you're going to help."

Omari choked. "Me?"

"Yes, you. Now get that food fest organized over there and make sure everyone gets equal share. We leave within the hour."

If Omari was good at anything it was following orders. Provisions were distributed and the expedition set off immediately. They journeyed through the verdant savanna, surrounded by large herds of gazelles, wildebeests and other animals of the grasslands. Elegant giraffes nibbled at acacia tips as zebras flitted about like nervous flocks. It was a beautiful land, more beautiful than any Kadira had seen. She realized why the baKenja had now decided to fight for it and themselves.

They camped at one of the areas designated on the map. Kadira and Omari set up their tent near the camp edge, building a large fire with gathered wood. Kadira leaned back on her hands, rolling her head to loosen the tension in her neck. A pair of warm hands grasped her shoulders and began massaging them.

"Thank you, Omari" she said.

"You're welcome," he replied. "You've had an interesting day."

"No more interesting than any of us."

"The fate of this journey is in your hands."

Kadira didn't reply. She was lost in Omari's hands, savoring his experienced touch.

"We can continue this in the tent," he said.

His words killed the mood.

"Get your hands off me," she hissed.

"I was just..."

"Get your damn hands off me!" she yelled.

Kadira shoved him away and pulled her dagger. "Enough of this farce. I'm taking my own tent."

Omari looked puzzled. "What of our agreement?"

"I'm leading the expedition now. I don't need your cover. Touch me like that again and I'll send you to the Cleave."

Kadira gathered her things and stormed to the Kashites.

"I need a tent," she demanded.

The acolytes smirked then gave her a tent. They sent servants with her to help her set up the monstrosity.

She went inside, spread out her things then sat hard

on her blanket, fighting back her tears. She wasn't mad at Omari; she was mad at herself. A few more minutes of his skilled hands and she would have gone into the tent with him. Nguvu deserved better than that. Olea deserved better from her mother. She had to be stronger. She would be.

When Kadira emerged from her tent the next morning, Omari was waiting for her.

"I'm sorry," he blurted out.

Kadira's embarrassment showed in her smile.

"No Omari, I'm sorry. I overreacted. You were just being yourself and I was letting you."

"So you won't kill me?" he said. The boyish smile returned to his face.

Kadira smiled back. "No, I won't kill you. But you have to respect my situation now, Omari. I'm a married woman. We had our time and now it's done."

Omari fell to his knees, touched his forehead on the ground then sprinkled his head with dirt, the sign of obedience among the Malian people.

"Get up!" Kadira shouted. "You're embarrassing!"

"Yes please, get up," Sebe said.

The Kashite priest stood behind her with his ever present acolytes.

"How far are we from Wadantu?" he asked.

Kadira took Nubia's map from her bag and unrolled it.

"At least two more days, maybe three. The map ends there. There is no route going into Wadantu."

Sebe gave her a sly smile. "Don't worry. We will find our way."

They set out late that day, taking their time breaking camp and enjoying a long, lazy meal. Despite their tardy departure they made good time, arriving at the next map point a few hours early. A shallow river flowed before them and they took advantage of the clear water to fill their gourds. They bathed as well, all except Kadira. She watched them all, comparing each man with the image of Nguvu in her mind.

Some were fit, others not. As always, Omari stood out, his perfectly proportioned body a gift from the creator. But none of them possessed the overpowering physicality of her man waiting for her in Sati-Baa. No one would, for Nguvu was bred to be who he was, one of a few that made up the Mansa's Shield, an elite group of shock warriors. She remembered the first day she saw them, one hundred men forming an ebony line of muscle and steel. They were magnificent.

Omari strolled over to her naked. He never quits, she thought.

"Aren't you going to bathe?" he asked innocently.

"No show for you today," she replied. She reached into her bag, took out a pange, then tossed it to him.

"Cover up your worm. I'm embarrassed for you."

Omari pouted. "You're mean."

He wrapped the cloth around his waist and stomped away.

The next day the road ended. The expedition stared into a wall of green, a thick tangle of trees, shrubs and grass that gave no hint of entry.

"Wadantu," Kadira said.

"How do we go into there?" Omari asked.

He was answered by the arrival of the Kashites.

"This is where I take over," Sebe said.

His acolytes bowed before him, presenting a small gold trimmed box. Sebe leaned close to the box, whispering to the object reverently. It opened on its own and the priest reached into it and extracting a crystal vial, a small grey chip contained inside. Kadira gasped.

"What is it?" Omari asked.

"A piece of the Creator's Ax," she whispered.

Omari shuddered. "How did he obtain such a thing?"

"It's like Nubia said, the source of Kashite power will ruin them."

Sebe stepped toward the forest wall. The crystal vial glowed. Sebe turned slowly side to side until the vial shined brightly. He raised the vial over his head and shouted.

"Open!"

The forest exploded. Trees shattered then fell away; shrubs ripped from the ground and tumbled to the right and left. Kadira and the others fought to control their mounts until the commotion subsided. When the air cleared a wide ragged road into Wadantu lay before them.

Sebe turned to them. "Follow me."

The Kashites resumed their position as leaders of the expedition. They unhitched the horses from the chariot and saddled them. The path Sebe blasted through the thicket was too uneven for the vehicle. Sebe and his acolytes entered Wadantu as their vanguard, followed by the Kashite spearmen and Auxite archers. The mercenaries brought up the rear with Kadira and Omari leading them. Though the Kashites advanced confidently between the ravaged devastation the mercenaries proceeded cautiously, their eyes trained more on the foliage to either side than on the road ahead.

The power of Sebe's charm was more evident as they advanced. The path ran for miles. Kadira had seen much in her days on the road and at war, but never had she seen such destruction.

"I remember a voyage I took beyond Kiswala," Omari began.

"Beyond Kiswala?" Kadira's eye narrowed. "Are you sure you want to tell me this? I know how the Kiswala guard their trade secrets."

"I am the only Mikijen here," he said. "No one will know, unless you tell."

Kadira shook her head.

"Our destination was a city called Tai on the Eastern Sea. There was a war; by the time we reached Tai it was rubble. The Kiswali were angry, of course, so they sent us ashore to see if we could salvage anything of worth. It was the worst destruction I'd ever seen until now."

"The destruction is not what concerns me," Kadira said. "I'm worried about who heard it."

The ragged road finally opened into a wide green field. A

group of steep hills rested on the horizon surrounded by small trees and some type of stone columns Kadira could not make out. It was the first sign of men.

"Eyes and ears open!" Omari shouted. "We may have company."

No sooner did Omari utter those words did the sound of hoofbeats break the eerie silence. Horsemen advanced on them from either side.

"Archers take the flanks!" Omari shouted. "Horsemen stand behind them!"

Kadira instinctively led a group of riders to the right flank while Omari took his riders to the left. She glanced at the Kashite; they took the same position with the exception that they had no cavalry. The spearmen backed the archers, their spears and shield at the ready. Sebe and his acolytes rested between them. They waited patiently until their attackers were in range.

"Fire!" Omari shouted.

Arrows took flight like startled fowl, arching overhead then falling into the ranks. The riders fell in large numbers, but continued to charge.

"Monsters!" someone shouted. "They're monsters!"

Kadira strained her eyes to see what was going on. The archers continued to fire; it was a few moments more before she could see what had unnerved them. These were not horsemen. They were a terrifying amalgam of man and beast; their bodies that of the great grass antelopes, their torsos man-like, their heads crowned with horns. They attacked brandishing shields, assegais, bows and arrows.

"What in the Cleave are they?" Omari shouted.

Kadira's eye narrowed. "I don't know, but they die like men. Riders, prepare to charge!"

The archers let loose one last volley, then ran aside. Before Kadira could kick her horse, it let out a loud grunt and ran toward their attackers. She put the reins between her teeth, took out her bow and loaded. The man-beast threw their spears toward her; to her surprise, her horse dodged them nimbly without breaking stride.

"Nguvu, what kind of horse did you give me?" she said between her teeth.

Her arrows found their marks, bringing down more of the creatures. Soon, she was too close, so she sheathed her bow and took out Nguvu's saber. She could see the faces of the creatures now, their angry eyes meeting her stare. This would be a battle with no quarter.

The man beast nearest to her did an unexpected thing. It leaped into the air, its shield and spear raised. Her mounted did the unexpected as well. It leaped also, carrying her upward. She hugged the horse's neck as it slammed into the man-beast. The man-beast fell first, no match for the horse's bulk. When they came to the ground, Kadira and her horse were atop the man-beast. Before she raised her sword, the horse began pounding the beast with its hooves.

"By the Creator," she exclaimed. At that moment, she realized what she rode and a wide grin came to her face. Nguvu had given her a great gift. He'd bought her a Malian warhorse.

Her glee was short-lived. The man-beast quickly surrounded them and attacked. A second surprise was gripped in the palm of her hand. Nguvu's sword cut spear and man equally, its sharp edge melting wood and flesh. Her warhorse fought as well, kicking, butting and biting in precision with her movements. In moments, the crowd about them cleared as those beasts still alive sought easier prey. Kadira took a moment to assess the battle; they were hard-pressed on either side with more beasts coming from the distance. She looked ahead to the hills. If they could make it to them, they would at least have the higher ground.

"To the hills," she shouted "The hills!"

She worked her way between the beasts and her cohorts, freeing those on foot to run. The other riders picked her plan and joined her. The Kashites were already fleeing for the high ground, leaving the Auxites to their fate. Soon, they were all running. The man-beasts followed; although they seemed to slow the closer they came to the hills. Omari worked his way to her. His arm was bloody, but he seemed otherwise okay.

"They're leaving," he shouted.

"That worries me," Kadira replied. "They may be driving us into another trap."

Omari laughed. "The only thing in front of us is those hills..."

The ground beneath them lurched. Kadira and her horse fell forward; luckily she and the beast were unhurt. Others were not so fortunate. She staggered to her feet.

"What is happening?" she said.

The ground shook again. Kadira looked ahead to the Kashites. They were no longer heading toward the hills; they were heading to the west toward another stand of woods. The ground shook again and Kadira staggered back. The hills were moving.

The ground trembled as she mounted her horse. Omari struggled to keep his still so she rode up him and lifted him on.

"Ride for the woods as fast as you can!" she shouted.

A deafening bellow emerged from before them. The hill was no longer a hill. It was a beast unlike any either of them had ever seen. It seemed made of earth and stone with a large single tusk protruding from its face. It looked at them and bellowed again. Nothing else needed to be said. They rode for their lives.

Kadira clung tight to her horse's neck as it bounded across the undulating ground to the woods ahead. The hill beast ran parallel to them each footfall causing the ground to ripple like water disturbed by a giant stone. She marveled at how the steed kept upright despite the vicious jarring. Others were not as lucky. Her cohorts tumbled from their horses, some killed by the fall, others when hundreds of pounds of horseflesh collapsed upon them. She searched for Omari and found him riding ahead of her. His mount stumbled about, fighting to keep its footing on the quaking earth. Kadira looked back from where they came. The antelope-men were there, following the fleeing interlopers at a safe distance. A few mercenaries fled in their direction, obviously more willing to take their chances against the horde than the stampeding monstrosity. They were met with spears and death.

Omari's horse faltered. Omari leaped clear, then struck the ground hard. The horse fell awkwardly, thrashing about for a moment before lying still. Kadira guided her horse toward Omari.

"Omari!" she shouted.

He stumbled around just in time to reach out. Kadira grabbed him, then lifted him onto the back of the horse. The beast grunted in protest but continued running, the extra weight having no effect on its speed.

"Thank you," Omari gasped. "What kind of horse is this?"

"A damn good one," Kadira said. Her attention was elsewhere. The hill beast was angling toward them. There was no way they could outrun it, if only because of its ground chewing strides. It was then she noticed that the Kashites were gone.

"Damn them to the Cleave," she shouted. "The Kashites have escaped!"

"No, they haven't," Omari replied. "Look!"

He pointed toward the beast. The Kashites stood in its path, the acolytes standing on either side of Sebe. The priest held the piece of the Creator's ax over his head.

"It won't work," she whispered.

She watched a few more minutes, then the beast shuddered. It uttered a deafening roar as it continued to advance. A moment later, it shuddered again. This time, it stopped then rose onto it hind legs. It roared again; Kadira thought she heard a hint of pain it its protest.

It shuddered again. This time it froze, locked on two legs. Sebe and his acolytes mounted their horses. This time, she heard Sebe's voice.

"Die!" he shouted.

A part of the beast head cracked then broke off. It tumbled down its body and crashed into the ground. The Kashites galloped away as the beast broke apart, its body becoming an avalanche of stone and blood. The morbid flow ceased far from them. When the Kashites reached Kadira and Omari, their faces were graced with confident smiles.

"The challenge has passed," Sebe said. "We can proceed to our destination."

"What about the..."

Sebe gestured over her shoulder. Kadira turned to see that the antelope men were gone. Most of her cohorts were either dead or severely wounded. Only she and Omari seemed capable of continuing on.

"Their share will be split among the living," Sebe said. "Come, we must reach our destination before nightfall."

The Kashites rode toward the rubble that was once a beast. Kadira hesitated.

"What are waiting on?" Omari said. "Let's follow them."

"I don't know, Omari," Kadira said.

Omari jumped from her horse and secured another from one of their hapless comrades.

"I've been through too much shit to go home empty-handed," he snarled.

He rode after the Kashites. Kadira watched him for a minute before rubbing her horse's neck.

"So what do you think warhorse? Should we follow?"

The horse grunted and followed Omari.

"Looks like this horse is braver than me." Kadira shrugged and let the horse have its way.

Kadira and Omari followed the Kashites into the new forests. She expected Sebe to clear a path for them as he did before but he made no move to do so. Luckily, this forest was not as dense as the other, with plenty of room to maneuver horse and man. She surmised that Sebe had spent considerable power bringing down the hill beast and a closer inspection of his face confirmed her suspicions. He looked as if he had aged decades within a few minutes. How long that would last was uncertain. The pieces of the Creator's Ax contained immense power. It was possible it could rejuvenate Sebe, but Kadira was ignorant of such things. She depended on her skill and what little nyama she could afford. Everything else was in the Creator's hands.

"We're going to be rich beyond our wildest dreams!" Omari whispered. "We started with one hundred, now there is only you and I. I can buy an island. Cleave, I can buy Kiswala!"

"How do you know Sebe will be true to his word," Kadira asked.

"He has been so far," Omari replied. "If you have doubts, then why are you still here?"

"Because I am bound to see this through," Kadira said. "And I don't think I can fight my way through those antelope men alone, despite this wonderful horse."

"Any animal that fight like that deserves a name," Omari commented.

Kadira patted the horse on its neck and it snorted in response.

"If we survive this, I'll name him, then give Nguvu a long night of my appreciation."

"You shouldn't talk that way around me," Omari pouted. "It's been a while."

The rest of the day was uneventful. They traveled until night, then made camp along a thin creek. Omari caught a pair of exotic colored fish that tasted as good as they looked and did not make them sick. The Kashites kept to themselves, eating whatever rations they brought then whispering intensely to each other. The acolytes seemed to be in some sort of disagreement with Sebe, leaning toward them with stern faces as they argued in their intelligible tongue. Sebe said little, responding with either a gesture or a word. He finally ended the conversation with a swipe of his hand. The acolytes went to their cots and slept, but Sebe paced between them. He was still pacing when Kadira awoke. He marched directly to her.

"Today we will reach our destination," he said. "You will have to be very diligent. I had hoped to have more protection at this point, but I did not anticipate such a resistance to our intrusion so soon. I hope you and your friend are as skilled as you say you are."

"You should know by now," Kadira replied.

Sebe frowned. "Then I will pray that you find more skills between here and our destination."

They ate a quick meal, then set out once again. At midday, the forest ended abruptly, replaced by a barren expanse. Something rose over the dirt and gravel. She strained her eyes to see.

"It is our destination," Sebe said. "Our journey is almost at an end."

They galloped across the wasteland until they reached the object. It was a temple, a small simple structure consisting of a flat stone on which five thick columns supported a stone conical roof. Kadira could see a pedestal inside. Though the building was sparse, the power it possessed was overwhelming. Kadira felt as if an invisible shield pushed against her as she tried to get closer.

"You two will stay here," Sebe ordered. "Kill anyone who tries to enter."

Kadira and Omari dismounted, and then took out their bows. Sebe and the acolytes continued to the temple.

"So this is it," Omari said. "This is how we get paid."

"I guess so," Kadira replied. "Looks like this will be the easiest part of the journey."

They had barely positioned themselves when Sebe returned. He held an object in hand, the bust of a man's head similar to those she had seen in Oyo, but with one significant difference. Instead of iron, this bust was made of material from the Creator's Ax.

"It's incredible!" Omari said.

"It's impossible," Kadira replied. It was also

foreboding. Such a concentration of the Creator's Ax was killing them as they spoke. That much she knew. It was also a quantity that could make its possessor insanely powerful, and it was in the hands of a Kashite. Suddenly the stacks of gold meant nothing. What use was it to be wealthy in a world that was soon to end? Kadira's shoulders slumped. Nguvu's words were true. This would be her last journey.

Sebe stared into the object, delight in his eyes. The strain of the last confrontation disappeared from his face and he smiled.

"For so long I've sought this, longer than any of you can imagine," he whispered. "The world is now in my hands."

He extended his hand toward his acolytes. They gave him a black cloak and he wrapped the carved head with it. The intense nyama was diminished; Kadira felt the invisible pressure lift. Maybe she would live after all.

"So you have come again," a voice said behind her.

She spun, her sword drawn. Three small men stood before them, each naked with the exception of simple loincloths. The men carried no weapons, only carved staffs.

"Kill them!" Sebe shouted, his voice filled with terror.

Kadira looked at the priest. "These men are not armed."

Sebe glared at her. "They are the most dangerous of all. Kill them!"

Kadira normally followed any order given to her when in a person's employ. It was the reason she harbored memories she'd soon forget. But this command seemed wrong. She looked at Omari for support.

"The Kashites are paying the bill," he said then shrugged his shoulders. He lifted his hand cannon and aimed.

The small man who spoke moved with amazing speed. He knocked Omari's weapon aside, then drove his staff into his chest, the bloody end protruding from his back. He snatched his staff free then attacked Kadira. Kadira desperately blocked his rapid thrusts, but it was obvious his was faster...and stronger. The staff struck her wrist and she dropped her sword; another blow landed across her thighs and she collapsed to her knees. The small man raised his staff; the bloody end aimed at her chest then hesitated. He slammed it on her shoulder and she collapsed to the ground. She clenched her eyes in pain.

"You will not stop me this time!" Sebe shouted.

Kadira tried to rise, but could only roll onto her side. The small men advanced on Sebe and the acolytes, their staffs raised high. Sebe threw the cloak from the carved head.

"I have it now," he snarled. "I'm stronger than you!"

He raised the head high and his acolytes fell to their knees. A triangle of light formed between them and Sebe. A similar shape formed between the small men and a magical confrontation ensued. A thick beam of light joined the two groups, raised a storm of wind and dust around them. Kadira watched in fearful fascination. Sebe trembled and his acolytes glowed; the small men stood still, no signs of any physical movement. Suddenly the acolytes were consumed in a blue white light then disappeared; Sebe fell to his knees, his arms struggling to hold the mystical head.

"You will not take it from me!" he screeched. "It is mine! It is mine!"

The small men advanced on Sebe. The Kashite priest began to glow, his features diminishing with each step. Soon he was a only the form of a man in blue white light, the head still suspended over what was left of him. The small men gestured toward him with their staffs and the essence of Sebe dispersed slowly into the swirling winds. The carved head fell to the ground.

Kadira rolled onto her back. So the Kashites were dead. She turned her head to see Omari lying still on his back, as handsome in death as he was in life. She looked up and the small men stood over her, their faces solemn. She took a moment to remember her family and a slight smile came to her face.

"I'm ready," she said.

The small men smiled. "It is not your time, Dogon."

One of the small men touched her breast with his staff. The pain dissipated and energy filled her limbs. She sat up quickly.

"Why are you here, Dogon," the man who spoke before asked. "We have an agreement."

"I am no Dogon," Kadira replied.

The small men exchanged confused glances.

"But you wear the stone," the small man said.

Kadira touched the amber stone given to her by Nubia.

"It was given to me...by a Dogon."

The small man grinned. "You are under their protection. That is good."

Kadira finally stood. Physically the men stood no taller than an adolescent child, but spiritually they towered over her.

"What you witnessed was not the end," the small man explained. "The one you know as Sebe is an old spirit, a creature of the Cleave. It craves the power it once knew and constantly seeks it. It will return again."

"You did not destroy it?"

The small man shook his head. "That which the Creator made cannot be destroyed, even that created in His anger."

"Who are you?" she asked.

"We are the Caretakers," the man replied.

The small man's companions left his side. They lifted the head and placed it back into the temple.

"If you know this thing will come for the idol, why don't you hide it?" Kadira asked.

"He must find it," the small man answered. "It draws it like a moth to light. If it cannot find it, it will cause havoc among the favored. That cannot be allowed."

The small man stepped toward her, his free hand extended. Kadira took it.

"You must go home," he said. "Your family worries for you."

Kadira smiled. "I'm sure they do."

She glanced at Omari and sighed.

"You favor him?" the small man asked.

"I did once. It's sad to see him this way."

"It was his fate," the small man said. "Your path still remains. Go."

His words were like a command. Kadira gathered her weapons, and then started for her horse. The animal had remained despite the turmoil that just occurred. She wasn't surprised. She mounted it and patted its neck.

"Let's go home," she whispered.

Kadira mount seemed as anxious to be out of Wadantu as she. It galloped across the barren lands of the temple, and then sped through the surrounding forest. Even when they emerged onto the ominous savannah where they fought the antelope men and faced the hill beast it did not slow. Unlike before the grassland was empty, but Kadira kept close vigil as her horse streaked across the expanse. Soon they were back to the dense forest. The gash that Sebe, or whatever it was, created was gone, replaced by a trail just wide enough for horse and rider. Kadira shuddered when she thought of the power of the Caretakers. They had to be connected to the Creator is some way. She decided not to dwell on it. They spared her life, which was more than she could say for everyone else.

"Keep running, warhorse," she whispered. "Don't stop until were out of this strange place."

The horse obeyed her order. It stumbled to a halt only a few strides into Kenja, panting hard. Kadira quickly dismounted then removed her saddle and bridle from the tired beast.

"If you ran off and left me today, it would be deserved," she said. Another surprise greeted her as she stripped the horse, two leather bags and a large gourd. The gourd contained fresh water, which she shared with her horse. The leather bags contained relief and joy. One bag was filled with food; berries, edible leaves and strips of dried meat. It was at least enough to last her a few days. She opened the other bag and a giggle escaped her lips. It was filled with gold dust. It was nowhere near eight stacks, but it was enough to make her journey worth it.

"We got paid after all,' she said to her horse. The horse ignored her, busying itself with consuming the thick green grass surrounding them.

Kadira set up camp and gave way to the fatigue and pain she'd ignored for days. She planned on setting out for Sati-Baa after a day's rest, but stayed at her camp for three days, resting and healing. On the third night, a strange sound woke her. It came from the direction of her food bag. She was about to rise when she heard her horse snort. There was a thud and a shout.

"Damn you, you crazy horse!"

The voice she heard was shocking and familiar. Kadira sprang to her feet and ran to the source of the sound.

"Omari!" she shouted.

Omari lay on his back, her warhorse standing between him and the food bag. He was filthy and he stunk, but he was very much alive. Kadira picked up the food bag and threw it to him.

"You're alive," she said.

"Of course, I am," he spat back. He opened the bag, reached inside and pulled out a handful of food then stuffed it in his mouth. A moan escaped his lips.

"Twigs never tasted so good."

Kadira pushed the horse aside. She sat beside Omari.

"How did you get here?"

"I walked," he said. "Thanks for leaving me, by the way."

"I didn't leave you. You were..."

Omari stopped chewing. "I was what?"

Kadira smiled. "Never mind. What do you remember?"

"I remember trying to shoot at those short men. The next thing I knew, I was lying on my back surrounded by them with that damn head on my chest. It felt like an elephant was sitting on me. Then one of the short men lifted it of me and told me to go."

"I'm happy to see you," she said.

Omari stopped eating and a sly smile came to his face. "Really? We should celebrate."

Kadira would have laughed if she didn't think it would give Omari the wrong impression.

"I'm not that happy to see you."

Omari shrugged, and then continued eating.

"Go easy on that," she said. "It's all I have. I'm going back to sleep."

"Alone?"

She shook her head. "Alone. And don't get any ideas. My horse will stomp you to death."

"I'm sure he will. I think that horse is Nguvu."

Kadira finally laughed. "I think you're right."

The morning came with a clear sky. Kadira and Omari broke camp; traveling together in silence for a while about midday Omari stopped walking and began looking about.

"I think I'll head that way," he said.

Kadira was puzzled. "What are you talking about?"

"I'm not sure, but I think Bashaba is that way."

"Bashaba?"

"It's a Kiswala port."

Kadira finally understood. "So you're not going back to Sati-Baa, then?"

Omari shook his head. "I think I'll rejoin the Mikijen. They're always looking for men and I'm familiar. Besides, a city like Sati-Baa is no fun without money."

Kadira remembered the other bag. She went to her horse then returned with it and the empty food bag.

"Hold this," she said, handing him the food bag. She poured half of the gold dust into the bag. Omari's eyes teared up.

"I could kiss you!"

Kadira drew back. "You better not."

The sight of money seemed to add a bounce to his stride.

"Then I'm off," he announced. "It was good riding with you again, Kadira. Things didn't turn out as expected, but then it never does."

Kadira nodded. "It never does. Good-bye Omari."

Omari bowed. "Good-bye, sweet lady. Tell that husband of yours he made a fine choice. And kick that damn horse for me."

Omari turned away and marched toward the northeast. Kadira watched him for a while, and then resumed her journey home.

The walls of Sati-Baa never looked so good. Kadira rode toward the walls surrounded by a stream of merchants, farmers and others heading to the city for their daily work. The lax guards barely paid her any attention when she passed through the gates. The patience she possessed throughout her journey home suddenly vanished, replaced by an urgent need to see her man and girl.

"Get us home fast," she whispered to her horse. He snorted a reply and trotted through the throng, gathering curses and shouts along the way. By the time they reached their alley, the horse was in full gallop and Kadira's heart pounded against her chest like a celebration drum.

"Nguvu! Olea! I'm home!"

She jumped off the horse and rushed into the house. It was empty. A bolt of fear struck her until she heard the rhythmic hammering. She sped through the house to Nguvu's shop. Her man's broad back was turned to her as he pounded a strip of red hot steel.

"Nguvu!" she squealed.

He turned and laid eyes on her, smiling as if he knew she would be there. She started toward him, but he held up his hand. Nguvu put down his hammer then went to the cradle, lifting Olea into his arms.

"My baby," she whispered.

Then Nguvu surprised her. He set her down on the ground.

"Mama's home," he said.

Olea gave her a look of recognition, clapped and smiled. Then she stood, her bowed legs wavering.

"Olea? Are you.."

Olea half stumbled and half walked into her mother's arms. Kadira could not hold back any longer. She cried like a child. Nguvu came to her and hugged them both.

"Welcome home," he said.

She kissed him full and long.

"Are you satisfied now?" he asked.

"Very much so," Kadira replied. "I'm home for good. There is no treasure greater than the one I hold in my arms this moment."

Nguvu nodded. Together they left the shop and entered their home.

# VENGEANCE

*Rebecca McFarland Kyle*

Throbbing in her temples awakened Obayana of the Fireclaws. Stomach-roiling stench she couldn't identify filled her nostrils. She cautiously opened her eyes, searching for enemies, summoning the fire within her to strike like a viper.

*Goddess curse it, I am still on the sea.* Obayana swallowed back a bitter taste as the ship beneath her heaved with the waves. Every day, she washed the salt from her ebon skin and wished the Goddess of Waters would speed their journey homeward.

*When I finish this onerous duty, I will never set foot upon a sailing vessel!*

This couldn't be the King Abinbola's ship. No Macavarian vessel built for the transporting Royals would have such a splintered punky deck as the broken planks that stuck on her silken robes as she shifted her slender body minutely sussing for damage, then reaching out her senses for more clues before she revealed she was awake. Her eyes accustomed quickly to the dark, she glanced first toward the fresh coppery stench of blood, standing out from the older reek of death and decay.

Eibhlin Starraker lay within arm's reach clad in queenly finery. The hand Obayana touched contained no fire of life. In the darkness, the black spread on her golden Royal robes could only be blood.

*Goddess, I have failed my Father and King Abinbola.*

A guilty part of her breathed with relief. Her pale-skinned nemesis would not be wedding her beloved Prince. But, her failure to protect Eibhlin could well mean war between Macavar and Creed.

Obayana sat up with a startled oath, grasping her head as the pain stabbed her like a sword between her eyes. Not Eibhlin, this was Caislinn, her cousin and maid who'd thought it prudent to don the Princess' finery since pirates were rumored to plunder this part of the seas. Still, where was her future queen?

"Help!" the man's cry brought Obayana unsteadily to her feet. An unfamiliar blonde haired sailor, clad only in a shabby shirt, was coiled up grasping his privates. Next to him, she saw one of her true charges, Eibhlin Starraker, unconscious, clad only in her cousin's plain linen chemise and that covering only the middle part of her body. Someone, probably the sailor, uncovered her breasts and her woman parts.

Obayana gave the sailor a solid kick between his legs, forcing some distance between himself and Eibhlin. He half rolled and scuttled away, clutching his manhood and moaning like a babe.

Fire sprang between her hands and she prepared to aim a lethal dose at the would-be rapist.

"No!" Eibhlin's gasped order stayed her. "This ship would flame like a tinderbox with us in the middle." She pulled up her sleeve, exposing a slim tanned arm and a sheathed knife.

One minute Obayana saw the blade's gleam in the dim starlight from a be-webbed porthole and the movement of Eibhlin's hand. The next, the weapon lodged in the sailor's throat.

Eibhlin rose, pulling the chemise down to cover the pallid flesh of her lower torso and retrieved the knife from the sailor's corpse. She wiped the blade on the cleanest portion of the man's shirt and held it at the ready. She surveyed the ship's cabin they were on, openly dismayed.

"We're on a slaver. The rumors of Creedans pirating Macavarian ships are true," Eibhlin announced, examining large welded rings attached to the wall and sniffing the air. She closed the cabin door, then pulled out her other knife and extended it, handle first. She glanced toward her cousin, stifling a sob. Her voice had only the tiniest bit of unsteadiness as she spoke. "Would you like the second?"

Obayana bridled at the question Eibhlin should know the answer. They'd both trained at Macavar's Sorcerial Academy, though Eibhlin was undisputedly her father's favorite of the two no matter how hard Obayana tried to please him.

"Sorcerers do not carry weapons."

"Even Master Tau would sanction a blade in a situation like this," Eibhlin murmured as she knelt next to Obayana's other charge, glancing between the child-like Royal and the door in case other assailants should appear.

Obayana bit back her reply. Eibhlin was always more privy to her Father's thoughts. Jealousy and anger set the fire in her blood to a near boil, but she knew Eibhlin was right, though her belly ached to admit it. Father prized a sword given to him by Eibhlin's mother, the Queen of Creed.

"Aja," Eibhlin's voice was soft as her pale slender hands, gently chafing Aja's deep molasses colored ones. Smells of earth and trees emanated from Eibhlin: Earth magic and healing.

The tiny princess awakened with a gasp, glancing at her surroundings with wide frightened eyes.

"Shhhhh," Eibhlin whispered, helping the child sit up. "Little Sister, we're all fine."

Obayana turned away from the maternal sight, staying her hand from reaching protectively to cover the spark of life in her belly. Princess Aja should never have been dispatched on this errand. She was still a child and second in line to the throne after Prince Tafari. A guilty part of her knew Aja accompanied her as a diplomat. Unlike her Father, Obayana could not find any love in her heart for Creed. Then again,

Master Tau had more than enough for them both.

She listened as Eibhlin described their situation to Aja, nodding agreement reluctantly. Someone drugged them at dinner and delivered the ship to the slavers.

"A handful of crew is left on this ship," Eibhlin finished. Obayana suspected she'd deployed more Earth witchery to determine that number. "Mother's defensive magic protected me from harm, but I don't know how long that will last."

Obayana caught Aja's wistful glance at Eibhlin. The pair formed an instant bond, dismaying particularly since it was obvious that liking was built upon a mutual dislike of Prince Tafari.

"If I had only known, Little Sister, I would have asked Mother to protect you as well."

"I think she must have," Aja answered. "No one touched me."

Eibhlin moved toward her deceased kinswoman, speaking softly as she began to place Caislinn's body in a more comfortable final repose. Eibhlin waited until she knew Aja was safe before she loosed her own grief. Commendable, but that still did not help with their predicament aboard this ship. Eibhlin spoke gently to a woman who'd never hear her voice.

"How did you dismiss Mother's spells, Cousin?"

"What in the name of Fire are you doing?" Obayana demanded, seeing both princesses tending to the dead when they should be planning on how to get themselves away from whoever held them.

"We're mind-calling for help," Aja explained in her childlike voice.

Once she tuned her ears, Obayana heard their plaintive mind-voices cast out across the sea. She unclenched her hands, fighting back the urge to bang their heads together until the two developed some sense. What in the name of Fire did they expect to accomplish by this? They should be leaving this cabin and killing every crewman they could find!

But, then, who would pilot the ship? Other than

Eibhlin's knives, what weapons did they have that wouldn't seal their own doom?

Creaking of boards overhead indicated the crewmen were awakening from whatever witchery Eibhlin's mother cast. Above, she heard a scuffle and a cry, then a soft thud on the deck. Obayana rose when she heard their cabin door open with a squeal from aged hinges. Whoever was coming was smart enough to shield himself with that door.

Obayana summoned fire to her fingertips, ready to defend when the face revealed was dark-skinned with hair so wild it looked like a bird's nest. Macavarian, at least part save for the pale gray eyes glittering like rain by the light of her fire. He was tall, clad in only a pair of short black breeches sailors wore, moving cat-silent save for the ship's betrayal.

"Stay away," Obayana hissed a warning. Fire snapped like lightning bolts between her fingers, illuminating the woman she stood above.

"I mean no harm," the stranger held his hands palms up in a gesture of peace. Though he spoke Macavarian, Obayana heard the Creedan lilt in his voice. So, he was a half-breed. That explained those eerie pale eyes. "I am Ashlan. I came from the *Venture* in response to distress calls."

Aja stood, settling her Royal crimson robes about her tiny body. Her impractical bejeweled braids clattered like wind chimes.

"I am Princess Aja, daughter of King Abinbola of Macavar," Aja said. "This is Princess Eibhlin Starraker of Creed and Lady Obayana of the Fireclaws. Any help your ship can give us would be appreciated and compensated."

Eibhlin nodded, but did not speak. Obayana saw her stand and realized she sustained some hurt after all. Her pale shoulders were bruised near as night-black as Obayana's flesh. Pity and jealousy warred within her.

"Are you injured?" Ashlan asked Eibhlin, his tone appropriately gentle and respectful.

"No," Aja answered, laying a protective hand on Eibhlin's shoulder. "The men tried—and they discovered it wasn't wise."

Trust, with just a bit of warning. Aja's wisdom startled Obayana, but she approved.

"What of the men on this ship?" Ashlan asked.

"Kill the ones who are left save for the captain," Aja ordered. "They are the ones who captured us, killed our companion, and attempted rape. We need to find out from the Captain who ordered this capture."

Ashlan nodded. "I will do as you ask. Rapists have earned their deaths."

"We gained our freedom," Aja added in a more clement tone. "But none of us have the skills to pilot this craft and we do not trust the captain to take us where we are bound."

"Where are you bound? I need to tell my captain." Ashlan said.

"Macavar," Obayana answered, but spoke no more.

Ashlan nodded. They followed him topside and watched as he efficiently dispatched four crewmen and tossed their bodies over the side of the ship.

"Did you attempt to rape the red-haired woman?" he asked each. Some replied with a 'yes,' others just turned their heads, shamed.

None resisted him. Whatever powers Eibhlin's mother deployed against them were prodigious. No wonder Father took such care training her children.

"There are three girls and the bound captain of the ship alive," Ashlan called down in Trader to a fair-skinned sailor who sat in a tiny boat alongside their ship. "They were taken captive by these men—and apparently regained control."

"Witches?" The man asked. His craggy upturned face was pallid in the moonlight. Obayana understood Trader well enough, but the man's guttural delivery turned the benign language into something animal and warlike.

"Aye," Ashlan's answer sounded reluctant. Obayana realized they had an ally and suspected it was the princesses who'd earned that allegiance. "And one of them can conjure fire. But we cannot leave them here. They do not have the skills to pilot this ship."

The sailor signaled *The Venture* to come in closer with a lantern. Once they were within hailing distance, Ashlan repeated the situation to his captain, Danil. Obayana realized they were dealing with Ruvakians. King Abinbola only recently began peace negotiations with the Northerners in the hopes their alliance would make sea trade safer from predation such as they'd just experienced.

"Three girls," the captain shouted across the distance. Obayana wondered at Ashlan's emphasis on the number.

"Aye, Captain." Ashlan called back. "Four to begin with, Sir. One of them was killed in the attack. They are no older than I."

"Does the sorceress give her oath she won't use fire on my ship?" Across the distance, Obayana could hear the mistrust.

Obayana stepped forward, called out to the Captain.

"I do, Captain. If you notice, I didn't set fire to this ship even when it attacked us."

"Young woman," Captain Danil's voice sounded amused even over the sound of the sea between them. "I do not think you are foolish enough as to set fire to what separates you and your companions from the sharks. My understanding is that those who earn robes such as yours are tested for their intellect as well as their ability to summon fire."

"The foolish ones generally incinerate themselves before the end of the training," Obayana chuckled. In fact, her Father seemed to have a positive knack in culling out the thoughtless, the easily angered, and the foolish. "Captain, I am Obayana the daughter of Master Tau. The two young women traveling with me are destined for the court of King Abinbola. One is his only daughter, Aja, the other will be the country's future Queen. I am certain he will reward you well."

"And what of the commitments I have made? I am a man of my word." Captain Danil continued. They were negotiating, Obayana knew. She was not a woman of trade, but she understood the dance.

"Extenuating circumstances," Obayana replied. "You will be on an errand of mercy for the Royal Houses of both Macavar and Creed. Think of the tale you can tell once you reach your home. And, since our countries are seeking alliance with yours, you may well be one of the first delegates.

"I suppose I can sell my goods as well in Macavar as Creed," Captain Danil called back. "I cannot leave women to fend for themselves. Too many slavers travel this route."

Aja stepped forward and stood beside Obayana. Even with her complicated arrangement of braids, the tiny princess did not reach her shoulder, but her voice was much bigger than her stature and her words rang out, beautiful and bell-like across the waves.

"I am Aja, daughter of King Abinbola. We are grateful for your help," Aja appeared at the rail and curtseyed to the Captain. "Now, I seek your word that we will go unmolested upon your ship. It is not only my honor I wish to protect, but that of the future Queen of Macavar, Princess Eibhlin Starraker."

The Captain bowed, then assured Aja speaking to the woman-child with the gravest of respect.

"No woman has ever been dishonored in my care and I will not let that happen now, Your Highness."

"We'll gather our belongings then, and say farewell to our dead," Aja said to Captain Danil. "If you will give us a bell, we will be ready to depart."

"Take until sunrise," Captain Danil told them. "Ashlan and Gigori will aid you."

Obayana watched as Gigori tied the skiff to the slaver and climbed aboard. He tasked himself with ridding the ship of the rest of the crew's bodies and did so with ease. Ashlan kept his post standing protectively beside Aja and Eibhlin.

Gigori came topside, a grieved expression on his face. "Captain," he called across to *The Venture.* "There are numerous skeletons in the hold."

"Slaves who perished, no doubt," Captain Danil

sounded saddened.

Obayana spoke up. "Captain, in Macavar, we build a pyre for our honored dead. I'm sure burning this ship will suffice."

"Indeed," Captain Danil agreed. "As soon as you are aboard *The Venture* and we have some distance, will you do me the favor of performing the task?"

Obayana nodded. It would be a great relief to release the power built up within her and on such a worthy target.

Gigori gently carried each skeleton to the deck, arranging the bones in restful positions. The tiny ones brought tears to everyone's eyes as the merciless sun came to expose their frailty.

Eibhlin spoke over each one, her eyes boring into the slaver captain's. "This man had four children at home waiting for his return." And: "This lad was the third son of his father, a noble house and a strong heart."

"Who are you?" She lingered over a youth's bones, her brow furrowed, tears streaming down her face. She touched the child's forehead, her eyes closed. "If only I had the skill to read these bones like my mother."

"We will give them back to the God of Fire as is our custom," Obayana said, once Eibhlin finished. "They will find their rest at last."

"The people of Creed prefer to inter their dead in the earth, but we cannot keep Caislinn's body until we reach Macavar," Aja said. "We have nothing to preserve her."

"The sea is part of the earth." Obayana detected the slightest trembling as Eibhlin looked thoughtfully down into a face with an uncanny resemblance to her own. "Perhaps the waves will return her home."

"Her name was Caislinn," Eibhlin spoke in a choked whisper. "She was barely fifteen summers. "She could dance from the gloaming until dawn. She played the lute like a bard and she loved a young man named Aron and hoped to marry…"

Eibhlin took a tremulous breath and continued. "She

was the one who suggested she don the finery made for me. Having the Lord Marshall as her father made her more cognizant of these things than I ever would have been. She was my cousin, my friend, the sister of my heart."

"Caislinn," Aja spoke next. "I was glad you were coming to court, because I knew from the first moment I saw you that you would be my friend. I will miss you."

Obayana paused. She could not think of anything as powerful and sentimental as the others, "I did not know you well, but you served your country with distinction and died with honor."

Obayana watched as Eibhlin gently removed the rings and crown from her deceased kinswoman and placed them back on her own fingers and head. She smoothed the girl's golden hair after the crown was taken off and kissed her forehead, letting tears spill down her cheeks.

Then they allowed Ashlan to pick Caislinn up. He let her slide gently into the ocean. Eibhlin and Aja sang a threnody, interweaving their voices in harmony, which brought tears to even the sailor's eyes. Obayana did her best to compose her face in grieved lines.

"Farewell, Caislinn," Eibhlin whispered. "I will tell your father you died well."

They gathered their belongings and ferried them over to *The Venture*. Among the trunks was a precious glass case bearing a massive fighting spear, heavily bejeweled in steel which looked like wood grain and clearly intended as more of an ornament than an actual weapon. Prince Tafari would never use the spear, since he had sorcerial powers, but Obayana knew he loved decoration and the gift would please him. Part of her wished they'd just leave the spear to blaze in the boat, but by rights it belonged to her lover and she could deny him nothing.

"A wedding gift for my brother Prince Tafari, from his bride Eibhlin," Aja explained when the sailors exclaimed over the case and the spear. Obayana saw her turn to Ashlan, who'd become her particular favorite, and ask. "The spear is the weapon of our Clan, the Firewings. What clan are you?"

"I do not know," Ashlan answered her as he hefted the spear to carry to the skiff.

*A bastard,* Obayana thought. Yet, she couldn't quite dismiss the only dark-skinned sailor on a Ruvakian boat. How did he get there? And, why did he look so familiar?

Obayana wasn't surprised the slavers had taken the lavish store of foodstuffs and casks of wines their ship carried for the voyage between Creed and Macavar. Their new hosts claimed these items. While the three of them would dine like princesses, there was more than plenty to share which hopefully would dispose the traders favorably.

"*Duskies,*" Obayana heard the guttural mutter in Trader, just loud enough for her to hear. "And Cap has to bring a sorceress as well."

"You don't refer to the Princess of Macavar and her lady as *duskies,*" Captain Danil had storms in his eyes. "And you don't think of any of these ladies as anything less than untouchable."

Obayana's tightened muscles eased. Virtue was not a value among sorcerers; however, the two princesses' vaunted virginity must be protected with her life. In the beginning when they had a contingent of Macavarian soldiers guarding King Abinbola's ship, she felt at ease. Now, she realized she must be vigilant every hour of the day.

Eibhlin Starraker was the first to come aboard the *Venture*. She'd donned the crown and the jewels and somehow managed to make her blood-spattered and torn chemise look like finery. Every man on deck bowed as she passed.

Aja was much more resplendent, but not quite as sure. Eibhlin was the one to reach out a hand and assist her onto the ship. When Eibhlin noted some of the men were not bowing, she spoke in a firm and precise voice.

"You will show Princess Aja of the Firewings the same courtesy as you have given me. Always."

Every one of them bowed.

Obayana followed, moving lithely from ship to ship

without assistance.

"This is Lady Obayana of the Fireclaws," Eibhlin provided introductions, bowing her head slightly as she had to Aja. "She is the daughter of Master Sorcerer Tau. In magical circles, her parentage and talent affords her rank and respect similar to ours."

Obayana glanced along the rank of sailors performing the required obeisance seeing mostly fear in their eyes. Superstitions were strong among the men who daily trusted their fate to the waters. Their original crew were accustomed to ferrying Father on pleasure cruises with King Abinbola and thought nothing of her coming aboard.

She didn't mind the Ruvakians' fear as long as it led to handling her with respect though she was well aware that too often that was not the case. She was a facile diplomat like Aja, who'd offer her smile like a benediction for all she met. Smiles, like respect, had to be hard earned. Obayana looked the men in their eyes, keeping her expression calm and neutral.

The slaver's captain was the last one to be ferried over. Before she departed, Obayana watched as Ashlan secured him at hands and feet with the chains he'd used in his own hold. Ashlan and Gigori held the man so as they rowed away from his ship.

The sailors hauled the man aboard like he was a catch they'd rather have cast from their nets. Obayana knew any one of them could have been captured and sold on the block like meat.

"Now you can set the ship ablaze, Lady Obayana," Captain Danil instructed. "I despise wasting a sea-worthy vessel, but that ship holds too many ghosts. It is a vile thing and probably could never be cleaned of the stench."

"I am honored to assist you, Captain Danil," Obayana saluted him as she'd seen men salute senior officers in the Macavarian sea-force. She then issued a thin stream of flame from her fingertips that widened into a tremendous gout once it struck the slave ship. The vessel lit the night for a good long time then finally died to ashes, which spread out like petals in the water as dawn came.

Captain Danil made the slaver watch. The man's face could be carved in ivory for all the emotion he displayed.

"Take him below and chain him up," Captain Danil instructed Ashlan and Gigori, who still held him. "Come ladies, I will show you to the best guest cabin on this ship. I presume you would prefer to remain together?"

All of them offered an affirmative answer.

"I regret I have nothing befitting your stations," Captain Danil opened the cabin door for them. "But you will be safe and as comfortable as we can make you. The door locks. I can even have your meals brought to you if you choose not to eat on the deck with the men."

Comfortable as he could make them was a small cabin featuring a central porthole with two double decker bunks on either side. The captain pulled up a hinged table from beneath the porthole that looked large enough for the three of them to take their meals on if they sat on the lower bunks. Obayana noted the porthole glass was clean and even the corners free of dust or webs. Rough-looking ivory sheeting with a single blanket made up their beds, but those items smelled of sea air and sunshine.

"Compared to the slave ship, this is heaven, Captain Danil," Aja smiled, patting a top bunk. "And the table is the cleverest contraption I've seen."

Ashlan arrived, announcing himself with a brief knock on the open doorframe and bowing. He held a small crimson bag which rang with the authority of gold when he dropped it on the table.

Full, Obayana noted. She doubted another coin would fit. Whatever else the half-breed was, he was honest.

"I believe these might belong to one of the ladies," Ashlan said. "I found them on the slaver Captain when we searched him."

"Ashlan, lad, I hate to lose your fishing expertise, but I'd like you to guard our noble passengers," Captain Danil said, nodding approvingly at the full bag. "I trust my men, but you've demonstrated how honest you are and I know you have much-loved younger sibs from the way you treat them."

"Ladies," Captain Danil said. "I will leave you to plot a course to Macavar with my navigator. Should you need anything, just tell Ashlan and we will endeavor to provide it for you."

Despite her gown, Aja swung to the top bunk like a monkey. A contented smile spread across her lips as she settled into the bedding.

"This is yours," Obayana tossed the coin pouch up to her. In her experience, Prince Tafari never carried coins, but one of the servants must have had the pouch in safe-keeping for Aja.

Aja drew the strings of the pouch open and exclaimed, sitting up so fast she nearly bumped her head on the ceiling.

"This is not mine!" She hopped down from the bunk, pouring a molten pile of freshly minted gold coins onto the table. One side bore two conjoined crowns in commemoration of the treaty wedding between Macavar and Creed. "Father made a first run of the wedding coins for the Royal family. Only he, Tafari, and I have some. Mine are back in the safe at the Palace! How would the slaver captain get hold of these?"

"That's a very interesting question we're going to have to ask the captain himself," Eibhlin replied. "I never even knew the coins were minted."

Obayana caught the two of them looking intently at the other. Mind-speech, she knew, could be open like their distress call which brought the *Venture* or closed. In this case, it appeared the Royals were leaving her out of the conversation.

Obayana shook her head vigorously in denial.

"It's not possible," Obayana said, her voice shaking. "You know that Tafari would not do such an awful thing."

"One of our guards was paid off, at least," Eibhlin reminded Obayana, answering a question they all had about how the ship was taken and sunk so easily. "The food was drugged. The taster, perhaps as well. Very few knew when Aja and I would be traveling."

Obayana started to offer further denial.

Aja's frown stopped her. The princess' eyes were narrowed in thought. "We'll see. Perhaps the slaver captain will have answers for us."

In that moment, Obayana caught a glimpse of the woman King Abinbola's daughter would be. She would never mistake a small stature and a kindly temperament for weakness again.

Still, she fought for her lover.

"It's not possible," she said, her voice shaking. "You know that Tafari would not do such an awful thing."

"We have to gather all the facts," Aja spoke reasonably.

"Let's get this over with then. Come with us, Ashlan," Captain Danil ordered. Then, as he passed his crew, he added: "The rest of you, stay with your duties."

"We were journeying from Creed to Macavar," Aja explained as they climbed down to the bottom of the hold. "Obayana and I were serving as escorts to Princess Eibhlin who is to marry my brother, Prince Tafari, the heir to our throne, to seal a treaty our two countries made more than twenty turns ago. Because we were warned the seas were dangerous, we exchanged clothing between Eibhlin and her maid, her cousin Caislinn. The last thing I remember was eating our meal. We had a taster from Father's court who wasn't affected, but we all felt sleepy and went to our cabins. We awakened with the ship taken and the attackers attempting to rape Eibhlin."

Eibhlin drew a long breath and continued the tale for the Captain. "Mother instilled defensive magic in me even before I started formal training under Master Tau at the Sorcerial Academy. Protection is a reflex now. The spell activated before I was even aware of what was happening. It seems the whole crew was lined up to rape the 'maid', so they all sickened."

They'd reached the spot where the former captain was chained. He looked much the worse for the experience.

"Release me so I don't soil myself." The slaver captain demanded.

"Did you afford the slaves you hauled that luxury?" Captain Danil asked in a deceptively mild tone of voice.

The man glowered.

"I'll release you when you're done," Captain Danil said. "Simply because I do not wish to soil my deck. Come to think of it, you're stinking up the hold now. I may chain you above decks in the sun if you don't cooperate with these ladies."

"We found this on your person," Aja showed the pouch of coins.

The man paled. "Look, I did what he asked—only the Princess got killed. That was all he wanted."

"I'm Princess Eibhlin Starraker," Eibhlin told him. "You killed my maid, the Lord Marshal's daughter. And none of our guard survived."

"Your guard took off," he replied. "They got their money and opted not to return to Macavar."

Obayana's belly flopped like a fish. Few would have the power and funds to arrange such a thing. Perhaps a Clan Chieftain, her father, one of the Royal family…

Aja's breath hissed out. "Who paid you?"

"I don't know," the man answered.

He *did* know. Obayana glanced at Princess Aja, who nodded. Her lips formed a tight line.

"I can make you talk," Aja threatened. Obayana could sense Aja's mind reaching out to the slaver Captain, like a tendril of fire moving toward unburned forest. "You saw what happened to your men when they touched Eibhlin without permission. Or perhaps you'd rather have Obayana question you?"

"I didn't meet the man who wanted this done directly," he answered quickly. The stench of his bowels filled the room and the captain shifted, his face flushing. "The coins were delivered to me by a man in a fancy black robe with a massive gold chain and he assured me that the Macavarian guard would give me no trouble."

"Did the man have a bald head?" Aja asked.

Obayana stared hard at her, but Aja merely glowered back. At the beginning of their trip, Aja would not have met her gaze for long. Now, she faced her without fear.

"He wore a turban," the slaver captain said. "But I saw no evidence of hair. He limped."

Obayana found herself staring at the space between two boards, sickness boiling up in her. Few with imperfections served King Abinbola. One such was Prince Tafari's steward, who'd gained his injury trying to stop Tafari's younger brother Blyds from falling down the stairs.

"I guess we'll just have to ask my brother directly when we get home," Aja said.

"Tafari would do not such thing," Obayana said, but she could feel a chill of doubt in her bones. Tafari and his steward were the only witnesses to the toddler's fall. "Tafari doesn't love Eibhlin..."

"What does love have to do with honoring the word of his King and country?" Obayana saw Eibhlin's blue eyes flash. "I love Abinbola as a father and Aja as a sister, and I loved little Chika...." She stopped, looking stricken, then shook her head to deny whatever thought arose there.

Obayana swayed with the motion of the ship, recalling the small skeleton Eibhlin lingered over.

*I know you.*

"You don't think we know that Tafari's your lover," Aja's voice cut. "If you don't want to be accused of being part of this conspiracy, I suggest you remain neutral until we are able to question him."

"You two are plotting against your future King," Obayana accused.

"No," Aja said. "We're talking about someone who might have committed treason. Three people had access to those coins. If Father wanted Eibhlin dead, he'd simply find a reason to behead her once she arrived."

"For instance, not caring for the man she is to marry?" Obayana inquired.

"I care for Prince Tafari's safety and welfare as any subject would," Eibhlin answered. "I do not care for his conceit, cruelty, or contempt for his subjects, but I will do my duty to the treaty."

"You cannot love or understand him as I do."

"You can have Tafari," Eibhlin's voice was glacier cold and precise. "All I need do is bear him a son and heir and do my part to rule Macavar wisely. I have no further desire for him than that."

"I'll bear his first born," Obayana's hand slid to her slender belly.

"You'd have to do that turns ago," Eibhlin's voice was kind. "Tafari has a handful of bastards among the palace staff."

Fire sprang to Obayana's hands. She wanted nothing more than to incinerate the pale-faced princess.

"It's true," Aja nodded. "Father's sent most of them away."

"If I sire a son first, perhaps Tafari will name my child the heir."

"The one who tried to assert her son was a member of the Royal family ended up falling down the stairs," Aja advised. "Tafari claimed it was an accident."

"You lie!" Flames flew from Obayana's hands. Still, she'd heard her father say more than once too many convenient accidents were happening in the court.

Eibhlin stepped between the two women, stopping the fire short of her upraised hand.

"By the Gods of Fire, I bind your power to your solemn oath to not use your powers on this vessel. Let your anger and jealousy turn upon you rather than harming others."

"How can you do that?" Obayana demanded, feeling her gift bind itself up in knots. "You should not be able to command this kind of power—I do not even possess that spell."

"Master Tau gifted it to me," Eibhlin answered calmly. "He thought some day I might need it."

"Father never gave me such a gift," Obayana felt the tears coming. "He loves you more than he ever did me."

"Perhaps he loved my mother more than yours," Eibhlin's voice was gentle. "But how could Master Tau not love one so much like him? He gifted the future queen of his country spells for her protection and those of her subjects. That is what he taught me."

"And turning my anger back on me?" Sweat poured down Obayana's face, burning her eyes, dripping down her cheeks, salty as the sea.

"Better than to harm innocent people—particularly when Master Tau's own daughter gave her oath," Aja spoke up. "I have the same spell, Obayana. So does Father."

"Does Tafari?"

"You would have to ask your father that question," Aja answered. "Or perhaps Tafari himself."

Captain Danil stepped in quietly, "I will gladly have Mihail place a lock on the cabin door across from the one Aja and Eibhlin share for you, Milady Sorceress."

Obayana bit her lip, then shook her head. "I was tasked by my King and my Father to protect both these women. I must do my duty."

For a moment, Obayana's and Eibhlin's eyes met. They were both tasked with a duty they neither asked for nor understood.

"Peace," Obayana extended her hand palm up toward Eibhlin.

"Peace," Eibhlin agreed. So did Aja.

"Our Fathers will sort this out by trial when we return," Aja said. "You trust their justice."

Obayana closed her eyes and nodded. Her father would want what was best for the Kingdom. Surely that would favor King Abinbola's son over a paltry plotting girl-child.

Still, part of her mind told her that neither Aja nor Eibhlin were traitors.

*What am I,* the thought recurred to her every single night as she slept across the room from the two princesses. *If I blindly side with Tafari?*

Sobbing awakened her. For a moment, Obayana considered just turning over, but it was little Aja who cried. She started to rise, to take the few steps across the room to comfort the younger woman, but Eibhlin reached her first.

"Shhhh," Eibhlin whispered. "You're safe. No one can hurt you."

"I don't want to go back. He'll come to my bed again."

"I'll see to it that you have more dogs," Eibhlin answered.

"Don't," Aja's voice was high-pitched and grieved. "The others died…"

"Then, you'll share my bed as my sister," Eibhlin answered. "I doubt Tafari will come there much."

Obayana closed her eyes tight and kept her body still and her breathing even despite hearing Aja's sobbing laughter. They were half-siblings, she knew, as all of King Abinbola's children were. But still what he'd done to his sister was wrong and wicked. That wickedness tempted her to his bed as they together laughed and plotted against the pale-skinned Creedans, but now she was seeing the results of his cruelty first-hand.

The next day, Obayana emerged from the cabin to see Ashlan training Aja to use a knife. Both princesses were clad in breeches and shirts cinched at the waist with their hair in kerchiefs and their feet bare like the sailors.

"The key thing to remember," Ashlan said to Aja. "Is where the blood flows closest to the skin." He raised his arm, then pointed to the veins near his groin, and finally at his throat. Obayana stared at a pattern of jagged raised scars on his back. Who was this half-breed sailor with the whip scars? An escaped slave? A criminal?

"And, if I wanted to strike his heart?"

"That would be a very tricky maneuver," Ashlan

answered. "You would have to be very lucky to strike between the ribs with a throwing knife. He pointed to a spot on his bare belly below his ribs. "You want to go for the heart, you use a longer blade and stab upward from here. It's like cutting meat."

Aja shook her head, "I've never done that—not even at dinner…"

"I think your next lesson will be with Cook," Eibhlin commented. "And, you are cutting your own meat from now on, Little Sister."

"What are you doing?" Obayana demanded. "You have the gift of fire—you're sworn.."

"I also have the gift of a brain," Aja replied as she tossed one of Eibhlin's slender blades toward a target fashioned out of planks. "And I choose the wisdom of knowing more than one way to protect myself."

Obayana opened her mouth, but Aja stopped her.

"I'll confess to Master Tau as soon as we arrive," Aja said. "If your Father chooses to punish me, I will accept his wisdom. Meanwhile, I will learn whatever methods of defense the sailors choose to teach me."

"Now, try again," Ashlan instructed.

Aja aimed the knife toward the target and struck close to the center ring. She caught a glimpse from the Princess and wondered if the child was thinking of her when she aimed.

Obayana stalked away toward the helm to see if she could determine if there was any progress toward Macavar. *The Venture* was smaller than the ship they'd traveled aboard and bounced upon the choppy sea. She'd never been bilious before, but she suspected she'd spend the entire voyage with her head hung over the rails if the seas didn't calm.

"Think of it this way," Captain Danil apparently overheard the conversation. "You don't have to entertain the youngling and she gets to work off some nervous energy. She'll sleep better and feel more secure."

Obayana exhaled a gusty sigh. "She'll be swearing like one of you as well."

"She's teaching my men to swear in your language, it only seems fair," Captain Danil chuckled. "Milady Sorcerer, our countries are trying to be friends. I think the tales of Princess Aja's goodness to my men will spread in my country like your wildfire and encourage that friendship. We all need the seas to be free of those who'd capture and enslave us—so this is a good meeting despite the circumstances, Yes?"

Obayana forced herself to nod.

"With this fair wind, we'll be sailing into your ports in a bit more than a fortnight."

"Thank you," Obayana grabbed at the rail before a wave knocked her overboard. She struggled to keep the sour-spiced meal Cook served for breakfast in her stomach. Her child needed the food.

"Perhaps it is better for you below?" Captain Danil suggested gently. "The drugs they gave you may well make you ill for a few more days. I have some cards if you would like to play or some wooden puzzles for you to work?"

Obayana shook her head, keeping her mouth firmly shut on her rebellious stomach. She carefully climbed the wooden ladder back down to the cabin she shared with the two princesses and laid down, hoping the illness would pass.

She awakened to Aja asking her if she would like some sup.

"Who tasted your lunch for you?" Obayana demanded. She'd taken over the task at breakfast since their taster disappeared with their guards.

"We did," Aja answered. "The sour cabbage and sausage was delicious."

Obayana felt the headache and nausea she thought she'd slept off returning. Prior to this, she had an entire staff to care for the two of them. Now, it was just her and the pair seemed bent on taking unnecessary risks.

"Let me go taste your meal," Obayana snapped. "I'm supposed to see to your safety now."

"Ashlan!" Obayana caught their titular 'guard' staring up at a rose-colored sunset. "Ashlan!"

"My apologies, Milady. I have never seen skies this color."

Obayana's eyes narrowed like a hunting lynx. Unless the skies were gray, the sunset was always this color. She considered every word each person said and assayed it for truth and worthiness.

Obayana made a gesture which Ashlan took as a command to tell her his story.

"I was born far North of here. I seek my homeland." Ashlan paused, looking confused.

*Is there something wrong with him?*

"Was your family outlawed to be cast so far from Macavar?" Obayana's curt question stung as badly as her power.

She watched as Ashlan bit back the angry retort. Hot summer breezes turned to ice around them as some power in him swelled with his anger. Obayana recoiled, chill-bumps rising fast on her exposed flesh. Her teeth chattered as she spat out the words: "What kind of abomination are you that your power is cold as snowmelt?"

"Milady Sorceress," Ashlan's tone was as chill as the wind swirling around them. "I'll get the meal so you can taste for the princesses."

Obayana waited for near half a bell before Ashlan arrived with a bowl full of soup the color of congealed blood.

"What is this?"

"Beet soup from Ruvakia," Ashlan answered. "I've tasted it. It's good."

Obayana glowered up at him. "You tasted the Princess' meal before I did?"

Ashlan nodded, calmly. "Cook and I gathered from your demeanor that I like both of them better than you."

"You—" Obayana took a spoonful of the soup and nearly spat the vile-looking stuff back at him. Salty, sour, and thick, like she imagined blood tasting. And the cursed waves were rolling again.

"Would you like me to serve the Princesses now, Milady?" Ashlan's voice was as wintry as those weird haunting eyes on a face she felt she should know.

Obayana made a gesture which was as close to acquiescence as she could get. Ashlan brought the bowls to Aja and Eibhlin and the pair of them pronounced the food delicious.

After sup, both resumed their defense lessons on the deck. When she started hearing thuds, Obayana rushed up the ladder half hoping one of them broke their neck.

Eibhlin was attacking Aja from behind. Aja stepped to the side and ably tossed the taller woman on the deck. Despite herself, Obayana gasped then saw Eibhlin's cat-like roll before she struck.

Sailors cheered as the Creedan rose from the deck. Eibhlin spoke breathlessly. "You have to learn how to land, too, Little Sister."

For a moment, Obayana knew Eibhlin saw her wide-eyed concern. She merely nodded at her arrival. Then, she went back to instructing Aja on how to hit the wooden deck without injury.

Seeing she was outnumbered objecting, Obayana absorbed herself in the scrolls Creed sent along with Eibhlin. They were mostly history and quite dry; however, it was better than seeing Eibhlin teach a sorceress how to fight. She saw no point in complaining to Father or King Abinbola, either. One could not always rely upon a straight-on attack, particularly in the palace. Even she began watching the lessons from her shaded spot on the deck.

Some part of her still watched for Eibhlin's undoing though now she dreaded reporting such to her prince. Still, when she saw her alone with the half-breed bastard both princesses treated like a brother, she crept to where she could hear.

Ashlan stared intently down at the sea. He slid his shoulders out of his shirt. So, the water mages wanted him? They could have him for all Obayana cared.

Eibhlin took hold of his bare shoulder moving between him and the sea. "Stop!"

Ashlan shook his head, trying to clear it of the melodic sounds coming from the rocks below.

"They call men to the sea to drown them," Eibhlin explained, moving the two of them from the rail.

"Honor the treaty," Eibhlin reprimanded the sea people. "You have protection from our countries as long as you do not harm any innocents."

"I---" Ashlan started to speak. "I am safe with them."

"Anyone can see you have a gift with the waters," Eibhlin answered gently, showing more warmth to him than she'd ever seen towards Tafari. "Your mother must have been very skilled, indeed, because Captain Danil and the crew all say you are one with the seas. But part of you is of the land as well. That part could weigh you down like the anchor that holds the *Venture* in place. You must learn about both halves before you choose one over the other."

Ashlan allowed her to take his hand and steer him where the others had gathered below to eat and exchange songs and stories. Obayana sneered when he took a place at the table, but said not a word.

So, his mother was technically Creedan since all water mages were fair-skinned. Obayana stored up that tidbit. Perhaps she wouldn't tell Tafari after all, but having some leverage with the Queen might be a good thing.

Then, Eibhlin discreetly passed her the piece of roasted poultry from her plate, the first thing Obayana found tasty the mad Ruvakian cook prepared. To that point, she'd subsisted on the dry bread Aja or Eibhlin brought her. That night, she joined the story circle the princesses started for the sailors and found her tale of the Goddess Gift of Fire to Macavar welcomed.

The next morning, Obayana's heart lifted at the sight of the Macavarian coast. She stood on the deck, drinking in the sight, willing the current to pull their ship into the dock faster. All her life, she'd been cloistered at the Sorcerial Academy, but that was nothing compared to the stifling confines of a trading ship surrounded by water.

"If you permit me," Eibhlin spoke at her elbow. "I will ask Master Tau to assign you to me."

Obayana nodded. Why was she offering this honor when she knew Tafari's child was in her belly? Then again, she'd be closer to her prince and Eibhlin could send her to his bed!

She was the first off the ship after Captain Danil. Her legs wobbled peculiarly at first on the stable ground, but she had no time for delays. She usurped the Captain explaining to the port authorities precisely who they were and what was needed. The man dispatched messengers to the Palace immediately. A coach accompanied by a contingent of Royal guards arrived before the next bell rang.

Aja and Eibhlin appeared hand-in-hand bedecked in royal finery looking every bit the princesses they were. They paused to thank each member of the crew for their kindness, receiving a fatherly hug from Captain Danil and abashed bows from the men. Standing at the end of the line, Obayana noted Ashlan held two cloth wrapped bundles.

Ashlan bowed to the two princesses and quietly handed over the bundles. The girls opened them to reveal a carved knife he explained came from the man-bone of an ice bear. Both thanked him profusely. Aja impulsively reached up and hugged him. Obayana saw the longing on Eibhlin's face and for the first time, her heart ached a bit for the other woman.

Obayana turned her face away, but she still listened.

"Ashlan, if you'd like to know about Macavar, I could get you a position on the Royal Guard," Eibhlin offered. "I know Aja would appreciate having you on her detail."

"No, thank you, Your Highness," Ashlan murmured, bowing once again. "My mother told me where I must go before I left the North."

"Where, then?" Eibhlin asked.

"To Creed," Ashlan answered her. "I'm going to find my mother's friend."

"If you need assistance, go to the Royal Library. It's public. Vicry, the librarian, knows more than anyone and if she doesn't know—she will find out. Tell her that I sent you. Good luck."

"Thank you."

*Trust Eibhlin to take care of the lost lambs*, Obayana thought. Tightness in her chest finally eased once they were surrounded by the crimson-coated guards. Losing the weight of responsibility for the two made her feel as light as the seabirds feasting on scraps from the harbor. Her powers returned to her in full force once they stepped on the land as well.

Aja requested Captain Danil join them in the coach as witness to their rescue. The slave captain was taken in custody of the Royal guards and would follow under far less pleasant conditions.

Obayana settled back into the luxuriant crimson dyed leather seat of the coach next to Captain Danil, grateful at last to be on familiar territory. The two princesses took the seat facing toward the crowd so they could look out on the crowd that was already amassing because of the news of their safe arrival home.

The Royal Palace stood above the city at the top of a high hill. Its roof was a gold-covered dome shaped like a flame extending high into the sky. Obayana noticed the old sailor captain turning to stare up at the palace with wonder-filled eyes. From a distance, it appeared several dozen *Ventures* would fit inside with room to spare. Gray banners, signifying mourning for the three of them, flew everywhere. As the procession passed, people tore down the gray and shouted jubilantly.

Women bared their breasts and danced alongside the street to the rhythm of hand drums, echoing down the hill like a herd of elephants.

*Father thought I was dead!* Obayana's vision blurred, watching the banners flutter in the wind. The idea had never occurred to her. She wondered why the two mind-speakers had not been in contact with someone similarly gifted in Macavar and realized that neither of them trusted her with the knowledge if they had.

News traveled fast in the Royal city, whether or not they'd been forewarned. She'd seen parades for the births of several of Tafari's siblings and mourning for all but Aja who died. Whether the occasion was joyous or not, her people gathered supporting each other.

Macavarians lined the Royal Mile a hill which led up to the castle, waving banners of all sorts and throwing flowers before the coach, so many flowers that the air was perfumed with them. Eibhlin and Aja played their parts, waving to the crowds. Obayana maintained her dignity and stared straight ahead, willing her eyes to dry and her countenance to reflect composure and wisdom.

"Praise the god of fire!" People shouted. A cacophony of drumming and hymns drowned out the clop of their horses on the paved hillside.

King Abinbola and Father shunned propriety and greeted the coach personally in the Palace's inner courtyard. His Highness had tears streaming down his dark cheeks. Was there more silver in his braids?

Obayana's heart ached to see the worry lines on her Father's normally calm face. He was old, she realized. His ebony skin did not show age lines, but for the first time she realized he had snow white hair marking age since she could remember. Father always jokingly called the King "grandson" since he'd trained Abinbola and his father in sorcerial arts. She let the two Princesses go first, unable to coax the wobbles out of her legs.

Aja bounded to King Abinbola and was scooped up like the favored child she'd always been. While the King was still young enough to have many more children, the loss of so many brought neglect to the women of his seraglio until he finally began pensioning off some of the least favored of the odalisques. Aja's half-breed mother was still there, but Tafari's had been gifted to Sango, the Chieftain of the

Fireclaws, who'd been missing from a sea voyage for more than a turn now.

"Obayana!" Father caught her in a tight embrace, his strong fingers stroking her short curls.

Obayana closed her eyes, savoring his warmth like a fire on a cold winter's day. Tears she'd held in check, dampened the silk of his robes. She pressed her face to his shoulder, hearing the quickened hammer of his heart.

"I thought you were lost to the seas," Father's voice resonated deep and rich. Obayana's heart soared as she realized he'd looked to her first, rather than either of the two princesses. "Until Eibhlin's messages finally reached us. Abinbola and I have kept the information to ourselves until we could speak with the three of you in person."

Obayana pulled away starting to speak when she saw Aja hand the red pouch of coins over to King Abinbola.

"Father-King," Aja said, curtseying low. "We were captured by a slaver who accepted this as payment for killing Princess Eibhlin."

By then, the guards bearing the slaver captain appeared. The man was already weeping and begging for mercy.

"We'll determine your case in open court before the people," King Abinbola declared. "It is fortunate you managed not to harm either of my daughters or I would have dealt more severely with you."

The court assembled in the main courtyard paved with multicolored mosaics of dancing dragons where marriages, coronations and other special events took place. In her lifetime, Obayana never saw a trial convene there, but she could see by the grim faces of the older Clan Chieftains that many had, particularly during the Firefang Clan Rebellion twenty turns before.

King Abinbola sat upon a dragon-shaped throne of gold, rubies, beryls and citrine. He was clad in red with a crown that glowed like flames. His hair was braided like Aja's, but threaded prominently with silvering strands. Before him stood Prince Tafari, looking handsome, but sullen. He was similarly clad as his father, but a circlet like Aja's topped his braids. It'd been so long, Obayana longed to run to him, to touch his face, hold him, but he'd merely glanced at her in passing. Enitan, one of the newest sorceresses, stood behind him now smiling proudly to be in the prince's company. Still, Obayana couldn't take her eyes from Tafari throughout the trial.

"My dear Eibhlin," King Abinbola rumbled to the two women who sat on smaller chairs on either side of him with his broad hands protectively on their shoulders. "We were grieved to hear that you and my daughter were killed on the sea. Imagine my delight to learn you're both alive and well."

Testimony about their attack followed from both princesses, then Obayana heard her name.

"Lady Obayana of the Fireclaws, Daughter of Master Tau," the Justiciar who presided over the High Court called her to the front. Tafari cast a traitorous look on her as she passed.

"I have nothing to add to what Princess Aja and Princess Eibhlin have said," Obayana responded to King Abinbola's questions. She quickly returned to her Father's side

Captain Danil took over afterward telling about the three women's rescue. He managed to commend Ashlan, who'd first heard the distress call and volunteered to check out the ship, to the King.

"What reward do you seek, Captain?" King Abinbola rumbled. "We are most grateful for the return of our daughters."

Captain Danil bowed. "Your Majesty, I seek no favor other than payment for these ladies' passage which your daughter has already graciously provided. I have three daughters and I would hope they would be similarly treated should they ever be in trouble."

The crowd roared with approval, Obayana noted. They probably wouldn't so much if they'd had Cook's beet soup every day.

"But, you've given this kingdom far more," King

Abinbola said. "These women represent hope for the future and peace between two kingdoms, so I shall fill your ship with the finest trade goods it my country offers and I'll see to it that each of your children receives a gift as well. And, if you are any example of the people of Ruvakia, I will be speeding treaty negotiations between our two countries along."

Another cheer from the crowd. Aja and Eibhlin both came forward to embrace Captain Danil. The silver haired seaman was smiling so broadly by the time he left the dais his teeth could be seen even in the back of the gathering. Obayana stepped forward at the last and extended her hand. Captain Danil smiled and bowed to her as he had the others, but she suspected he was as glad to be rid of her as she was him.

Then, King Abinbola questioned the slaver who'd captured the three.

"What precisely were your instructions?"

"I was to kill the Creedan princess," the slaver Captain said. "The others were mine to do with as I chose."

Obayana felt her stomach drop. For the first time since the trial started, she took her eyes away from her lover as she felt the spark in her belly burn out and die within her. Her vision narrowed. She awakened with Eibhlin looking down at her, expression concerned. They were in one of the garden rooms overlooking the courtyard. Obayana rested upon a couch. While the room itself was empty, guards crowded every entrance. It was the most alone any Royal could ever be in so public a venue.

"Please don't tell," Obayana begged her.

Eibhlin nodded. "You'll have your moons in a day. It'll be more painful than most, but the healer will have herbs for that. I'm very sorry for your loss, Obayana."

Obayana swallowed, realizing Eibhlin meant more than just the babe.

"You should rest," Eibhlin said. "I'll tell them you've just had too much heat."

Obayana shook her head. "No, I need to see the end

of the trial."

"They took a brief recess," Eibhlin offered her hand to help her rise. "Father Abinbola and Master Tau are discussing what should be done."

They walked together back out to the courtyard. Eibhlin nodded to both King and Obayana's father, indicating all was well. Obayana hated their concern and the suspicion of her weakness, but she'd rather that than have them know the truth. Father gestured for a guard to bring her a chair. For once, she was sitting like a princess.

"What other ships have you taken?" King Abinbola demanded, continuing his questioning of the slaver.

"I can't remember," the slaver captain started to say.

"Shall I summon a mind-mage to force the memories from your brain?" King Abinbola made a gesture. "You've noted my daughters can call ships to their aid from a distance. What do you suppose someone with similar gifts could do to you?"

*TELL!* The combined mind-voices of Aja and Eibhlin sent shivers down Obayana's spine. The crowd stilled hearing them as well.

Obayana's heart fluttered. Now she knew why King Abinbola chose a half-breed mind-mage for his seraglio. He wanted children with mixed powers such as Eibhlin and her Starraker siblings possessed.

"No, no, Your Majesty," the slaver captain was visibly shaking even from the distance. He began naming ships.

"My son was aboard that ship!"

With each name, it seemed more came forward calling out names of the slaver's victims. Far too many hands raised among the nobly clad in the audience. Many had called out names of family members they'd lost to the slavers. Others had younger children in tow.

But, the slaver saved the worst for last.

King Abinbola rose from his throne, his formerly impassive face flaming with anger. Obayana caught the flare of sparks between his hands and knew who the skeleton

Eibhlin had lingered over belonged to.

"Prince Chika was aboard that ship," Obayana heard the murmur everywhere. "Along with the Fireclaw Chieftain Sango and his daughter."

"Dear Goddess," Eibhlin's gasp filled the silence, her face ice pale. "Father King—there were many skeletons aboard his ship, but one was a boy of no more than seven. I haven't my mother's skill, but I *knew* him."

King Abinbola strode to face the slaver. Despite the silver in his hair, he moved powerfully, his expression purposeful.

"And what happened to my youngest son aboard your ship?" the King's voice was deceptively soft, but every word was pronounced with care.

The slaver captain murmured something even the King could not hear.

"Repeat that!" King Abinbola thundered, fire dancing around his body in a deadly nimbus.

"The youth didn't survive the hold," the slaver could barely speak. "The Princess identified his skeleton though she did not realize it."

"Were you ordered to kill Prince Chika as well?"

"Aye," the slaver captain admitted. "But I thought he would bring a fair price from the brothels like the Chieftain's daughter did."

The crowd gasped and surged forward only to be held back by the Royal guards. Obayana could almost smell the bloodlust in the air. She shifted minutely away from her father. He'd summoned enough fire to set a dozen prisoners ablaze though he didn't not glow with the power like King Abinbola.

"Can you point out the man who gave you the commission to take these ships and kill Princess Eibhlin?"

He didn't have to. Tafari's steward started a halting run. Tafari raised his hand and fire snapped from his fingers, but that flame was intercepted by Obayana's Father.

"Master Tau," the crowd murmured.

"And who purchased the other slaves?"

The slave captain listed off names and countries. Only one was a Creedan lord named Redburn.

"Master Tau, we have no further use of this," King Abinbola pointed to the slave captain. "Don't make it quick."

Father didn't even look at the slaver captain. A thin scream erupted from the man's throat like a lone wolf's howl. Smoke poured from his mouth while blue flame slowly bloomed at several points about his person. The wail only died when the man's body fell to embers and blew away on the wind.

"Your Majesty," Eibhlin said. "You've my word Father will deal severely with Lord Redburn and he will free those of your countrymen enslaved there." She stepped aside to speak to a man in Creed's green, who hurried away with her instructions.

"Tell me, Steward," King Abinbola's voice was deceptively mild. "Who sent you on this errand?"

"Prince Tafari," the man's voice shook. "Your Majesty, I beg you—I was only doing what the man you swore me to obey ordered."

King and Master shared a glance. The steward's death was much quicker and kinder. He went up like dry kindling soaked in oil.

Prince Tafari started to edge away, drawing a knife from his robes when his attempts to summon fire sputtered futilely. A phalanx of Royal Guards appeared from everywhere blocking him. None laid hand on the Royal, but it was clear from their drawn swords they'd lay steel on him if he moved.

"I would never do such a thing, Father, Eibhlin, you have to believe me," he spoke pleadingly.

"Oh I did," Eibhlin spoke from where she stood.

"She seduced me!"

Obayana stiffened when Tafari's finger pointed straight at her.

"It was Obayana's idea to do away with my unwanted

Queen so we could wed."

Obayana rose, feeling as though she was going to faint again. King Abinbola stared at his son, faint hope on his face. That faint hope was enough for her to see her death.

"You lie, Tafari. I thought you wanted the peace between our two people as much as I did even if you didn't want me. I believed you until I saw this." Eibhlin tossed the pouch of coins at the prince's feet. They spilled out like a pool of fire. "Those coins were a limited run for the Macavarian Royal family only. King Abinbola and Princess Aja have theirs. How do these coins come to the hand of the slave captain?"

Prince Tafari scarcely looked at the pouch before he dropped to his knees. "Father, have mercy. You made this arrangement with King Jaydan even before I was born..."

"And you would shatter the peace we fought so hard to build all these turns?" King Abinbola's voice rang out over the square. "By murdering the only daughter of the woman who saved my life during the Rebellion?"

"And, what of my other brothers and sisters?" Princess Aja demanded. "What happened to them?"

"Accidents," Prince Tafari answered defiantly. "If anyone has any word otherwise, let them come forward and accuse me!" He must have thought his status would prevent this, but the crowd had turned their faces from their prince.

One by one, frightened servants and guards stepped forward telling of seeing Prince Tafari pushing a younger sibling down the stairs, throwing another one who'd 'accidentally drowned' into the water.

"You killed them all," King Abinbola's voice was hollow. "What serpent did my loins bring forth?"

Tafari's mother, who stood with the new Fireclaw Chieftain, attempted to edge away. Guards seized the pair of them, dragging them off.

"Please, Father," Tafari said. "I will wed Eibhlin Starraker and honor the treaty."

"You are not worthy of her," King Abinbola rose from his seat. "Or of the crown I would bestow on you. Prince Chika was a better man than you at seven. You are no son of mine. Choose, Tafari, the fire or the spear!"

"Father, no!" Tafari was on his knees. "Eibhlin, tell him…"

"I would tell him that you've entered your sister's bedroom at night on more than one occasion," Eibhlin said. "I'm sure there are others who'd step forward with testimony of your abuses."

Hands rose throughout the audience. Women of both noble and common births stepped forward ready to testify. Obayana lost count at a score. She refused to look past that number.

"Aja still has her precious maidenhead!" Tafari shouted.

"And I have nightmares every night about your hands upon me," Aja stood facing Tafari. "I want no man now!"

"The fire or the spear," King Abinbola repeated. "Choose or I will have Master Tau make the choice for you."

"Spear!" Tafari wept out the word. The heavy wedding gift appeared from Obayana did not know where. King Abinbola glanced at the two princesses who were most wronged by him.

Aja and Eibhlin huddled together whispering urgently. They turned, holding the spear together.

"Obayana," Aja said. "I believe Tafari has wronged you as much as either of us."

Obayana stared at the two women's gift. Sorceresses did not use bladed weapons, but they were offering her vengeance—and most of all, dignity and respect for herself and her house. She stepped forward accepting the blade and recalling the lessons Ashlan gave the two princesses on the ship.

Then she turned to face Tafari with the bejeweled spear in hand. She could make it quick or prolong his death. Everything in her said to let him bleed out like the slaver captain burned, but there'd been enough death today. More would follow as King Abinbola rooted out those his son corrupted and replaced them with loyalists.

Taking a deep breath, Obayana plunged the spear through his belly and upward to his heart. Tafari let out a high-pitched scream, then went silent. Obayana let go of the spear and her former lover fell to the mosaic tiled courtyard, blood darkening the red of his robe, then flowing out to fill in the cracks of the mosaic with crimson.

She took a deep breath and stepped away, turning her back on the man who'd used her and abandoned her. She nodded thanks to the two princesses as she departed the courtyard, bowing to the King and her father.

"Long live King Abinbola!" Princess Aja led the cheer for her father.

Two hands grasped her as she made her way back into the cool and dark of the Palace. Aja and Eibhlin held her between them like sisters.

"I'll claim your child and raise it as my heir," Aja offered in a whisper. She hadn't sensed the healing energy Eibhlin sent through the palm of her hand and the scent of cinnabar which clung to the air masked the quieter herbal smell.

Obayana shook her head, allowing a single tear to burn a course down her cheek. "That child fled my womb when Tafari accused me. Besides, he could turn out to be like his father."

Father and King Abinbola followed them into the chamber.

"Milady Eibhlin," Abinbola bowed deeply to her. "I know you have always thought of me as a second father, but would you consider becoming my wife?"

"Your Highness," Obayana felt Eibhlin release her grip so she could curtsey deeply. "I am honored by your offer, but I will always love you as my father and honor you as such. If you wish, I will remain as friend and counselor to my little sister," Eibhlin offered a compromise. "However, I request that you allow me to accompany Lord Summermoon to recover the captives at the Redburn estate. Many will need a healer. Perhaps I can also find some of the children taken to the brothels and aid in their restoration."

"I will dispatch enough guards to make certain you are safe," King Abinbola agreed.

With another quick curtsey, Eibhlin disappeared no doubt to shuck off her finery and rush to join the rescue party.

King Abinbola's eyes flashed with anger. "It is a pity I have no other sons to offer her. I believe she will make sure the treaty holds, but our line could use healers as well as warriors."

Obayana slipped away, taking the path through the Royal Gardens, which was generally quicker to the Sorcerial Academy than the streets shared with the commoners. Even if the princesses' joined faith redeemed her, she knew there would be whispers. The day was hot and uncharacteristically bothersome after becoming accustomed to the cool sea mist on her face. She found herself drawn to the cool places within the maze with a central fountain.

She'd passed the bit of water magic many times, but seldom paid attention to King Abinbola's lost consort and only true love. *Camialle* the name engraved in marble beneath the fountain which hosted the statue read. If she recalled, the woman was lost in the Firefang rebellion twenty turns ago.

Obayana stared up into eyes the color of rain, of dove's wings, or the still ocean on a cloudy day.

"Cinders!" she swore, recognizing those eyes, realizing the chill Ashlan emitted was frozen water—ice.

"You're the second one to stand so long in front of this place," an elderly gardener with rheumy eyes commented. "A sailor was here for what seemed like a bell before the garden closed to the public. If he wasn't dressed common, I would have thought he was the young King himself."

"Goddess!" Obayana ran for the harbor as fast she could. She'd sworn never to take a ship again, but she must go to Creed!

# Death and Honor

*Ronald T. Jones*

The scout leader presented the bloody head to his superior.

Keersi Jiyan, commander of the First Army of the Goyo Kingdom, clutched the grisly trophy by its tuft of frizzy hair and lifted it from the soldier's grasp. She held the head up for scrutiny and narrowed her eyes in concern.

Four horns protruded from the head, positioned at the crown down to the forehead. The vacant eyes were humanlike, save for their scarlet coloring that betrayed this creature's demonic heritage. The rest of the face took on the characteristics of a serpent, with it sloping outlines, elongated mouth and scaled skin texture. The head's size, along with its weight, bespoke the creature's immensity.

Keersi had never encountered a Zorsi, but rumors traveled to her from a variety of sources; rumors alleging the Zorsi's height and girth, their incredible strength and sheer, indomitable prowess in battle.

The commander of the First Army tossed the head aside where it landed on a dirt packed surface with a thunk and rolled into a refuse filled ditch.

An ignominious resting place for so fearsome a visage.

The scout leader threw the discarded head a scalding glance. "We ambushed that thing and its party in the Sasund

Valley. They raided a village a day earlier, slaughtered and ate every man, woman and child." The scout leader looked like he wanted to spit, but held his discipline before the commander.

Keersi hid a grim smile, her sentiment mirroring the soldier's. She turned to Luotunde, her second. "It's true then. The Zorsis have entered the war."

The grizzled veteran folded his enormous, battle-scarred arms across a chest wider than two men shoulder to shoulder. "If the Zorsis have become involved in the affairs of men, then that means the Phulani must have offered them something quite valuable."

"Yes, like their souls," Keersi scoffed.

"The Phulani have no souls." Luotunde's brow knitted tensely, amplifying the usual severity of his eyes.

Decades of animus toward the Goyos' traditional enemy were etched with a finely honed blade into the second's glaring expression.

Keersi, relatively new to the Western Lands, never shared Luotunde's lifelong aversion to the Phulani. If anything, she hoped that one day the opposing kingdoms and the coalitions they led could put aside their hostilities and exist in peace.

Unlikely…at least in her lifetime.

She placed a hand on Luotunde's shoulder, breaking the spell. "We have some planning to do."


Ten thousand campfires lit the flat land, their flickering ubiquity reflecting the stars of a clear night sky.

Keersi and her generals huddled beneath the largest tent in the camp where they were gathered around an unfurled map on the floor. Dancing torchlight illuminated the map's outlines and illustrations. Chess pieces dotted the map. Keersi loved the game and was quite proficient at it. She approached war in the same manner as the game.

Scouts arrived throughout the evening, providing

updates on enemy movements. With each new bit of information, a general would reach over and move a chess piece representing a friendly or enemy army to a new point on the map.

As her officers debated deployment and attack strategies, the jade pendant necklace hidden beneath Keersi's tunic began vibrating. She put a hand to the pendant as if to soothe its insistent tremor, but knew a gentle touch would do no good.

Of the officers present, only Luotunde spotted the motion and his keen eyes glinted with knowing.


An hour later, when the officers retired to their tents, Luotunde remained behind.

Keersi stared at the map, pretending to study it intently, hoping her beloved mentor would take his leave.

"The pendant spoke, am I correct?"

Keersi looked up at her second-in-command, her mouth open to speak, but failing to form words.

"This is a day that I have always feared." Bits and pieces of Luotundes gruff manner flaked away, revealing patches of emotional vulnerability. "It speaks, but you do not have to respond!"

"I'm sorry," Keersai muttered gravely. "But I must." She drew up, facing the big man squarely. "I have to confront them. I have to."

"No, you don't!" Luotunde snapped. The cracking whip of his voice would have struck terror in the bravest of soldiers.

Keersi merely smiled at the veteran with deepest affection.

Luotunde had discovered her all those years previous, a lone, frightened girl, fleeing from her homeland. He took her in, fed and sheltered her, treated her like a daughter. He tutored her in the ways of war as well as the ways of life. He was indeed the father she should have had.

"Please, I don't want you to worry. You trained me well. The king would not have placed me in charge of an army if you hadn't."

"Leading an army is one thing, fighting multiple opponents by yourself is another." Luotunde's lips tightened with anguish. "At least let me accompany you…"

Keersi's eyes flashed objection. "No, I need you to command in my absence…"

"Then let me assign you a bodyguard…"

"Luotunde, I'm going alone." The note of authority in her voice silenced the old general. "You will stay behind and prepare the men for battle. I will not accept assistance from you or anyone else. That is an order."

"It will be as you wish, Commander," Luotunde conceded, trying to veil the pain in his tone. "But understand this; a Zorsi army will march through the Akkan Forest in six days. They're going to link up with Phulani forces and use the forest as a staging point for an assault on the regional capitol. That's where we'll meet them. I expect you back by then."

"If I'm not," Keersi began softly. "I fully expect your inspired leadership to carry our forces to victory."

Luotunde lingered for a moment. He pulled a curved dagger with a leather bound hilt from his scabbard and extended it to Keersi. "Additional protection."

She hesitated. "That's your prize blade."

The general practically forced the weapon in her hands. "It will only be a prize if it aids your survival. Take it."

Keersi reluctantly gripped the knife's hilt.

Without a word, Luotunde turned and departed the tent.


Keersi alighted from the camp shortly before dawn, informing the night watch beforehand that she had to go on a mission of utmost urgency.

While questions leapt from the guards' curious faces

like locusts from a calabash, they held their tongues and watched the commander gallop into the darkness on a black steed.

Well armed she was. She rode equipped with a two swords forged from Damas steel, a pair of Zan throwing knives, a bow, a quiver of arrows, and of course, Luotunde's dagger. She wore a lamelar torso vest, a black leather loin covering, matching leather shin and forearm guards and sturdy brown sandals that laced up to her knees.

Admittedly, she wasn't so well armored, but that was intentional. She knew quite well the caliber of the opponents she would soon face. Additional armor of the plated type she was accustomed to wearing on the battlefield promised more hindrance than aid.

Keersi needed every ounce of agility her sleek, sinewy physique had to offer.


She pushed her laboring mount hard, across rolling, grassy plains and rocky plateaus. She forded rivers and negotiated steep hills. The mild, periodic vibrations of her pendant grew stronger and more sustained the closer she moved to her objective. All the while she wished she could just rip the thing from her neck and toss it away.

When she stopped to rest her horse, she partook very little of her rations. Strips of meat and diced plantains registered in her mouth as bland as the water she gulped. Nothing existed for her but the imminent confrontation. Neither pleasure nor discomfort could pry her iron bound focus from the grim task ahead.


Night came and went.

Keersi's pendant thumped with unending insistence, heralding the completion of her journey. She pulled up on her horse's reins, reducing the mount's speed to a cautious trot when she happened upon a village…or what remained of it.

Most of the thatch roofed huts were partially of wholly scorched. Skeletons lay sprawled about, displaying a gruesome assortment of injuries. Skulls bashed in or perforated. Ribs broken. Cleanly sheared off limbs. The bones gleamed stark white beneath a morning sun, indicating that what dreadful attack devastated this assuredly blameless community was not a recent one.

Keersi spared no more than a sliver of curiosity at her surroundings. A marauding army or slave raiders, or a combination of both. The perpetrators were of no consequence to her.

She brought her horse to complete stop and leapt off the animal's back, landing nimbly on her feet. She removed both swords from the saddle scabbard, slid them into her hip sheathes, and hooked a throwing knife to her belt. She grabbed her bow, notched an arrow, ventured several paces from her horse and waited.

Her pendant had gone silent, but she knew it was not because the danger had passed.

Four men on horseback approached from the opposite end of the village. Three were younger, the rider at the forefront, considerably older.

Keersi's heart quickened, her jaw clenching; otherwise her face remained set in stone.

The younger men wore sleeveless gray tunics with brown billowy slacks tucked into matching brown boots. The older man's garb consisted of a flowing black robe. Hardly appropriate attire for the heat and humidity of the Western Lands.

Then again, Keersi knew that the elder was shackled with far too much discipline to allow an unaccommodating climate to affect him.

Like the peoples of the Western Lands, the men ranged from dark brown in complexion to rich mahogany.

The older man shared Keersi's burnt sienna hue.

Unlike many Westerners, the riders' faces like Keersi's, tended toward long, their features narrower, their woolen hair more loosely textured.


The horsemen halted twenty paces from Keersi.

Four sets of eyes fixed on the woman. Hostile, contemptuous eyes.

Keersi stared back, unwavering, unflinching.

In her homeland, for a woman to have held a male gaze without averting would have earned her a vigorous lashing.

"Lower your eyes you impudent cow!" The younger brawny man to the elder's far right growled in Mosalian, a tongue Keersi had neither heard nor spoken in years.

Keersi's gaze shot to the speaker named Umed. She bared teeth in an unsettling display of challenge. "Why don't you try to lower them yourself?"

The large man unsheathed a sword with a curved blade. "I'll damn well shut them permanently!"

The elder lifted a hand to restrain the sword wielder. He looked Keersi up and down. "You expose your skin like the infidel wenches in this land," he stated, his baritone voice a bristle of judgment. "You confirm what I have always thought you to be: a whore."

Rage brewed inside Keersi. She was a victorious military commander, honored and respected by kings and queens, nobility and commoners, officers and soldiers. How dare this old dog reduce her and her achievements to a vile epithet.

"Turn around and leave this place," she warned with barely controlled calm.

Her eyes swept the riders, starting with the old man, Suli, then moving to Umed, Kalhad, and Jumir.

"This is intolerable!" Jumir shouted, whipping out his sword. "It's time to shut this slut up!" He spurred his horse forward, exhorting a battle chant that advertised he would give no quarter.

Keersi back pedaled rapidly, elevated her bow and loosed an arrow.

Jumir slapped the arrow aside with his sword.

Keersi notched a second arrow and let it fly.

The charging horseman brought his sword about, slicing the shaft in half within an arm span of his chest.

Jumir proved as uncannily quick as he was impulsive.

Keersi dropped the bow and pulled out her swords fleeting seconds before Jumir thundered into stroke range.

He swung ferociously as he rode past.

The commander met the blow with both swords and the still air rang with the clamor of clashing blades.

Keersi whirled from the contact to see Umed bearing down upon her with sword raised.

Somehow she thought this would be a fairer contest, that they would come after her one at a time.

Obviously, her foes did not think her worthy of being accorded the honor of fair combat.

She ducked beneath Umed's swing, the breeze from his blurring blade swishing across her back. She rolled to the ground; half twisted and flung the sword in her left hand like a spear.

The sword struck the right flank of Umed's horse and the animal reared up in a screech of pain, tossing its rider.

Keersi gritted her teeth in disappointment. That could have been Umed's back had her toss been a little higher and more centered.

Muttering a heartfelt apology to the horse, Keersi sprinted toward Umed, intent on finishing him before he recovered from his fall.

Jumir galloped for a second pass, forcing her to contend with him instead.

Keersi deflected a series of hammering blows from her opponent before she slashed beneath his guard, tracing a cut across his side.

Jumir cried out more in rage than pain and dismounted, swatting his horse away.

Before the animal was clear he charged Keersi, slicing

the air in front of her.

Keersi moved back, ducking and weaving, trying desperately to parry the eye blinking swiftness of her opponent's blade.

He bent low and Keersi's teeth gnashed at steel biting into her right thigh inches above the knee.

Jumir sneered and leaned in for a thrust to the heart.

Keersi stumbled backwards out of the other's reach. She saw a recovered Umed running to reinforce his brother, before she hit the ground.

Jumir plunged his sword toward her in an overhand swing.

The commander blocked the strike, snapping a foot to Jumir's knee.

Jumir tottered sideways just as Umed's broad form filled Keersi's view.

She jumped to her feet in time to block Umed's sword. But the strength of his blow was monstrous, and Keersi's grip on her blade faltered at a crucial instant. Her sword flew out of her hand

Keersi dropped and swept a leg in a crisp, arching kick, tripping Umed at the ankles as he bulled toward her.

She rose and made a dash for her sword. She heard rapid footfalls behind her and sensed that they did not belong to Umed.

Reaching down in full flight, she scooped up her blade, and spun, swinging blindly, burying gleaming, unyielding Damas steel deeply into Jumir's neck.

Keersi extracted the blade and an arterial gusher poured from Jumir's fatal wound.

His eyes glazed over with death and he fell forward, landing on his face.

A vengeful yell escaped Umed's lungs. He rushed the woman, his face locked in distorted fury.

Keersi braced for the big man's attack. Her pendant thrummed a warning, alerting her that Kalhad was entering the contest.

She dove to one side, eluding a stroke from Umed that would have cleaved her down the middle.

Meanwhile, Kalhad dismounted with a small battle ax in hand and walked forward. With his free hand, he grasped a pendant hanging from his neck, the same jade object as the one Keersi wore.

Muttering a string of words in a dead language, a shimmering blue light coursed through the ax and blazed outward in a whorl of blue fire.

Detecting Mosalian magic, Keersi's pendant erected a barrier around her, blocking the incoming flame.

The jarring force of the fire bolt's impact swatted Keersi dozens of paces until she crashed through a burned out hut.

Keersi rose shakily, her body wracked with pain. When last she saw Kalhad, he could barely conjure a strong enough spell to stir dust. Now, he was a full fledged battle-mage with a mastery of his pendant that Keersi at once feared and envied.

Keersi's pendant was a gift from her grandmother, who believed a woman could manipulate the chaotic forces of magic as effectively as a man. With time to learn magic she would have had the expertise to unlock the full power of her pendant. Unfortunately, circumstances did not grant her the time she needed and as a result her pendant's capabilities were severely limited. It could block an attack, not launch it, and it only protected her from Mosalian magic.


Umed burst through the ruins of the hut with murder radiating bright as torchlights in his eyes. He didn't see the whore. He swept his sword in scythe-like fashion through layers of debris searching for what he hoped was a dead or dying woman.

"Where the hell are you!"

He heard a faint rustle and turned to the sound's source

in time to receive a throwing knife between the eyes. *Thuck.* Amid a bloody mist, Umed fell backwards instantly dead.

Keersi emerged from the side of the hut, walked over to Umed's wide-eyed corpse and plucked the throwing knife out of his head. "I'm right here you bastard."

A gust of wind swirled around her.

Keersi looked up to see Kalhad, encapsulated in a blue aura, floating toward her.

The air around him crackled like kindling in a fire.

"My foolish brothers," he declared disdainfully. "They should have let me deal with you first. Alas, pride can be an instrument of suicide." The battle-mage swung his ax in a downward stroke, generating an iron dense bubble of boiling hot air pressure.

At Kalhad's command, the bubble zipped toward the woman with the speed of a shooting star.

Keersi threw herself out of the bubble's path. What remained of the hut burst in a fiery cloud of ash and splinters when the bubble struck it.

Her shield protected her from the blast, but could not prevent the impending shockwave from tossing her end over end like a thrown pebble skipping across water.

Blue flame rippled from Kalhad's ax, dredging a molten path toward where Keersi lay bruised and battered.

She tried to roll, avoiding the directed fire, but too quickly did it capture and engulf her in a writhing blue blanket.

Her shield held, but not for long, she feared. Either the shield would fail and the fire would incinerate her or the rising heat would bake her like a stuffed pig in a kiln.

Keersi struggled to her feet, slowly, laboriously defying a pounding fist of flame-laden pressure. Drawing on a burst of strength, she leapt out of Kalhad's literal line of fire, took quick aim and hurled her throwing knife.

The battle-mage directed his ax, a jet of flame issued forth, and the blade ended its flight in a spray of liquefied metal.

Keersi gripped her pendant. She needed to strengthen her shield. Her grandmother told her that the pendant's power could be amplified with a thought. If she concentrated hard enough perhaps she could…

Kalhad unleashed another fire bolt.

The commander squeezed the pendant until her knuckles paled. The shield, fueled by the power of her concentration, suddenly expanded.

The bolt slammed into the enlarged, extra-fortified barrier, deflecting back to the battle-mage.

Kalhad found himself wrapped in an inferno of his own creation. At the heart of a fireball the battle-mage flailed, his agonized cry almost pulling a morsel of pity out of Keersi's ice encrusted heart.

In seconds, Kalhad fell silent and what dropped from the sky was a charred lump roughly shaped like a man.


Keersi closed in on the remaining horseman with deadly purpose.

Suli climbed down from his horse, and unsheathed a forearm length wide bladed double edge sword. His movements were casual, yet underlined with a certain methodical grace. With a slender, elegant hand, he stroked his gray beard, his opaque robe swaying gently in the breeze.

"Was this worth it to you, old man?" Keersi demanded venomously. "The deaths of your sons?"

Suli's demeanor displayed no indication that he felt anything at all for his fallen progeny. "Honor is worth more than life," he explained stoically. "When that honor has been stained, only death can wipe it clean. Your death will restore the luster of the honor you have soiled."

Keersi's eyes narrowed in exasperation and reflection. What had been the crime that precipitated her flight from her homeland? Questioning the traditions that kept the women of her country in virtual slavery? Giving her heart to a man not of her family's choosing? Wanting to learn the arts of war and magic? Skills forbidden to women?

Were such desires, concerns, ambitions in a woman truly so terrible as to warrant her death? She could only shake her head sadly.

"You fought superbly," Suli admitted, permitting a glow of approval to mitigate the harshness of his countenance. "Regretfully, every second you breathe is an affront to your family."

"Well then, I'll have to keep breathing then, won't I?" Keersi lunged when she came within strike range.

Suli barely made a motion to deflect the sword flying at his mid section.

Keersi followed up with short, swift thrusts and slashes, all of which Suli parried without taking a single step. His arm moved as if it were independent of the rest of his body.

The commander went for her opponent's legs.

Suli leapt above the sword sailing beneath him with an astounding agility belying his age.

Keersi attacked with a backhand to the neck only for her blade to be halted by Suli's blade and shunted aside with laughable ease.

Sweat streamed down the woman's face and body. She panted from her exertions, while Suli, every bit the master swordsman she remembered appeared little winded.

Now it was Suli's turn. The old man's sword flashed like silver fire.

For every ten incoming blows, Keersi managed to block, one slipped through her guard. Blood splotched both arms from the cuts she received from Suli's precision assault. Her chain linked vest armor was tattered with slashes.

Suli ended a flurry of strikes with a brutal kick to Keersi's chest that landed her hard on her back.

Keersi's vision clouded with pain, her breathing reduced to sputters. Her chest throbbed fire.

Through a stunned haze, she saw Suli approaching, positioning his weapon to deliver a deathblow.

She saw something else. An object falling from the sky…a spear. It was heading straight for her opponent's back and Keersi uttered not a single note of warning.

Whether it was the look on Keersi's face, or unusually perceptive senses that gave warning, the old man stepped aside, just avoiding the projectile's bite.

The spear, taller than a tall man with a shaft as thick as a human shinbone pierced the spot where Suli just stood.

Inhuman grunts and shouts preceded the appearances of six horned, scaly-skinned, serpent featured creatures with hulking, muscled bodies. Two were armed with long spears, the rest carried blades with gleaming rounded edges. What little armor the new arrivals wore amounted to thinly padded black leather. Their gaping, slavering mouths revealed rows of sharp, curved teeth.

"What are those abominations?" Suli queried with revulsion.

Keersi rallied to her feet, urged on by a new threat. "Zorsis, "she replied. "They must be part of a scouting party."

The Zorsis let loose a combined roar before charging.

Ordinary humans would have been struck dumb with terror at the sight and sound of them.

Suli ducked a spear thrust by a Zorsi on his right flank at the same time blocking the ascent of a round blade from a creature that slipped behind him. He promptly impaled the spearholder in the chest, whipped his sword out and slashed the other Zorsi across the gut, carving through leather and flesh, spilling its innards.

Keersi rolled forward, and jumped up within inches of a startled Zorsi that had clearly not expected so bold a move. She jabbed the point of her sword beneath the creature's chin, driving it up through the top of its thick skull.

Pulling the sword out posed a problem she didn't have time to address. She flipped away from the falling Zorsi and yanked the spear of the out of the ground.

A Zorsi lumbered in her direction, its blood-crusted sword waving overhead.

Keersi thrust swiftly, in and out. The Zorsi crashed to the ground with a fatal wound where she presumed its infernal heart to be.

The commander dashed back to the first Zorsi she killed and yanked her embedded sword out of its chin.

No ordinary humans these were.

The remaining two Zorsis measured their attacks.

One swung its spear like a club, the tip grazing a section of Keersi's lamellar just below her collarbone. The commander shot forward before the Zorsi could bring its spear about. She stabbed the creature through its rib, eliciting a howl of agony.

Suli avoided a wild succession of strikes from his sword-wielding foe.

The Zorsi, much bigger than his deceased comrades, tried to use its mass to overwhelm the small human. It struck hard and fast, driving the human back.

Suli stumbled, presenting an exposed side to the Zorsi.

The creature focused on that opening and aimed his sword at it.

Having lulled his foe into thinking he was vulnerable, Suli glided parallel to the Zorsi's thrust. He executed a pirouette, slicing a gash across the Zorsi's back, severing its spine. The Zorsi collapsed as if invisible strings holding it upright had been cut, the lower half of its body locked in paralysis.

Suli plunged his sword through the back of the Zorsi's neck, finishing it off.


Despite the massive injury to its rib, Keersi's beastly foe lashed out almost as a reflex action, cuffing her on the side of the head.

She reeled from the contact, but maintained enough presence of mind to pivot out of the way when the Zorsi tried to pin her with its horns like a charging bull.

Like any large animal, this Zorsi was at its most dangerous when wounded, as if it could get any more dangerous than it already was in optimum health. It was also enraged to the point that any sense of calculation it possessed, meager though it seemed, all but vanished in a whirlpool of blind frenzy and fury.

The Zorsi spun around.

Keeri felt herself fading. She shook off the encroaching blackness with ferocious effort.

The Zorsi was upon her, sword reared back to strike, its savage shadow spilling over her like a precursor to disaster.

She bent her legs in a combat stance and met the Zorsi head on, burying her sword in its lower torso, before the creature could take her head.

The Zorsi's breakneck momentum carried Keersi to the ground. She managed to land in a way that prevented her from being flattened by the creature's bulk.

Lying on her stomach, emitting pained moans, Keersi sluggishly brought her legs underneath her in an effort to rise.

From the corner of her eye a figure much smaller than a Zorsi bounded toward her.

Suli saw his opportunity and took it. The woman was obviously wounded. Now that those foul beasts were no more he could finish what he started.

He darted toward her without hesitation, blade poised to slice through her back.

At the final second, with the old man looming over her, Keersi hopped to her feet.

Suli's expression transitioned from smug arrogance to disbelief. He locked eyes with Keersi, and then looked down to see a sword lodged halfway in his stomach, the hand gripping it pushing it deeper.

Keersi snatched the blade out and shoved the man to the ground in a fit of pique.

Her rage diminished as she stood over Suli. From the nature of his wound, death was going to be slow to claim him.

"Others…will…come for you," Suli croaked through quivering lips.

"I'm sure they will," Keersi replied with a mix of resignation and defiance. "And I'll be ready for them."

Animalistic grunts flittered through the air, signaling the presence of more Zorsis.

"You…won't…leave me to those…beasts?" Suli uttered weakly.

Keersi's gaze turned heated. "I damn well should!" She paused in consideration before taking out Luotunde's dagger. She knelt beside the dying man, lifted his head, and cradled it. "I've hated you all these years. Yet, a small part of me still loves you…father."

She slit her father's throat and watched him die a mercifully quick death in her arms.

A trio of Zorsis emerged into view from a distant part of the village. More appeared soon after.

Keersi counted up to thirty. The rest of the scouting party.

Wounded and exhausted she couldn't outrun them for long on foot. The horses had scattered, further reducing her chances of escape.

She glanced at her father's reposeful face. "It looks like the stain on our family's honor will be removed after all." She smiled faintly in bitter amusement. "You always did get what you wanted." Resting Suli's head gently on the ground, Keersi stood. She picked up her father's sword to add to her own and proceeded to advance toward the Zorsis.

"Let's see how many more of you I can kill before I join my father and brothers in death!"

Yelling their frightful battle cries, the Zorsis thrust their weapons overhead, their mouths gaped wide, baring full sets of flesh-shredding teeth.

They charged in uncoordinated fashion. It was a footrace to get to the human prize.

Keersi maintained her casual stride. A soothing calm draped over her even as her muscles tensed for combat.

High pitched noises intermingling with the clamor of charging Zorsis, caught her ear.

The sounds came from above. Keersi looked up and saw whistling flocks of arrows darkening the sky. The arrow volley arched at its highest point and rained groundward in a murderous drizzle.

Zorsis dropped and tumbled to the surface, their bodies bristling with arrow shafts. The deadly storm continued. Arrows slashed through flesh. More Zorsis fell, their battle cries heightening to death wails. A trickle of survivors tried to turn and run. Arrows screamed past Keersi, burrowing into their wide backs, ruthlessly ending their retreat.

A Zorsi, lacking the wit to play dead, stirred amid its

downed comrades, trying to rise. An arrow shaft protruded from its upper chest. A second arrow penetrated beneath the first one and the Zorsi crumbled to the ground. This time it stayed still.

Keersi looked behind her.

Bare chested Goyo light infantry soldiers approached with fleet footed assuredness, their bows notched and directed upon the dead Zorsis.

A cluster of heavy infantry in chest armor, bearing wide bladed spears with large oblong leather hide shields, followed close behind the archers. The latter group established a protective cordon around their commander while the archers continued forward into the killing zone to assess the slaughter they inflicted.

Keersi's astonished gaze fell upon a particularly large Goyo soldier in the regalia of an officer and stayed there.

"You disobeyed my order, Luotunde," she scolded, somehow unable to give the weight of sincerity to the displeasure on her face.

Luotunde drew back with a look of wounded innocence. "Not at all, Commander. I heard rumors of Phulani troop movements in this region. I sent soldiers to investigate and decided to join them at the last minute. I had no idea we would just happen upon you out here in the middle of nowhere."

"No idea?"

Luotunde stuck to his story. "None whatsoever, my Commander."

Keersi gave in to a smile. "You're not a very good liar, you know."

"Which makes me ill suited for the intrigues of the king's court." The officer studied Keersi with deep concern "Are you all right?"

Keersi nodded. "I'll live."

Luotunde looked around, spotting human dead in addition to Zorsi. A human corpse in black garb snagged his attention. "Was that…?"

"Yes," Keersi preempted, staring at the corpse, her gut churning with conflicting emotions.

"Is it over?" Luotunde asked.

Keersi tore her gaze away from the body. "I wish I could say it is, but it's not. I have a lot of relatives."

Grim silence fell over the pair until a soldier arrived to report that all Zorsis were dead and that there were no more threats in the area.

Luotunde clasped his hands in satisfaction. "Good. I think we can head back to camp, now. It seems those rumors of Phulani activity this far north were just that: rumors. Permission to withdraw, Commander?"

Keersi straightened, shedding some of her fatigue, putting on her command face. "Permission granted. Let's get out of here… and Luotunde."

Her second-in-command looked at her.

"Thank you."

Luotunde shined a broad grin. "You're embarrassing me. Come, we have a campaign to finish." His levity faded immediately as he turned and shouted orders to the soldiers to clear out.

# Queen of the Sapphire Coast

### Linda Macauley

Kala, pirate queen of the Sapphire Coast, stood upon the white sand of the nameless beach and looked about herself.

She looked at her ship, the *Assegai*, rocking gently on the crystal clear water of the bay. She looked down at the white sand beneath her toes, and then raised her gaze up and beyond, to the palm fringed jungle that led to the interior. She looked at the corpse of the ragged white man at her feet. He who had but recently expired. She wondered if what the white man had told her was true or if the tropical sun had burned his brain or the poisoned fruit he had eaten in his ignorance had driven him mad.

They had seen the smoke from the deck of the *Assegai* earlier that morning. A long, thin column that rose high into the cloudless blue sky.

A lookout had yelled and pointed. The smoke was rising from one of the small and nameless islands that dotted this part of the Sapphire Coast.

"Probably cannibals," Tergu, her helmsman grunted.

Kala had been inclined to agree. There were no large communities living amongst the chain of small islands. Only a few savage tribes who used their canoes to paddle from one island to the next. She was about to instruct the helmsman to hold steady on their course and pass the island by, but then, on a whim, changed her mind.

"Take us closer. It is early in the day for a cooking fire, and a large one at that."

Tergu grunted unhappily but did as he was bid. If the mistress of the *Assegai* wished to investigate the strange smoke, then it was not his place to dissuade her. Like the rest of the crew, Tergu worshipped her.

Even as he swung the tiller, he cast an admiring glance at the woman who stood beside him.

He knew men swore that Kala was a lioness in human form, but he always thought of her as a cheetah of the veldt. Tall and sleek. Sinuous, graceful, deadly. Her ebony skin glistened. Her short hair was today hidden under a red silk turban she had wrapped around her head in deference to the fierce heat of the sun, and it not yet midday.

Her feet were bare and the loose doeskin breeks she wore came only to her knees. A sleeveless white blouse completed her costume. She wore rings of gold in both ears and gold bracelets upon her wrists. She little resembled the feared pirate queen most knew her as in these waters. Her history was well known on the Sapphire Coast.


Her father had been the chieftain of a small kraal, set amongst the rolling greens hills of a verdant savannah. Araq slavers had come in the night. Raiding the village, murdering her mother and father in their bed. Slaying all in the village, sparing only the young boys and girls. Her elder brothers died defending her. Kala, along with the other youths, was shackled and dragged, screaming, away from the burning village.

Flailing whips and sharp blows transported them from the grasslands to the jungle and thence to the coast, where the slavers had beached their ships, awaiting the return of their chain gangs of despair.

Chained in the filthy hold of an Araq ship already the white hot flame of revenge had begun to smoulder in Kala's heart. She was the daughter of a chieftain. The descendant of a proud warrior race. In her sixteen summers, she had hunted lions alongside her brothers, protected their herds of cattle and goats from slinking hyenas and marauding leopards. She was no timorous native girl to beat her breast and sob her heart out, bewailing her fate.

Kala had always been a skinny child, and had grown into a slim young woman. The shackle about her left ankle was not tight. The second night of the voyage, scraping the skin of her heel raw, using her own blood to lubricate the restraining iron, Kala freed herself. She knew the leader of the slavers held the key for the lock that secured the long chain. The remaining members of her tribe gathered around her as she whispered to them in the darkness.

The leader of the Araq slavers died when Kala opened his throat with his own knife. Like a cat she crept back to the hold with the keys to her tribesmen's shackles.

Once freed, they followed the daughter of their chieftain up upon the deck and like ebony spectres crept around the ship, using the purloined blades of their owners to slay their captors in silence.

When the sun rose the next morning, all the slavers were dead, their bodies flung over the side to feed the sharks.

All this Tergu knew, for he had been one of the youths with whom Kala had been captured. With the slaver's ship beneath her feet and vengeance still burning bright in her heart, Kala had vowed to slay every Araq she came across. In the years that followed, she made good on her promise. Together with her tribesmen she captured Araq slave ships. Raided their coastal villages, ransacked the slavers baracoons. Once, together with a flotilla of pirate vessels from Tortarge, she had even led an assault on a major Araq trading port.

Her name was a byword for terror amongst the Araqis. She slaughtered them wherever she found them. Giving no quarter and asking for none.

Tergu knew that his Captain was now in her twenty-second year and as far as he could judge her hatred toward her sworn foes had slackened not one iota.

Few of her original tribesmen still survived to serve her, most had been slain in their battles on both land and sea. But Kala was never short of volunteers, her raids against the Araq's brought in much plunder, plunder she had little care for, but brought her crew the best of everything. Good food, strong rum, the soft flesh of women. The merchants of Tortarge were always glad to see the sails of the Assegai on the horizon. She only took crew from the natives of her own land. Many of whom had either been themselves enslaved or lost children and loved ones to the chain gangs.

"It could be a trick," Tergu suggested. "A ruse to lure us in." The price on Kala's head was high. Araq Men O'war and privateers, mercenaries in truth, had hunted the *Assegai* before.

His Captain shrugged carelessly. "We are still far enough off shore. I only wish to get close enough to see the cause of the smoke. It looks like a signal fire to me."

"A brave lot, who signal in these waters," Tergu countered. "They guide the cannibals to a feast, and have the fire already lit."

Kala laughed. "Oh you are a gloomy soul today, my friend." Then she pointed. "Look you. There's a man on the beach. A white man. He waves to us."

Indeed Tergu could now see the figure Kala's sharp eyesight had pinpointed. As the *Assegai* sailed sedately closer to the beach all the crew could see that one man stood alone upon the sand, and his signal fire beside him appeared to be the burning remains of a longboat.

"He stands strangely," a new voice said.

Kala and Tergu turned to the speaker. It was Yango, the huge, shaven headed Matabele warrior who was Kala's lover and second in command of the Assegai. Clad only in a short leather kilt his muscles rippled under his dark skin. He too had once been a slave, a gladiator in the arenas of Roma, one of the favourites of the crowd, before he had escaped and made his way back to the land of his birth. Now the big man grunted. "He must be injured. He uses a crutch to support himself."

As the *Assegai* sailed closer to the shore the others could see that he was correct. The lone white man, now kneeling at the water's edge, was indeed supporting himself with the aid of a stick.

"Drop anchor here," Kala instructed. "I will take four men and go ashore in the rowboat."

"Is that wise?" Tergu wondered. "It could still be a trap, there might be men, waiting, hidden in the tree line."

"I will go with you," Yango said. "I need to stretch my legs."

"Tell the men to launch the boat," Kala ordered Tergu.

To Yango she said, "Let us arm ourselves, and be alert for any treachery."


Four men rowed whilst Kala and Yango sat in the bow of the small boat and peered intently at the approaching beach and the man who knelt there. He raised a hand and waved weakly at them.

"How can he be so sure that we are friendly?" Yango asked.

"Perhaps he has been marooned here for so long that any company is welcome." Kala suggested. "Even ours."

The big warrior beside her grinned. "Lucky for him he's not an Araq, hey?"

"Then I would throw him on his own signal fire," the woman agreed.

Their boat passed into the shallows and the slight swell guided them onto the smooth white sand above the waterline. No sooner had the hull scraped the sandy bottom than Kala and her companion vaulted over the side and approached the kneeling figure.

With her hand on the hilt of her cutlass Kala surveyed both the man in front of her and the edge of the jungle behind him.

Yango had been doing the same. "I see only one set of tracks."

Kala nodded.

The kneeling man gazed up at her. "Thank the Gods. I thought you had not seen my smoke. I thought you would pass me by."

He was gasping and a trickle of blood ran out of the corner of his mouth as he spoke. His left leg was twisted badly below the knee. Kala suspected it was broken near the ankle. The ragged marks in the sand behind him showed how much of an effort it must have taken to drag himself down to the water.

The man was white, as testified to by his pale skin and blonde hair. He had a weeks' worth of beard on his face and his eyes shone with the burning intensity of those afflicted with fever. He spoke in the common tongue of the coastal ports, though his accent made some of his words hard to understand.

He was dressed in rags, breeches ripped almost to pieces, a once white linen shirt torn and stained with blood.

Kala knelt down before him. "Who are you and how came you here?"

One of her men handed her a waterskin and she pulled out the stopper and handed it to the other as he began to speak.

"I am Jakob, late of Tortarge. I sailed on the *Redhawk* under Ironhand, our captain."

"I know of him," Kala interrupted. "Though we've never met."

The wounded man peered at her. "Aye. I know you, too. You're Kala, whom men call the pirate Queen of the Sapphire Coast. I saw you once, in Tortarge, just before you sailed out with a dozen ships to sack the port of Tubal." He coughed as he spoke and more blood trickled out between his lips. Rising the waterskin he took a sip, sighed and continued.

"The *Redhawk* is gone. Caught in the storm that battered this coast a week back. Drove us onto the Siren Rocks. The hull fair ripped apart under us. Ironhand and a few others managed to get clear in a long boat. I was one of them. Tossed about like a cork we were, at the mercy of the storm and the sea. We thought the Gods were smiling on us when we beached here. That was before we found the damned ruins."

"What ruins?" Kala raised an eyebrow.

Jakob gestured behind himself, at the jungle. 'In there. We went in there, looking for fresh water, some game to kill for food. Ten of us went in. Only I have come back out."

The pirate Queen and her lover shared a glance.

"What happened to the others?" asked Yango.

The kneeling man was about to speak when he was taken by a coughing fit. He cried out and gasped as blood spurted from his mouth and he clutched his chest with his free hand.

"We found the treasure," Jakob gasped weakly. "Like a dream it was, lying there for any to take." He groaned again and his breath came in pants. He was dying, they could all see that. Kala suspected the white man had broken ribs, the fragments of which had punctured his lungs. In an unaccustomed display of tenderness Kala leaned forward and put her arm around Jakob's shoulders, holding him as he fought against the coming of the long darkness.

"Treasure?" she queried.

Jakob looked at her and smiled a sad smile.

"Aye," he breathed. "Lying there for the taking."

Then he coughed once more and died.

"He came out of the jungle here," Yango pointed, "and used his flint and the kindling he had gathered to set the long boat a'fire. He must have had it prepared, on the off chance he saw a ship passing by. He probably spotted our sails on the horizon after sunrise."

Kala nodded in agreement. Gestured to the bright yellow fruit lying scattered around on the sand. "He didn't know these are poisonous."

It was Yango's turn to nod. "White men I've met know little about such things. But these wouldn't kill him, just make him vomit his guts up."

The black warrior knelt down himself and ripped off the remains of the dead Jakob's shirt. He began to run his hands around the torso and stomach. "Ribs are broken." His hands moved lower. "The shin bone is fractured, the ankle shattered. He must have been injured during the storm he spoke of, or mayhap he fell when they went into the jungle."

Indeed there was heavy bruising all over Jakob's torso. Kala doubted the man would have lived, even had he been attended by a competent healer.

"He spoke of treasure," one of the oarsmen noted. "Ruins. In the jungle somewhere."

"He also said that ten men went in with him and only he came back out," Yango observed dryly. He looked at Kala.

The pirate captain arched an eyebrow in return. "We'd never forgive ourselves if we didn't investigate his claims."

"He was probably delirious from the Derketos apples."

"And if he wasn't?"

"I hardly imagine the local cannibals would have missed a pile of ruins filled with treasure. They like their gold and silver trinkets as much as anyone else."

"Perhaps they are a'feared of the ruins and will not approach them, you know how superstitious the coastal tribes are."

Yango sighed. There was going to be no denying his captain, he could see that. "Let us go back to the Assegai, gather more men and weapons."

Kala grinned at him. "Just so."


Fifteen men and one woman made their way along a narrow jungle trail.

Kala and Yango were in the lead, with thirteen stout warriors behind them. Their mode of attire and choice of weapons varied from man to man, depending on personal preference or tribal upbringing. Some carried a cutlass and dagger, whilst others preferred the short stabbing spear and spiked war club. Some even bore the animal hide shields of their homeland. Many of them also carried powerful bows or crossbows.

Dressed now in a leather bodice, with sturdy sandals protecting her feet and a cutlass swinging from a scabbard at her side, Kala looked every inch the pirate Queen most of the Sapphire Coast knew her to be. She had removed the silken turban she had worn earlier and also divested herself of her earrings and gold jewellery. She wished for nothing to impede her in combat. A turban could slip over the eyes; an earring could be grasped by an enemy.

Yango strode along beside her, the big man pushing stubborn branches out of their way. A short sword was thrust through his silken waist sash and a thick hafted trident was clasped in his hand.

They had left the beach some time ago, over a turn of a sand-glass if Yango was any judge. Sweat dripped down his forehead, small insects flew in to feast on the salt. He thought of Jakob, the dead sailor from the Redhawk, wondering if his Gods were pleased at the manner of his funeral pyre. It was better than being left on the sand, he decided, being slowly devoured by crabs and seabirds.

He heard Kala make some noise in her throat and glanced that way. Still walking she indicated the trail before them. "Footprints. Some booted."

Yango peered at the soft earth underfoot. His captain

was correct. The imprint of both boots and naked feet showed clearly.

"All heading the same way as us," he said. He didn't have to make mention that none of the prints went in the opposite direction, Kala would have already noticed that.

She kept her voice low, that the men behind not overhear. "Perhaps they reached the ruins and were attacked by a party of cannibals, they are all over these islands, like scavenging hyenas."

"A pity Jakob died before he could tell us," muttered her companion.

It was past midday when the party from the *Assegai* finally arrived at the ruins of which Jakob had spoken.

The trail ended abruptly and Kala let forth an involuntary gasp as she saw the ruins for the first time.

Built of marble blocks the buildings were in a sad state of disrepair, jungle vines and creepers having wormed their way through the stone and broken apart the mortar that bound them together. Roofs had fallen in, walls had crumbled, and the paving stones were raised and broken in places. Yet still an air of majesty hung over the place.

"Who the hell built this?" Yango voiced what they were all thinking.

"I have heard," Kala replied slowly, "that the sons of the serpent, driven from the lands of men, would oft times seek out places like this. Islands, remote, deserted. There they would build their temples and continue to worship their dark God."

Yango gave her a look; behind him some of the crew began to mutter amongst themselves. One man snapped his fingers three times, to ward off evil spirits. At which Kala laughed.

"Oh come now. It's broad daylight and the sun is shining, whoever heard of ghosts or goblins venturing about at this time of day. Whoever built these ruins have long turned to dust."

Her laughter had broken the somber mood of her men. They grinned at their captain and each other sheepishly.

"Yango," she continued, "do you take some of the men and do a sweep around the edge of the ruins. The rest of you split up as you will and see if you can find that treasure the white man was babbling about."

Her lover called some men to him and moved off to the right, as he went he called back. "What are you going to do?"

A pointed finger supplied his answer. "I'm going to investigate that temple there."

His eyes followed the direction she indicated. They came to rest on a circular building. Some of the wide pillars had toppled and the domed roof had long since collapsed. A set of broad steps led from what must have been a small plaza, up and through an arched doorway. Like the other buildings it was covered by jungle growth, vines and creepers, some of which sprouted red or orange blossoms.

"If there's treasure to be found anywhere," Kala called to him, "it will be in the temple. You know how priests love to hoard their gold."

He grinned back at her. "Aye. I'll join you shortly." So saying Yango and five of the crew began to walk around the perimeter of the ruins. Despite his apparent unconcern, he was cautious. Jakob had said that nine others had entered the jungle with him, reached the ruins, found some unspecified treasure. Yet Jakob had fled the ruins, carrying no treasure, and as yet Yango had seen no sign of the bodies of the other nine men.

As she walked around fallen marble blocks, or clambered over tree roots, Kala had the same thoughts running through her head. If Jakob's companions had been killed in this spot, where then were the bodies? Her initial suggestion of cannibals returned to her. Those flesh hungry jackals would have taken the bodies with them, back to their villages for the whole tribe to feast on. Kala shuddered. She hoped if such was indeed the case, that all of the men had been killed here. Those captured alive by the cannibals were frequently cooked that way.


The pirate Queen stood inside the crumbled temple and surveyed the scene before her.

A statue had once stood on a raised dais, that much was certain. Made all of pure white marble the figure itself had toppled over and shattered. Kala walked over to the dais and then stepped up on to it. Five more steps took her to the opposite side and she looked down to see what form of man or woman the statue had been carved in.

A sharp breath hissed between her teeth. Although the carved figure was now in three separate pieces the design of the statue was still plain enough to see. A woman. The face carved so skilfully that the countenance was as real as Kala's own. A cold visage, haughty and arrogant, yet in place of the expected tresses of human hair the scalp was adorned with a spiked crest. The skin too seemed covered in minute scales. The hands and feet looked normal enough, until a closer inspection revealed the reptilian webbing between the fingers and toes.

"So I was right," Kala murmured to herself. "This was a temple of the serpent folk." Legends had it that long eons ago the race of men had fought against the serpent people in a long and bloody war. Man had been victorious and the remnants of the sons of the serpent had scattered across the wide world. As the centuries passed the serpent people became little more than a dark folk tale, until, as Kala and her crew had this day, someone stumbled over the remains of one of their hidden lairs, built far from human civilisation.

Kala shivered as she looked at the fallen statue. So human and yet so alien. Kala wondered who the image was based on. A real person or one of their deities? She shrugged, what did it matter, the serpent folk had vanished from the sight of men for thousands of years before she was born.

Turning away from the statue, Kala got on with the serious work of seeking out the treasure of which Jakob had spoken. She had seen nothing of it so far.

Having walked all around the temple area and finding nothing except jungle creepers and animal droppings Kala shook her head in disgust and retraced her path back outside to the plaza.

She was just walking down the marble steps when a scream erupted from another part of the ruins. This was quickly followed by more, and not all from the same throat. Cursing, the pirate Queen unlimbered her cutlass and began to run in the direction the cries were emanating from.

Yango and the men with him had likewise heard the screams of their fellow crewmen.

"Back to the plaza," the large warrior shouted and without waiting for a response leapt over a crumbled wall and raced headlong in the direction of the temple.

When Kala arrived at the location from whence came the screams she skidded to a stop in amazement.

Two of her crew lay motionless upon the bare earth, and judging from the wounds inflicted on their bodies they would not be rising again. The remaining three were still battling the foe that had slain their companions. Yet what that foe was Kala could not quite make out.

One of her men thrust a spear at something just in front of him. Kala could see only a blur of colour. There was a vague suggestion of an outline but it blended so well against the jungle behind it that she was hard put to describe what it was she was looking at.

Movement behind one of the other men and as he turned he was knocked from his feet. Without warning his throat opened and blood spurted high into the air. There was something astride his chest, a large form. As the blood spurted some of the form changed colour to match the bright redness.

A chill ran through Kala, thoughts of djinns and jungle demons filled her mind. For an instant she hesitated but then the third man began to wrestle with another changeling form. Crying out in fear and anger she raced forward.

Yango dashed toward the screaming and yelling. Running around a crumbled wall he came upon an odd sight. He saw Kala swinging her cutlass at thin air. A downward slash, followed by a backhand then a forward stabbing motion. To the big warrior's surprise, he saw blood covering the captain's blade as she pulled her cutlass back. A blurred shape shimmered in front of her, a mixed hue of colour, as though the jungle itself had come alive and was attacking her. Then the shimmering form coalesced into a creature out of nightmare!

It was a lizard, as tall as herself, and although it had a tail longer than its body it walked upright on two legs and instead of forelegs had a pair of very human looking arms, even if the hands did end in razor sharp talons. The face – if asked Yango would have been hard put to say whether it was reptilian or human – there were traces of both species in those features.

The bodies of her crewmen lay unmoving at her feet, only Kala still stood and even as she slew the creature before her Yango realised that two more lay in wait. To his eyes they appeared as no more than a shimmer amongst the green of the jungle backdrop, yet those shimmers moved to encircle Kala. As his captain whirled to defend herself from a second creature the third came upon her from the opposite side. Without thinking, Yango raised his trident and hurled it with all his might at the spot he judged the third creature to be. The heavy trident flashed through the air, and for a moment seemed suspended in it, then another lizard form materialised and collapsed, the all too human hands clasped around the haft of the three pronged weapon that was buried deep in its chest.

Slipping his short sword free of his sash Yango ran forward to aid Kala, but there was no need. The pirate Queen stood panting over the twitching body of the second lizard creature.

At the sound of his approach she turned with her sword raised, a wild look in her eyes.

Yango held his hands up. The sword lowered.

"What manner of creatures are these?" he asked as he pulled his trident free of the one he had slain.

"The last of the serpent folk, I think," Kala replied. She bent to her fallen crewmen but quickly realised there was nothing she could do for them. Throats were torn out, chest cavities torn asunder.

"I thought the sons of the serpent resembled men more than reptiles?"

She shrugged. "So the legends would have us believe, perhaps they are wrong. Perhaps the creatures never looked like real men at all."

Yango had noticed something else. "Look here. Each of these things wears a necklace. This one is of gold, and this one, and by the Hydra is this one not of rubies?"

Crouching down beside him Kala reached out and fingered the red stoned necklace. She chuckled mirthlessly.

"What?"

"I see it now," she said. "Jakob's cryptic mumblings. Did he not say that the treasure was just lying about, to be picked up by anyone?"

The other shrugged, not understanding her point.

"These creatures have the same abilities as the chameleon," she continued. "Imagine you're walking along and you see this ruby necklace, hanging on a tree. But when you reach out to pluck it off, that tree comes alive and tears out your throat."

Yango's eyebrows went up. "So these creatures are intelligent?"

"I'd rather not wait around to find out," Kala said. "Do you collect these trinkets and we'll be off and round up the rest of the men. I suddenly have no desire to linger on this island any longer."

All they found were corpses.

"There must be many of these things," Yango said.

"At least our lads made them pay dearly. Look you, almost every spear has blood upon the tip and every cutlass is red to the hilt," Kala made these observations with grim satisfaction.

They were once more standing in the plaza, in front of the steps that led up into the temple area that Kala had explored earlier.

"I see a silver bracelet sitting atop that marble block," Yango jerked his head. "And a gold chain in the dust to the left."

"Neither of which was there when I was here before," Kala noted.

Yango grunted, he had suspected as much.

"We must make a run for the beach," he told her. "It is our only chance."

An unladylike snort answered him. "We'll be lucky to get away from these ruins," she said.

Even as she spoke vaguely human-like shapes had begun to materialise around them.

"Into the temple," Kala whispered fiercely.

Together the pair sprang forward, dashing up the marble steps. Yango used the butt of his trident to shove back a lizard creature that snapped at them as they rushed past. Once inside the temple proper Kala jumped up onto the dais and spun around. Yango joined her and they stood back to back, breathing heavily, fearful of what might come next, but not willing to greet the long darkness without a fight.

Shimmering shapes crept around them on all sides. Claw prints magically appeared in the dust that lay thick on the floor of the temple. Necklaces and bracelets and other accoutrements floated in the air, as though to entice them to step forward and take them up.

The pair of them didn't move. Kala's cutlass was raised and ready to strike. Yango's trident was clenched in both hands.

"Mayhap I attack them and you slip away in that moment," Yango suggested. "Leave your sword, run like the devil himself was after you. You could make the beach, I know you could."

"Ah, Yango," Kala half turned and offered him a dazzling smile. "Do you think I would leave you to face death alone? You love sick fool." She leaned over and kissed him upon his cheek.

Suddenly the air in front of them shimmered and changed colours, a vague outline became a solid shape. Then all around them the reptilian creatures slowly became visible. They surrounded the pair on the dais. Cold, unblinking eyes stared malevolently into their own.

"I think the time for running has passed," Kala muttered.


A sibilant hissing broke out amongst the creatures arrayed before them. Some slipped aside as a smaller member of their kind entered the temple.

Kala gasped and Yango simply stared.

In form and figure the new arrival was identical to the toppled statue at their feet. Save that this creature lived and breathed and moved with sinuous grace. The same cold, arrogant features, the slim and supple limbs, as human as their own, the skin coated in a fine sheen of glittering scales. As she walked past the other creatures they crouched down upon the broken marble floor, gently lowering their heads, as though royalty was passing them by. She stopped a short distance from the dais and inspected the two who stood upon it.

"Will your kind never stop hounding us?" she hissed.

Kala and Yango exchanged a glance. "We came in search of treasure, nothing else."

"There is no treasure here."

"Save for trinkets such as this?" Yango held up the necklaces he had collected. "These are worth a fortune."

The serpent woman blinked. "To us, they are just pretty baubles."

"Our kind lust after baubles such as this," Yango assured her.

"How many more of you will come?" she hissed.

"If you let us pass, none." Kala replied quickly.

"You think me a fool, human? Tell me what I wish to know and you shall die swiftly, that is all I will offer." The voice was as cold as the look upon the serpent woman's face.

Kala's chin came up. She was the pirate Queen of the Sapphire Coast, she would show fear to no one. "I say this once and mark my words for they are as iron. If we do not return to our ship others *will* come. Many others. They will bring steel and fire. They will raze this island to the ground. You may kill some of them, but not all. My men are the fiercest warriors on the Sapphire Coast, blood and death is as food and drink to them. I see you and I see your people. You are few. You have the power of the chameleon, but where will the chameleon hide when all the jungle is a'fire, when all the trees are burnt husks and the grass is a smouldering carpet of ash. Think on this, O'queen of serpents."

Silence followed Kala's outburst. The female creature in front of her giving no indication that Kala's words held any import.

Then she sighed. "My people have suffered enough. This island is our last resting place, we have no other. If I slay you, then perhaps others will come, and do as you have foretold. If I let you live, you may go back to your ship and thence return, with fire and steel yourself. These few poor creatures you see before you are all that is left of our race. Females all. Our males are all dead. There are no sons of the serpent, only daughters, who will never bear children of their own. What guarantee do I have that you would not come back, seeking revenge for those of your men my sisters have slain? Or go forth and tell all the world that there are yet serpent folk still alive on this island."

Kala hesitated, wondering what to say, that would assure the serpent queen that she would keep her word.

Before she could frame an answer, Yango spoke up. "I will stay behind. As hostage to Kala's word. If she breaks it, slay me."

"Yango, no!" Kala shook her head.

The serpent queen looked back and forth between them. "You are mated?"

"She is my woman," Yango agreed. "I am her man."

"If he stays, then so do I," Kala assured the other.

Whatever fateful decision would have been made by the serpent queen was never voiced, for at that moment the cries of men echoed through the ruins.

"Kala! Yango! Kala! Yango! Where are you?"

"Men from our ship," Kala spoke quickly. "They search for us, we have been overlong in returning to the beach. Disappear into the jungle, O'queen, we shall say nothing of your presence here. Make haste, they are almost upon us."

The serpent queen hesitated. The voices came closer. With a few hissed commands, she issued orders to the others around her. Like ghosts they turned about and slipped away through the ruins, their chameleon abilities making them vanish in an instant.

The queen met Kala's gaze. "I have little faith in the word of a human."

"Why are the others not as you?" Kala asked.

"Because I was born of woman, while they were begat of the snake."

Kala stared at the other. Her mouth opened to frame another question, but before she could do so the serpent queen had turned away.

"Leave us in peace," were her last words.

Kala, with Yango beside her, met Tergu and two dozen men in the centre of the ruins.

"We must make haste back to the ship," Kala told them. "This island is infested with cannibals. They have killed the others, Yango and I were lucky to escape."

Tergu cursed. "One of the men from your party staggered out of the jungle. He waved to us for help. By the time we got ashore, he was dead. Slashed to pieces he was, I'm surprised he managed to get back to the beach. I gathered the men about me and we came in search of you. Lucky we did. We haven't come across any of the cannibals; they must be a'feared of a large party."

Kala nodded. "Indeed. Come, let us leave this place. Jakob was delusional, those apples he ate poisoned his brain. There is no treasure here, and the cannibals killed all his companions."

It was at that moment that Kala realised Yango must still have hold of the necklaces he had taken from the slain serpent folk. She glanced at him, expecting to see the jewellery in his hands, but when she did so she saw that his hands were empty.

As though reading her thoughts the other smiled and slyly pointed back at the temple. "There is nothing of any value on this cursed island," he said aloud.


The *Assegai* lifted anchor and sailed with the outgoing tide. In the west the sun had already started to set, turning the ocean into a pool of liquid amber.

Kala, pirate Queen of the Sapphire Coast and her lover Yango, stood upon the stern rail and watched the small island slowly disappear in the distance behind them.

"I thought you might want to take revenge for the deaths of our men?" Yango wondered.

His captain sighed. "We lost men, they lost sisters. I think both sides are to blame. Besides, I gave my word."

The big man nodded. "Aye."

The island was but a tiny speck now.

"Farewell," she said. "Daughters of the serpent."

She felt Yango's arm slide around her waist and leaned into his embrace. Above their heads a strong wind caught the sails of the *Assegai*, snapping the canvas taut, carrying the vessel and its crew toward the setting sun.

# Ghost Marriage

*P. Djeli Clark*

Ayen ran, her bare feet kicking up a cloud of ash colored dust across the parched earth. Behind her, the hooves of horses thundered like drums, drawing closer despite her desperate strides. When the rope slipped over her head, she was struck with terror--a primal fear, droned into her since she was a girl. She grabbed at it, frantic to free herself. But a harsh pull jerked her back as the noose tightened, cutting off her breathing. She went down, tumbling in an awkward heap that left her long legs splayed out from beneath her goatskin skirt. She coughed and sputtered, inhaling thick choking dust as she fought for air, fingers grappling futilely at the coarse fibers biting into her flesh. From the corner of an eye she caught sight of her captors.

They were three men, bundled in dark robes with cloths of yellow, deep blue and crimson covering their faces. The one holding the wooden pole with the noose had jumped from his horse, its sleek black body speckled with flints of gray. He ran up eagerly as she backed away, scrambling on bruised palms and feet as best she could. But a cruel twist of his pole wrenched her neck, slamming her head down in an explosion of dust and pain. She cried out in prayer to the One Nhialic. Of all those who had abandoned her, she did not count the great Creator among them. Or at least, so she hoped.

She laid there, with her face pressed to the earth,

watching her captor approach cautiously, the way one would a frightened calf that might bolt at first touch. One of his eyes was ruined, a useless bit of white flesh covered by a flap of skin. But the other, dark and trained on her, glittered with excitement. She imagined that beneath his crimson face wrappings he grinned just as fiercely. Reaching her he quickly pressed her down, ignoring her cries of struggle as his knee dug into her back and his hand palmed her bare scalp. In one fluid movement, he loosed the rope about her neck, replacing the scratchy fibers with something cold and heavy but no less constricting. Finishing, he moved from atop her and stepped back, exclaiming in satisfaction.

Ayen struggled to sit, keeping her eyes on him. Her hands went up, feeling the metal clasped about her neck and the length of linked chain extending to her captor. Her heart fell in despair. Janjawa slavers. Who else but they would be out here, on the scorched lands beneath this merciless sun, where only the banished and forsaken--like her--were forced to walk alone. She cursed her carelessness. All knew Janjawa roamed here, hunting for slaves for their coffles to be driven to faraway markets and sold beyond the known world--at least the world as her people, the Djeng, knew it to be.

A fierce tug came on the chain as the Janjawa called to her in his tongue, a mashing of incoherent sounds no more known to her than the bleating of goats. She gazed at him coolly, but did nothing. She had watched many a stubborn cow do the same—become a rock, refusing to be moved when they did not wish. You could learn a lot from cows and rocks, if you paid attention.

The Janjawa's good eye creased. She imagined now beneath his wrappings he scowled. Another strong yank of the chain pitched her forward, sending her flat to the ground. Still she lay unmoving, refusing even to sit up. From atop their horses his companions laughed, calling out what sounded like jeers. This only annoyed her captor further. He stalked towards her, a long stick now held high, readied to lash her obstinacy. She laughed and cursed as he came, damning him and any children that passed from his shriveled loins to the hottest, most barren and scorched lands beneath Nhialic's gaze. She was Ayen of the Akok! A Djeng! One of the First People and Lords of Men! And she would die here today than live as a slave! She gritted her teeth, waiting for the blow.

And then, he disappeared.

It was quick. One moment, the Janjawa stood there, the next his body caved in and burst apart--clothing, flesh and bone, all violently rendered to pulp as if crushed in the grip of an unseen hand. Blood spurted in every direction, and she gasped as it washed over her, sickeningly warm and unnaturally wet.

Malith. So he was here after all. But then, when did he ever leave?

Ayen blinked, wiping the gore from her eyes. One half of her face was covered in dusty earth; the other in blood. Rising to her knees, she gazed about. Her Janjawa captor was spread out in every direction, like soft *aror* porridge. His companions fared little better. One lay flat on his back, eyes open and staring to the sky, his glistening entrails torn out and entangled like fleshy roots with those of his horse. The third Janjawa lay crumpled awkwardly beside his bloodied steed, outstretched arms holding his decapitated head as if trying to retrieve it. One among them, however, had lived. Ayen turned to see a lone horse, a blur of black with speckled flints of gray, speeding away in the distance.

"Run," she whispered. "Flee from me, for I walk with the dead."

Faint laughter echoed in her hears. It was not a good laugh, the kind that brought feelings of mirth. Instead it was filled with a coldness that cut like a dulled blade.

"Malith. When did you come to so enjoy slaughter?"

Her ghost husband only laughed harder.

It took time for Ayen to sift through the Janjawa's bloodied entrails like some seer. Malith had whispered for her to do so, in his odd way, a voice that was not really a voice that she strained to hear. She supposed that was how the dead in their land fought to reach the ears of the living. She found the bit of metal he claimed would be there and fit it into a hole on the collar around her throat. With a turn, the iron ring broke apart and fell away, landing heavy upon the ground. She rubbed her neck and whispered out a thankful prayer, relishing her freedom.

Her eyes went to the other dead. Curious, she reached out to one, gingerly undoing the crimson cloth that covered his face. She'd heard so much of the Janjawa, who moved south from the far western desert to the lands of the Djeng in their incessant quest for slaves. Many claimed they were half-men and beasts, marked by their gods with serpent snouts or goat horns they hid beneath their head-cloths in shame. But what she saw now was just a man. His skin was as ebon as hers. And though his features were not as broad and beautiful as the Djeng, his face bore no unnatural traits. Only the thick black beard that enveloped his chin and mouth marked him as remarkably different. Her fingers played along three hoops of gold entangled in that rich mass, each twice as large as her thumb and etched with designs--markings perhaps of his clan, or tokens to his gods. Whatever the case, he was now dead, and would have no need of them.

Grimacing, she undid the shining rings, one at a time. Gold held no meaning for her. But traders claimed outlanders were as ravenous as suckling pigs to a sow's teat over it, which might prove useful. Among the Djeng more importance was placed on beads or shells--like those that made up her *Alual*. The loose bodice of stringed together red and sky blue glass beads fringed in white draped her long and slender body from shoulders to thigh, with a broad strip of yellow studded here and there with *gaak* shells that hung down the front to her knees. It was her prized possession, given to her by her mother upon her first marriage to Malith.

The morning of Ayen's dowry ceremony thirty young men, Malith's family and friends, arrived at her dwelling in a single line, jumping and singing poetry. Malith stayed away, as was custom. In his place his father, brothers and cousins came to barter. Her initial bride wealth was one hundred head of blue horned cattle. She'd been offended. One hundred blue horns was no small number, but her family was respected enough, his wealthy enough, and she certainly pretty enough, to earn twice that. She'd voiced this to her mother and her uncles agreed, convincing her father not to accept.

The next day, Malith himself came to their dwelling, alone and stunning in the tight-fitting *Malual* corset of red and black beads that seemed to amplify his taut lean frame. Her sisters had pinched her to keep her face calm, lest her pleased smile give away their bargaining position. Still, he'd seemed quite sure of the outcome, a knowing smirk on his face as he led his final addition to the dowry. It was a full-grown bull, its horns a series of remarkable red and white stripes. Red and blue horned cattle were common, but striped ones were exceedingly rare. There were men who would trade a thousand head of cattle and two daughters for it. The offering was enough to make her father and uncles lose all composure, and they hurriedly gave assent. Her sisters allowed her to smile then.

It was a good marriage, but all too brief. Tragedy stole Malith away, leaving her a widow. "Nhialic injures, Nhialic heals," his mother had intoned, as Ayen sat grappling with her grief. The woman had lost more than one child in her long life, some before they even left her belly. And she had developed a way of accepting God's unknowing will that helped her endure over the years. Ayen could only hope for a bit of that strength.

Her ghost marriage was agreed upon by both families. She'd yet borne no children for Malith, no one to carry on his name. They had tried, but no seed had planted. Now she would marry his older brother Yar, who already counted three wives. Any children she bore him would belong to Malith, and fall under his lineage. It was a certain demotion, even if out of ill circumstance and not spite. She would enter a new household as a young co-wife and by no means an equal, not among women who already held eight children between them. But she accepted it in silence. She would be a good wife to Malith, even after his death.

Only he seemed unwilling to embrace this fate.

The first sign came on her new marriage night, during the ritual that would bind her to Malith's spirit. A strong gale had sent up a sheet of dust so thick people fled to their homes for cover. Six goats died, all belonging to Yar, their mouths and nostrils suffocated in dust. Old women clutched to charms and men whispered prayers, calling it an ill omen.

Other misfortunes quickly followed. *Dhok* cats carried off several of Yar's calves in the night. Another day some ten blue horns were found dead, after grazing on poisonous *koor* shrubs. That these odd happenings began with Ayen's arrival in his household only placed blame at her feet. People whispered when she walked past or refused to meet her gaze. Mothers clutched their children in her presence and spat on their faces, a sign to ward off evil. Even her co-wives kept their distance. Many whispered it was Malith, refusing to accept his place among the dead or hers in the living. He clung to her they said, like a tick to a cow, sucking the life away of all nearby.

Then Yar's eldest son took strangely ill. He lingered with fever for three days before dying. And Yar could endure it no longer. He chased Ayen from his home, pushing her out at the edge of a spear. People watched as he shouted at her in his grief, calling her an *apeth*. In their tongue, it could mean witch or witchcraft. For her, it simply meant cursed. She fell to the ground trembling and sobbing at his rage. Then it happened.

Yar's spear flew from his hands. It spun high into the air, hovering for a moment, before falling with incredible force. Ayen watched as the tip of the spear found Yar's gaping mouth, piercing him right through, emerging from the back of his neck and embedding itself into the ground. He stood there, impaled and oddly bent back, a look of disbelief still on his face.

Ayen fled that very day. Yar's mother had insisted.

She claimed to do it for Ayen's own good, for if she stayed there, people would surely kill her. She'd bundled her with water skins and food, telling her to flee back to her parents where she might be safe. Ayen thanked the woman between her fright and tears, wailing her endless apologies. The elder woman had only shaken her head, saying Ayen would have to find a way to bring her tortured son the peace he needed.

But Ayen had not gone home. She could not return like this, carrying with her the vengeful spirit of a dead husband. Who knew what harm she would bring? No, she'd decided to go elsewhere, away from the clans, away from any Djeng. She needed help that was beyond them. There was someone however. Someone she had heard people speak of, a sorceress who lived deep in the scorched lands. They called her the Blood Woman.

Retrieving the golden rings from the dead Janjawa, Ayen used his robes to wipe her face clean. It was then her eyes spied the gleaming thing at his waist. She reached out and tugged it free. A knife, its hilt crafted of polished ivory. It sat in a golden scabbard studded in red and green gems that winked at her in the sunlight. Unsheathing the blade, she found a curving length of steel near long as her forearm. She let it tumble back and forth in her hands, impressed with its weight.

Among the Djeng, weapons were not common, even spears. But boys were gifted knives, to help ward off predators that stalked goats or cattle. She'd pestered her brothers as a girl to show her how to use one, and had become well acquainted with which end was which. Placing the blade back in its sheath, she tucked it into a green beaded sash about her waist. Out here in the scorched lands, it might prove useful. She took the Janjawa's crimson head-cloth as well, wrapping it about her face and over her scalp, where the first bits of new growing hair provided little protection from the stinging sun. From their water skins, she drank heartily, keeping a watchful eye on the vultures already circling above. They would draw larger predators, like giant *kör* cats that ran on four legs but attacked on two; their powerful jaws could crush a bull's neck and would make short work of her. Replenished, she gathered herself up and set out again.

There were no more Janjawa. Nor did she spy any predators; better yet, none spied her. Once that night she heard the mournful baying of *ayolgal*, long haired wolves her people believed were the spirits of mistreated dogs. She crouched against a crag of rock that sat like a lone island, clutching the knife and prepared for a fight. But the baying soon died away, and she curled back to sleep and into Malith's arms.

In her dreams, Malith was more than a whisper or a laughing madman. He was strong and full of passion. And when she woke, her body would ache longingly in remembrance. She'd been ashamed and confused at the first dreams, when she was yet married to Yar. Was it unfaithful to love a dead husband? Her nights with him were her only refuge, even as he made her waking days a misery. Now, abandoned and alone, she welcomed his embrace whenever she closed her eyes. Yet it only made what she now sought that much harder.

The next morning was quiet. Malith was there as always--a tangle in the back of her mind that would not let go. She tried to speak to him. But as often, he was silent. Other than small lizards that skittered between the deep cracks that fractured the dry earth like an eggshell, she was alone. So this land would remain, until Nhialic remade as Dengt sent the rains that would nourish it, providing a brief flowering of life. This was proving to make her journey a punishing one.

Her water was near consumed, along with her food--bits of *ayup* bread, dried *tuk* fruit and *kuin* porridge. She'd tried to catch one of the lizards; but this was their land, and they evaded her with ease. At this rate she fretted she'd soon be forced to eat her skirt.

*Where is your help now Malith? Can you not keep me from this slow death? Or am I to join you in the next life?* Silence was her only answer. *Selfish*, she thought bitterly.

It was some two days later, snaking her way through

a wide, dried out riverbed, that she realized she was being followed. She more felt than saw her follower, his presence markedly noticeable in this empty place. She fought to make him out in the distance but could not, the land bending and shimmering under the relentless heat. Not tall enough to be a man. Some predator then? A wave of dizziness washed over her and she swooned, catching herself. Her food and water had been exhausted the previous night. She'd awakened with her belly cramping in hunger and her throat dry, trying to drink its own saliva.

Her eyes scanned for a place to run. But this flat land offered no escape. She cursed, drawing the Janjawa knife from her waist. Her body was too weak with hunger and thirst to fight, but weaker still to run; she would have to stand her ground. Whatever beast thought her an easy meal would get a fight, and to the victor went the feast. She crouched low, saving her strength for the battle to come. As her pursuer came into view she squinted to see clearly.

Ayen gasped. Was this some trick? Deceptions of malicious spirits that inhabited these lands? Or was she delirious, the heat and hunger taking its toll? What she was seeing now wasn't possible. It *shouldn't* be possible.

Walking towards her was a bull. But not any bull. It was white, with thick long horns curving up from the sides of its head. Polished smooth, they were covered with crimson stripes that bled down the front of its face and traveled on to its back. Even without the broad colorful bead collar around its thick neck, she would have recognized it. This was Malith's bull. This was Malith's murderer.

She had been with his mother, helping pound seeds, when the shouts came. Men were running, carrying Malith between them. He looked as if he'd been bathed in blood. It erupted from his mouth and poured from a deep gash in his belly as his eyes rolled madly in his head. In those frantic moments, she'd only caught a few words. The striped-horn bull, Malith's great pride--twin to the very one added to her dowry--had attacked him, goring him with one of its massive horns. Their healers could do nothing. That night Malith fell into slumber, and never woke with the dawn.

Seeing her husband's murderer again sent Ayen momentarily numb, a thousand questions filling her thoughts. Then something inside gave way, like a weak bit of mud tasked with holding back a river. She screamed with a rage she couldn't control. Her hands sought rocks, but there were none. They settled instead on the flat squares of dried riverbed, hurling them in anger. It was said long ago a Djeng hunter killed the mother of a buffalo and the mother of a cow. The buffalo in anger chose to remain in the forest and attack man from there; the cow was craftier, entering man's home and making man its servant. Among Djeng, cattle were wealth-- sacred, protected, revered. But not this one. Not today.

Bits of earth shattered or bounced off the bull's hide, but he did not slow his approach. Small bells attached to his horns jangled and rang, making an odd discord of music to accompany her screams. He finally stopped just short of her, standing there silent, head tilted and staring at her with one dark eye. How long she stood there pouring out her resentment and pain Ayen did not know. But grief could only sustain so long. Her legs gave way and she collapsed to her knees, panting for breath, her throat so dry it felt as if she'd tried to drink the dust beneath her.

"Why are you here?" she rasped. "Have you come to torment me?"

The bull responded with a terrific snort, pushing air forcefully through its nostrils. Its familiar animal scent wafted past her on a hot wind, as if to assure what she saw was no delusion of a shattered mind. Then suddenly, it tapped the ground with a hoof. Once. Twice. Then again.

She looked up, curious. The bull was driving his thick hoof into the dried earth--digging. She watched perplexed as he carried on his work. Then there was an amazing sight. Wetness pushed up from the parched soil like blood from pricked skin. It turned to vapor instantly, unable to survive the scorched plain. But as the hole grew deep, more wetness appeared. Water this time, spurting and bubbling to the surface--an underground spring or a bit of river from the last rains, trapped beneath the earth.

Ayen scrambled towards the tiny well, pulling down the Janjawa cloth as her blistered lips reached eagerly. The water was warm, but wonderfully real. She drank, sucking from the earth as a babe would her mother's breast. Dirt and grit and small stones found their way into her mouth, but she filtered through them. She'd never tasted anything so beautiful. When she could take no more she rolled over onto her back, staring at the sky. Beside her, the bull began to drink as well, using his long tongue to take in gulps at a time.

She closed her eyes and said a prayer of thanks. When she opened them again, she found her husband's murderer, her savior, hovering above. How the bull had come all this way, and why, she couldn't begin to guess. More important, what did he want? As if hearing her thoughts, he bent his head to nudge her gently with a horn. When she didn't move, he did so again, with more force. It took a moment for her to understand, but then somehow she suddenly did. The beast was telling her to get up, to get onto his back.

How she managed to do so she would later hardly recall. When she was young, her brothers would laugh as she vaulted onto the backs of their bulls. It had been a favorite trick. But this act took all the meager strength she yet had. At long last she sprawled atop the bull's back, her long limbs spread out across his broad frame while her head rested on his hump. She lay panting, thoroughly exhausted from the effort.

"This changes nothing between us," she said wearily. And her mind spun away to darkness.

Ayen dreamt. Of home. Of family. Of Malith. Even Yar. The two were proud Djeng men, running alongside their cattle. She stood between, rooted like a tree as they passed on either side. Then the striped-horn bull appeared--a monster rearing up before her, his eyes hot embers as thick black saliva ran from his mouth. He charged, screaming with the voice of a hundred horrid beasts. She pulled her Janjawa blade then and slashed his throat. The wound bled blackness and the bull fell away, sinking with the shadowy blood into the earth.

Ayen's eyes fluttered open to stare at a brown sky. No. It was mud. A roof, rounded like the inside of a cone. The walls were made of the same, one continuous rounded structure that would reach little more than her head were she to stand. From its walls hung the decorated skulls of small creatures, stitched together pouches of leather stuffed with leaves and other things she could not name. She was in someone's home. And she lay on a thick set of skins, soft like goat fur but much larger. Struggling to sit up she was cut off by a voice.

"So, you have decided to stay among the living, spirit girl."

Ayen snapped her head about to find a woman. She was old, with skin that wrinkled and sagged even as it sought to cling to her gaunt frame. Breasts, shriveled and long past the time they could nourish children, hung like sacks of flesh almost to her waist. She sat with her legs crossed, a long dark red-brown cloth around her waist, and an endless tangle of colorful beads, silver bracelets and other jewelry about her neck, wrists and ankles. But it was her skin that stood out-- a deep crimson that extended even to her hair, which hung in thick molded tubes of clay that gathered at her shoulders.

"Blood Woman!" Ayen gasped. This was her indeed-- the sorceress of the scorched lands.

"So many have named me," the old woman replied in a flat voice. Her dark eyes barely blinked as she handed over a roughly hewn wooden cup. Ayen took it and drank, thankful to wet her throat.

"Though if they care to look close enough," she continued, "they may notice it is not blood that covers me." She reached down to two small bowls. One was filled with something soft and white, reminding Ayen of old thickened milk. The other contained a coppery powder. She mixed the two and began smearing it across her bare breasts.

"The butter fat only needs a bit of ochre to make *otjize*," she said. "It restores life and protects against Mukuri's fiery eye."

Ayen watched, only now noticing the old woman's skin wasn't red at all. In places where the ochre-mixture had not yet smeared it was dark--like burnt wood. Yet she was no Djeng. The length of her face and flatness to her nose marked her as different, as did her curving eyes.

"Here." She offered over an earthen bowl of murky soup and a misshapen lump of what looked like bread. "Eat, spirit girl. I have fed you as I could these past two days." Ayen's eyes rounded. Two days? "But your belly will want more now that you have wakened."

Ayen took the food but hesitated, tales of witches who tricked travelers with savory morsels filling her thoughts. But as the scent sent her stomach to crying out, she gave in. The bread was hard to chew and the broth overly salty, but she ate it all--even the small chunks of meat she could not name by taste and thought better not to ask.

"Flesh is hungrier than spirit," the old woman murmured, those dark eyes drinking her in.
"You speak Djeng, but you are not," Ayen said, crunching a bit of bone and sucking out the marrow. Gods! She'd eat the splinters too if she could.

"I come from the far south, spirit girl. Beyond where the Djeng have roamed. But I have long lived in these lands, and learned well the tongues of those who dwell here."

Ayen said nothing. What little she'd heard of the Blood Woman held true. That she was a sorceress from some far place who now lived alone among the wild beasts of the scorched lands. Some said in exile for a misdeed done to her people. Others claimed she was the one wronged.

"My tale is not for your ears, spirit girl," she said, reading Ayen's ponderous look. "Rather you should be telling me what brings you here. In my time I have received many. Yet none have arrived as you, Ayen of the Akok."

Ayen stopped chewing, a soup-soaked piece of bread

perched on her tongue.

"How do you know me?" she stammered.

The old woman reached for a hanging flap of animal skin, pushing it back to reveal the outside. It was dusk, and in the distance the sun was beginning his descent into the belly of the fractured earth. But the old woman was gesturing much closer. Standing outside her home was the bull. He used his muzzle to push up the dirt, stopping briefly to give them a passing glance.

"The one who brought you named you," the old woman said. "When he came, bearing you upon his back, you were more in the next life than this one. I might have let death claim you--a mercy. But he pleaded I bring you back."

Ayen frowned. "He named me? You can speak to him?"

"When I claimed to know the tongues of those in this land, I did not mean only we who go on two legs," the old woman replied. "He speaks in his own way, if any bother to listen. His kind called the scorched lands home long before the Djeng. He knows how to survive in this harsh place, certainly better than you. Should count yourself blessed for such a friend."

"That monster is not my friend," Ayen said, more venom in her voice than intended. Just looking at the bull brought her anger flowing back. She held onto that in place of strength. "Did he tell you how he murdered my husband? Did he tell you how he stole my life from me?"

The old woman nodded. "He spoke all these things and more. The other bull that bore his markings, they were brothers. Did you know? Twins born of the same womb. Among you Djeng, he is prized for his markings. But among cattle, they are outcasts, shunned even by their mothers. His brother was all he had. Then your husband took him away, a gift for your bride wealth. He was angry, afraid. In rage he lashed out, wounding your husband. He had not meant to kill."

Ayen sat, unable to form words. To Djeng, cattle were

sacred, and cared for like no other possession. But never did she think they carried such feelings. She watched the bull dig about in the earth, and wondered what lay beyond the depths of those eyes. For a brief moment, a deep sadness replaced her anger, a pity she'd reserved thus far only for herself. But it broke fast as her gaze roamed to his great curved horns. The red that tinged those sharp ends; was it stained too with Malith's blood?

"What does he want from me?" she whispered. "Why is he here?"

"I would think that plain, spirit girl. He has come to make penance. He has pledged his life as yours until it is met. He seeks forgiveness."

Ayen gritted her teeth, shaking her head. "That is not something I can so easily give."

The old woman shrugged. "Those matters are your own, spirit girl. I have delivered the message as asked. Better we speak on the business you have with me."

Ayen looked to the woman, who stared back in her unblinking way. "If he has truly told you all, then you already know."

"Perhaps." She lifted a bony finger, jabbing it forward. "But I want to hear you say it."

Ayen swallowed, rolling across a knot sprung up in her throat. All this way she'd come, knowing well her intent. Yet when asked, the words buried and hid beneath her tongue.

The old woman sucked her teeth in annoyance. "If you cannot say it, then you cannot truly want it." She turned away and Ayen reached out, clutching her arm.

"Unbind me from Malith," she said, each word cutting like a blade. "End my ghost marriage and free us from each other, in this life and the next." The knot in her throat loosened as she spoke the words aloud, but she took no joy in it. *Forgive me Malith.*

The old woman nodded solemnly. "I can do this thing."

Ayen released her grip and a thankful breath. To risk

the vengeance of Malith's dishonored spirit carried great risk, none any Djeng would take. But the Blood Woman, it was said she had no fear of the living or the dead.

"I thank you," she said graciously.

The old woman snorted. "You may thank me with payment. Or did the stories of me not make that plain?"

Ayen nodded. The Blood Woman did no biddings for free. She always exacted a price.

"My family has cattle," she offered. "Once the marriage is undone, they could bring...." She trailed off as the old woman cackled, showing large perfect teeth.

"Are you to marry *me* spirit girl? What good are cattle here?"

Ayen grappled for an answer and remembered the rings she'd taken.

"I have gold."

The old woman shrugged with disinterest.

Ayen became desperate. "I can clean...cook... serve..."

The old woman scowled. "Now you take me for a Janjawa, so that I need servants to fetch my water and knead my bread." She held up a quieting hand before Ayen could start again. "I will name my price spirit girl. You will meet it."

Ayen stared at the sorceress, who suddenly seemed as dangerous as her reputation. When she nodded in acceptance, the old woman smiled wide, the way a jackal would at a meal that had wandered carelessly into its den.

"Gold, fine cloth, cattle," she mocked. "Those that come offer me things I care little for, things important in their world...not mine. Now what can you give me?" Ayen flinched as the old woman's fingers ran along her arm. "Skin still carries the softness of youth. What it would be to live in such soft skin again. And eyes, still sharp. How would the world seem from behind them?" She put a hand to Ayen's belly and frowned. "A troubled womb, though. You will bear no children."

The words were idly said, but to Ayen they still cut sharp. So it was true. She was barren. Lost in her own thoughts, she almost did not realize the old woman's hands had stopped--on her forehead.

"These!" she exclaimed. "I want these!"

Ayen frowned, her own hand touching the same space.

"My markings?"

The old woman nodded. Her fingers traced the raised beaded dots that rose across Ayen's skin. They spiraled into a pattern across her forehead and down her cheeks. They were common adornment of Djeng women, received upon leaving girlhood. She remembered the day her mothers and aunts marked her with the sharp hot knife after her first bleeding. The memory still filled her with pride.

"No!" Ayen shook her head, pulling away. "They are all I now own!" It was truth. Among the Djeng these markings gave meaning. They named her as Akok. A woman.

The old woman's eyes were hard black stones. "I am no haggler. Accept my demands or leave."

Ayen met her stare, taken aback by its coldness. There would be no argument. With reluctance she lowered her gaze and the old woman palmed her forehead tight. The words she whispered were foreign and brought pain--slicing her skin. She clenched her teeth and balled her fists tight, trying not to cry out. Then it was done, and old woman pulled away. Ayen touched her forehead. The skin was now smooth--naked. Across from her the sorceress sat grinning, the markings now adorning her wrinkled flesh.

"Your offer freely given is accepted, spirit girl."

"I gave you nothing free," Ayen said bitingly.

The old woman narrowed her eyes. "True enough. We should begin." She rose, setting her many beads and jewelry to rattling. "Unbinding the dead from the living is no easy thing. And it will be less so with you, spirit girl."

"Why do you call me that?" I am as much flesh as you are." Ayen had endured the seeming jibe. But her patience had vanished with her markings.

The old woman cackled, rifling through the hanging pouches on her wall. "Flesh you are, but your other foot is rooted firmly in spirit." She rounded about, meeting Ayen's puzzled look. "Have you not wondered how your Malith is able to enter back into our world? Ghost marriages among Djeng are common. Yet how many like yours?"

"So I thought," she muttered at Ayen's silence. "The spirit realms are many, some say endless. We of flesh contain not enough spirit to walk them, much as they cannot walk ours. But you are more spirit than most. I can see it about you, even now. Strong, pulsing with life. This is how your Malith reaches into our world--through you."

Ayen listened, momentarily at a loss for words.

"How did this come to be?" she asked frightened. "Was I cursed? Did I wrong--?"

The old woman waved away her words. "No more cursed than the singer with a sweet voice. So you were born. I can teach you of it, if you wish."

Ayen shuddered. She wanted no such thing. This spirit curse--damn what the old woman said--had brought her nothing but ill. Then something came to her.

"Could a spirit enter a dream?" she asked.

The old woman shrugged, going about her work. "Possible. The dream world is closer to the spirit world."

Ayen recalled her nights with Malith. His warmth, his touch--

"I will need your help," the old woman called.

Ayen pushed away those thoughts and rose. She was remarkably rested. But as expected the rounded roof brushed her head, causing the old woman to smirk.

"You are a tall one."

"I am Djeng," Ayen replied. *And even with my markings, you will not be.*

Night had long fallen as Ayen knelt beside the sprawling pattern of white powder that now adorned the earthen floor of the old woman's home. Candles rendered from the fat of some beast marked it, as did sharp edged silver amulets. The pungent smoke of some burning herb escaped its bowl in curling wisps of white, choking the air alongside the old woman's incantations.

Through a slit in the animal hide door, Ayen looked upon the stars in the night sky. She could make out the bull as well, keeping a silent vigil. The claim that this beast had journeyed across the scorched lands seeking absolution seemed madness. Yet what else explained his constant presence? She had asked if a price was exacted from the bull to relay his message. The old woman had nodded, but said no more.

As always, Malith was there, a faraway but close presence. She'd feared he would lash out when he realized her intent. But he had done nothing. Perhaps, Ayen mused, he wanted this as much as she.

"It is time," the old woman declared. She lifted up a small flat disc. One side was plain and dull; but the other was a wonder--like the surface of water that did not ripple. The old woman called it a mirror.

"Spirits are vain," she said, handing it to Ayen. "And cannot resist their reflections. But what more are they in our realm than reflections? One look and the mirror will trap them. But take care." Her voice turned stern. "Do not the look upon the spirit when trapped, for he will seek to enter you. I will lead him elsewhere."

She turned and gave a series of shrill whistles. After a long while it was answered with a squeak. Ayen looked down in surprise to see a mouse entering the small house. No larger than her hand, it scampered to the old woman who seized it up quickly. It twitched and squealed, but a few whispered words sent it unnaturally still.

"Your Malith will enter here." From her waist she pulled a small dagger with a hooked end. "When he does I will end this small life. As it dies and enters the spirit world, it will draw away your husband's spirit with it. Do you understand?"

Ayen nodded. So this is how her marriage would end...

in blood.

"Good. Now, call him."

Ayen took a deep breath and did so. At first there was no answer. She called twice more. Still nothing. Perhaps he would not come she feared--and half hoped. Then, in a rush, an unseen presence filled the small space, casting a shadow and bending the flames of the candles. That familiar cold laughter sounded in her ears, and she shivered. Malith...

"Dead husband!" the old woman called out. "Come, show us your face! Let your wife look upon you now as she did in life!"

The presence about them stirred stronger, sending a slight gale that made the candles dance and flicker. The pungent smoke that filled the air swirled about them as the laughter grew louder. And there, above the white markings, a shape began to form.

Ayen inhaled sharply. From the midst of the smoke, there appeared what looked like a man. He towered above them, a vague outline of a torso, a neck and a head. She struggled to glimpse his face, but he had no more features than he had flesh.

"Now girl!" the old woman hissed. "Call him to you! Make him look!"

Ayen gripped the overturned mirror, her breath caught in her throat. "Malith," she stammered. At her voice, the spirit turned towards her. She searched for some recognition of her dead husband, some slight resemblance, but there was nothing. With a whispered apology, she pulled forth the mirror and held it high.

A terrible wail rose from the spirit that made her insides quiver as its ephemeral form was pulled towards its reflection. The mirror shook and it felt to Ayen as if someone was pushing strongly from the other side. Then in a moment it was done.

"Good," the old woman said. She turned her gaze away as she held up the mouse. In her other hand was the dagger. "Here restless spirit," she coaxed. "I have found a new place for you. Come now, so you can find peace."

Ayen looked into the glazed eyes of the bewitched mouse, which reflected the mirror and the swirling spirit trapped within. Beneath her breath she joined the old woman, urging Malith into the small creature so that this grim work could be done. Suddenly the mirror shook violently, nearly flying from her hands. There was a terrific groan and then without warning--it exploded.

Ayen was thrown back, her bloodied hands holding only a piece of the glass. The rest flew out like sharp blades, shredding the mouse and burying themselves into the old woman's arm. She cried out and brought her head forward, meeting the gaze of a large bit of mirror that sailed past her vision. For a moment, she seemed to go numb. The veins about her neck bulged beneath her skin like serpents as her mouth opened wide in a silent scream. A convulsive shudder shook her body and her dark eyes rolled back until only the whites showed. Then she went still, breaking into a wide grin as a cold laugh escaped her lips. Ayen felt her stomach go hollow. She knew that laugh.

"Malith," she dared. The old woman turned, tilting her head unnaturally to the side and glaring with bone white eyes. Ayen grimaced. The mirror had shattered and she'd looked inside. Malith had entered her, not the mouse.

"Malith," she tried again. "You can't stay here. You have to go." Outside, the bull snorted loudly, stamping his hooves and shaking his head. She spared him a glance, but crept forward slowly. Maybe she could reason with Malith. Maybe she could convince him to go.

The old woman suddenly erupted into spasms. Her fingers went to her face, gouging the flesh beneath the crimson ochre and cutting gashes into her cheeks. She screamed and thick black liquid poured from her nose and mouth, reeking of death. Ayen thought she would gag. In a sweep of air the old woman was hoisted back, flying from her home and into night. Ayen followed, scrambling through the door into the outside. There she found the old woman being tossed about, her body slamming the dry ground repeatedly like some doll. She tried to get close but the bull leapt up, blocking her path. In frustration she managed to make her way around him. But by then it was too late.

Ayen scrambled over, frantic and speechless. The old woman was bruised and broken. White bone showed where it pierced the flesh of one leg. Another jutted within her neck, causing it to swell. Her dark eyes were wide as she spit up the putrid black liquid. She reached out, grabbing Ayen and dragging her down as she tried to speak through broken teeth.

"Not Malith," she rasped. She repeated it again and again, until the last breath escaped her.

Ayen pulled away from the corpse's grasp, confused and shaking. Not Malith? That couldn't be. She could still feel him, unseen yet stronger than ever. But wait. No. Something was different. Something wrong.

She shivered. The air seemed colder. Dead. Almost Stifling. And a feeling of dread filled her within. Gods above and below! The old woman was right! This was not her husband! This was not Malith!

"Who are you?" she dared.

The voice was immediate, a whisper that rumbled.

*Your husband, my wife,* it mocked.

She shook her head. "You're not Malith."

*I never claimed to be.*

Ayen shuddered. Nhialic preserve her! "Who are you?" she demanded again.

That cold laughter filled her ears. *Nameless.*

"Nameless?" She fought to stop her voice from trembling. "Are you another of the dead then, who does not rest?" Something unseen suddenly grabbed her by the throat, lifting and pinning her harshly to the wall of the earthen dwelling. She choked and gasped for air, as all around the voice snarled and raged like a starved beast.

*Frail thing that lives and rots. I am beyond life, beyond death. I am the Hidden, the Dweller in the Dark, the*

*Nameless, for were I to reveal to you my true self, your mortal soul would shrivel and burn away.*

Ayen fell as she was released, gasping for breath.

*I knew this world when it was yet young,* the voice roared, *one of the first beings, before mortals, before even your cursed gods. It was ours to rule, to ravage. We waged wars of such horror the land trembled, belching fire that boiled seas and scorched the skies. We were glorious. Then the new gods came, usurpers, seeking to make this realm over as their own. We crushed many, trampling them to dust. But they were cunning. They tricked us! Banished us! Leaving us to wander in nothingness, never to walk these realms again!*

Ayen winced at each word, laced with such emotion. Hate. Pain. Anger. Deeper than any she'd ever known. Any she ever thought possible.

*But we are also cunning,* the voice hissed. *Across seas of time we have searched for someone like you, child of flesh and spirit. We felt your presence at your very birth, a ripple across the realms, and waited until our chance. When your priests sought to bind you to your dead Malith, I took his place.*

Ayen recoiled in horror, recalling the day of the ritual, the ill wind and the omens. It had been this…thing! This was the presence she'd felt all this time. And in her dreams she had let it touch her…she had let it…  She choked back the bile rising in her throat.

"You killed Yar. His son. Why?"

*For the same reason I killed the horsemen that would enslave you. Why I killed this witch who would have taken you from me. We are bound now, my wife. And I have great use of you.*

When the voice laughed again, Ayen covered her ears, praying so she would not weep.

It was near dawn when they set out. Ayen turned back once to gaze at the trail of smoke in the distance. Nameless commanded she set the old woman's home ablaze. It commanded many things now, and she obeyed. It was stronger, pulled further into the world by the old woman's spells, and by her. But it still couldn't leave its lightless prison. Not yet. That's what she was for.

She flinched each time Nameless called her wife. Yet that's what she was now, bound to it by magics intended for her dead husband. The deaths that sent her fleeing her village were all its design. It wanted her here, in the scorched barren lands, where its power was greater. Most of all, it wanted freedom.

There was a place, it claimed, where the walls of its prison were weak. For time beyond time, its kind had beat upon those walls, seeking to tear them down. But they were always unable. Now, through her, they would try again.

Days passed. She was afforded only brief snatches of rest before being awakened harshly. Refusal brought punishment, unseen straps striking with such fury she blacked out. She'd become too fatigued to even eat. But her mouth was pried open, the food shoved down, leaving her throat raw and her teeth bloodied. More than once she'd feared she would die. But Nameless would not allow that, not yet. Instead it wanted her mind to shatter beneath the strain, leaving her a beast that reacted only to pain and the lash.

Her only other companion now was Malith's murderer. Nameless had allowed her to take the bull. During her brief moments of rest when their gazes met, he seemed to speak to her, making her remember who she truly was--Ayen of the Akok. A Djeng. One of the First People and Lords of Men. Somehow she would survive this.

Ayen did not know how many days came and went. Wherever they now walked, there was no life, not even the calling of insects at night. It carried a silence that spoke for its emptiness. She was draped over the bull, her food and water near done. And there was none to be found in this dry lifeless place. But then they stopped. And Nameless spoke.

*Here. It is here.*
Ayen lifted her head, looking about through bleary

eyes. In the horizon the sun was a fiery ball falling into the earth. The land about her was barren, littered with fine black rock like sand. She slid off the bull and put her bare feet to the ground, which burned hot beneath. But she endured the pain as she endured so much else.

*Behold Shad Lahar! Here my fortress stood, swallowing all beneath its shadow!*

"I see nothing," Ayen rasped wearily. "Just a dead land."

She readied herself for the blows to come for her insolence. But instead she was seized from her feet. She felt her body soar up at great speed, the wind beating her face so fierce tears streaked across her cheeks. When she finally came to a stop she hovered high in the sky, the sun now so close she thought she might reach out and burn her hands upon it. Beneath her was the world, as Nameless hissed in her ears.

*Look close wife. What do you see?*

Ayen looked. Across the barren land was a great mark, as if a giant had taken a blade and scarred the earth. It stretched out in every direction, made of one line that looped itself into patterns like a knot.

*The mark of the young gods, across my great city! A seal to keep it trapped and hidden forever from this realm. But no longer! Already I am able to reach to it, pulling it from the void as I pull myself forth. Do you see now wife? Do you see what is coming?*

Ayen trembled. She could see it well. It was like mist slowly taking form--a looming monstrosity of black stone with sharp fingers that cut into the sky. It covered the land as far as she could see. All within it things stirred, creatures with hideous faces and twisted mouths, teeming and writhing in a dark mass. And above them all was the greatest horror of all.

The thing looked like nothing Ayen could have stolen from any nightmare. It was a giant, a massive being of pale grey flesh, long and shaped like a worm. Arms curving as snakes flowed out from it, wrapping about the stone structure.

Two great wings opened wide from its back, drowning all beneath in shadow. Crowning its monstrous body was a head hidden behind a carved mask of iron that took on a new face by the moment, each more terrifying than the last. Ayen did not need to be told who this was.

"Nameless," she whispered, gazing upon the god in awe and horror.

That cold laugh filled her ears. *Soon this world will have a name for me, and men will bite out their tongues rather than utter it.*

Ayen was released, falling so fast she didn't have time to scream. She was dropped onto the ground, not gentle but at least alive. She staggered to her feet. The dark city was all about her. But it was not here, not fully, not yet. It hovered partly in this realm and the next, trying to break free of its prison. She could push her hands through its walls. And the horrid creatures that lurked within swarmed about her like smoke. Some walked on two legs, others on many more, misshapen mockeries of men and beasts. Orifices like gaping mouths filled with gnashing teeth gaped where eyes should have been, and in their many hands they carried savage weapons.

All of them would eventually break free she knew. And she would be the cause. Her presence weakened whatever barriers held the two realms apart. Soon they would collapse, and these horrors would come pouring out. This is what she would give birth to. If Nameless was the father of this nightmare, she would be its mother.

"No!" she whispered, shaking her head at the madness of it all. "This will not be!"

With careful hands, she gripped the knife at her waist, sliding it from its scabbard. She let a finger run across its edge, cutting the skin easily. Yes, this would do if she had the resolve. Nhialic pray she did. Nameless had not thought to take the weapon from her; such a thing could do it no harm. But it did not know her strength, and to what limits she would go. Indeed, she had not known until this very moment. Only, she would have to be quick.

Bringing up the blade, she placed it on her neck, the cold iron seeming eager to bite her skin. The cut would have to be deep, so that when she spilled her blood death was assured. She whispered a prayer, prepared to drive the blade home when something knocked her down hard.

Ayen fell sprawling, the bull standing over her. He stamped his hooves and shook his head. She scowled. Was the beast to betray her now? When she again readied the knife, he struck again, knocking the blade away. She gasped in exasperation, readied to lash out. But he had latched onto her skirt and was tugging hard. When she managed to break away there was a tear as the goatskin shredded. Items she'd tucked away spilled out, falling to the ground below: three golden rings, the scabbard to the Janjawa knife and something that glistened, which the bull stamped his hoof at.

It was a bit of glass, from the old woman's shattered mirror. She'd taken it, thinking perhaps she'd like to glimpse her face again one day. But what use was it now?

She looked at the bull perplexed. "What do you want?"

He stamped his hoof again at the mirror and snorted heavily. She recalled the old woman's words. The beast could talk in his own way, if any chose to listen. As she looked down again at the mirror, he slowly walked forward, lowering his massive head until it rested on the Janjawa blade. And in that moment, Ayen suddenly understood. Penance was what he sought, the old woman had said. To atone for taking Malith's life, he had pledged his own.

"You would do this?" she asked. "For me?" His unblinking eyes stared up in answer. Ayen nodded once in silent acknowledgement, and wasted no more time.

She snatched up her knife and the piece of mirror and turned to stare up at Nameless. With the blade to her neck, she drew on all her strength and screamed out her defiance. The monstrous being turned its attention, untangling its great body from the city and surging towards her. Even unsubstantial as it yet was, when that massive horrid iron mask reared up before her she nearly fell away in fright. The voice thundered.

*You need only wait a few moments longer, wife, and I will grant you death.*

"Or I take my life now!" she spit back. "And leave you in your prison!"

Nameless snarled with the fury of a tempest. *Just a thought and I can grind the bones in your frail flesh to powder, leaving you alive only long enough to be of use!*

"I have another idea, husband."

From behind her back, she brought up the bit of mirror, letting the spirit gaze at its reflection. Nameless let out a deafening howl and the face before her began to waver, collapsing into mist. The old woman had showed her this trick. The mirror captured spirits. And for all its power, Nameless was still spirit! Its vaporous body quickly lost shape and flowed speedily into the glass with all the strength of an unleashed river. The force of it staggered her to her knees, but she held strong until it disappeared inside.

She released a thankful breath, but the work was partly done. Like before, the mirror would not hold such a powerful being. Already it trembled and shook. Turning she found the bull gazing at her. His head dipped lightly, an acceptance of what as to come. Ayen turned away and lifted the mirror, letting him gaze fully at the spirit trapped within.

The bull's eyes rolled back until only the whites showed, and thick black liquid that reeked of death poured from his nostrils and mouth. She scrambled away, as he made unearthly sounds and his body kicked and flailed wildly, echoing into the night. Nameless. Trying to break free. But the bull held him, fought him, and kept him there--just long enough for her to act.

Ayen was no warrior. But as all other Djeng, she'd grown up around cattle. The trick was to come from behind, where they couldn't twist their heads to see. Then it was just a simple matter to leap up upon their backs. And if you could grab the horns, there was something to hold to. She managed it as easily as when she was a child, holding tight as the possessed bull struggled madly. Draping her arms about his thick neck, she pressed the Janjawa blade into the soft flesh.

"Farewell husband," she whispered, and with one wide sweep, opened the bull's throat.

She was sent flying, landing on her shoulder in an explosion of pain that made her scream. Fighting from blacking out, she looked up in time to see the bull's front legs give out--blood flowing in torrents from the gash in its throat. Out too came the black liquid, disappearing into the ground that drank it eagerly. It was as the old woman said: in death the bull was taking Nameless with him, out of this world and back to its dark prison. Far across the blighted landscape lines glowed bright in the black earth--the sigil that held Nameless and its city, coming alive to trap them once again. Then abruptly, all fell silent.

Ayen looked around. Nameless was gone. So was the dark city. The sigil too no longer glowed. She raised her scraped and bruised body, one arm dangling uselessly as she stumbled over to the bull. It sat, tongue hanging from its mouth, as blood poured freely from the wound she'd inflicted. She nestled against him, cradling his head and running a hand across those long red-striped horns. He *was* magnificent. Pressing her lips against an ear, she whispered inside.

"I forgive you."

It was all she could manage to say. And it was no lie. That must have been enough, for those knowing eyes turned to regard her before his body went heavy, and finally still. She whispered a proper Djeng prayer for his spirit--Malith's murderer, her savior. It was done. She was free. And with the coming dawn, somehow she would find her way--

Ayen's thoughts were drowned away as a sudden roar pierced the stillness. Beneath her the land trembled and heaved as if alive. Something was rising out of the earth. Something immense. Something dark. Her mind formed the coming horror before it could be seen. Nameless!

The spirit erupted from the earth in a geyser of swirling

black sand, bringing a second night to the dark sky. It towered before her like an angry mountain, raging and cursing in endless tongues, struggling to claw its way free. Ayen fell back in terror, wondering if her battered body could yet flee. But even as she watched, Nameless's prison pulled like a leash, trying to draw it back inside. The world itself seemed to bend and stretch as the ensnared god strained against it, struggling to claw free. For a moment, Ayen feared it would succeed, either that or the whole world would be wrenched apart. Then with a sudden force the prison grabbed hold of its captive, and the opening Nameless had managed to create began to collapse. The god howled in anger and defeat as it was drawn back into the void. Before vanishing, it surged forward one last time, and the iron mask that concealed it slid apart, revealing what lay beneath.

The blood drained away from Ayen's face as she stared into the many faces of Nameless, each more horrid than the next. When the scream finally erupted from her throat, she found she couldn't stop. She was still screaming when darkness claimed her.

Ayen blinked her eyes open to find the sky, bright and blue with the sun above. She was moving, but she did not walk. She fought to turn her head, finding her neck stiff. People surrounded her. Some wore dark robes and veiled their faces. Others wore little and made their faces known. Their skins ranged from brown to ebon. But none looked to be Djeng. When she tried to rise, a hand touched her shoulder.

"Be easy," a voice came. "Your shoulder has been set back in place, but you should not place weight upon it." Ayen looked up to find a woman. Much of her face was hidden by rounded bits of silver stringed to beads that rattled as she moved. She looked perhaps her mother's age with near bronze skin and lips stained black. Her mouth worked as she chewed on something continuously, while eyes as silver as her coins stared down.

"Where...?" Ayen rasped, her throat dry. The woman brought forth a water sack, letting some dribble onto her lips.

She licked away the first few drops then drank until she could talk. "Where am I? Who are you?"

"I am Zara of the Amazi," the woman replied. "You are in a caravan bound for the East lands, near the Green Sea."

"The East lands," Ayen repeated. She strained to lift her head slightly, gazing about. She was in a cart, pulled along by a large shaggy beast with curving downturned horns. On either side of them were more women, two figures, each wrapped in blood red cloth with spears and curved swords strapped to their backs. They rode atop giant brown-striped lizards that walked upright on two legs. One of them, a woman with a conical silver helmet, turned an ebon face etched with golden marks to spare Ayen a glance, before returning her gaze to the landscape.

"You take me to a slave market?"

Zara snorted. "You wear a Janjawa veil and blade but name us slavers?"

Ayen looked down to where her hands clutched something at her waist. The knife.

"You would not release it," Zara said, "even when we found you, lying with a dead bull in the barren lands. We carried you with us, wondering if you would wake. That was seven days past." Ayen gasped. She seemed to be in the habit of losing time.

"Who are you, girl?" Zara asked. "You look Djeng, but you wear no markings of womanhood. And cattle-people rarely wander alone, or so far." She paused, frowning beneath her veil of coins. "The night before we found you, there were ill omens, unearthly voices. Some claimed to see ghostly visions in the distance, a dark city...."

Ayen listened, clutching her knife tight as memories flooded her thoughts. When the woman stopped, she finally answered.

"I am Ayen of the Akok. Thrice married. Once to the living. Once to the dead. Once to a god." Zara's eyebrows rose, as did those of some nearby who whispered to each other while stealing glances.

"Your face is youthful," the woman noted. "But you wear ages upon it."

Ayen looked to her curiously and the woman pulled something rounded and small from her robes. A mirror. Ayen stared within, pushing back her veil. It had been some time since she'd shaven her scalp, as was common to Djeng women. Now a fine bit of hair grew like a field of wild grass. Only it was as white as bone, near silver. So too were her eyebrows. She ran fingers over them in wonder.

"The price of looking upon the face of a god," she murmured.

She returned the mirror and eyed the older woman with interest.

"What business do you have in the east, Zara?"

"We go to the Zaar." Ayen shook her head, not understanding. "A gathering for wise and holy women," Zara explained, "strong in matters of magic and spirit. All here are." Ayen looked around at the caravan, only now noticing there were no men among them.

"Strong in magic and spirit," she repeated.

"As are you," Zara replied. "More than one woman here has noticed as much. It is not by chance, I think, that we have found you here in this barren land."

Ayen felt that as well enough. Spirit girl, the old woman had named her. Curse it may have been, but perhaps Nhialic had set her on this path with purpose. Suddenly she wanted to know more. She needed to know more. No Djeng could speak to her on this. But the women of this Zaar....

"Can I come with you?"

Zara met her question with silence, before nodding. "I feel it may be best that you do."

Ayen thanked her, taking a moment to dwell on her hasty decision. There was nothing for her at home. To her people she was still cursed, and no man would have her as a wife. She would remain at her family's compound, spending life as her mother's attendant. No. If this bizarre journey taught her one thing, it was that there was much to learn in this world. Besides, she had never before seen a sea. Her eyes wandered back to the strange older woman.

"Zara, how is it you speak Djeng?"

The woman gave her an odd look. "I do not speak Djeng, child. Nor are you speaking it now. You speak Amazi, the very dialect of my own clan, with ease as if you were born to it." Ayen glared, only now realizing her mouth forming unfamiliar sounds. "You have spoken that and many other tongues in your sleep these past days. It has been... remarkable...to hear."

Ayen could only stare back in wonder. Nhialic keep her! What was this? You looked into a face of a god, she reminded herself. Who knew what other changes may come?

"Three husbands you claimed to have," Zara said, breaking her thoughts. "Is one of them then the father?"

Ayen glared at the woman perplexed. "Father? How do you mean?"

Zara frowned. "You must know you are with child."

Ayen felt every part of her body tremble as she shook her head. "That's not possible," she whispered hoarsely. "I am *barren*."

Zara lifted a bejeweled and painted hand to Ayen's belly, feeling about. "Barren you may have been, but this womb now carries life. Freshly planted, but strong. I ask again, who then is the father?"

Ayen said nothing, a hand moving slowly to caress her belly as her eyes wandered across the sands that seemed to

rise and fall like her thoughts, in boundless waves.

# Raiders of the Sky Isle

*Cynthia Ward*

I am Indel the Trader, and I was the first to see the sky isle's return, thirty years agone. But I never guessed what a change it would bring to our world.

The sky island came in the dolphin season, when the sky reflects the color of the sea, deeper than attis-flower blue and brighter than sapphire. I was on the Trade Road, the current which sweeps up from the south to caress the thousand-mile length of our island, Sethena, flowing past the long curve of the great archipelago, the Teroe Isles and Kalishi'is and the rest. My ship had sails and full thirty rowers: strong women and men of New Aricuse, with bronze-tipped spears at their sides and bronze knives in their belts, ready for pirate or savage, kraken or sea-dragon.

I sat at the stern of my triaconter--of course the merchant does not row or chant the time--and kept watch. We were sailing athwart the wind, and so our sails were lowered and my view unimpeded. On the cloudless horizon, the smoking peak of Ynae rose into view. Northwesternmost island of the archipelago, it grew larger as we drew nearer; and I jerked at the sight of it. For the mountain was strangely altered: malformed, and thrice its wonted height.

Then a blue seam appeared between the old and new portions of the volcano, and the enigma resolved itself: in the sky above the mile-high volcano was another mountain. This mountain had two sharp peaks, one above and one beneath, as if the latter were a reflection of the former, strangely overlaid upon the sky.

My stomach tightened.  What sight could be more horrifying than an island that rode only upon the winds?

Though I gave no command, my time-keeper ceased to chant, and my rowers ceased as one to ply their oars; then as one they cried with the time-keeper; *"Bithuva!"*

We were far too young ever to have seen it, but we all recognized the island in the air; only one island ever traveled upon the unseen currents of the sky, and Bithuva's legend was so fearsome that I did not chastise my rowers for ceasing to draw the oars and sitting gape-mouthed as half-wits.

As we stared, an avalanche of stones began to fall from the sky isle's under-peak:  yellow boulders that from our distance looked like nuggets.  And lightning-bolts fell too, as thick as rain, and as uncannily silent.  An avalanche may be started with tools; but lightning from stone was magic, and magical lightning in such profligate quantities was impossible.

So we saw that the dreadful old tales were true.

The Bithuvans had command of a potent magic that our own people had lost with the sinking of Amuria.

The boulders and lightning struck the green slopes of Ynae, and the golden shore where the natives had their villages; and everywhere the lightning struck, thick black columns of smoke sprang up, so that in moments it seemed the volcano must have erupted, setting half the forest aflame, and every village.

Avalanche and silent lightning-storm lasted but seconds; and as they ceased, the sky filled with distance-tiny shapes.

My stomach clenched and a sour taste filled my mouth. I could not have imagined an act more dreadful than stepping into the sky; yet here were scores, hundreds, of flying men.

We could not see the figures in the sky well enough to judge their sex, yet we knew the fliers all were male; for they must be warriors, and always the Bithuvan warriors were men, though everyone knows it is women who are the natural fighters, with their ferocious instincts to protect their young. And we could not see this either, but we knew the winged men were throwing spears to kill the Ynaean men, and swooping down to steal food and capture women.

"Come about!" I cried; and my women and men came to themselves. The time-keeper resumed her chant, and the rowers thrust their oars in the sea, and brought my ship swiftly about. The rowers' speed did not slacken, though now they fought the ocean-current; sweat flowed down their spines like mountain streams, and I seemed to hear the muscles cracking between their shoulders. I drew out my lodestone to set a direct course, an insane course: straight across open water to Sethena Island.

But directly must we return to our fair city. For the sky isle Bithuva was set upon the same course.

\*\*\*

Five days brought us into New Aricuse Bay. The city of New Aricuse sprawled unaware, a white cat peacefully napping in the oak-green lap of the Sethenan Mountains. I went home.

I had remembered her hours aright; my elder sister was there. I spoke one word: "Bithuva."

Within an hour, the Assembly was gathered, the Twenty, the representatives of the Twenty Clans, summoned by the Warchief of New Aricuse. I spoke to the Twenty of what I had seen. Before I could finish, the Twenty were shouting, and it wasn't anything useful they said. "Kidnappers!" "Pirates!" "Butchers!" "They'll burn our city!" "They'll kill us all!"

"Enough," my sister called, my elder sister, Amala, the Warchief of New Aricuse. Her low voice could be loud and resonant, when she willed it, and with one word she silenced the women who represented the Clans of New Aricuse.

Of course, her presence was no small part of her ability to silence the Twenty. Warchief Amala was fully as tall as our ancestors are said to be, and as nobly black of skin, and strong, and beautiful. Young she was for her post, thirty summers; at twenty-five she had become the youngest Warchief in all New Aricusene history, and even the legends of Amuria, the lost continent of our ancestors.

Seeing us together, you would not have guessed that we were sister and brother, for my body was soft, my complexion brown, my height inferior; not unless you noted that we had identical eyes, tilted and amber, betraying Teroese blood.

Warchief Amala silenced the Twenty, but not long: "How can we stop the Bithuvans from destroying New Aricuse as they have three times before?" they cried. "The Bithuvans fly. Bithuva itself flies!"

"Had we made preparations after any of Bithuva's three previous visits," the Warchief replied, "we would not be in this predicament. At least this time we are forewarned of the sky isle's approach. But it takes six days for Bithuva to travel from Ynae to Sethena--the sky isle will be here tomorrow. If we would avoid destruction, we must pay tribute to Bithuva."

"We are the Aricusene. Our ancestors ruled the Amurian Empire. We do not pay tribute. We demand it!"

"Amuria sank over five hundred years ago," Amala said. "Her thousand mages and hundred thousand legionaries are muck, the Great Talismans long lost." The Clan leaders protested, but my sister would not let them cling to their dreams of ancient glory. "Old Aricuse ruled Amuria, aye," she said, "but New Aricuse is no great power. Our army numbers but twenty-five hundred. And our warriors cannot fly. The most powerful magician of Amuria could not have suspended a dozen women in the sky without a Great Talisman. No, my lady clan-leaders, we must parley with the winged men of Bithuva. We must buy them off with slaves and gold and grain. It is a small price to pay, to save New Aricuse and the life of every Aricusene."

"Never!"

The argument went on for hours; but in the end, the Twenty acceded to the Warchief's counsel. And Amala and I walked wearily back to our Family House, to find our younger sister, Tai, waiting for us, her amber eyes wide with fright at the rumors that had flashed like fire through the city, since my rowers came ashore; and so I had it all to tell again.

Our little sister was a magician, no stronger nor weaker than any other in New Aricuse; which is to say, as weak as a barbarian witch. The few spell-casters of New Aricuse bear little resemblance to the wizards of history, the powerful, terrible Talisman Mages of Old Aricuse.

"I cannot believe the Twenty agreed to pay tribute," Tai said, hugging herself as though perishing of cold on this warm summer evening. Short and slight, with brown braids and tan skin, she seemed more child than woman, though she'd reached her twentieth year.

"They had to agree, once they were done strutting their pride," Amala replied. "But hours it took to persuade them to pay tribute, and I know I will never be able to persuade them to build higher towers, or any other defense, because the sky isle comes always at unexpected times: once after a century, another time after two hundred and fifty-five years, once after seventy-three years." Her face grew grim. "Perhaps nothing we could do would protect our city from Bithuva." She looked at me. "Indel, you described how the sky isle struck Ynae with silent lightning on a clear day. The histories tell of firestorms raining from the sky isle, of magic swords that bend and break our blades like willow switches--the Bithuvans use magic we lost when Amuria sank. Yet history also tells us the Bithuvans have no talismans." She looked at our sister. "How then can the winged men wield such powerful magic?"

Tai shivered. "I cannot imagine."

"A deal with the Goddess's Darkchild," I said.

"No." Amala shook her head. "Such bargains are only myth. How I wish we had not lost the ancient knowledge of Amuria."

Over five centuries ago, the great continent of Amuria sank beneath the World-Ocean--some say because the Goddess punished Old Aricuse for hubris, others because the mages created a Great Talisman so powerful they could not control its energy and thereby destroyed Amuria. No one knows. The thousand Aricusene warriors who survived became our ancestors only because they'd been scouting the newly discovered Sethenan archipelago, vanguard for a conquering army that never arrived.

"What if the Bithuvans refuse our offer of tribute?" Tai cried. "You must have some plan, Amala. You are the Warchief."

Amala spoke quietly. "I have only twenty-five hundred warriors, and Bithuva will be above New Aricuse tomorrow. So I must find some way to make them accept our offer."

\*\*\*

In the morning, I broke fast alone in the shade of our grape arbor. In the distance, the sky isle Bithuva hung over the western sea, a gleaming gold flake in the sunlight, a day-star beneath the sinking crescent moon. By evening, the sky isle would be overhead. I could not stop thinking of the dream that woke me: of white New Aricuse stained red and black with flames and smoke and blood, and the shadow of Bithuva over everything, even my sisters' lifeless bodies; and myself rising helplessly into the sky, captive of the winged men.

The great doors of our Family House swung open, and a double column of thirty warriors in dress uniform marched out, the Warchief's escort, all men today, honored as men never would be in any other situation; and before the men marched Amala.

"Sister!" I heard my voice with surprise. Amala looked at me, face impassive under the ornamental headdress. I studied her fine uniform, the bronze breastplate chased with gold, the gilded sword-hilt, and said, "You go forth to seek parley with the winged men. Let me take you in my triaconter."

She nodded. And so it was that Warchief Amala went out to meet the Bithuvans in my ship, seated between two rows of warriors whose strong strokes drove my vessel swiftly westward; she sat with me at the stern, near a pile of branches, dry and green, and a large stone bowl, lidded.

I asked Amala, "Have you seen our sister this morning?"

"I had Tai brought up to the High Fort last night. You too may shelter there from the winged army, if you wish."

"The High Fort?" It stood in the mountain pass east of New Aricuse, three thousand feet above the sea. I suppressed a shudder, and swallowed the sudden sourness that coated my tongue. "Thank you, no."

Despite my dread of Bithuva, I grew somnolent in the heat of the sun, and succumbed to the weariness of too many days with too little sleep.

Then Amala's voice startled me awake: "Indel, behold."

She pointed ahead, and I saw that the sky isle, though still distant, was grown huge, a bulking mountain impossibly floating in the sky, with a few dark shapes winging about its twin peaks, one above and one beneath.

I looked at my sister's hand-picked warriors, all male, and felt only more afraid. In the Amurian Empire, only women were warriors; but the New Aricusene are not so numerous that we can restrict who may learn the art of war.

The Amurian mages would have made short work of the winged men. But they never heard of Bithuva; the sky isle never passed over Amuria, only the Sethenan archipelago discovered in the months before the continent sank.

Amala removed the stone lid from the wide bowl and spread tinder and dry twigs upon the exposed coals, breathing upon them until small flames consumed the tinder and caught on the twigs.

"Indel, put wood on the fire," she said, already doing as she ordered.

The flames bit into the dry wood. They rose, flickering around the leafy green sticks we laid loosely atop the dry; black smoke poured up, and the winged shapes turned toward us.

I remembered the winged men, plunging to Ynae to plunder and kill; and I shivered, wondering what mad whim had brought me out to meet the only unconquerable foe the Aricusene had ever met.

"Halt!" the Warchief cried; and her warriors drew up their oars, pale blades dripping golden light, and shipped them.

Then Amala drew her gold-hilted sword and laid it flat beside her, and rose up in my triaconter with a lithe grace that made it seem she had spent her life at sea; and she raised up her arms to their utmost reach and showed her empty hands to the approaching foe.

And her thirty warriors laid their bronze blades down beside their bronze-tipped spears, and stood up empty-handed. We were helpless! But I wouldn't let the winged men drag me into the sky. My left hand crept to my hilt--

"You too, Indel," Amala said, and I put down my sword and slowly rose, cursing the weight of my belly that made me clumsy.

The Warchief cried, "A parley!" in Aricusene, and Teroese, and a dozen other languages of the archipelago, and started over again, her voice as patient as the waves that break rock to sand.

The winged men of Bithuva drew closer, and closer, and I could not restrain my trembling. They were big, sharp-faced warriors, clad only in bright-colored loincloths with fringed and embroidered fabric hanging down fore and aft; I wondered if they eschewed armor out of foolhardy arrogance, or because the weight was too great for their wings to support, though these were astonishingly long and broad. Their bare chests were disproportionately huge, banded with muscle.

The winged men wore mismatched jewelry, and the ruddy-skinned, flame-haired man at their lead had a gold torc about his neck. The winged men's skin tones varied from pale olive to black, and their hair, which rose above their heads like bird crests, varied from white to copper to black; and whatever the color of a Bithuvan's crest, it matched the feathers of his wings. The Bithuvans carried spears and swords, and the blades and points were a peculiar, shining, almost silvery gray-white.

My trembling increased. It was true; the Bithuvans had magic weapons.

"A parley!" Warchief Amala cried, come back again to the Aricusene tongue as the Bithuvans circled above us. A throbbing wind from their wings slapped my face, filling my nostrils with a sharp dry smell and blowing a dust of fine feathers in my eyes.

Someone above called out in a strange language that croaked like a raven and shrilled like a hawk, speaking no words I could understand; yet I knew their meaning: "I am Krech'k't, son of the King of Bithuva, and I have authority to speak for him. How is it that a *girl* addresses me?"

I blinked, and lowered my aching arms to rub my eyes, 'til I saw that the speaker was the red Bithuvan in the gold torc, addressing us by means of some spell unknown even to Amurian legend. I squinted, looking for a metal pendant of intricate twists and knots--a talisman, necessary to power any strong spell. But I saw only a clutter of simple, ill-matched jewelry, such as you may find on any sea-pirate.

Amala answered the red Bithuvan: "I am Amala, a Chief of New Aricuse, and I have authority to speak for my city."

"Then I will listen to your words, though a female has no business leading even wingless crippled men. But I will not listen for long. Speak quickly!"

"My lord, there is no need for your people to burn or loot New Aricuse," Amala said. "We will pay you tribute, to spare our land and city."

The red Bithuvan stared at her in silence for a long while, as if he were considering.

Then he said, "The King of Bithuva will spare your pathetic island if you pay us a thousand pounds of gold, a thousand bushels of grain, a thousand barrels each of water, wine, and olive oil, and a thousand women. And one thing more--"

"A thousand women!" cried one of Amala's warriors.

"A thousand pounds of gold!" I exclaimed.

"Silence," Amala said in a low voice which nonetheless struck us quiet; then she called up to the red man: "What is your last requirement?"

Krech'k't said, "That I have *you*."

I gaped at him.

Amala said, "Agreed."

*"No!"* I shouted.

"Be silent when I am speaking to the king's son!" Amala didn't look at me, but kept her face raised to the enemy leader. "Please ignore him, my lord."

Krech'k't never looked at me. "Have your tribute ready by this evening," he told my sister. "We will take it then, girl. And I will take you."

***

"Amala, you cannot do this!" I cried, striding across the antechamber of her suite.

She was out of uniform, dressed only in gilded sandals, gold bands about her wrists, and a simple, elegant gown of white and deep blue silk that sharpened her Amurian beauty. She stood, watching me, and said nothing.

"I suppose you have weapons hidden somewhere about your person, as if the winged men will not check," I said. "But even if they find no weapon, do you think you can overcome an army of winged men by killing their prince, or taking him hostage? Do you think they would let you hold their prince captive for so long as a minute? By the Goddess, the sky isle will soon be here. *Hide* yourself, woman. They'll be content with the slave-girls and grain and gold."

"Indel, don't talk like a fool. Neither their king nor their king's son would be content; and so the Bithuvans would destroy New Aricuse with their magic. Anyway, their mages would find me immediately. They command magic of unknown strength."

"Unknown strength?" I forced myself to laugh. "Because their island flies through the sky? Is it required that all isles be fixed to the ocean floor?"

"Do you, who witnessed it, forget the power of their magic? Do you forget their army of winged warrior--"

"For the Goddess's sake, Amala," I cried, in despair, "do not do this thing. You don't even bed men."

"I will, to save New Aricuse. Oh, Indel, let us stop this ridiculous argument." Amala raised a steaming stoneware cup from a low table. "I--"

"Thank the Goddess you're drinking silphion and wild carrot tea. At least you'll bear no winged monstrosity--"

"This is an infusion for quite the opposite purpose."

"What?" I stared at her a moment, turning her words over in my mind; then I grabbed her wrist, spilling hot tea on her hand and mine. "Do you think you can conceive an army of winged Aricusene in one night?"

"Let go." Her free hand shoved me back so hard, I had to release her wrist to keep my balance. "Indel," she said, "you have spent the afternoon with your winecup--no, do not deny it, your breath reeks like a rowers' tavern. You should not be in the city any more than Tai. I know you are nervous of heights, but please, go to our sister at the High Fort."

"What--you think I--*I'm* not afraid of heights!" I said. "Tai is the coward in our family."

"Tai is braver than you think," Amala said. "And stronger." She put aside her cup. It was empty. "While you,

Indel, are drunk and carrying bronze." She raised her voice: "Guards!"

Immediately two armed women stepped into the antechamber. "Warchief?"

"Summon my escort. And four more warriors."

They saluted and were gone.

"Four more warriors?" I said.

"To hold you here, or take you up to the High Fort. You shall be allowed no opportunity to attack the Bithuvan king's son."

I felt as if I would shatter, like some painted winecup dashed to the tiles. "Don't do this, Amala."

"I do not break my word, Indel."

"I know." I admitted it at last. "Oh, sister, do you take care!"

She smiled crookedly. "Always, brother."

There was a knock at the door. "Your escort, Warchief."

I embraced Amala as I had not in a decade; not since I was thirteen and she fifteen, a raw recruit bound for her first battle. I thought her arms would crush me.

I swallowed, against the feeling that came into my guts at the thought of the High Fort, against the feeling that made me want to hold Amala until she said she would not go to the Bithuvan king's son, save with her sword in her hand and her army at her back.

I released her, and said, "Sister, I will go to Tai."

"Keep her safe," Amala said, and left.


\*\*\*


My escort let me keep my sword and gave me time to don a heavy cloak against the cold of the heights, but they marched me up the pass so quickly, I thought my laboring lungs and wine-swelled gut would rupture; certainly I burned the drunkenness out of my veins. I saw a number of carts drawn by slaves or goats, bearing the children and worldly goods of wealthy Aricusene fleeing over the pass, or to their villas in the cool mountains, as if high ground could save them from winged raiders and an island that floated in the sky. I wished I had one of the lost horses or camels of Amuria beneath me. I wished I were in a cart with high sides and a roof.

Though I had no desire for a glimpse of the world falling away from us, the twists and turns of the mountain road sometimes left me facing that vertiginous drop; and the oak trees which grew along the road weren't always there to hide the edge. Oddly, these glimpses of the edge, and the mountains and sky beyond, failed to disturb me. Finally, I realized I didn't mind the glimpses because I wasn't at the edge, in sight of the drop.

I began to enjoy the views from the mountain road.

Then I looked up.

I didn't look up again. Above New Aricuse Bay hovered Bithuva Island. It was so high, the highest peak of the Sethenan Mountains was below the level of its downthrust peak; yet so huge that, despite distance, the island in the sky seemed about to crush us.

\*\*\*

I was staggering and gasping, sure my lungs must burst with every step, when we reached the gates of the High Fort. The red granite edifice had been built by the first generation of New Aricusene, in imitation of the spired white marble citadels of their lost city, but I did not pause to admire its lofty towers; I wanted only to put myself inside its opaque walls.

The gate-guards admitted us into the courtyard, and somehow I found breath enough to shout, "Tai!" I was glad to see my younger sister again, even if she was chanting a spell and making magical gestures at a uniformed woman, and sure to embarrass herself.

She fell silent. The warrior leaped into the air. And, impossibly, stayed there.

"Indel!" Tai turned to me, and an enormous smile came over her face, lighting it so it seemed brighter than the sun. "I have put two thousand warriors in the sky."

I couldn't help it. I burst into laughter. "You've put most of our army in the sky? I see one warrior above us. And that is your limit, little sister."

Tai's smile had vanished. "Always, you have mocked my strength. But those warriors are in the sky above us, cloaked in the spell of invisibility."

I smiled indulgently. "Tai, now is not the time for pretend--"

"Please, Indel." She made an intricate gestured, then touched each of my eyelids. "Behold."

"Goddess!"

The sky was full of uniformed warriors, row upon row of women and men standing in midair, their bows in their hands. The bronze arrow-heads and cuirasses shone red in the sunset, for the sun-goddess is not blinded by mortal spells.

"Impossible!" I cried, rounding on Tai. "You do not have such power. No one has since Amuria sank."

Tai laughed delightedly. "My power has grown enormously since I came up the pass. Last night, I put the entire garrison of High Fort in the sky. Now I can keep two thousand warriors invisible and in the sky for hours, and myself with them."

"In one day you have become the most powerful mage the Aricusene have seen since the art of talisman-making was lost with Amuria? No, Tai, you have put an illusion-spell on me."

But Tai never could hold an illusion for more than two seconds, and they were all still up there, two thousand wingless flying warriors in the uniform of New Aricuse.

"Goddess," I whispered, struck by realization. "The

sky isle is a Great Talisman. The greatest ever created--"

Tai's joyful expression broke like a terra cotta statue flung against a wall. "Why must you belittle my every achievement, Indel?"

"You know the Amurian mages were powerful only because they had resources we do not. Or <u>did</u> not, until the sky isle drew near. Goddess, Tai, it is a great thing you have discovered."

She smiled, tremulously. "Do you really think so?"

I put my arm about her shoulders. "Of course."

Her smile vanished. "Then the magicians who live upon the talisman-isle must all be powerful mages, wise and dreadful with experience."

I stared at her in shocked silence. Why had I not realized this? Why had I not held my tongue? Why did I always have to find some way to wreck any pride or joy my little sister gained?

"It doesn't matter," Tai said stiffly. "Either way, I fly with the warriors to Bithuva."

"No!" I said, though it was clear Tai would heed me no longer. "Our army has its own magicians--"

"Don't you remember? The last three died six months ago, in action against the united Teroe Isles. That union is broken, but for all Amala's efforts since, her army has gained no recruits with magical talent. It is so rare--"

"You don't even know which end of a sword is which," I said. Already, I was belittling her again. The thought set my heart aching, and I changed my next words. "Our sister will never allow you to go into battle, Tai."

"Amala forbade me to leave the High Fort," Tai said. "But she is not here to enforce her order, and her Second-in-Command, Pesena, agrees with me, that I am needed in the sky. I am going," she declared, and with a wave of her hands she stepped into the air.

*Keep her safe*, Amala had said to me. As if she had known what Tai would do.

She had known, I realized suddenly; and she had

agreed to lie with the Bithuvan king's son so our enemies would expect no trouble from another quarter while our "Chief" was their hostage.

"Wait, Tai," I called. I swallowed. "I'm going with you."

"You?" she said, incredulously; but she descended to me, and raised her hands to cast the flying spell.

\*\*\*

It was not really flying, such as the winged men do. It was stepping upon air that felt solid where you placed your foot, though you saw nothing beneath your sole. But my sister and the warriors of New Aricuse called it flying; and it was difficult enough to do, when you're suspended about a Goddess-damned *distant* valley. And everyone around me had spent the day at practice, moving in midair. Thank the Goddess Tai was beside me, to keep me from blundering into the warriors' ordered ranks, and to right me when I started dizzily to reel.

"Watch the warriors, Indel," she murmured as I battled dizziness and nausea and a terror that made me want to scream without end. "Study the movements of their limbs."

Well, at least the warriors were *above*. I studiously did not look down.

"Why are Bithuvan warriors all men?" Tai softly asked. I said nothing, focused as I was on remaining upright when naught save invisible air held me in the sky. "They want us to pay them women--are few Bithuvan girls born?"

"Perhaps," I said, though that would be unnatural. I thought on the contemptuous way the Bithuvan king's son had addressed our sister. "I think only men are warriors because the Bithuvans do not like women."

We walked in silence for several minutes above the valley, at which I never glanced. Then Tai's small hand closed suddenly on my wrist, halting me.

"Look!" she whispered, and I saw that we stood, cloaked in her invisibility spell, only a few yards from the sky isle.

Bithuva seemed barren of civilization; the double-peaked mountain showed no sign of habitation, save the mouths of caves gaping everywhere, and the winged spearmen, who wove a net of defense around the sky isle.

***

The Bithuvans flew their patrols, oblivious to two thousand warriors spreading high and low, and around to the far side of the upper and lower mountains of Bithuva. Like the enemies of Old Aricuse, the Bithuvans had no idea of the existence of an invisibility spell.

A line of Bithuvan men flew up from the field behind New Aricuse, slow and labored under their burdens of gold or grain or barrels or bound slave-women, which they carried into a large cave-mouth. Tai and I stayed well away from the winged men, for I had only my sword; and neither of us had armor, only her strange new magical strength to shield us--if it did not fail.

It did.

It failed as the hand-signal was passing among our warriors that all were in place for our attack. A harsh voice suddenly rang out, seemingly from everywhere and nowhere, incomprehensible, impossibly loud. Then the enemy looked about themselves, wide-eyed, as if finding a new world revealed all around them; and then they threw their spears.

The magical gray spear-points pierced bronze breastplates like old linen. Our dead fell, to lie still upon the air.

But many of the gray-tipped spears gave only glancing wounds, or missed entirely; and our warriors reacted quickly, loosing a flight of arrows.  The winged men wore no armor, and our arrows were more accurate than their spears, and had a longer range; and our quivers were full.  Wings folded and bodies plummeted.

Tai cried, "The invisibility spell is gone!" as if we might not have noticed; and she began chanting and gesturing, seeking to restore her illusion.

The winged men drew their magic swords and rushed our warriors.  A second flight of arrows further reduced the Bithuvans' numbers.  But still there were many hundreds of winged men to close with our warriors; and the silvery-gray blades cut through bronze armor and blades like butter.

The thunderous harsh voice spoke again.  Though it still spoke in the strange Bithuvan tongue, I understood the words this time; and by Tai's sharply-drawn breath, I knew she did, as well.

"Foolish little witch-girl, to think yourself a match for a true magician."

"Where are you?" Tai shouted.  "It is easy to call insults from hiding.  Show yourself, coward."

"No!" I screamed, hoping to drown out Tai's provocation.

I failed.  In a flash of light and heat, a red-skinned man with gray wings materialized three yards away.  The evening light was failing, but I could see the red winged man clearly, as though he still glowed with the light of the instantaneous-travel spell.  He was ancient, his crest gray, his hawkish face folded into more seams than all the Sethenan Mountains may claim, but clearly he was kin to the arrogant prince; and he was possessed of a frightful vitality that showed itself in his supple and arrogant posture, and in his maliciously merry black eyes.  Horror came over me as he raised his hand and I realized he would surely destroy Tai's flying-spell and send us all plunging to our deaths.

But Tai was already gesturing, and as he raised his hand, her fists struck together before her chest, and lighting flashed out from them, streaking toward the Bithuvan mage.

He gestured, and the lightning divided, splintering around the red fire that blazed out of his fingertip; and he was not touched by the remnants of Tai's spell, nor was his red fire deflected by her lightning.

I shoved Tai aside.

Then I screamed and went spinning as the Bithuvan mage's fire-bolt blasted my right arm to ash. I heard Tai screaming my name, and the Bithuvan mage's harsh, mocking laughter.

I screamed again, in the knowledge that I should not be spinning; Tai's spell should have meant only that I fell upon solid air. I tried to stop my spinning, despite my missing arm and spraying blood and the pain that turned my vision black. I spread my arm and legs, and that slowed me; and my scrambling feet found invisible solidity.

Madly blinking, I cleared my eyes of dizziness, just as my sister flung fire like a wall at the winged mage.

He dissolved it and, still grinning with baleful pleasure, threw a lightning-bolt that made Tai's earlier lightning seem a small gold needle. He wanted to duel, that was clear; he wanted to duel because he expected to win, and would take cruel joy in crushing a weaker foe.

My baby sister.

Tai gestured, and the winged mage's lightning-bolt vanished; a second gesture did nothing I could see, but the Bithuvan mage grunted and shook himself, and raised his arms for another spell.

Despite my terror and pain, I sensed that they were no longer aware of my existence, or of the groups of Bithuvans and Aricusene fighting all about us; yet I knew that if I threw myself at the winged mage, he would notice me--see the motion out of the corner of his eye, or sense me with some defense-spell--and he would destroy me before I came near him, as easily as I might reach out and flatten a gnat between my palms.

With my left hand, I drew my sword.

I threw.

A sword is no spear, or throwing-dagger; my blade tumbled horridly, its length and balance suited only for cut and thrust. It had little chance of doing damage if it struck the mage; it had less chance of touching him at all. But I am ambidextrous; so my sword came close enough to catch the mage's eye or twinge his defense-spell. He reacted, twisting at the hips to splinter my blade with an ice-bolt.

Tai blasted the distracted mage to dust.

The winged men screamed as if they felt his death; and every winged warrior turned toward Tai as if he were not embroiled in deadly combat.

And every Bithuvan warrior sheathed his magic sword and bowed to my sister, wings sweeping above his lowered head.

"What is wrong with them?" Tai cried, looking wildly about. "It must be a trick--Indel, do you see other mages?"

"No!" I said, looking around as desperately as she.

I thought of the mage's vast arrogance, and his resemblance to Krech'k't. Who must be his son. If the mage was the winged men's leader, and he had a son, why would the winged men surrender to us upon his death?

*Son of the King of Bithuva*, Krech'k't had called himself. Not prince; not heir.

"Tai," I said, "the Bithuvans must have only one mage at a time, and the mage must be their king, even if that mage is only a 'girl.'"

***

Our warriors also suspected treachery, and cut the Bithuvans down from behind, until Tai cried out, "Goddess, they've *surrendered!*" and Amala's Second-in-Command, Pesena, screamed, "Stop! We are not butchers!"

Our warriors ceased the slaughter, even as Tai cast a swift spell to catch the Bithuvans whose wings had gone still with death or injury; and she healed the wounded, both Aricusene and Bithuvan, as if she were one of the mightiest mages of lost Amuria. Now the Bithuvans looked at her with something very like worship; and I knew that if their king had won, he would have healed no one. But Tai spent spells as recklessly as if she had never known one to fail.

And no healing-spell failed her, until she treated me. She stopped the pain, but she could not make bone and muscle out of thin air. She could only heal the burned flesh and seal the stump of my arm without scar or lingering ache.

Then: *"Amala!"* Tai cried suddenly, and was off like the legendary flying horse of Amuria, running down the sky toward New Aricuse. The winged men tried to follow her, but the Aricusene warriors barred their way with such weapons as remained unbroken; and Tai turned about to face the winged men. The translation spell was gone with the Bithuvan mage; but Tai made it clear to the winged men that all but one of them must remain here, under the watchful eyes of the Aricusene warriors, until she returned.

I followed Tai and her chosen Bithuvan down to New Aricuse, though the earth plunging up toward me brought me near to emptying my stomach. But I did not. Perhaps it was because I was dazed by the loss of my arm, and no small amount of blood with it; perhaps it was because I was afflicted by the exhaustion that follows seeing your dearly loved sister almost slain, and cannot be banished by any healing-spell. And I was sick with fear that my other sister, as dearly loved, was dead, at the vengeful hands of the dead mage-king's son.

\*\*\*

Tai's winged man called to his fellows at the eastern gate of New Aricuse, where they hovered above the torch-lit field and the pavilion of their late king's son; and the son's guards cast down their magic spears and swords, and descended to kneel on the ground, making a full and profound obeisance to Tai. And they did not rise, though the Aricusene warriors Amala had left in the city promptly swarmed through the gates to surround them, and set spear and sword points against their skin. Tai told our warriors to do the Bithuvans no harm, as long as they remained in their posture of surrender; and then she stepped onto the field and ran into the Bithuvan pavilion, with me close on her heels.

We almost collided with Amala. Tai and I fell upon her, shouting with relief, and her arms went about us.

"Oh, Indel," she said quietly. "You have lost your arm."

I said, "Where is Krech'k't?"

"When I heard Tai's voice, giving orders, I strangled him."

I looked at her, dressed in her white and blue silk gown, and said, "Did he--"

Tai interrupted, to tell her what had transpired in the sky.

Then Amala strode from the pavilion.

"Bithuva is conquered," the Warchief of New Aricuse cried, her low voice ringing with triumph, and her amber eyes glinting like a hawk's.

Her warriors raised a cheer to shake the heavens, and nearly rock Bithuva from the sky; a worrisome notion, with the isle now directly overhead.

"The sky island is ours!" she called.

Cheers rose again; but I did not join my voice to the warriors'.

*Ours?* What were we to do with Bithuva? How should we keep the sky isle, when it flew ever onward? And what were we to do with its inhabitants, still bowing down to Tai? Winged men could not easily be kept slaves.

"Ours," Amala continued, "but we haven't much time before the sky island is gone. Step forward and let my sister grant you flight, if you would come onto Bithuva and travel the world!"

My head jerked and my stomach clenched.

"What is this?" I demanded. "What do you mean?"

Then I realized it. Amala had hoped to capture the sky isle since first I told her of its return.

So I thought, until I saw the exhilaration in her eye. Then I knew this was a far older folly, dating from our childhood, when our tutor first told us of the sky isle. And now that New Aricuse had defeated Bithuva, Amala was foolishly spinning out her childish fantasy for the swelling crowd.

"Amala," I cried, "you don't even know where the sky isle flies--"

"What does it matter?" she shot back like an arrow. "It will be the greatest adventure an Aricusene could have since our ancestors lost Amuria and won a new home." She looked upon her warriors with eyes that were brighter than a signal-fire. "Who will go with me," she called, "and discover the world?"

No one, I would have said. No one would want to stay in the sky when they could step back onto solid ground; and no one would want to ride upon an island that moved through the air.

No one, I would have said; but I would have been wrong. Many wanted to travel upon the sky isle and discover the world, our little sister among them. ("How can I turn my back on such power?" she asked me. "In New Aricuse I am a joke, but on Bithuva I am a mage!" And a queen, I thought; but did not speak.)

And there was room enough for the many hundreds of Aricusene who wanted to go with Amala, for the upper and lower peaks of Bithuva were honeycombed with spacious caverns and labyrinthine tunnels. And, while the winged men would not be abandoning Bithuva, most every other inhabitant *would*: all the women recently torn from Ynae and other islands of the archipelago, and most of the other women, including many who were nursing winged boys. For all the alienness of their speech, the women from unknown lands made it clear that they had no desire to stay with the winged men. Even the old women did not want to continue with the sky isle on its journey. These were ominous portents; but when I said as much to Amala, she laughed and said I should not worry. No men, she said, even winged Bithuvans, were a match for Aricusene women.

We found no abducted Aricusene among the old women, but that was not entirely a surprise; Bithuva had last raided New Aricuse eighty-seven years ago. We found no winged women, nor any girls, with wings or without; we could not determine if girls were never sired by the winged men, or if the Bithuvans killed female infants because they believed that only men should have wings, or believed that girl-children had no worth.

Tai laid her palm on Amala's lean belly, and said, "You will know the answer to this mystery, when your daughter comes in nine months."

I could not speak, for the thought that, however willing she may have painted herself, my sister Amala had been taken against her will.

Amala looked upon me, knowing me too well not to know my thought. But she did not speak of what had occurred; she only touched my remaining arm and said, "Come with us, and be uncle to my child."

"I will not risk my life on such a foolish adventure," I said. "And I wish you would not risk the heir of our House."

Amala whispered, "Oh, Indel, do not let your fear of heights stop you."

"I'm not afraid!" I shouted. "I went up to Bithuva, did I not?" My stomach grew queasy as I remembered spinning in mid-air, and my long swift descent to the field outside the city; and the nausea increased as I contemplated spending the rest of my life in the sky. "I have a good life here, Amala. As you do--one with far greater responsibilities than mine. How can you abandon your duty, Warchief?"

"What kind of Warchief would I be," Amala said

quietly, "if I did not learn everything I might of the sky isle--the mightiest weapon known to all our long history?"

"And I shall be with her," Tai said, "seeking to learn the secrets of the Bithuvan mages."

"Oh, Goddess, I shall lose you both. Don't throw your lives away on a foolish fancy, sisters!"

Tai locked her arms about me and burst into tears, and Amala said, "I will miss you terribly, Indel. But I shall not stay. And I have not neglected our family."

And my elder sister gave me a statement she had drawn up, I know not when, that placed the House in my responsibility until our Family selected a girl-cousin from another branch to become Family leader and owner of the House; and her statement granted me the right to live there always.

So I am well sheltered, now that I am too old and fat to ride the Trade Road of the current, though I have no sisters or nieces to provide for me. Thirty years ago they went, Amala and Tai, with three thousand other citizens of New Aricusene, and the three thousand winged men, and all the tribute gold and grain and wine and water and oil which the winged men had gotten into their storage-caves before Tai became their mage and queen. My sisters are long gone, and my travels meant I never found a man to stay at my side; but my years on the Trade Road have left me comfortable--even wealthy--in my own right, and so the young men overlook my overlarge belly and missing arm and advanced years when I want one in my bed.

No, I lie; it was not my age or body or travels that brought me to this. Some still call me one of the heroes of the Battle of Bithuva; but about me they are mistaken. None must stay with me, when sooner or later he must see the coward in me.

Too, I am not often in New Aricuse, even in retirement.

I have never stopped thinking of how I turned my back on the chance to see things no Aricusene, even of Amuria, had ever seen before, only because of fear. Fear of leaving my comfortable rut.  Fear of the unknown--a thing shameful to the memory of my ancestors.  Fear of seeing my elder sister birthing the child of her rape.  And, most shameful yet, my fear of heights.

The sky isle will return again.  The last cycle of its journey was eighty-seven years, and I will never live so long as to cover such a span.  Yet I pray to the Goddess for a short cycle, and my sisters safely back, that I may see them once more before I die; and I think of what my sisters told me before they ascended to the sky isle.

"You guessed right, Indel," Tai had said.

I had not understood, until Amala had explained:  "The sky isle is indeed a Great Talisman, storing magical energy in the intricate recomplications of its tunnels."

Now they are gone with Bithuva, three decades gone.  I spend my days among the vines of the House arbor, or, more often, in the villa I bought in the mountains, where I live alone save for the slaves that maintain it; and I remember how always a different time has stretched between visits of the sky isle.  And every night I dream Tai has discovered that Bithuva may be steered like a triaconter, and will return with the morning.

But what is this?  Do I dream by daylight?

I see a shadow in cloudless sky, sharp-pointed as some gemstone at top and bottom; and I see my sisters, Tai and Amala, both as impossibly young as the ageless mages of Amurian legend as they descend toward me.  And I see they are accompanied by another, a young woman who has wings, and the tilted amber eyes of our House.

I reach up.  I will fly with them.

OYABAKIN

# BROOD

*Balogun*

Mistress Oyabakin deftly blocked the barrage of punches and kicks aimed at her face and belly, her muscular arms coiling, python-like, around the lean arms of her son, Akinkugbe.

"It is not speed, but timing that wins battles, Akin," Mistress Oyabakin said as she side-stepped to evade a quick back-kick. "You will see as you grow into manhood that speed decreases, while timing experiences growth for all the days of your life."

The martial arts mistress' dark blue wrap-skirt made a popping noise as she exploded forward. Mistress Oyabakin pulled her aṣe from her right palm just as it struck Akin in the chest to avoid hurting him.

The boy slid backward a few yards and then tumbled head-over-heels, coming to rest on his haunches.

Mistress Oyabakin sauntered over to her son.  A long braid – which had come loose from her tightly plaited, Mohawk-styled hair – danced across the left side of her face with each confident step.

The war mistress extended her hand out to Akin.  The

boy grabbed it and Mistress Oyabakin pulled Akin to his feet.

"I cannot wait to tell my schoolmates about our sparring match, Iya," Akin said. "They are in such awe of your power!"

"A barrel with just a single coin is noisy," Mistress Oyabakin began. "A barrel full of money makes no sound at all."

Akinkugbe contemplated his mother's words for a moment and then nodded. "Yes, mother. I understand. I will keep our training sessions between us."

"Good," Mistress Oyabakin said. "Now, let's go get cleaned up and…"

*"Oyabakin, the Oba of Ede needs your help!"*

Mistress Oyabakin turned toward the source of the voice that interrupted her. "Bankole, my sister-in-law is in need of her midwife. I have already given your wife all the herbs she needs for a healthy baby and a safe delivery."

Baale Bankole's chin dropped to his chest as he lowered his gaze.

Mistress Oyabakin studied her elder brother's face. The usually jovial man seemed consumed by sadness and worry. His short, coarse hair was speckled with grey, while it was completely black the month before, when Mistress Oyabakin last saw him, and darkness encircled his puffy eyelids.

"Jolaade is not…herself as of late," Chief Bankole said.

"Explain," Mistress Oyabakin demanded.

"As you may know, since her installment as Oba of Ede, Jolaade has become loved and admired as a just and benevolent king and is one of the Alaafin's most loyal and effective representatives," Bankole replied.

"So I have heard," Mistress Oyabakin said.

"When she made her pregnancy known to the citizens, they were nearly as elated as we were and a great celebration was held in the baby's honor," Chief Bankole said. "I could not have been happier with my wife...my *king*...until a fortnight ago."

Baale Bankole folded his arms across his chest and paced back and forth. "Jolaade began to become consumed with anger...and a *meanness* that I had never before witnessed. Before the citizens of Ede, she was still her kind, just and witty self. However, to those close to her – the palace staff, her midwife and I – she became increasingly cruel and even began striking me when she was cross – which was almost all the time!"

Mistress Oyabakin placed a hand on Akin's shoulder. "Son, go fetch my bag from the house."

"Yes, Iya," Akin said. "Ekaaro, Uncle Bankole!"

"Ekaaro, Akin!" Chief Bankole replied.

Akin turned on his heels and sprinted past his uncle's carriage, which was constructed of ebony and trimmed in brass. The boy stopped briefly to run his hands along the smooth, sinewy backs of the horses tethered to the vehicle before continuing on.

"And what does the King's midwife have to say about this change in your wife's behavior?" Mistress Oyabakin inquired.

"Oyelola has nothing to say, Bankole replied. "She's

dead."

"What?! Mistress Oyabakin said, her eyes widening in shock. "When? How?"

"It happened two days ago," Bankole sighed. "Oyelola came for Jolaade's final examination. As she proceeded to check the baby's position in Jolaade's belly, my wife became belligerent. She cursed Oyelola and accused her of trying to hurt the baby."

Chief Bankole turned his back to his sister. His shoulders shook, as did his voice, as he continued to speak. "Oyelola demanded that Jolaade calm down. Jolaade reprimanded Oyelola for making demands of her king and, in the next moment, she pounced on the old midwife – like a lioness on the back of a gazelle – and sank her teeth into Oyelola's throat."

"No!" Mistress Oyabakin gasped. "Yeye Oyelola helped deliver *me* into this world; she helped deliver my *son*! Why am I just now hearing about this?"

"Because no one else knows," Chief Bankole replied. "There was so much blood! So much...I-I dragged Oyelola's body out of the palace and buried her myself in Jolaade's garden."

"Bankole...no," Mistress Oyabakin said, shaking her head. "This is all wrong."

"What would you have me do?" Bankole said, throwing up his hands. "Expose my wife – the beloved Oba of Ede – as a murderer?"

Chief Bankole shook his head as he hammered his right fist down into his left hand. "The people would be devastated; Jolaade would be dethroned and probably beheaded; and Ede's enemies would see such a debacle as a perfect opportunity to strike."

"Spoken like a true politician," Mistress Oyabakin said.

"We cannot all be warriors, little sister," Chief Bankole spat.

"I would much rather be a warrior than a *worrier*," Mistress Oyabakin countered.

"I tell you what...succeed in helping my wife and I will resume my warrior studies," Bankole said, smiling.

"Are you sure?  You might break a fingernail, or lose a chest hair during a training session," Mistress Oyabakin snickered.

"You are the epitome of wittiness," Baale Bankole said, rolling his eyes.  "You should consider applying for a position as the Alaafin's quipster."

Akin returned.  Tucked under his arm was a small bag made of crocodile hide.  The bag had a long strap made of thick suede.  Akin handed the bag to his mother.

"Mo dupe," Mistress Oyabakin said, thanking her son.

"Ko tope," Akinkugbe replied.

"Now, go to the Warriors' Compound and find your father," Mistress Oyabakin instructed.  "Tell him that I had to go to Ede because Oba Jolaade is having...complications and needs my assistance."

***

The evening air in Ede was cool and dry, yet as Mistress Oyabakin stepped through the gateway of the palace, her bag slapping against her left hip with every movement, a moist blanket of blistering heat fell over her.

*It is as I feared,* she thought. *Dark spirits are at work here!*

The portcullis slammed behind the war mistress and her brother.

"Jolaade's chamber is this way," Bankole said, pointing toward his right. "She is usually napping at this time"

Mistress Oyabakin followed Chief Bankole up a short flight of marble stairs and then down a long hallway with a mahogany floor and walls. Sunlight poured through the thatched roof, illuminating the hallway.

At the end of the hall was a door made of polished bronze.

"This is Jolaade's chamber," Bankole whispered. "Please, enter quietly. Loud noises seem to set her off."

"Alright," Mistress Oyabakin whispered in reply. "Open the door and let us tip-toe in."

Chief Bankole pushed the door and it slowly slid open.

Mistress Oyabakin rushed past the Chief and stormed into the room.

"Ekurole, Oba Jolaade!" The mistress shouted. "Your sister-in-law has arrived!"

Chief Bankole's jaw went slack. He shook his head and then shut the door behind him.

Oba Jolaade rolled out of her plush bed, which sat at

the center of the capacious chamber. A crimson cloth was balled up in her tightly clenched fist.

The Oba was completely naked. Her full breasts, heavy with colostrum, swayed back and forth as she waddled toward her sister-in-law and her husband.

Jolaade's dark brown belly was as big as a ripe pumpkin and hung low on her pelvis.

Baale Bankole dropped to the floor, pressing his forehead to the hot marble. "Ekurole, Your Highness. Please, forgive our intrusion. My sister wishes only to ensure the health of Your Highness and of the baby."

Mistress Oyabakin did not bother to prostrate in salutation, as was customary among the citizens of the Oyo Empire, when greeting someone of a higher station.

"I would think you would have better manners, Mistress Oyabakin!" Jolaade spat as she wrapped the red lace cloth around her waist.

"And I would think you would know better than to put on that tight wrap-skirt," Mistress Oyabakin snickered. "You look like a whale in a mermaid suit."

"What?!" Jolaade screamed.

The Oba's face twisted into a mask of fury. She stormed around the room, knocking over racks of expensive clothing and snatching the silk covers from her bed.

Mistress Oyabakin threw back her head and laughed heartily.

"What, in the name of Olodumare, are you doing?" Chief Bankole hissed.

"Trust me, big brother," Mistress Oyabakin whispered.

The Chief nodded and then crept into the shadow of a nearby corner.

Oba Jolaade whirled around.

Mistress Oyabakin studied her.  Her face was no longer her own.  The face that leered at her was of a pallid, grayish-pink hue.  Her eyes had become round, black pits.  In the middle of each pit floated a bright red dot.  The corners of Oba Jolaade's mouth were stretched to each conical cheek – the lips curled back to reveal a mouth full of long, needle-like teeth.

Mistress Oyabakin reached into her bag and withdrew something, which she clutched tightly in her right fist.  "My goodness!  You are so hideous I am sure that when you were born, the midwife slapped your *mother's* ass instead of yours!"

The creature that was Oba Jolaade unleashed a high-pitched wail – like a baby crying for its mother's milk – and then charged.

Mistress Oyabakin flicked her right wrist and opened her hand.  A cloud of bluish-green smoke rose from her fingers.

Jolaade stormed through the teal cloud.  The powder covered her face and the Oba's body went limp.

Mistress Oyabakin darted forward and caught Jolaade's unconscious body just before her rotund belly slammed to the floor.

Jolaade's face returned to normal.  Mistress Oyabakin cradled the king's body in both arms and carried her to her bed.

"Mo dupe, for the assistance, big brother," Mistress Oyabakin called over her shoulder.

Chief Bankole crept out of the dark corner. "I apologize. I was frightened. I have never seen anything like that! Her face..."

"It was not *her* face," Mistress Oyabakin replied. "That was the face of the thing that festers in your wife's womb."

"What?" Chief Bankole shouted, taking a step backward. "What...*thing*?"

"Abiku – the Death Bringer; the tormentor of parents; the murderer of children," Mistress Oyabakin replied. "An abiku spirit has taken up residence in Jolaade's belly and has taken your baby's spirit hostage. If birthed, it will look like the fruit of your loins, but it will, most certainly, not be."

"What do we need to do?" Bankole asked.

"*I* need to travel to Ikole Orun," Mistress Oyabakin answered. "There, I will kill the abiku and rescue your child. *You* need to make sure no one enters – or leaves – this room until I return."

"How will you reach the spirit realm?" Bankole sighed. "We do not possess the apere ayorunbo."

"The apere ayorunbo is only necessary when you need to *physically* travel to the plane of spirit or to traverse long distances instantaneously," Mistress Oyabakin replied. "Only my *spirit* will travel to Ikole Orun. My flesh will remain here, with you."

"How?" Chief Bankole inquired.

Mistress Oyabakin reached into her bag and withdrew a silver flask. "This is extract of the iboga plant mixed with bark from an iroko tree. After I drink this, my body will fall into torpor as my spirit separates from my flesh. My spirit will then travel sideward into Ikole Orun.

"And why, exactly, do you possess such a concoction?" Baale Bankole asked, raising an eyebrow.

"I made it years ago in anticipation of one day needing to kill an opponent in the spirit plane." Mistress Oyabakin replied.

"You frighten me," Chief Bankole said.

"A ki i ṣe oto eranko gan-n-gan; bi a ba he igbin ada la nna a," Mistress Oyabakin chanted. "Do not conduct a feud with an animal halfheartedly; if you fight a snail, kill it with a cutlass!"

"Like I said – you frighten me!" Chief Bankole replied.

Mistress Oyabakin touched the flask to her lips and then took a large gulp of its contents. She slipped the flask into a pocket in the interior of her blouse, frowning as the bitter liquid swirled around her tongue.

Chief Bankole grabbed a large, forest green pillow and laid it behind his little sister's back.

Mistress Oyabakin lay back on the pillow and then closed her eyes.

In the next breath, the plush bedding and the soft pillow behind her head had given way to something hard and the sweltering room had become bitter cold.

Mistress Oyabakin opened her eyes. She was lying on a marble floor of a reddish-amber hue. The ceiling above her was made of a translucent, ruby-colored substance that ebbed and flowed like a gentle ocean tide.

Mistress Oyabakin sat up and perused her surroundings. She was in the center of a hallway that seemed to stretch nearly half a mile in both directions. Although it was obvious to the war mistress that she was indoors, the gentle breeze on her face – which carried the scent of mint, jasmine and kola nut – gave her the sensation of being deep in the forest.

A distant whimper broke the serene silence in the corridor.

Mistress Oyabakin sprang to her feet. She examined her surroundings with more care. Each end of the hallway appeared to veer off to the left and to the right.

The warrior-woman closed her eyes and focused on the whimpering sound. Keeping her eyes shut, Mistress Oyabakin began to slowly pivot, circling her hands in front of her chest as if she was rolling a small ball between her palms.

Scores of gossamer tentacles caressed Mistress Oyabakin's arms and face. She reached out, returning the caress, and the tentacles encircled her fingers.

The tentacles gently tugged, coaxing her forward.

Mistress Oyabakin followed the force of the pull, allowing the tentacles of sound to guide her to their source.

After a long walk – which seemed to last an hour – the tentacles loosened their grip on her fingers. A moment later, she felt them fade away altogether.

Mistress Oyabakin opened her eyes. Before her – sitting on his haunches – was an emaciated old man with flaccid, cocoa skin. The man looked up at her and smiled weakly.

"I am dying," the man sobbed.

"I know," Mistress Oyabakin replied. "You must die in heaven to be reborn on earth."

"But something has torn me from the womb of my mother and imprisoned me in this tomb of never-ending corridors," the old man sighed.

"Can you walk?" Mistress Oyabakin asked, pulling the man to his feet.

"Yes, I-I think so," the man grunted.

*"No, I think not!"*

Mistress Oyabakin propped the man against a wall and then slowly turned toward the strong, alto voice.

Oba Jolaade stood with her arms crossed over her bare breasts. A wrap-skirt was around her waist. The reddish-amber cloth seemed to meld into the floor.

"Where are you taking my son?" The woman spat.

"*Your* son?" Mistress Oyabakin hissed. "This is the child of Oba Jolaade, king of Ede, and of her husband, Chief Bankole! They want their son back and *you* gone!"

"You are insane!" The woman shouted. "I *am* Oba Jolaade! Son, come to me; we are leaving!"

Mistress Oyabakin placed a gentle hand on her nephew's shoulder. "That is an abiku spirit. The wicked creature that imprisoned you in this place. Do not listen to it! If we don't return you to your mother soon, you will die here, forever lost to the eternal cycle of life, death and rebirth."

"The abiku spirit sent this woman to murder you, my love!" The creature said. "I have come to rescue you and to return you to the comfort of my womb, where you belong!"

The old man grabbed the sides of his head with both hands. "I do not know what – or whom – to believe!"

Mistress Oyabakin grabbed the dying man around his

throat, her fingers digging into his loose flesh. "I tire of this! Why don't we just cut him in half and then you take one part and I take the other?"

"No...please," the old man begged.

A broad smile spread across the abiku's face. "I think that is a splendid idea! At least I will have a *part* of my son to cherish."

Mistress Oyabakin released her grip on her nephew's neck. "Do you see now, my nephew? No mother would agree to sever her child in half. That thing is *not* your mother!"

The abiku began to convulse violently. "No! You interfering witch!" The voice was that of an angry child.

The face and body of Oba Jolaade melted away, revealing the hideous face Mistress Oyabakin had witnessed earlier in Jolaade's chamber.

The abiku's monstrous visage sat upon the stout frame of a toddler.

The creature spat a string of obscenities as it charged forward, baring its needle-teeth and slashing with its clawed fingers.

Mistress Oyabakin somersaulted backward, kicking the abiku in the chin with the instep of her left foot.

The creature flew backward, crashing to the floor with a loud thud.

Mistress Oyabakin darted forward, crouching low.

The abiku staggered to its feet.

Mistress Oyabakin wrapped her arms around the abiku's waist and snatched the creature off its feet, hoisting it onto her right shoulder.

The abiku bent forcefully at the waist, slamming its forehead into the right side of Mistress Oyabakin's lower back.

A terrible pain ripped through the war mistress' kidney and clawed its way down to her pelvis.

Mistress Oyabakin collapsed onto her buttocks.

The abiku flipped onto its feet, landing back-to-back with Mistress Oyabakin.

The creature spun around and then wrapped its stubby arms around Mistress Oyabakin's neck, catching her in a powerful, vise-like choke.

Darkness descended upon the war mistress. Her brain cried out for oxygen-rich blood to nourish it and to bring back the light.

The warrior-woman beat back the encroaching unconsciousness and grabbed the abiku's ankles with both hands. She slammed her torso backward, pushing off of the balls of her feet, as she yanked the abiku's ankles forward.

The tremendous push-pull pressure threw the abiku spirit off balance. The back of the creature's skull slammed onto the floor. A sickening crunch followed.

Yellow gore splattered across the floor.

The abiku's grip loosened on the war mistress' neck.

Mistress Oyabakin whirled around on her knees to face the abiku spirit.

The creature's red-orb eyes rolled around wildly in their pits and the monster's long, pointed tongue flapped loosely across its face.

Mistress Oyabakin exploded forward, launching a

flurry of powerful elbow strikes at the abiku's throat, jaw and temples.

Each strike met its mark.

The abiku released a weak, child-like cry and then lay still.

Mistress Oyabakin struggled to her feet and then limped to her nephew, who was cowering against the wall, with his face buried in the palms of his hands. Mistress Oyabakin extended her hand to the old man and the old man grabbed it with shaky, crooked fingers.

"Come on," Mistress Oyabakin said. "Let's deliver you to your mother."

The war mistress drew the flask from her interior blouse pocket. She opened the flask and took a sip. A moment later, darkness overtook her.

***

Mistress Oyabakin awakened.

She was back in the Oba's chamber.

Jolaade was fast asleep. Her breathing was slow and rhythmic and a hint of a smile was on her face.

"You're back," Chief Bankole said, hugging his sister. "How did you – and the baby – fare?"

"Your child has been returned to you," Mistress Oyabakin said, leaping to her feet. "The abiku spirit is dead. My work here is done."

A hand grabbed Mistress Oyabakin's wrist. The grip was powerful.

Mistress Oyabakin looked toward the source of the grapple. Jolaade was sitting up, her free hand rubbing her big belly. Her expression was a mask of pain. The bed-sheets beneath her were soaking wet.

"Your work is not *quite* done," Oba Jolaade sighed. "My water has broken; I need you to help deliver this baby!"

"Oro ti aboyun ba so eni meji lo so o," Mistress Oyabakin chanted. "Whatever a pregnant woman says is said by two; how can I deny such a request?"

"Mo dupe!" Oba Jolaade replied.

Mistress Oyabakin nodded. She then nudged Chief Bankole's shoulder. "Leave; go practice a thousand sword strikes! I will send for you when the baby is born."

"A thousand…"

"Remember what you said about resuming your training," Mistress Oyabakin said, interrupting him. "Now, go!"

Chief Bankole nodded and then jogged out of the chamber.

Mistress Oyabakin tossed her bag onto the foot of Oba Jolaade's bed and approached the king. A broad smile was on her face. "I swear…a warrior's work is *never* done!"

# The Sickness

*Valjeanne Jeffers*

The Bini warriors crouched in the high grass of the savanna. They'd passed the Fula borders a mile back, and now were a hundred yards from the Adobe mud city. At the forefront they were armed with sword and shield, behind them the archers readied their bows.

General Chinua led the army. To his right was Nandi, a tall woman with braided hair, high cheekbones and full lips and her ebony-skinned husband, Sula, his head shaved in the traditional Bini custom. To Chinua's left was Nandi's older brother, Tomi.

A wide gateway led into the Fula kingdom. It was deserted.

"Where are the guards?" Nandi hissed.

"I don't know," Chinua replied. "But I won't return without Fula blood on my sword!"

The Fula had been violating the Bini borders for month. Three men traveling from the bush to their village had been attacked. Livestock had been stolen. And last week they'd actually tried to kidnap Effiwat and Iverem—the Oba's own daughters. Only the vigilance of the Bini guards had thwarted their efforts.

The General raised his arm and flung it forward... the

warriors crept through the grass. As they came abreast of the city, shields were snatched back from multicolored doorways. Fula warriors, armed with bow and arrows, emerged and took deadly aim. Men poured out the gateways.

General Chinua rose and gave a loud battle cry, echoed by his warriors...those Bini with bows and arrows began picking off the less agile Fula. The rest surged forward—engaging the Fula in hand-to-hand combat.

Nandi, the famed daughter of Oba Adegoke, charged into the fray. With a howl she leapt up and stabbed her first opponent in the chest, whipping her sword around to take the head off a second...

The Bini warriors fought their way to the gate, Nandi slashing and chopping though the enemy, and inside the city to the conical palace—slaying any who dared challenge them. Women and children watched the invaders from doorways. Inside Oba Gardiah's palace, they swept past chambers cordoned off with rich fabrics... to his throne room.

Gardiah's five personal guards surged forward. *"Enough!"* he shouted. "There has been enough bloodshed this day!"

The Oba met their gaze. He was a portly man, given to arrogance and vanity. His people followed him more from fear, than respect. Beside him stood a tall man dressed, despite the heat, in a hooded garment.

Nandi's eyes were drawn to him. Only the shadow of his visage, and red eyes burning like coals, were visible from his cowl. This was without doubt Gardiah's fabled witchdoctor, Atsu. The sorcerer who'd murdered his own twin in supplication to a demon to gain his power.

*An evil,* evil *man,* she thought. *He doesn't even look human.*

General Chinua raised his head proudly. "Your army is defeated, Gardiah. Your lands and all you have are now forfeit to Oba!"

The big man smiled slyly. "Such a high price! Perhaps we can come to a more reasonable agreement, eh?"

"I should gut you!" the general snarled. "You have violated our borders— insulted our women!"

"Careful, *dog!* Remember your place! You are no chief!"

In one smooth motion, Chinua blurred to the throne and pointed his sword tip at Gardiah's huge belly. "When I speak, it is Oba Adejoke's voice you hear and *his* commands. You will compensate us for your men's thefts. From this day forward, your village belongs to the Bini kingdom. We will collect a tribute each month. One of our messengers will visit you soon, to map out the terms. Do not harm him—not if you value your life and the lives of your people."

\*\*\*

They rinsed the blood of battle from their dark skins and supped on roasted yams. Although offered food, they'd refused to eat in the Fula village, for fear of being poisoned.

Now, the soldiers fed the fire with sticks. It would keep the scavengers away. Leaning against a tree to their right, was Gardiah's tribute: two bags heavy with cowrie shells, that they would take turns carrying home.

The night was cool, and the air sweet. So they sang:

*We are mighty*

*The enemy has been crushed*

*beneath our feet*

*His cries echo in our ears*

*We are mighty...*

Nandi, the Oba's eldest daughter, smiled, Sule beside her. She was the only woman there. *But soon there will be others. My rise in their ranks has caught the eyes of my sisters—those like me would rather hold a sword than pound yams and stir vegetables.*

Her joy at fighting alongside her husband, Sule, made victory that much sweeter. And their win, had extended the Oba's rule.

*Their defeat will be good news to share with father.*

A full, bright moon silhouetted the Jackal berry and Marula trees. In the distance, a lion roared. Sule grinned. "Ah, our brother congratulates us for bringing the Fula low!" The warriors roared with laughter.

"Gardiah is not such a big man now," Tomi said, "with his tribute on our backs!"

"Our village will prepare a feast in our honor!" another warrior, Chika said.

Tomi smile slyly. "Yes, I'm sure your wives will greet you with many succulent *treats.*"

They laughed again raucously. Sule looked sheepish at the men's subtle innuendo, and Nandi reassured him with a glance.

A chill lightly brushed her spine, and her smile froze. Since leaving the Fula's village, Nandi had had the feeling that they were being followed.

But she hadn't spoken her forebodings aloud. After all, she'd been visited by the preternatural once before. It was how she'd realized her dream of becoming a warrior. And how she'd become the only woman ever to serve in the Bini army.

She searched the savanna with keen eyes. *Perhaps he is visiting me now? Perhaps—*

Her thoughts were cut short by a loud wind, that blew

through their camp, quenching the fire. The moon and stars winked out, leaving them in total darkness and total silence—an eerie, unnatural stillness without birds or predators.

Now there was no sound but their ragged, panicked breathing, as if they were afraid to break the silence.

*What has happened?* Nandi reached out for Sule's hand, a hand she could no longer see.

Then she felt it. A heavy, malevolent presence watching them, directly in *front* of them, studying them as if they were little more than insects.

It vanished. The moon and stars returned, and the warriors cut their eyes at each other. But their lighthearted mood and thrill of battle were gone too. No one spoke as they bedded down.

\*\*\*

It began the next day, the weakness, fever and coughing. By the time the warriors reached their village borders, they could barely stand. The disease spread quickly, attacking men, women and children with equal vigor.

Nandi alone was mysteriously immune to the illness. But her father, the Oba and mother, Mariama, were not. His other three wives and their children were stricken as well. Even Bolajl, the village witch doctor, was so sick he could barely get out of bed.

\*\*\*

Nandi sat on the floor beside their bed, sponging Sule's face with cool water. Her husband had slipped into unconsciousness that afternoon and now lay in a near comatose state, babbling with fever.

*How I wish it were me instead! My heart feels like it has been stabbed with a dagger over and over!*

There was a loud cough behind her. She turned to find their serving girl, Poady, her eyes listless and hollowed out by the illness. But the girl's eyes burned with something else too. Resentment.

*They all think I am evil spirit that has brought this illness to my people. How quickly they forget!* For just last year it had been Nandi, who saved her village from slaughter by the Edo... aided by Ogun, the god of war.

"The village elders request your presence," Poady said sullenly, and left without Nandi's permission.

*She takes liberties because she knows I have fallen out of favor with the elders.*

Outside, to the right of her father's ivory palace under the palm tree, sat Oba Adejoke with Bolajl on his right. The elders were gathered around her father, two on his left and two on his right. Those villagers strong enough to stand stood outside the circle. As Nandi approached, they glared at her and cleared a path.

The elders and Oba Adejoke were also feverish and had lost weight. But the sickness did not diminish their severe demeanor. Only their chief looked sorrowful as well.

The first one, Hodan spoke from her father's left. "Daughter, we allowed you to fight, to take up sword and shield that rightfully only a man should hold. We violated long held Bini customs, the customs of our ancestors. This has brought the wrath of the gods down upon us."

"May I speak—?"

"I am not *finished!* " Hodan thundered. "It is the decision of Oba Adejoke and the village elders that you be stripped of your tribal birthright and banished into the wilderness. Speak your final words."

"It was because of *me* that you are not dead now or Edo slaves!" Nandi blurted.

"Gifts from a *demon!*" Bolaji shouted back. "And see the price we've paid for it! *Go!* You are no longer Bini! Leave this village and take your affliction with you!"

Tears streamed down her face. *Banished...?* "And what of my husband?" she sobbed.

The witchdoctor shook his staff at her and coughed. "You have no husband, no possessions! You will go now with the clothes on your back!"

Without another word, she turned and stumbled away.

\*\*\*

The young woman had been walking for hours, when she came upon a stream. She was not hungry but she *was* thirsty, for the day was hot and dry.

*And when hunger does come how will I feed myself, without a weapon?* Nandi knelt, scooped some water with her hands and drank. Afterward, she washed the tear tracks from her face.

Dispiritedly, she stared back down at her reflection in the water. A panther's image stared back at her.

She recognized him.

In the next moment, Ogun, the god of war appeared before her as a tall, powerfully built man with skin the color of midnight. A rope of iron hung from his thick neck.

"Nandi," he rumbled in a basso profundo voice. "I am here, daughter."

She bowed her head, "Ogun, you honor me once more! Please tell me, what has happened? Why is my village dying"

"It is sorcery, most foul and evil! The witchdoctor, Atsu, cast a spell upon the Bini in revenge for your victory, and the humiliation of his Oba."

"But I was untouched by his magic!"

Ogun smiled down at her. "I cloaked you, my warrior."

She gazed at him in confusion. "Ogun, why did you not cloak *all* of us?"

"Because, it is your destiny to do battle with him."

He instantly transformed into a huge black panther. Nandi jumped astride his back and wrapped her arms about his neck.

"Tonight," he said, "we travel to the spirit world..."

They rode with the wind, far from her home, passing trees with glowing bark and tops that grew further than her eye could follow... across blue sands... through lands with the earth above them and the clouds beneath their feet... Finally they came to a wall of fire. Nandi gripped Ogun's even neck tighter. But she did not cry out.

The panther leaped through the fire... emerging into a dimension with a starless sky and blood red moon. Beneath them lay smooth mahogany dirt without wrinkle or crevice.

Nandi climbed off Ogun's back. Yards ahead stood a castle gleaming whitely in eldritch moonlight. With a gasp she realized it was crafted from human bones. She felt *him* watching her again, the cold, inhuman presence she'd felt once before. Atsu.

Ogun vanished.

*Be brave,* the god whispered in her ear. *You must enter the castle. Once inside you will know what to do.*

She was afraid. But she was also angry—angry that anything human or inhuman would try to strip her of what she'd fought so hard for. The ancestors had smiled upon her.

But her village—her village was dying. Her mother and father were dying.

Sule was dying.

*Atsu is trying to steal my world! I will give my life to defend it.*

A sword appeared in her hand, forged from the iron about Ogun's neck. It was a thing of a fearsome beauty with a shimmering edge and a grip of woven iron.

The god's bass voice spoke in her ear again. *"My daughter, tonight this is your sword. Use it well."*

From out of the night they came, shadow warriors with amorphous shapes and holes for their eyes and mouth. They attacked. Nandi whipped her sword back and forth—stabbing and thrusting, through the demon's minions. The creatures shrieked horribly as she stabbed them, melting over her body, leaving a sticky, foul smelling dew on her skin.

*There are too many!*

Her lungs burned, her arms ached but she fought on grim faced. The castle seemed further away than ever...

Suddenly, the ground beneath her parted like water... Warriors with the heads of panthers and bodies of men rose like avenging spirits... to fight alongside her.

She reached the doorway of the castle. Unexpectedly, a strong push was all it took to open it. Inside the walls were smooth and white. Like the outside, the interior of the castle was made of bones. There were no lamps. But at the end of the hallway, a jewel glittered on an intricately carved ebony pedestal, illuminating all about her.

Nandi walked slowly toward the stone. As she drew closer, the castle morphed into a structure of ivory and gold. Fine soft rugs lay cushioning her feet. Languid song caressed her ears.

*"Come Nandi,"* myriad voices whispered. *"Nandi, come...*

Feelings of power and sensuality washed over her. She felt the stone's longing. *It wants* me. Nandi stood before the jewel and saw herself inside it. Indomitable. Immortal.

*"All this is yours,* the voices whispered, *Sweet Nandi. Strong Nandi. Take me, fight with me at your side."*

*"Forever."*

She reached out to snatch the stone from the pedestal. And hesitated.

*Take it!* The voices hissed. *Take it now! Take it and live forever!*

Nandi lifted her arm, and brought Ogun's sword down upon the the jewel—shattering it.

A hideous shriek flooded her ears. Atsu's cowled visage appeared, huge and diaphanous, his mouth stretched open in a scream. Shards flew past her like drops of blood. Inside she saw faces, the souls of those trapped inside. She glimpsed her father, her mother, the elders... and Sule...

The walls of the castle crumbled, screams echoing in her ears. Clutching Ogun's sword Nandi turned and raced back the way she'd come. Suddenly, Ogun was there as a panther. With his sword in one hand, she leaped on his back, and wrapped the other about his neck...

\*\*\*

She awoke to find herself outside her village. Ogun at her side. The sword had vanished from her hand, and now was coiled about his neck.

Nandi looked at him with questioning eyes. "Is it over? Are my people well now?"

"It is done. When you destroyed the jewel, you freed the pieces of their spirits trapped inside. It was written that you were the only one who could do this. Your village is whole again."

"I understand.  Once Atsu made them sick, he fragmented their souls and snatched them away from their bodies. A healthy spirit will not dwell inside a sick body."

The war god nodded approvingly. "He wanted your power for himself and this was ultimately his defeat. He lowered his guard enough so that you could break the spell."

"I sent your village dreams, they will welcome you home with open arms."

She stared at him incredulously. *I've only been gone a few hours!*

Ogun read her mind. "Time flows differently in the spirit realm. In this world, you have been gone for three days."

Suddenly Nandi's face became hard, and she bared her teeth. "I saw Atsu!" she hissed. "He still *lives!*"

"He is weak. There will be other battles. This one is over."

She turned away, her brown eyes still thoughtful.

"Speak your heart, Nandi. I am listening."

"I couldn't find the Atsu's castle alone—couldn't even defeat his warriors without you." Now she gazed into Ogun black eyes. "This was not my victory. It was yours."

The god of war smiled his beautiful, terrible smile. "What would have come from all my efforts, if you'd made the wrong choice? And the choice was yours alone to make. Nandi, you are a mighty warrior. But not all wars are fought with a sword."

"Go now, my daughter, you have been missed."

# KPENDU
## A Dossouye Story

### *Charles R. Saunders*

Dossouye sat in the middle of an elaborate corral that also served as a pasture. A carpet of lush grass surrounded her. Patterns pleasing to the eye were carved into the logs from which the enclosure was constructed. A soft breeze sighed through the grass-blades.

Dossouye was not alone. Gbo, her war-bull, lay in front of her. His legs were folded beneath the huge black bulk of his body. His head, armed with formidable, wide-curving horns, rested on the grass. His nose touched Dossouye's knees, and his warm breath wafted across her skin.

Dossouye's hand lay against the war-bull's forehead, just below the boss between his horns. Gbo's eyes were closed. He had not opened them that day.

More than thirty rains had washed through Dossouye's life. She was no longer the young woman who had departed from her native land of Abomey, on the other side of the Ilodwe continent. But she was a long way from old age. The muscles beneath her ebony skin remained supple, even though the angles of her face had become sharper, and the glint in her dark eyes harder.

Animals like Gbo aged far more quickly than humans. He had seen half of Dossouye's rains – which made him ancient by the standards of his kind. Dossouye had never known a war-bull to live as long as Gbo had.

But now ...

Three rains had passed since the last time Dossouye had ridden Gbo into battle. She had given him the pasture, in which he could live the rest of his days in comfort. Since then, Dossouye had learned to ride horses, for the wild buffalo in this part of Ilodwe were resistant to domestication, unlike the ancestors of Gbo's breed.

A day earlier, Gbo's legs had suddenly failed. And he had not moved since. As well, he had stopped eating and drinking. Soon, Dossouye knew, the war-bull would stop breathing.

Dossouye had not left Gbo's side since his collapse. The women she had made into warriors brought food and water to her. And they nodded in respect to Gbo, whom they revered nearly as much as they did their leader.

The time for mourning was growing short, though. Danger was imminent. Dossouye was well aware that she was needed now more than ever. Yet she could not allow Gbo to die alone.

She spoke softly to him in the language of Abomey, which she now heard only when she was dreaming. She had raised and trained Gbo since the time he was a wobbly-legged calf. They had saved each other's lives on innumerable occasions. The bond between them was as deep as possible between human and animal. Now, death was about to break that bond.

Gbo opened his eyes then.

Dossouye looked down at the milky film that glazed his orbs. That, and the white hairs that speckled his snout, were the only signs of the age that had ravaged the war-bull from within. His body still looked strong on the surface, and the tips of his horns appeared lethal enough to rip the flesh of any foe.

A weak *whuff* escaped Gbo's mouth. Then he closed his eyes. And Dossouye could no longer feel the touch of his breath against the skin of her leg.

Tears filled Dossouye's eyes. But she could not shed them.

Not now ...

Then she heard a footfall in the corral. And she looked up.

\*\*\*

The woman who stood at the entrance of the corral was tall and muscled like a lioness. Form-fitting armor made from hardened leather encased her frame, and a plain black helmet capped her head. A scabbard belted to her waist held a long, straight sword. The broad-featured face exposed by the helmet was deep umber in hue. Normally, that face would bear a stern, uncompromising expression. Now, however, it expressed sympathy and concern.

"He is gone, Sigaza," Dossouye said to the other woman.

Sigaza bowed her head.

"I am sorry, Dossouye," she said in a low tone.

Neither woman said anything else for a time as Dossouye stroked the thick boss between Gbo's horns and spoke soft words in her native tongue, which Sigaza did not understand. Finally, Dossouye moved the war-bull's head from her knees to the grass, and rose to her feet.

Dossouye was tall, but the top of her head only reached the level of Sigaza's eyes. Nor did Dossouye match the other woman's musculature, which possessed strength more than a match for that of most men. Yet never once had Sigaza bested Dossouye in the dozens of practice-duels they had fought. For Dossouye's quickness was almost preternatural, and her lean frame carried a deceptive strength of its own.

Unarmored, Dossouye was clad only in a length of black knotted around her waist. The unshed tears still shone in her dark eyes. The time to allow them to fall would come later – if she and those who followed her managed to stay alive in the next hours.

"A life ends – and a battle begins," Dossouye murmured.

Sigaza nodded. As the two women walked out of the corral, Dossouye turned and looked at Gbo. Already, flies were beginning to settle on his huge carcass. Dossouye resisted the urge to rush back and sweep the buzzing insects aside. But there was no time.

*No time …*

\*\*\*

Like a noose of steel, a host of armed men encircled a cluster of *ilimas* – spires of rock that jutted from the ground like the fingers of huge, buried hands. Dwellings were scattered like pebbles among the *ilimas*. So were gardens and corrals. People moved purposefully within the stronghold. The sun glinted from the various types of weapons and armor borne by the inhabitants.

Beyond the *ilimas* lay fields that bore crops that had grown abundantly until a few days ago, when an attack of malignant *kyame* – sorcery – left withered, colorless husks in place of *teff* and *fika* plants. Only one field remained untouched, and that one was guarded by men like the ones who formed the iron ring around the community the intruders were there to subdue.

Nearly a dozen huge cages on wheels were bunched behind the intruders' lines. The oxen that had pulled the cages to the battlefield were unhitched. They munched placidly on grass left untouched by the magic's blight. The wheeled pens stood empty – for now.

From a rise in the rolling landscape, two men closely surveyed the scene of impending battle. One of them looked like a boulder that had been carved from basalt: squat and round, but also solid, with scarcely any excess flesh beneath the leather-and-iron armor that encased his body. His helmet bore an elaborate crest fashioned from the feathers of a falcon – the only accouterment that designated him as the commander of the intruders.

The second watcher was small only in comparison with the other man. His nut-brown skin stretched tightly across a frame that was rangy, but not thin. Though he was slightly taller than his companion, he seemed diminished by the other man's bearing. The multi-colored beads that decorated the lean man's armor presented a telling contrast to his commander's utilitarian gear.

"They'll be coming out soon," said the lean man, whose name was Kengi.

The commander, who was called Muhalu, grunted in response.

"It's a good thing we're getting rid of them," Kengi continued. "Women living without men ... who ever heard of such a thing?"

"*They* have," said Muhalu, gesturing toward the stronghold.

Kengi snorted in derision.

"No, Muhalu," he said. "It is their leader, that Dossouye woman, who put that notion in their heads. With that devil-beast of hers gone, her army of women will be no match for us."

"The devil-beast has not been seen in some time," said Muhalu. "But still, no one has been able to defeat Dossouye and her followers. Only our numbers, along with the sorcery of Thloko, has enabled us to have an advantage these women will not be able to overcome."

"By Ishimandi!" Kengi cursed. "I'd like to kill them all!"

Muhalu gave his subordinate a hard glare.

"Keep that wish to yourself, Kengi," he grated. "Unless you prefer that the Tiputi pay us with death instead of ivory and gold."

"As you say," Kengi muttered, looking away.  Then he sketched a salute and descended the rise without saying another word.

\*\*\*

A scowl settled on Muhalu's blunt features as he returned his attention to the besieged stronghold.  In all the rains he had seen as a leader of sell-swords, this was the most bizarre task he had ever undertaken.  But then no one had ever offered richer rewards than the Tiputi, a sinister cult that was spreading rapidly through southern Ilodwe.   Though the Tiputi were secretive, they were also influential – and extremely wealthy.

When a masked member of the Tiputi approached Muhalu in the southern city of Nkhata, the sell-sword was tempted plunge his sword into the man's body.  But Muhalu knew that such an action would mark him for death.  And even though the prospect of death was part of his profession, he was not anxious to throw his life away so cheaply.

As he considered what the Tiputi wanted him to do, and contemplated the magnitude of the reward the cult was offering, Muhalu had difficulty deciding whether he had been favored by the gods, or cursed by the spirits of evil ancestors, to be the one the Tiputi had chosen.

Like nearly everyone else in the south of Ilodwe, Muhalu had heard of the women known as the Muringaka – the Freed Ones.  He was aware, as well, of their leader, Dossouye, who had come from the north astride a beast of a kind never before known to have been tamed.

*Devil-beast and devil-woman*, Muhalu thought as he continued to gaze at the *ilimas*.  Local legends held that the *ilimas* were haunted by the spirits of those who had been too wicked to merit an afterlife in the Bush of Ghosts.  Many people – women and men alike – believed such a place to be a fitting abode for such nonconformists as the Muringaka.

Despite his negative opinion of Dossouye, Muhalu was not one of those detractors. He cared little about the existence of the Muringaka, as long as the women did nothing to interfere with his concerns as a leader of sellswords. Now, thanks to the riches the Tiputi had dangled like bait, his concern was the capture and defeat of the band of women who had set themselves apart from the dominance of men.

Now he heard the footsteps of someone approaching the rise. His ears told him it was not Kengi, coming back to raise more annoying questions and misgivings. This tread was lighter, more furtive – and it was accompanied by a clicking sound.

Muhalu turned and saw a cadaverous-looking man swathed in a cowled cloak that was the color of fresh blood. Dozens of tiny bones were sewn in to the crimson fabric, accounting for the clicking noises. The only flesh that showed was that of his hands, sienna-brown in hue. A mask craved from white wood covered his face. The only features on the mask were thin slits through which its wearer could see, breathe and speak.

This was Thloko, the Tiputi *njulu* – sorcerer – who had hired Muhalu's sellswords and was accompanying them to lend his arcane talents to the completion of task. Muhalu instinctively disliked the *njulu* … but then in any case, he had not been in the habit of cultivating friendships with those who sought his services.

"They will come out soon," Thloko said, his tone halfway between a whisper and a hiss. "They will not allow themselves to be defeated by starvation. It will take more – much more."

"They will fight like devils," said Muhalu. "Because you want them to be taken alive, many of my men will die."

"As you know, the ones who survive will be well-rewarded," Thloko retorted.

Muhalu had no immediate response to that observation. Still, he had something else to say.

"You could help more –"

Thloko cut him off with an impatient gesture.

"We have already discussed that, sell-sword. I have done what I can in eliminating their food supply through sorcery rather than burning, which would have alerted them too soon. And I concealed our approach until we had them surrounded. The rest is up to you, for our purposes require that no sorcery touches these women, other than what we have already planned."

Muhalu gazed at his employer for a long moment.

"When they come out, we will be ready," he finally said.

"See that you are," Thloko responded curtly. Then the *njulu* turned and descended the rise, the bones that covered his garment rattling eerily with each step he took.

\*\*\*

Dossouye stood before her assembled Muringaka. Even in the midst of her grief over the death of Gbo, and her apprehension over the sudden and unanticipated arrival of the invaders, her heart swelled with pride at the sight of the warrior-women who faced her. Armor made from leather and metal encased bodies that ranged from slight to muscular to voluptuous. The women's hands gripped spears, swords and bows with a confidence that came not only from hours of practice, but also from having survived combat. They also carried light shields that were curved in a way that would deflect rather than bear the brunt of an enemy's blow.

Nearly all the races of southern Ilodwe were represented among the Muringaka: from squat, jet-black Ibwabwa to brown-skinned Kikwati to willowy, sienna-skinned Okini, with many variations and admixtures as well. Although the women's expressions were grim, their eyes could not conceal the fear and defiance that warred within their hearts.

For the Freed Ones had seen the size of the horde that surrounded the *ilimas*.  And they had seen the cages ...

Dossouye was clad in black leather armor reinforced with rectangular plates of steel.  It offered her protection, yet it was also light enough to allow her to retain her agility, which was the foundation upon which her formidable fighting skills were based.  Her cap-like helmet was in her hand, and her shield lay on the ground, waiting to be picked up.

Two women flanked Dossouye.  One was Sigaza, who towered over Dossouye but did not overshadow her.  The other was shorter than Dossouye, and so thin that she appeared at first glance to be an effigy fashioned from black sticks.  All *njulu* were bone-thin, due to the extreme physical demands their style of sorcery imposed.  This one's body was nearly naked, but the swirling designs of white clay daubed on her dark skin made her appear to be completely clothed, for the designs extended from her feet to her clean-shaven scalp.  The Muringaka – including even Dossouye – were careful not to look too long at those swirls ...

This was Vulyuwa, a *njulu* who had fled from Kubata, the City of Magic, rather than submit to the deviant lusts of one of its overlords. Even though she was no warrior, Vulyuwa still sought sanctuary with the Muringaka, and they accepted her.  Now, Vulyuwa's face showed the strain of maintaining the unseen magical barrier that that  had prevented the invaders from immediately overrunning the *ilimas*.

Dossouye leaned toward the *njulu*, and spoke to her in a low tone.

"Are you certain you can do it?"

Despite the intensity of her concentration, Vulyuwa managed a grim smile.

"Nothing is certain, Dossouye," she said. "I will do my best."

"That is all I ask," said Dossouye.

Dossouye turned to the massed ranks of the Freed Ones – an impressive sight, even considering the odds against them.

She knew they could never be the equals of the *ahosi*, the women-warriors of Abomey, who were trained from childhood in combat skills. There were no children among the Muringaka, however. Their social order was not yet sufficiently stable to allow for the nurturance of young ones.

"My sisters," Dossouye said, loudly enough to be heard throughout the *ilimas*. And the warriors were, indeed, as close to her as blood-kin could ever be. She had rescued, trained and nurtured them. She was their mother, their sister, their teacher, their friend. Even having acquired their prowess later in life, though, the Muringaka were formidable.

"Who are we?"

"The Muringaka!" came the answer from nearly a thousand throats.

"The men gathered outside want us for their own. Will they have us?"

"No!"

"How will we defeat them?"

"Any way we can!"

"When will we submit to them?"

"Never!"

Dossouye sheathed her sword and donned her helmet. Along with the other Freed Ones, she went to the area where their steeds awaited. She mounted her horse, a powerful black stallion bred for war. The horse responded instantly when she pulled the reins. She had been riding this animal since the time it became clear that Gbo's health was failing. The horse was a courageous beast. But it was not – and could never be – Gbo.

But this was not the time to long for her war-bull. With a grim expression fixed on her face, Dossouye led the Muringaka out of the *ilimas*: past the rough rockfaces, past the faded images painted on the stone long ago by unknown hands … images that were the source of the tales about the spirits that were trapped in the crags.

After Dossouye and her warrior-women departed their stronghold, only Vulyuwa stayed behind. Eyes closed in deep concentration, the *njulu* muttered incomprehensible, yet fearsome, words while her hands shaped intricate symbols in the air. As Vulyuwa chanted, the whorls on her skin spun in concert with the quivering of her muscles.

\*\*\*

*He loped swiftly and tirelessly across terrain that was unfamiliar and fleeting. Yet he knew what his destination was to be, and he knew he would get there. He already missed his home, even though he had only been gone for a short time. He knew he might never see his home again. But a promise had been made. And once made, it had to be kept.*

*The urge that both drove and guided him was unerring. The shape he wore caused the beasts of forest and savanna to avoid him. And he, in turn, shunned the locales of women and men. He would continue to do so until he reached his destination.*

*Necessity pushed him to greater haste. The circumstances leading to the fulfillment of the promise had developed over a long period of time. Now, events had changed suddenly. And the need to see the promise through had become drastic.*

*He moved even faster than before. He hoped he would arrive in time …*

\*\*\*

A grin split the usual stolidity of Muhalu's features as he gazed intently at the *ilimas*. Even from the distance of his vantage point, the commander's keen eyes detected movement. Tiny figures were beginning to emerge from their stronghold. Sunlight glittered from the tips of weapons, and puffs of dust marked the progress of horses' hooves.

The plume atop Muhalu's helmet bobbed as he turned to Kengi. Excitement glittered in the commander's eyes.

"They are coming out at last!" Muhalu exulted. "Now we've got them!"

"But why are they coming out *now*?" Kengi wondered, his initial enthusiasm suddenly tempered by caution.

Muhalu paused a moment before speaking again.

"Does that matter?" he demanded.

As if in answer to the commander's question, the warrior-women fanned out, forming a long, single rank with their leader at its center. When the line was complete, the women halted their mounts and remained unmoving, as though awaiting some occurrence of which only they were aware.

"They're making it easy for us," Muhalu said contemptuously.

He then pulled a spiraled horn from his belt. He lifted the horn to his lips and blew three short, sharp notes that reverberated across the battlefield. It was the signal for his men to attack.

In a display of disciplined motion, the intruders surged forward. The impact of their horses' hooves against the ground sounded like muffled thunder, drowning out the steps of the foot-troops who followed the mounted men. And still their foes did not move.

Suddenly, Muhalu felt a faint vibration beneath his feet. Kengi felt it, too. Before Muhalu could wonder aloud about what was happening, the front ranks of the invaders abruptly fell flat, mounts whinnying in pain and surprise while their riders shouted in consternation. In the blink of an eye, an orderly advance was reduced to chaos as more invaders went down in the face of the unseen force.

At first, it appeared that the invaders had collided with an imperceptible wall. But as the moments passed, it became clear that the power was pushing against the invaders, forcing them to retreat or be crushed.

For a moment longer, Muhalu stared at the swiftly progressing disaster. Then he turned to look for Thloko – who was standing directly behind him. Muhalu's initial shock at the *njulu*'s sudden appearance, without so much as a single rattle of a bone to betray his approach, gave way to a burst of anger that superseded his fear of the Tiputi sorcerer.

"Do something!" Muhalu roared in the command-tone that intimidated his underlings.

The *njulu*'s mask regarded him impassively.

"I am," Thloko whispered.

\*\*\*

Vulyuwa stood as rigid as the stone spires that surrounded her. She was alone in the stronghold; all the other Muringaka were with Dossouye. Vulyuwa's arms were raised high above her head. Her fingers curved into stiff claws. Her eyes were closed in concentration and her teeth were bared, though no sound escaped her mouth. The white swirls that covered her skin twisted and spun as she drew upon their power to push the protective barrier toward the invaders. She could sense them retreating in the face of inexorable *kyame* – magic.

So intent was the *njulu* on her task that she was unaware of the filaments that were beginning to poke through the ground near her feet. Corpse-gray in color, they resembled worms or eyeless snakes ... or, perhaps, animated blades of grass. More of them emerged silently – scores in all.

Abruptly, the filaments grew in length. Then they wrapped themselves around Vulyuwa's body, obscuring the white swirls. The *njulu*'s eyes snapped open. Her concentration broke, and she lost control of the magic that had created and maintained the barrier.

With a pang of despair, Vulyuwa realized that the barrier had suddenly dissipated. To rebuild it, she needed total focus of her sorcerous strength. That was impossible now. The *njulu* needed all the internal resources she could muster to stay alive even as the gray filaments encased her and bore her to the ground.

She knew who had sent the filaments to bind her. She had not suspected that the Tiputi sorcerer's *kyame* could do much beyond the blighting of the Muringakas' fields. Otherwise, would he not already have done it?

Vulyuwa was prone now. The relentless filaments covered her completely, like a burial shroud. One of them was attempting to slither between her clenched teeth and work its way inside her mouth. Despite her hopeless position, Vulyuwa continued to struggle against the loathsome grasp of the filaments. If she could somehow extricate herself before the invaders pressed their attack ... But the filaments were squeezing tighter ... tighter ...

\*\*\*

Dossouye cursed in the names of several deities from the other side of the Land of Trees when she saw that many of the invaders pushed back by the barrier were now rising to their feet and regrouping. Some of them remained on the ground, crushed flat by the unseen *kyame*. But it was quickly becoming clear that the barrier was no longer moving forward ... and had, indeed, disappeared.

"Something has happened to Vulyuwa," cried Sigaza, who was at Dossouye's side. "That Tiputi *njulu* must be more powerful than we thought."

"Then we will have to be more powerful than *they* think we are," Dossouye said calmly.

The mounts of both warrior-women tossed their heads in anticipation of the fighting that seemed imminent. They were fierce war-horses, trained to fight as extensions of their riders. Again, Dossouye wished it were Gbo she was riding.

Again, she thrust that distracting thought aside.

Neither she nor Vulyuwa had believed that the expansion of the protective *kyame* barrier would, in itself, be sufficient to defeat the invaders. Even so, the women had hoped to demoralize their foes, and kill enough of them to negate their advantage in numbers. Many of the sell-swords had, indeed, fallen ... but not enough to even the odds against the Muringaka.

And the invaders were no longer demoralized. Taunts and jeers rose from the throats of the men as they surged forward.

Along with the other Muringaka, Dossouye quickly observed that the invaders were utilizing unusual tactics. Instead of advancing as a single unit, they broke into teams of three: two of whom were armed with swords, spears and shields, and the third with a large net. The connection between the nets and the wheeled cages could not have been clearer.

Even as the invaders drew nearer, Dossouye relayed a quick command to the Muringaka. The ones who were armed with bows moved their mounts forward, while   the others remained motionless. Bowstrings twanged. Feathered shafts sped toward the enemy. Arrowheads plunged into the armor and exposed limbs of the men carrying   nets.

Cries of consternation rose from the invaders as net-wielders fell from their mounts. Not all of the archers' marks were hit, however. And some of the ones who went down were wounded, not dead.

When the Freed Ones loosed their second volley, the invaders responded quickly. Shields interposed in front of the net-wielders deflected most of the arrows. Still, more of the net-wielders fell.

Dossouye did not order a third volley. And no return arrow-fire came from the invaders. Ordinarily, the lack of retaliation-in-kind would have puzzled the *ahosi*. But within the parameters of this battle, it was understandable. The invaders' purpose was to capture rather than kill. The warrior-women's purpose was to kill rather than be captured.

"Forward!" Dossouye cried.

The opposing forces clashed in a way that had never before been seen on any battlefield. Even as the Muringaka strove to cut down the invaders, their foes did not engage them directly. When the sell-swords came close enough, the net-wielders tossed their snares toward the Muringaka. Instead of flying through the air, the nets floated as though buoyed by a nonexistent wind. The women-warriors lashed out with their weapons – then stared wide-eyed as the nets suddenly swooped down and enveloped them.

The moment one of the nets caught its prey, all struggles ceased, and the victim lay inert in a cocoon of mesh. At that juncture, the other members of the invaders' teams stood guard over their captives until other invaders carried them away. Then the net-wielders, who carried more than one of their devices, moved off with their companions in search of other quarry.

Some of the nets missed their targets, for after the initial onslaught some of the Muringaka were able to avoid being snared. When that happened, the nets would hover for a moment, then flutter uselessly to the ground. The women-warriors took care not to touch the fallen nets.

"There is *kyame* in those nets," Dossouye said to Sigaza.

The big woman nodded.

Then a net flew toward Dossouye.

\*\*\*

*Even though the battle was still distant from him, his supernatural senses were awash in the blood, the pain and the fear that the fighting produced. He did not know whether he would arrive in time, even though he had redoubled his speed, and the terrain through which he ran had now become little more than a variegated blur of emerald, umber and gold.*

*He did not consider what could happen if his arrival came too late. The possibility of that consequence did not – could not – occur to him. It was impossible ... yet he had much more ground to cover before the* ilimas *would be within his sight. What he would do when he reached his destination depended on the circumstances he found. Even so, he knew there would be killing – and repercussions.*

*He continued his journey of urgency, knowing that when he reached his destination, his life would change forever.*

\*\*\*

Dossouye flung her shield at the descending net. She had previously loosened the shield's straps in anticipation of the need for such a maneuver. The shield slid easily from her arm, and the net wrapped itself around the speeding object. The shield's momentum carried it – and the net – away from Dossouye.

Her stallion reared, forehooves churning as it shied away from the *kyame* imbued in the nets. As Dossouye quickly brought her mount under control, she saw that her ploy with her shield had succeeded. Wrapped in the mesh of the net, the shield dropped to the ground. The net did not detach itself. It lay inert, harmless.

"Do as I did!" Dossouye called to her Muringaka.

Sigaza was the first to heed Dossouye's suggestion. Slamming her sword into its scabbard, she loosened the straps of her shield and hurled it at the net floating closest to her. The moment shield touched the net's fibers, it became ensnared and fell to the ground.

Even as the shield dropped, Sigaza slashed downward with her sword. Its edge sheared through the neck of the net-wielder. As his severed head fell away, a crimson geyser shot upward from the stump of his neck. Then Sigaza's steed whirled, and she cut another invader from his saddle. The third member of the net-team chose to retreat rather than suffer a similar fate.

Although she was being hard-pressed by foes of her own, Dossouye nodded approval at the alacrity with which the Muringaka followed her suggestion. Soon after the capabilities of the ensorcelled nets became apparent, the idea of using flung shields against them had occurred to her. But she could not be certain it would work until she attempted it herself. Now she knew the tactic was effective. She also knew that the advantage it provided would be fleeting.

Because of the time that was necessary to loosen the shield-straps, some of the warrior-women continued to fall prey to the nets, and were carried away to the wheeled cages. Also, discarding their shields made the Muringaka more vulnerable – but not to the same extent they would have been had the invaders been fighting to kill rather than capture.

Dossouye knew that the Muringakas' only chance to retain their freedom was to kill a sufficient number of invaders to cause the surviving sellswords to reconsider the worth of the payment they were promised.

She led by example.

\*\*\*

Muhalu cursed bitterly as he surveyed the chaotic battlefield. The plans that had seemed so sound when he had conceived them were coming apart like a pile of dust in a windstorm. The Muringaka who had been rendered helpless by the nets were already loaded into the cages. But there were not enough occupants in those cages … not nearly enough. As well, too many of his men were falling in death, while too few of the women-warriors were falling captive.

And now, that damnable trick with the shields had seriously reduced the effectiveness of the nets. Many of them lay inert on the ground, having captured shields rather than women. And the net-wielders were being cut down before they could regroup to retaliate.

The women's leader, Dossouye, was not difficult to spot. Search for the largest number of fallen sell-swords, and that was where she would be. Muhalu understood now that it was not the devil-beast that had made Dossouye so formidable in combat. It was her quickness and her skills, regardless of what type of mount she rode.

When fury gripped Muhalu as it did now, no one – not even Kengi – dared to approach him. But a rattle of bones behind him signaled that someone was willing to accept that risk.

The commander turned and glared at Thloko. Angry words formed in Muhalu's mind. Before he could speak them, however, Thloko silenced him with a gesture. Even though Muhalu strained to make his voice heard, he found himself unable to utter so much as a croak. The subtle pressure that constricted his throat ended only when he stopped trying to speak.

Yet despite this demonstration of the strength of his *kyame*, Thloko appeared diminished, as though his bone-bedecked cloak was swathed over less physical substance than it had been scant hours before. The *njulu*'s mask hung loosely, but it somehow remained in place. He swayed slightly, as though it was costing him greatly simply to stay on his feet.

Even in this debilitated condition, Thloko still inspired unseemly dread in Muhalu ...

Then the *njulu* spoke.

"Cut off the head of the serpent, and its body will die."

With that, Thloko turned and departed. The clacking of the bones on his cloak lingered as a haunting echo.

Well did Muhalu understand the meaning of the Tiputi's words. Previously, Thloko had wanted the Muringakas' leader, Dossouye, to be captured along with the others. Now, the *njulu* wanted Dossouye dead. With their leader eliminated, the morale of the warrior-women would vanish, and they would become easy prey.

This was a command with which Muhalu was eager to comply.

***

Dossouye waited as a clump of sell-swords pounded toward her. The burly man in the lead could only be their commander. As Muhalu and the others came closer, she could discern the hatred and rage graven on his face. She also noticed that the surviving net-wielders had withdrawn from the forefront of the fighting. She realized then that it was her death, not her capture, that her foes now sought.

*So be it*, she thought grimly.

She glanced toward Sigaza. The other woman nodded, indicating that she, too, understood the invaders' new priority. Sigaza also understood how she and Dossouye would respond to the changed circumstances.

Muhalu's sword swung toward Dossouye in a vicious swing that would have cut her in half had it connected. But it cleaved only air as Dossouye dodged its arc. Her stallion bumped into the steed of her foe, throwing both horse and rider momentarily off-balance.

Although the intruder swayed precariously, he did not topple from his saddle. Instinctively, he raised his shield to deflect the counter-stroke he anticipated from the warrior-woman. But Dossouye chose not to waste energy with an attack that would not have been effectual. Instead, she thrust the point of her sword straight toward the unshielded part of Muhalu's body. His own sword barely managed to bat the lethal stab aside.

Shieldless as she was, Dossouye should have been at a disadvantage against Muhalu, who was stronger and better-protected. She was able to compensate, though, by maneuvering her mount to the unshielded side of the man's body and, relying on her flexibility and agility to evade his sweeping sword-strokes.

Frustration soon mingled with the fury on the commander's face as he struggled to engage withoverwhelm the warrior-woman. Their blades clanged again and again in a song of steel. Far too often, Muhalu was forced to duck away from the death-dealing jabs of Dossouye's blade. Faced with Dossouye's speed, Muhalu's shield was becoming more of an encumbrance than a safeguard.

At least he did not have to be wary of additional attackers. His men were fully engaging the other Muringaka who rallied to their leader's side, and to the one next to her who was larger than many men.

A cunning gleam suddenly flashed in the commander's eyes. Wheeling his mount in front of Dossouye's, he lashed out – not with his sword, but with his shield. The heavy object crashed against the head of Dossouye's stallion, tipping the animal off-balance. Dossouye was barely able to leap free from her saddle as her stricken mount toppled to the ground.

The *ahosi* landed on her feet, but she had to struggle to maintain her balance while evading the flying hooves of Muhalu's steed. Then she heard a crash beside her. She did not have to look to realize that Sigaza's horse had also fallen.

The rearing mount of her foe dominated Dossouye's field of vision, as did the enemy commander's upraised sword and the hate-filled snarl that twisted his features into a grotesque mask of vengeance.

*\*\*\**

*He was closer ...*
*He was closer ...*
*He was THERE!*

\*\*\*

The creature materialized suddenly, as if from nowhere. At first, its form could barely be perceived: vague impressions of a huge black bulk and sweeping, ivory-colored horns. Dossouye was so thoroughly astounded that for a moment, she was unable to move.

*Gbo?* she thought incredulously.

Fortunately, Dossouye was not the only one immobilized by surprise. Otherwise, Muhalu could easily have cut her down in her tracks. Even as the Muringaka and the sell-swords stood dumbfounded, the apparition whirled toward Muhalu's horse, which was still balanced on its hind legs. The tip of one of the creature's horns tore through the exposed abdomen of the horse. Shrieking horribly as its intestines spilled out of the jagged gash, the horse tumbled to the ground. Muhalu threw himself free, but he landed awkwardly and lay momentarily stunned.

The horse's scream galvanized Dossouye into action. She immediately drove the point of her sword into the throat of Muhalu. As she twisted the blade out of the commander's flesh, the resulting gush of blood told her he was dead.

Then she turned to Sigaza. And her vision blurred in sorrow at what she saw. Sigaza's steed thrashed weakly. Both its forelegs had been severed. Sigaza lay unmoving at the side of the animal. Her eyes were open, but unseeing. Her head twisted at an unnatural angle on her broken neck. Unlike Dossouye, Sigaza had not landed on her feet when she leaped from her falling mount.

A tide of fury surged through Dossouye as she turned to the field of battle. The black apparition was ravening though the ranks of the intruders: knocking down horses, tossing their riders into the air, trampling any foes unlucky enough to find themselves in its path of devastation.

Their commander dead, their will broken, the sell-swords scattered as the apparition and the vengeful

Muringaka pursued them, their shouts of triumph superseding the despairing outcries of their victims. Dossouye remained where she was, with her worst enemy and her best friend both lying dead at her feet.

"Gbo?" she whispered aloud. "No, it can't be ..."

As if in reaction to Dossouye's confusion, the apparition broke off its assault and headed toward her, leaving the Muringaka to finish the rout of their foes. The closer the creature came, the clearer it was to Dossouye that this was not some revisitation of Gbo. This animal was, if anything, taller than the war-bull – but not as bulky in conformation. Its horns swept in a wider arch than Gbo's, though blood dripped from them just as it had from the war-bull's natural weapons during battle. As well, the apparition's horns lacked the heavy boss between them that was characteristic of Gbo's kind.

Despite those differences, however, the mysterious creature bore a strong first-glance resemblance to Gbo. Yet as the apparition stepped carefully among the wounded and dead, Dossouye could discern another point of disparity. Gbo's eyes had been expressive, but still those of a beast. In this creature's eyes gleamed intelligence and awareness far beyond that of any animal.

The apparition stopped in front of Dossouye. It pushed its snout – narrower than Gbo's – toward her. Dossouye reached out and touched the warm flesh of the animal's nose.

And then she was ... *elsewhere*.

\*\*\*

Thloko reeled in shock and disbelief as he watched his – and the Tiputis' – schemes crumble like dry clay. His sell-swords were being cut down like stalks of grass. The wheeled cages contained dozens of warrior-women, still helpless in the nets that entangled them. But the cages were hardly filled to capacity.

*Still, these might be enough*, Thloko thought desperately. *Even a smaller number is better than returning empty-handed …*

The *njulu*'s *kyame* was weakened, but not totally depleted. If he could divert enough of the surviving mercenaries to maneuver the cages out of the Muringakas' territory … if he could conjure some sort of barrier that would impede the vengeful warrior-women's pursuit … if he could do those things, then his purpose would be at least partially fulfilled, and the reckoning he would face at the hands of his fellow Tiputi, and the entities they served, would be less harsh.

Looking toward the cages, Thloko steadied himself and marshaled what remained of both his physical and sorcerous strength. His mind reached out to Kengi, who remained alive and was attempting to rally the sell-swords. His hands began to move, and his fingers traced impious designs in the air. His heart beat faster in exultation as his *kyame* coalesced.

*I can do it*, he thought as he saw outlines slowly becoming visible. *I can do it …*

"*You!*" a harsh voice shouted behind him.

The sound snapped Thloko's concentration. His designs vanished. The commands he was projecting into Kengi's mind were cut off. Enraged, Thloko turned to face the interloper. And beneath his mask, his mouth fell open in astonishment.

Vulyuwa stood before him. Though she, too was debilitated, she was not as close to exhaustion as the Tiputi. The whorls painted on her bare skin had faded, and their movements were hardly visible. Fragments of the filaments that had nearly killed her hung limply from her limbs.

Her eyes blazed with an eldritch incandescence. Before Thloko could make any move to defend himself, Vulyuwa's *kyame* assaulted his mind. All his thoughts were laid bare to her scrutiny … including the objective for which the Tiputis hired Muhalu's sell-swords to capture as many Muringaka as they could.

Disgust twisted Vulyuwa's features as she saw a

distorted vision of scores of Freed Ones lying naked and spread-eagled on their backs, their wrists and ankles staked to the ground. She saw shadowy, unspeakable shapes hovering over their prey. She saw the shapes drift downward ... not to kill their victims, but to impregnate them, to force them to bear half-human, half-demonic offspring that would devour their mothers and grow to wreak havoc in Ilodwe, enabling the Tiputi to become overlords ...

With an inarticulate snarl of outrage, Vulyuwa thrust out her arms, laced her fingers together, and began to squeeze. Although she was standing too far away to touch Thloko, her *kyame* reached him, constricting his mask against his face.

The bones on Thloko's cloak clattered as he struggled against Vulyuwa's *kyame*. But he had expended the last of his *kyame* in his attempt to organize a retreat with the captives. He found himself unable to prevent his mask from cutting off his breath. As its edges sliced into his lips and eyeballs, he was unable to utter anything more than a thin, melwing outcry as the mask finally shattered – along with his face.

The bones rattled one last time as the Tiputi *njulu* collapsed in a lifeless heap at Vulyuwa's feet.

***

Dossouye was in the midst of a clearing in a forest of shadows. Black-barked, leafless trees thrust upward like spears planted in ground that was shrouded in gray fog that swirled around her feet, as well as the hooves of the ivory-horned beast whose nose she still touched.

She pulled her hand away from the animal's snout. The moment that contact ended, the creature stepped back ... and began to *transform*.

As Dossouye stared wide-eyed, the beast's bulk diminished. The apparition rose to it hind legs. Its limbs were changing as well, from bovine to human shape. The wide-spanning horns shrank back into the sides of a head that was reshaping itself: snout collapsing into a smaller nose; forehead rising, hair receding until it covered only a head that became round rather than flat. And the hoofs of the apparition metamorphosed into hands and feet.

When the shape-shifting was complete, a naked giant of a man stood before Dossouye. His skin was black as jet, and the thews that rippled across his broad frame promised power that extended beyond human limitations. The features of his face were coarse, even brutal. Yet the gaze his eyes cast upon Dossouye glowed with warmth and amity.

Dossouye's knees weakened. She had to will herself to remain on her feet. Once before, she had known a bovine that could become human ...

*It cannot be*, she thought.

"Who ... *what* ... are you?" the *ahosi* asked in a near-whisper.

The man smiled.

"My mother is Marwe," he said in a sonorous voice. "And my father is Gbo."

Dossouye's mind reeled in shock at those words.

Marwe ... an *imandwa*, a spirit-being capable of taking the shape of either a woman or a bovine. Marwe ... who had used her magic to beguile both Dossouye and Gbo in the vast forest known as the Land of Trees through which the *ahosi* had wandered before coming to the lands beyond its eastern fringes. Marwe ... who had been Dossouye's lover in human form and Gbo's as a bovine. Marwe ... who, in her bovine form, had given birth to a calf that resembled Gbo.

Dossouye had helped to deliver the calf when Marwe suffered difficulties during the birthing. Then Dossouye and Gbo departed, leaving the *imandwa* and her offspring behind. Though they were seldom absent from her memories, she did not believe she would see either of the *imandwa* again.

"My mother told me about you and Gbo," the *imandwa* said. "She told me that one day, you would have need of me."

"Is Marwe ..."

"She is still alive, Dossouye. And she has had other children. She misses you, but she is not alone."

"Did she bind you to me?"

"No. When I sensed the danger you were in, I came to you not by compulsion, but by my own will."

Dossouye's thoughts raced. Given the numerous arcane events she had experienced in her native Abomey, and the Land of Trees, and in these eastern and southern lands, she did not question how the *imandwa* could have known of her plight, and traversed the great distance from the forest, or matured to manhood in little more than ten rains. Nor did she question why they were in this vague shadow-forest rather than the battlefield in the shadows of the *ilimas*. *Vudunu* or *kyame*, magic was magic.

"What is your name?" she asked.

The *imandwa*'s grin grew broader.

"It is a name my mother found in your thoughts," he replied. "My name is Kpendu."

Now, Dossouye smiled. In the language of her native Abomey, "*kpendu*" meant "gift." The word "*gbo*" meant "protection." It was so much like Marwe to have given a name like this to her and the war-bull's offspring.

"I thank you, Kpendu, for saving my life – and those of so many of my Muringaka."

Kpendu nodded in acknowledgment.

"Will you return to Marwe's forest?" Dossouye asked.

"If that is what you want, Dossouye. But I believe you will have further need of me."

Dossouye pondered those words, and realized that Kpendu was right. Much needed to be done in the wake of the sell-swords' intrusion. If one enemy force could locate and attack the Freed Ones' stronghold, so could others. As well, she believed that the Tiputi were not yet done with the Muringaka.

"I agree, Kpendu," she said. "But I pledge you this: I

will never put a saddle or bridle on you."

"Just as well," said Kpendu. "I would never have been as comfortable with those things as Gbo was."

Then the *imandwa* transformed back to bovine form – a war-bull unlike any that had ever been bred in Abomey. This time, Dossouye was better prepared for the sight of the shape-change.

Kpendu stepped toward her. She laid her hand on his snout. And –

\*\*\*

She was back on the battlefield.

"Dossouye?"

"Dossouye"

"Dossouye?"

The *ahosi* blinked. Her hand was still on Kpendu's snout. She kept it there as she turned to face the one who was repeating her name. It was Vulyuwa.

The *njulu* appeared haggard and weary, barely able to stand upright. In one hand, Vulyuwa held a large fragment of the mask Thloko had worn. Concern was evident in Vulyuwa's eyes as she gazed intently at Dossouye.

Looking beyond the *njulu*, Dossouye saw that the Muringaka were effectively dealing with the aftermath of their victory. Some of them guarded clumps of sullen-looking enemy survivors. Others were pulling nets away from entangled warrior-women. The ensorcelment of the nets had disappeared with the death of the Tiputi *njulu*. Now, they were mere agglomerations of string that tore easily in the Muringakas' hands.

The wheeled cages were empty. Corpses of combatants and their mounts littered the ground like broken toys scattered by petulant children. The moans of the wounded echoed. Because the intruders had striven to capture rather than kill, fewer Muringaka had died than would have been usual in a battle like this. Even so, Dossouye mourned the deaths of the Freed Ones who had depended on her guidance.

Already, she missed Sigaza ...

As carrion-birds wheeled in the sky in anticipation of an imminent feast, Dossouye looked into the eyes of Kpendu. Now she understood why the gaze he returned in bovine form would never be that of a beast. She pulled her hand back from the *imandwa*'s snout, and returned her attention to Vulyuwa.

"How long was I ... gone?" Dossouye asked.

"Long enough for us to be afraid that you had been caught up in some final *kyame* from this one," Vulyuwa replied.

She held up the shard from Thloko's mask. But the direction of Vulyuwa's gaze indicated that the Tiputi *njulu* was not the only object of her suspicions.

Indeed, Vulyuwa was the only Muringaka who stood near Dossouye and Kpendu. Of course, they had no reason to distrust Dossouye. But Kpendu's sudden appearance, and his resemblance to Gbo, was unnerving, even though Kpendu's intervention had turned the tide of battle in their favor.

The eyes of Vulyuwa and the other Freed Ones asked the same, unspoken question of Dossouye: *What are we to do now?*

Dossouye grasped a handful of the hair on Kpendu's shoulders and vaulted onto his back. She straddled the bull with the same easy grace with which she had sat upon Gbo.

"Hear me, my sisters!" she said, her voice ringing across the field of victory.

The Muringaka stopped what they were doing and gave their full attention to their leader. Blood leaking from her wounds, the leather of her armor hacked, its steel plates dented, she looked like a deity of war astride some mythical beast in the aftermath of an apocalypse.

She laid her hand on the head of her mount.

"This is Kpendu," she said. "The spirit of Gbo lives within him."

The eyes of the Muringaka reflected acceptance of those words, though Vulyuwa, for one, believed there would be more to tell later. And Vulyuwa had not yet told Dossouye, or anyone else, what she had seen in the mind of Thloka.

"We have won a great victory here," Dossouye continued. "But we must leave this place that as our home, for others may come here to try to destroy us. We can defeat any foe ... but we need to find a place where we can be who we are, without having to fight forever."

She paused. Her gaze swept her surroundings, and she caught the glance of each of the Muringaka.

"Together, we will find that place," she said.

A ragged cheer rose from the ranks of the Freed Ones as Dossouye raised her blood-dripping sword above her head. Beneath her hand, she felt a rumble of agreement and approval from Kpendu.

***

Dossouye and Kpendu stood in front of the huge heap of stones that marked the burial place of Gbo. Other, smaller, piles lay atop the remains of the Muringaka who had died at the hands of the sell-swords. The living Freed Ones had already departed. Dossouye and Kpendu would catch up with them.

The surviving intruders were also gone. Their wheeled cages were loaded with the sell-swords' own dead rather than the captives they had come to claim. Only Thloka remained within the shadows of the *ilimas* – in ashes. After Vulyuwa told Dossouye what the Tiputis' intentions had been, the two women agreed that Thloko's corpse should be dismembered and burned.

Dossouye stood beside Kpendu, who remained in bovine form. The *imandwa* had not taken man-form since the brief interlude in the shadow-forest. They both agreed it would be better, for now, that the Muringaka believe that Kpendu was a magical beast that contained Gbo's spirit.

Dossouye laid both hands on the stones.

"Goodbye, Gbo," she said. "I know you would have enjoyed the battle we fought here."

Kpendu rumbled agreement. Then Dossouye swung onto his back, and they left the battlefield, and the *ilimas*. Behind them, Dossouye thought she could hear a faint "*whuff.*"

But it may have been only the wind.

# Griots: Sisters of the Spear Bios

## Marked

**Sarah Maklin, Author:**  Sarah A. Macklin is a writer and artist toiling away in the salt mines of Blythewood, South Carolina. She's the artist of the upcoming graphic novel based on the young adult novel Amber and the Hidden City. The nameless warrior from Marked was her first foray into Sword and Soul but it certainly won't be her last.

**James Eugene, Artist:**  James Eugene is a native of Elizabeth, New Jersey, and the founder of NeoArtStyleDesign. His digital work as well as traditional art is about communication and transition. However, the ultimate goal of his work is to bring all people together. He considers himself to be an entrepreneur, visual artist, Web designer, writer, and teacher.

James lives and works in Atlanta, Georgia, and he spends his spare time organizing arts shows, writing, and designing. His current projects include 2 seperate 2D projects (including his own), illustrating a children's book series, writing a screenplay, designing an independent apparel line, creating a line of limited edition prints, and producing games & graphic novels for iPad platforms.

# The Antuthema

**Dennis Brown, Author:** D.S. Brown is a true lover of the written word. For him, writing is a passion. He wakes up well before dawn, first to exercise his body, then to exercise his mind. He sets himself before his keyboard, and reaches for mental dexterity, complexity, and passion, pulling from DIDEA, the Dimension of Ideas. He crafts involved, convoluted, but very entertaining drama, action, or romance, whatever comes to mind. This is his fiction. Then, he may switch and concentrate on facts, common issues that are relevant to the common person. He will write zealously about that which he feels is of vital importance to everyone, not just a privileged few. All he would ask of you, his partner in this writing adventure is this ... take a moment to discover his work. It is his sincerest desire that you find favor with what he writes.

# The Night Wife

**Carole McDonnell, Author:** Carole McDonnell holds a BA in Literature from SUNY Purchase and is a writer of Christian, supernatural, and ethnic stories. Her writings appear in various anthologies, including So Long Been Dreaming: Postcolonialism in Science Fiction, edited by Nalo Hopkinson and published by Arsenal Pulp Press; Jigsaw Nation, published by Spyre Books; and Life Spices from Seasoned Sistahs: Writings by Mature Women of Color among others. Her reviews appear at various online sites. Her novels are the Christian speculative fiction, Wind Follower, and the alternative world novel, The Constant Tower. Her other writings include, Seeds of Bible Study: How NOT to Study the Bible, Spirit Fruit: Collected Stories by Carole McDonnell, Blogging the Psalms, A Fool's Journey Through the Book of Psalms, and My Life as an Onion. She also writes children's e-picture books with her husband, Luke McDonnell

**Luke McDonnell, Artist:** Luke McDonnell has been a cartoonist for more than 30 years, working with DC Comics, Marvel Comics, and other companies. He is married to Carole McDonnell.

# The Blood of the Lion

**Joe Bonadonna, Author:** Joe is the author of Mad Shadows: The Weird Tales of Dorgo the Dowser, epic fantasy with a film-noir twist; Three against the Stars, classic space opera in the tradition of Edmond Hamilton and E.E. "Doc" Smith; and Waters of Darkness, with David C. Smith, a sword and sorcery novel of piracy and the high seas. All books are available from Amazon in both print and Kindle editions. A brand-new tale of Dorgo the Dowser, "The Book of Echoes," appears in Azieran Presents: Extreme Sword and Sorcery—Artifacts and Relics, a Kindle-only anthology. He is currently writing stories for several shared-world anthologies, and is working on his first "Dorgo the Dowser" novel. "Blood of the Lion" is his first sword and soul story. Joe is on Facebook and Google+, and occasionally writes for Black Gate Online. His blog is at: www.dorgoland.blogspot.com.

# Lady of Flames

**LaTreka Cross, Author:** LaTreka Cross is a wife and mother living in the Metro Atlanta area. Lady of Flames is her first published work. She can be reached on Twitter: https://twitter.com/LaTrekaCross, Facebook: https://www.facebook.com/LaTrekaCross, Email: treka21@yahoo.com or by visiting www.latrekacross.com.

**Stacy Robinson, Artist:** Stacey "Blackstar" Robinson is an MFA candidate at the University at Buffalo. His work examines the African-American form through various mediums. By comparing and contrasting pop culture aesthetics with AfroFuturism he utilizes the African American experience to create narratives that construct a space of healing from Black trauma.

# A Subtle Lyric

**Troy Wiggins, Author:** Troy L. Wiggins is from Memphis, Tennessee. He was raised on a steady diet of comic books, fantasy fiction, and role-playing games. This is his first publication. He currently resides in Daegu, South Korea, where he teaches English.

# Zambeto

**JC Holbrook, Author:** J. C. Holbrook began writing fiction in 2009 with the creation of her "Astronaut Tribe" series. Her short stories appear in Genesis II and O.T.H.E.R.S. magazine. Her documentary films include "Hubble's Diverse Universe" and "Black Sun." She currently is a professor in Cape Town, South Africa.

**James Mason, Artist**: A graduate of Columbia High School in Decatur and Georgia Tech in Atlanta, James "Mase" Mason is best known as the writer and artist of the Urban Shogun comic series. In addition to his work in the mobile design field, he also serves as colorist and co-writer of the Street Team comic and is the lead designer of the independently produced video game "Street Team: Reign of the Iron Dragon."

# The Price of Kush

**Sylvia Kelso, Author:**    Sylvia Kelso lives in North Queensland, Australia. She mostly writes fantasy and SF set in analogue or alternate Australian settings, and likes to tinker with moral swords-and-sorcery and elements of mythology. She has published 8 fantasy novels, including Amberlight and The Moving Water, which were finalists for best fantasy novel in the Australian Aurealis genre fiction awards. Her short stories appear in Australia and the US, including anthologies from DAW and 12th Planet Press. Her novella "Spring in Geneva," a riff on Frankenstein, appeared in October 2013 with Aqueduct Press. She has just signed a contract for the 4th book in the Amberlight series, Dragonfly, with Jupiter Gardens Press.

# Old Habits

**Milton Davis, Author:** Milton Davis is owner of MVmedia, LLC , a micro publishing company specializing in Science Fiction, Fantasy and Sword and Soul. MVmedia's mission is to provide speculative fiction books that represent people of color in a positive manner. Milton is the author of eight novels; his most recent The Woman of the Woods and Amber and the Hidden City. He is co-editor of four anthologies; Griots: A Sword and Soul Anthology and Griot: Sisters of the Spear, with Charles R. Saunders; The Ki Khanga Anthology with Balogun Ojetade and the Steamfunk! Anthology, also with Balogun Ojetade.  MVmedia has also published Once Upon A Time in Afrika by Balogun Ojetade.

**Hasani Claxton, Artist:** Hasani Claxton was raised on the Caribbean island of St. Kitts. He studied Business Management at Morehouse College (1999) and Law at Columbia University (2003). While serving as an Assistant

District Attorney in the Bronx, he began taking evening classes at the School of Visual Arts in Manhattan. In 2005, he decided to pursue his passion full time, enrolling in Academy of Art University in San Francisco. He earned his Bachelor of Fine Arts in 2009 and later that year attended the Illustration Master Class at Amherst College. His commissions have included book illustrations, album covers, a mural for an installation at the Carolina Children's Museum in Puerto Rico, as well as private portraits. In 2012, his work was selected as the People's Choice for the Black Art In America Juried Art Exhibition and displayed at the Harlem Fine Arts Show. He was a semifinalist in the 2013 Bombay Sapphire Artisan Series. He is a member of the Portrait Society of America. He currently resides in Baltimore, Maryland.

# Vengeance

**Rebecca McFarland Kyle, Author:** Born on Friday the 13th, Rebecca McFarland Kyle has lived with black cats most of her life. She and her husband of thirty years live with four felines between the Smoky and Cumberland mountains.

As a career researcher, she explored diverse subjects, from automobile crash statistics to animal waste recycling. Her serious writing began in the 1990s. She has published both non-fiction and fiction and is currently working on two young adult novels.

# Death and Honor

**Ronald T. Jones, Author:** Ronald T. Jones is a science fiction writer and author of three published novels, Chronicle of the Liberator, Warriors of the Four Worlds, and Subject 82-42. He has also written short stories ranging from fantasy to steampunk. Originally from Chicago, Ronald currently inhabits fifteen different realities simultaneously.

**Charlie Goubile, Artist:** Fredrick Charles Goubile (aka FAB) was born in Alabama in 1981. An Army Brat, he spent his youth moving around the southeast states, even spending some years in Germany. After graduating high school in Virginia, he joined the Army himself as a graphic designer. After 6 years of military service, he left to pursue a career in multi-media illustration. He went on to work on a variety of projects from comic books to animation and live action films. He also produced his first creator owned project, the graphic novel "Blackbird." Since then he has teamed up with writer Daniel McNeal to form the creative duo Kid Monster Creations, their first project is the space adventure "Corsairs," which will be released as a graphic novel.

# Queen of the Sapphire Coast
Linda Macauley, Author

# Ghost Marriage

**P, Djeli Clark, Author:** P. Djeli Clark is a would-be historian who resides in Washington DC, by way of Brooklyn, by way of Houston, by way of Staten Island, by way of Queens, by way of Trinidad & Tobago. An overly long mild-mannered doctoral candidate by day, P. Djeli Clark manages to escape his humdrum existence of lecturing to students and grading papers whenever possible through writing. Fantasy remains his favorite genre, and his influences range from Robert Jordan to Charles Saunders to NK Jemisin. Djeli has published stories in such markets as Daily Science Fiction, Every Day Fiction, Hogglepot and Heroic Fantasy Quarterly. He is a veteran of the groundbreaking Griots: A Sword and Soul Anthology and has also published in the 2013 anthology Steamfunk. You can find him unpacking issues of race, gender and politics in speculative fiction over at his wordy blog, The Musings of a Disgruntled Haradrim...

**Jason Reeves, Artist:** Illustrator, Art Director, Writer, Jason Reeves is an up & coming Comic Creator. Carrying over his meticulous, action-adventure, super-hero influenced style, his production company 133art (www.133art.com) is set to take on the comic industry.

Born in New Orleans , LA , Jason graduated fro the New Orleans Center for Creative Arts (NOCCA) at the age of 16. Moving from the south to Los Angeles, he honed his craft by working with a variety of clientele around the industry, such as: Hasbro, USA Network, Devil's Due Publishing, Urban Style Entertainment, USAToday, Marvel/Upperdeck, & Esquire Magazine to name a few.

Other credits include cover art for the Hero Initiative/ Skybound's 'the Walking Dead #100' Event, A piece of art for Esquire magazine's review of The Dark Knight Rises, poster art for Heavy Metal's 'The Art of Agent 88' hardcover, and 'OneNation: Old Druids' released on Comixology.com.

# Raiders of the Sky Isle

**Cynthia Ward, Author:** Cynthia Ward has published stories in Asimov's Science Fiction and

Witches: Wicked, Wild & Wonderful (Prime Books), among other anthologies and magazines. She has published articles in Weird Tales and Locus Online, among other webzines and magazines. Her story "Norms," published in Triangulation: Last Contact, made the Tangent

Online Recommended Reading List for 2011. With Nisi Shawl, she coauthored Writing the Other: A Practical Approach (Aqueduct Press),which is based on their diversity writing workshop, Writing the Other: Bridging Cultural Differences for Successful Fiction

(http://www.writingtheother.com). Cynthia lives in the Los Angeles area. Her website is http://www.cynthiaward.com.

# Brood

**Balogun Ojetade, Author:** Balogun is the author of the bestselling Afrikan Martial Arts: Discovering the Warrior Within and screenwriter / producer / director of the films, A Single Link and Rite of Passage: Initiation.

He is one of the leading authorities on Steamfunk – a philosophy or style of writing that combines the African and/ or African American culture and approach to life with that of the steampunk philosophy and / or steampunk fiction – and writes about it, the craft of writing, Sword & Soul and Steampunk in general, at http://chroniclesofharriet.com/.

He is author of five novels – the Steamfunk bestseller, MOSES: The Chronicles of Harriet Tubman (Books 1 & 2); the Urban Science Fiction saga, Redeemer; the Sword & Soul epic, Once Upon A Time In Afrika, two Fight Fiction, New Pulp novellas – A Single Link and Fists of Afrika and he is contributing co-editor of two anthologies: Ki: Khanga: The Anthology and Steamfunk.

Finally, Balogun is the Director and Fight Choreographer of the Steamfunk feature film, Rite of Passage, which he wrote based on the short story, Rite of Passage, by author Milton Davis.

**Sheeba Maya, Artist:** Sheeba Maya is an illustrator, fine artist, and graphic designer specializing in digital painting and portraiture. She is best known for her portraits that appear to be oil paintings, but are actually digitally rendered. Her traditional portrait work is praised for it's high level of realism and accuracy while her illustrative style is often described as mystical and otherworldly. A master of her craft, she has created portraits of political officials, corporate figures, celebrities, as well as website illustrations, book covers, and editorial artwork.

Along with working on a personal body of work and for-client commissions, Sheeba is developing a series of online courses, webinars, and in-person workshops to teach her digital painting technique.

# The Sickness

**Valjeanne Jeffers, Author:** Valjeanne Jeffers is a graduate of Spelman College and the author of the SF/fantasy novels: Immortal, Immortal II: The Time of Legend, Immortal III: Stealer of Souls; and the steamfunk novels: Immortal IV: Collision of Worlds and The Switch II: Clockwork (includes books I and II).

Valjeanne's fiction has appeared in numerous anthologies including: Steamfunk!, Griots: A Sword and Soul Anthology, LuneWing, PurpleMag, Pembroke Magazine and Possibilities. Her two latest novels: Mona Livelong: Paranormal Detective, and Colony: Ascension An Erotic Space Opera will be released later this year. Preview or purchase Valjeanne's books at: http://www.vjeffersandqveal.com

# Kpendu

**Charles R. Saunders, Author:** Charles R. Saunders is the pioneer of Sword and Soul, having had his first Imaro story published in a small-press magazine in 1974. Novels in the subsequent Imaro series include Imaro; Imaro: The Quest for Cush; Imaro: The Trail of Bohu; Imaro: The Naama War; and the forthcoming Imaro: Vengeance in Velanga. Other novels include Dossouye and Dossouye II: The Dancers of Mulukau. His work has appeared in various magazines and anthologies. He lives in Dartmouth, Nova Scotia, Canada. His website is: www.charlessaunderswriter.com.

**Stanley Weaver, Jr., Artist:** Stanley Weaver, Jr. is a self taught artist who produces various art work for many independent labels. Stanley draws some of the most expressive and dynamic African American themed characters. Stanley is also a great story tellers with his pencils. Stanley work can be seen in some character designs/redesign of some of the best known independent projects. Currently, Stanley is penciling 6 Deep issue#2, working on the Dziva Jones project, Punxs of Rage and the on-going Street Team series.